SHADOWS OF THE NIGHT

"Would you hold me, Blane? I feel so safe in your arms."

Blane knew the danger of their contact, yet he complied, embracing Shannon tightly and possessively. He wished once again that she hadn't become involved in this dangerous war, but he was glad she was in his arms for the moment. He brushed kisses over her forehead, her cheeks, the tip of her nose, and her chin. His face caressed hers, his hands stroked her back and arms, and he inhaled her sweetness.

As if she had been a kitten, Shannon snuggled closer and silently encouraged more stroking with her reactions. Her fingertips teased over his shoulders and back. Then she closed her eyes and let her senses absorb the stirring sensations he was creating within her. As her head rolled to his pillow, their lips touched lightly.

Savoring the feel of her flesh, he moved his fingers over her face and down her neck to journey over her arm. His hand found hers and brought it to his lips. He kissed each finger, then her palm, then worked his way over her wrist and up her arm.

Their surroundings were forgotten. The war was forgotten. And forgotten, too, were any reasons they might have had to deny their blazing passion . . .

JANELLE TAYLOR

Destiny's Temptress

ZEBRA BOOKS
KENSINGTON PUBLISHING CORP.

ZEBRA BOOKS are published by

Kensington Publishing Corp.
850 Third Avenue
New York, NY 10022

Zebra and the Z logo are trademarks of Kensington Publishing Corp.

Twelfth printing: March 1996

Printed in the United States of America

20 19 18 17 16 15 14 13

Acknowledgments:

Sylvie Sommerfield, for the loan of many books from her personal library.

The Augusta/Richmond County Library staff, for their unselfish and untiring help when deadlines are pressing.

The Chambers of Commerce in Wilmington, Charleston, and Savannah, for their assistance with obtaining historical and local information about their cities.

And my readers, friends, and booksellers who have been so patient and helpful while I was too busy catching up from 1984 to answer their letters and calls and to make appearances in their areas.

Chapter One

Washington
August 1864

Shannon Greenleaf thought she understood the risks involved in her attempt to sneak into the White House near midnight to speak privately with President Abraham Lincoln. For days she had been denied a meeting with him, and she doubted that her written messages pleading for a short conference had reached his busy hands. As a loyal Unionist, she felt she deserved a show of manners and consideration. She was fatigued and angered at being put off on this crucial matter, for both her money and her patience had worn thin. It was time for desperate and clever action, and Shannon was bold enough to take them.

To facilitate swift movement and concealment, the nineteen-year-old Georgian had dressed in dark blue male attire that almost matched her eyes. She had twisted and stuffed her long red hair beneath a felt hat, then blackened her ivory face and hands with soot. And in order not to pose a threat to Lincoln, she was not carrying a weapon.

Shannon had observed the massive white structure for several hours, knowing that somehow she would have to reach the second floor. By now, she was familiar with the guards' patterns and felt she could slip past them, but she still had one major problem to surmount. She would have to make a rapid and stealthful entry.

The windows on the first floor had been closed and locked at dusk. Those open on the second floor were inaccessible. Four third-story windows offered hope and excitement. According to what she had learned, the third floor contained servants' quarters and guest rooms. Yet only one of the four had remained dark throughout her vigil.

Waiting until the sentry had passed, Shannon whispered a prayer and raced behind the shrubs near the eastern side of the building. There was no time for delay. She removed her boots and hid them beneath the bushes, then, with silent thanks for the numerous days she had played tomboy with her brothers and for the countless hours of forest training she had undergone with Hawke—she deftly began climbing a sprawling Magnolia. She gingerly straddled a selected bough and, tightly grasping both sides of it between shaky hands, she lifted her hips and slid her body forward, repeating the process many times as she gradually inched herself along its surface.

Tonight her anxiety hampered her usual skill and confidence. A splintered nub from a broken limb snared her pants and slowed her progress as she stopped to untangle herself. Each time she encountered an offshoot, she would cautiously raise that leg and pass it over the obstacle. She was acutely aware that her daring plot was fraught with many perils—including that of being shot before she could reveal her identity or motive. Inwardly, she cursed the full moon above her, even though its light allowed her to climb more easily.

Shannon was compelled to cease all movement as the sentry made his next round, despite her precarious position. Within a few feet of the tree, the guard halted and leaned against the building while he lit a cigar and leisurely smoked it. To retain her stability, Shannon squeezed her quivering thighs around the bough supporting her, locked her ankles together, and clung desperately to the bark surface with her hands. She kept warning herself not to tremble or disturb her balance and she was almost afraid to breathe, lest the erratic sound be overheard and reveal her presence.

The Southern beauty knew she must succeed. This war had stolen too much from her. Her father and oldest brother were dead, and her other two brothers were missing. Corry could be dead, or dying; Hawke had vanished years ago. As she waited for the sentry to leave, her troubled mind wandered to the past.

Hawke. . . . Shannon's tender heart surged with love and anguish . . . They had all been surprised in '56 when her father, Andrew Greenleaf, had returned from Texas with a half-blooded youth of fourteen who could put many grown men to shame with his prowess, physique, and looks. To everyone's amazement, he had immediately adopted WindHawke, son of a whiteman and the Indian woman, Flaming Eyes, who was the daughter of one Comanche chief and the sister of another. Two years had passed before Shannon and her brothers discovered that Hawke Greenleaf was their half brother. By then, it hadn't mattered to them.

Andrew Greenleaf had met Flaming Eyes in 1841, while she was working as a cook and laundress at a Texas fort. She had been using her job as a means of spying on the soldiers for her family, and the tales of her daring feats had intrigued young Shannon. For two months the ill-fated lovers had shared a bittersweet romance and fiery passion.

11

Andrew had not known of his son's existence until the Mexican War, when he renewed his liaison with the Indian beauty. And when Kerry O'Shannon Greenleaf died in 1854, Andrew was determined to recover Flaming Eyes and WindHawke. Finally locating them after two years, Andrew had found that his secret lover was dying and that hostilities between Indians and whites were increasing perilously. Flaming eyes had persuaded her son to move to Georgia with his father so that he would survive and benefit from his father's love and guidance.

Shannon had often recalled the words of Flaming Eyes, which Hawke had repeated to her: "Go, my son; live to see many new suns and to learn many new things. Our lands and ways are vanishing with the slaughter of our people. If it is the will of Grandfather, He will recall your feet to these ancestral grounds." After Flaming Eyes had died, Andrew had brought his third son home to live and work at Greenleaf, the family plantation, withholding his identity for two years.

Hawke's birth had come eleven months after Corbett's, a fact that sometimes troubled Shannon. Hawke had related many secrets to her that his mother had related to him: Andrew had loved Kerry deeply, but had feared for her life each time their lovemaking had conceived a child. The loss of their fourth one had been the cause of Kerry's death, which had proven Andrew's fears to have been well-founded. Andrew had not meant to fall in love with a second woman. As was the case with many men during and following their wives' pregnancies, Andrew had believed that he was merely sating his physical needs while protecting his wife's health and life. Yet two months later, both he and the Indian beauty knew they had fallen in love.

Andrew had tried to forget Flaming Eyes after he left Texas. He wondered how it was possible to love and need two women desperately. When Shannon was born in July

12

of 1845, he was still dreaming and yearning for Hawke's mother. Those feelings increased in 1846 when he discovered their love child, who was then four years old. After the war, he stole visits with his second family as often as he could create logical reasons for them.

The fates of all of them had changed dramatically when Kerry and Flaming Eyes died within two years of each other. Andrew's relationship with women were never the same again. If he saw one, it was usually one he had hired for a few hours to assuage his needs.

Andrew Greenleaf's four children were more fortunate; they all became fast friends. Hawke taught the three Georgians how to blend into their surroundings, to track, to fight like warriors, to handle knives and countless other defensive measures that he had learned during his warrior training. Since neighbors were ignorant of Hawke's paternity, they expressed open scorn for the handsome young man who spent too much time with Shannon and attracted too much attention from their daughters, sisters, and sweethearts. Hawke was a male who could easily impassion a woman's blood and heart—if that woman did not view him as a brother. The sons of those genteel neighbors despised him, though they wisely respected and envied his physical prowess. Shannon often mused that if her eldest brother, Temple, hadn't been on the front line at Shiloh, he could have used the skills Hawke had taught him and survived.

Honor and courage could be so lethal, so demanding, so confusing at times, Shannon would bitterly reflect. As they had been expected to do, Temple and Corry had accepted their duties to their father and their country without a second thought or a debate. But the nineteen-year-old Hawke had refused to fight to the death for a cause and people that he didn't know or understand, and her father had reacted blindly and rashly—and selfishly.

Andrew had been raised in the same manner he had

raised his two eldest sons. He placed great importance on displaying paternal obedience and respect; on defending loved ones, lands, and the family name; on protecting family pride and honor; and on evincing physical and mental competence. Andrew had been taught that a man did such things, no matter the cost or his personal desires. He had ingrained those same beliefs and traits in his two eldest sons.

Andrew regretted that in a time of weakness and vulnerability, he had made a terrible mistake by yielding to his physical urges and falling in love with the object of his desire. He had paid an enormous price for ignoring the tenets of his upbringing, and his pride had suffered greatly. He had been determined to spare his sons from such mistakes and sacrifices and had wanted Hawke to prove that he was worthy of the Greenleaf name and blood—worthy of their acceptance, respect, and love.

Hawke had not viewed the war in the same light as his father and half brothers. To the half-blooded Comanche male, it was irrational that people battle to the death over slaves or over a division of tribes. Hawke could not see why the whites should kill each other because the southern white tribe wished to split from the northern white tribe. He could not dress in a white man's uniform and wage lethal battles over such foolishness. How could he fight for the ideals of men who considered him as low as the black slaves? Why should he be forced to prove his honor and prowess?

Andrew had been angry and hurt at Hawke's decision not to fight. He had insisted that Hawke side with the Union and had accused Hawke of bringing disgrace to the Greenleaf name with his refusal. Andrew had felt it was crucial for Hawke to publicly prove his courage and honor. It had seemed to Shannon that Hawke's going off to war with his brothers would be some sort of test of his loyalty to and love for the Greenleafs. Shannon believed that her father had felt Hawke's actions might somehow redeem his lost honor or at least justify the birth of a bastard son from an adulterous relationship. Andrew had wanted Hawke to become a war hero whose reputation and competence could never be ridiculed or denied. He could not understand Hawke's refusal.

Andrew and Hawke had argued bitterly, and their verbal battle had exposed to Shannon many secrets from their entwined past. Perturbed and disappointed, Andrew had struck Hawke across the cheek as if to provoke his defiant son with a challenge. He had wanted to embarrass or to anger Hawke into obedience. When this ploy did not work, Andrew had rashly disowned and rejected Hawke in a final attempt to gain his son's submission, ordering Hawke to return to his mother's people and adding, "If they'll allow a coward among them." He then continued, "I will not allow a son of mine to blacken the Greenleaf name. If you do not care enough for your family and home to fight for them, then you do not deserve them. Prove I was not wrong to give you life, to bring you into my home and heart. Prove you are a real man, a real Greenleaf, or leave my sight forever."

Shannon and Hawke had been crushed by that unfamiliar side of their father. Tragically, Hawke had obeyed that parental command and had left that night in March of 1861. What demons had possessed her father that awful night and had forced him to behave so differently, so insensitively? Shannon had often wondered.

Before sailing to his death, weeping over his dark behavior and his loss, Andrew had vowed to go after Hawke upon his return to Boston, where he had moved the family at the outset of the war. Then, together, they would rescue Corry. After Andrew's death, his reasons for acting and speaking so cruelly and confusedly that night remained a mystery. Yet Shannon had always felt

15

there must have been some logical reason. She wondered if she would ever see Hawke again. How she longed to soothe his torment with part of the truth. How she wished he would come home . . .

The guard finished his cigar and crushed it beneath his dusty boot. He stretched and yawned, then moved away. After he vanished around the corner of the building, Shannon exhaled to relieve her tension and quickly resumed her previous actions. As the limb narrowed and lessened in strength, it began to sway. Shannon sighed a prayer of relief for her meager height and weight, although she had always hated being referred to as "that dainty redhead." She cautioned herself to move carefully, for she was very much aware of the hard ground far below her.

The limb angled to the left, placing Shannon within two feet of the open window to her right. She grasped an overhead branch and slowly pulled her quivering body upright. Before continuing, she steadied herself. Then she placed her right foot on the sill and flung her weight in that direction, stifling a shriek as she landed straddled across the wooden surface, as if she had thrown herself astride a bareback horse with a spine of oak.

Shannon glanced inside and was relieved to find the nearby bed empty. Prussian blue eyes squinted to pierce the darkness. Sighting no threat or hindrance, she threw her other leg over the sill and placed both feet on the floor. As she hesitated a moment to catch her breath and to slow her racing heart, she speculated that the worst part was over; she was inside the White House. Now, all she had to do was locate Lincoln's private quarters and persuade him to listen to her. Having been reared to respect and follow the orders of her elders, Shannon believed she needed the permission and approval of

Lincoln before she could head into Rebel territory, though her solitary flight from Boston had been a different matter.

When her eyes had become accustomed to the dimness, Shannon moved around the bed toward the closed door. Suddenly a powerful arm banded her body just above the waist and her slender back was jerked against a hard chest, driving the air from her lungs. For an instant, Shannon feared her ribs would be cracked. Her right arm was imprisoned at her side and the left one was captured just below the elbow in a grip of iron that mutely threatened to break the bone. The sharp blade of a large hunting knife was at her throat. Her captor had moved without sound and with the swiftness and success of a highly trained warrior, Shannon realized, one whose prowess could challenge and perhaps defeat Hawke's.

Considering her opponent's strength, she knew she dared not struggle and incite a battle. From her position, she could tell that he was very tall and extremely muscular. But if she hurriedly explained her behavior, she would be safe, she believed, just as soon as she could breathe and speak.

"Where do you think you're going, little Reb, sneaking in here like a contemptible Comanche? Davis want his lads to die young?" a surly voice questioned at her left ear. The man's grip tightened painfully.

Shannon lost her breath again within the vise of his arm. In a strained tone, she replied, "I must . . . see Pres . . . ident Lincoln. It's urgent."

As the cold blade lightly touched her clammy skin, his grip applied more pressure. "Urgent enough to sneak into my room and risk death?" the voice inquired sarcastically. "Who sent you?"

"No one. When the guards and staff refused to let me see him, I tried to contact him by letter. When that failed, I sneaked inside," she explained in a muffled

17

voice. "I'm unarmed. I only want to talk," she hastily added. Shannon tried to inhale and refill her lungs, but his steely grip prevented it. She was alarmed by this unseen peril.

Testing the intruder's claim, Blane Stevens's left hand shifted up and down her shapely frame and he was startled that it was a woman's voice, fragrance, and figure that assailed his senses. Keen perception warned him to be patient with this rash invader. Without a weapon or strength, she posed no threat to him. Blane placed the knife in its sheath and tried to turn her to face him. He had been leaning against the side of the window frame in pensive thought and had caught sight of her slipping across the lawn to shinny up the Magnolia. Now he wanted a look at this reckless vixen who smelled of jasmine and climbed a lofty tree like an agile bobcat.

Shannon used that moment when his grip loosened to pitch forward, then backward, to throw her captor off balance. Then she raced for his door. Before she could open it, she was seized and thrown to the bed. Pinned under a stalwart body, she was powerless. "I must see Lincoln. It's a matter of life and death," she panted breathlessly.

"I'm sure it is," the icy voice sneered. "Who are you? What do you want from the President? You Rebs don't give up easily, do you?" Why did some females view spying as glamorous and exciting? he wondered in disgust.

"It's personal," Shannon replied obstinately. "Get off me."

"Am I dreaming, or are you a woman?" he asked, laughter edging his voice when he realized how helpless she was. He would teach this little wildcat a lesson! When she didn't respond, his right hand held her wrists captive above her head while his left hand moved over her squirming figure. "Very nice," he remarked playfully. "Any chance your face is just as pleasing?" he asked to

18

provoke her.

Shannon warned herself not to shout or scream, actions which would alert and summon guards who would carry her off to prison before she could get to Lincoln. This rogue was just another obstacle. She told herself to stay calm and cool, for she would surely find a way to trick him. "Get your bloody hands off me or I'll kill you when I get free," she warned.

Blane was amused and intrigued. "Such an attempt would certainly liven up a dull evening." Blane chuckled, curiously enjoying this crazy encounter. He knew that few women would have the mettle or skill to climb a towering tree and steal into the White House. His previous feelings of exhaustion and ennui vanished. After what he had seen and endured lately, he realized he needed a spark of excitement. Lord, he was tired of the killing and fighting, and tired of his responsibilities to friend and foe.

"I demand to see the President," Shannon remarked sternly.

"You demand, my little Rebeless?" he taunted. He could smell the soot on her face and hands, and silently admired her daring and cunning. From what he could tell, she was less than five feet five inches tall and weighed a touch over a hundred pounds. He noted that her felt hat had been knocked from her head and he wished for more light to determine her age and looks. A smart man could tell a lot about a woman from her eyes and mouth. The moonlight suddenly streamed across the bed to reveal flaming hair to match the temper he was encountering. And he heard the undeniable inflections of culture and dialect in her voice, which piqued his curiosity.

Shannon wiggled beneath his tall body and pulled on her wrists to free them. He was immensely strong and stubborn. "You're heavy. I can't breathe. I told you, brute, I'm unarmed."

"There are weapons, and there are . . . weapons," he teased. "If you want to breathe again, you had best answer my questions."

"You wouldn't dare slay a woman right under Lincoln's nose," she asserted bravely. Shannon was acutely aware of the man's rich voice, his powerful physique, his manly scent. She found this battle fascinating, for she had always enjoyed matching wits and wills with men. Let him have his fun and show of power, she told herself. Soon . . .

As his mouth brushed against hers, he murmured devilishly, "How was I to know you were a conniving female before my knife slipped across this blackened throat? Indian fighters are trained to attack rapidly and lethally, especially if they're in a foul mood." His teeth nibbled at her earlobe as he inhaled her sweet fragrance. To intimidate her, Blane remarked casually, "'Course it's been a long while since I had me a woman, and I could interrogate you later—much later," he warned deceitfully. If she thought this mission would be simple and quick, he would prove her wrong, he decided. Soon he would have her weeping, trembling, and begging to tell him all he wanted to know. When he finished with her, she would think twice about spying again! "Yep, I could use a tasty woman to soothe my woes tonight." One hand deftly unbuttoned her cotton shirt, then his tongue flicked over a nipple.

Shannon inhaled sharply. As if it had been a soldier called to attention, her breast responded instantly to his bold action. "How dare you!" she panted in dismay, thrashing angrily beneath him. "Release me this instant. I know important people," she threatened desperately.

"So do I, love," he retorted. Concentrating his attention on unnerving and terrifying this Rebel spy, he ignored Shannon's struggles as he shifted his mouth

20

from one breast to the other several times. Despite her slender figure, she was nicely rounded where it mattered, he found. His mouth covered hers as she was about to speak. Then his tongue darted between her lips and his hand released hers to wander into her hair.

Shannon comprehended his misconception and intended to correct it soon, but now she was puzzled by his sudden gentleness and ardor. She found the mingling of their mouths enticing and briefly allowed the pleasant sensation to continue. Unlike those who had kissed her before, this man possessed talented lips and hands—those of an expert lover, she realized. She wondered about his looks, age, and character. Why was he here and behaving in this brazen manner? What an arrogant, crude rake! She believed that revealing her identity would afford her protection from his vile treatment. When his mouth drifted to her ear, Shannon vowed, "I'm not a Rebel. I came from Boston on a vital matter. Please stop and listen." Her voice quavered with apprehension and vulnerability.

Blane leaned backward. "If that isn't a Southern accent, I'm Jeff Davis. You're playing a dangerous game, little Reb. Surely you know how this break-in appears. I'll have to hand you over to the guards . . . unless you give me good reason not to." Blane's body was reacting passionately to Shannon's scent, feel, kiss, and voice.

Shannon panicked. If they tossed her into prison . . . "I am from Georgia, but I'm with the Union," she argued truthfully. "I came to seek the President's help and advice. The Confederates have captured my brother; they're holding him at Danville Prison. They've already slain my father and older brother. I have to get to Danville." Shannon wondered how far she should go to obtain his trust and assistance. If she lost Greenleaf and Corry, what did life matter? Without family, home, and money, what kind of destiny would she face in a war-torn country, especially if the South were defeated and she couldn't prove her claims? If she must play the temptress to entice him to help her, so be it! After all, tempting and complying were two different things. And against such a powerful man, those were her only weapons, just as he had teased.

There was something in her voice and words that tugged at him, though he retorted, "You steal into the White House with a wild story like this?"

"It's the truth!" she protested. "I was desperate. I was going to offer my services to Mister Lincoln in exchange for his help with rescuing my brother. Let me up; I'll explain everything."

"You mean you'll try to escape," he refuted.

"Damn you, then bind my hands! Just give me time to talk. I'm from the South, so I can be of assistance to the President. I know many important people and leaders. They would never suspect I was assisting the Union. With a little help, I could get in and around. I'm not a fool; I know I can't do this alone." Shannon had learned that in some situations it was unwise for a woman to reveal too much courage, aggression, or intelligence. She had to pretend she needed and wanted help. But once she was inside Rebel territory, she would rescue Corry and take him home to Greenleaf. All she needed was a travel pass, weapons, supplies, and the names or locations of Unionists who offered rest and food.

When the man lapsed into silence, Shannon pressed, "I've met President Davis, Robert Toombs, General Bragg, John Breckenridge, and Joseph Johnston. I've also met Robert E. Lee. They all knew my father from the Mexican War; they've visited our plantation. With luck, they'll remember me. Even if I can't get any valuable information for President Lincoln, I might acquire their help with freeing my brother before he dies in one of those awful prison camps. To protect our lands from angry Confederates, Father made certain that they believed we were loyal Southerners. I know you think one life doesn't count for much during a war, but it does to me. Please help me." She was appealing to his masculine ego, and hopefully to his conscience.

Blane was off Shannon instantly, pulling her to her bare feet. He gently pushed her into a chair, then pulled her arms between the spindles. After removing his belt, he secured her hands behind her back. Then, after locating his mask, he donned it to protect his identity, hoping that this little hellion didn't already know who and what he was. He lit an oil lamp and visually scanned her features, then frowned as he noticed that the soot she had used had rubbed off on him as well. Blane poured water into a basin, grabbed soap and a cloth, and scrubbed Shannon's face until it was pink.

Shannon winced in discomfort and wiggled. "Hold still," he commanded. "I want a good look at you. Faces are one thing I never forget. For your sake, little vixen, I hope you told the truth. If there's one thing that riles me as much as Comanches, it's a treacherous woman who thinks her beauty and charms will protect her."

Blane couldn't decide why he was taking the time and energy to listen to her. There was no way she could be of any real help to him or the Union. He had gotten into this repulsive war because of his determination to help a woman—the one woman he cared about. Perhaps he listened because this minx had snared his curiosity. Perhaps he wanted a woman's company and conversation tonight. Perhaps he yearned to gaze upon something unmarred by the war. Perhaps he wanted more . . .

Shannon clenched her teeth as the man's keen eyes roamed her features, eyes that appeared the color of maple stain and filled with green flecks. How she wished she could see and study more of his face. He was well built and she estimated that he was probably three or four

23

inches over six feet and weighed about one hundred and eighty pounds. Dark blond waves with reddish gold highlights peeked around the edges of the black mask. Thick, silky hair teased his blue collar and fell over the top of the mask. Shannon noticed that the area of his chest that was exposed by his unbuttoned shirt was hairless and its golden surface appeared smooth and hard. His hands indicated that he was a man accustomed to physical labor, a man of immense dexterity. His shiny, trimmed fingernails told her another pleasing fact—he practiced cleanliness. The timbre of his voice caused her to question his birthplace, for it sounded as if he might be Southern, or perhaps Southwestern.

Blane Stevens was astonished by Shannon's incredible beauty. Perhaps it was a good thing he hadn't seen her face and figure earlier! he mused. She had large, expressive eyes, as dark blue as a Federal uniform. She had the kind of eyes that instantly drew another's vision to them, eyes that would change from a mellow cornflower blue to a Rebel flag blue according to her emotions. Their mesmeric shape and color were in striking contrast to her fiery hair and pale skin. There was a tiny smattering of very light freckles over her nose and cheeks, which supplied her features with an air of innocence and youth. Her skin was the color of heavy cream, its surface unflawed and rose petal soft. Her lower lip was fuller than the shapely upper one, which would give her a sensual pout if she chose. He noted smugly that he had guessed her height and weight correctly.

Her hair once again captured his attention. It fell to her waist in mischievous curls, its texture almost crinkly. The crown's strands were trimmed shorter and lay in wispy curls across her forehead. Its color reminded him of the mountains in the West, which became vermillion shaded when the rising or setting sun beamed down on them. She was exquisite, highly desirable. And although

24

she appeared delicate, Blane knew she was plucky and resilient. A vulnerable Southern belle who needed help . . .

His greenish brown eyes helplessly lowered to her partially exposed bosom and a noticeable gleam filled them. Old Jeff Davis sure knew how to pick his spies! What naïve lad could withhold a secret from this disarming angel, this magical temptress? It would be a shame to confine such beauty to a stifling cell. Yet, such beauty and skills could prove dangerous if she were allowed to operate on susceptible Union soldiers.

"If you've memorized my anatomy, sir, would you mind buttoning my shirt?" she inquired scornfully, glaring at her arrogant foe whose greedy gaze was eyeing her like a sumptuous treat about to be devoured.

Muffled laughter sounded in the room. Blane knelt before her and obeyed, to her surprise and his. "I sure am sorry you weren't sent to work on me," he jested, caressing her scarlet cheek. "Yankee prison can be a rough place for a ravishing, though misguided, Southern lady. Drop this wild tale and give me your name, age, and mission."

Shannon narrowed her blue eyes and clenched her teeth. She started to refuse but realized that would be foolish. She was trapped in the room of a man who viewed her as a Rebel spy and perhaps as a woman to be used as he desired. To get to Lincoln, she would have to get past this vexing male whose gaze and manner were alarmingly disturbing.

Stalling for time and an opportunity to escape, she gave him a few facts. "Shannon. Nineteen last month. I've been trying to see President Lincoln for over a week. If you'll check, my ignored messages might be lying around somewhere. If not, the staff should recall a pesty redhead who's been here many times. I have little money left. And I can't return to Boston for personal reasons. I

25

was hoping to exchange favors with the President—my assistance for his."

"What about your family? Who's letting you gallivant over the land disguised like this?" he probed, hunkering before her.

She remarked contemptuously, "Almost my entire family has been annihilated by this travesty. My older brother was killed during the Battle of Shiloh in the spring of '62. Last May, my younger brother was taken prisoner at Chancellorsville. A friend got a message to my father that he was being held at Danville in Virginia, a horrible place. We kept hoping and praying that the war would end soon, but it didn't. Last October, my father decided more arms and better pay might give the Union the edge to win this vicious conflict. He sailed from Boston for England to sell future cotton crops of Southern loyalists to earn money for Union supplies. His ship was attacked and sunk by a Rebel blockade runner. I waited and prayed as long as I could, then I had to act. My brother's all I have left, except for . . . a few friends. I was hoping the President would help me get through the Rebel lines so I could at least discover if he's still alive. If so, I plan to find a way to get him out of that wicked place. If I fail, I can work and provide him with food and supplies. Don't you realize how many prisoners die under those horrid conditions? Is that sufficient, Mister . . . ?"

"You plan to travel through enemy territory for weeks, then single-handedly rescue your brother from a Confederate prison?" Blane queried in disbelief.

"I know how to ride and shoot. All I need is a contact here and there for rest and food. In return, I'll report anything I see or hear to the President. I read the newspapers and magazines, so I am familiar with the treatment given female spies on both sides. I know they aren't shot or hanged. Besides, I am . . . was a Southerner. We have a plantation in Georgia. Please

26

convince Mister Lincoln to help me." Shannon wondered if she was making a mistake by trying to enlist Lincoln's aid. She had gotten this far alone; maybe she didn't need anyone's help or permission. She could take care of herself under most circumstances, but a ravaged land with crazed soldiers was not a normal situation. If only Hawke weren't in Texas; he would help her. He wasn't afraid of anything or anyone. Why had her father shamed and rejected him? she wondered once again. It wasn't like Andrew Greenleaf to be so volatile and cruel. Hawke would know what to do. But for Shannon, getting to Savannah would be easier than getting into Comanche territory, and if Hawke returned, she knew it would be to Greenleaf.

Blane eyed Shannon up and down several times. There was a ring of verity in her tone. Yet he sensed she wasn't being totally open and honest. "If this tale is for real, you're mighty naïve. Don't you realize there's no way you can get to Danville? Don't you own a mirror? I doubt you could get five miles without being ravished, or at least robbed and left stranded, or captured by Rebs. Then you might join your unlucky brother," he stated harshly, envisioning this vital creature enduring such an ordeal.

Angry lights flickered in Shannon's deep sapphire eyes. All she wanted was to get out of this room and this uncomfortable situation. "Why don't you let the President decide if I can defend myself and be of assistance to him?"

"How could you defend yourself against numerous men when you couldn't even fight off one?" he challenged to awaken her dreamy mind.

"Not all men are as strong or as mean as you— especially not Southerners! Gentlemen help ladies, not assail them! No Rebel officer would shoot me or attack me!" she fiercely declared.

"Would you like me to prove you wrong?" he

speculated as he unbound her hands and jerked her against his chest.

Blane didn't stop Shannon when she tore off his mask and threw it to the floor. She immediately wished she hadn't. Despite the sooty smudges, his good looks stormed her troubled senses instantly. His full lips formed a devilish half-grin, as if he recognized his effect on her. She noted that his flesh had been bronzed by the sun and wisps of his thick hair lightened by it. Physical and mental superiority radiated from his strong, angular features. He was freshly shaven, even to the deep cleft in his squared chin, and Shannon saw that a thin, white scar snaked along his left jawline for two inches. His eyes were sparkling with mischief. For a while, Shannon felt breathless and weak.

Blane's eyes fused with Shannon's, and neither spoke or moved for a time. It seemed that each was assessing the other, in looks and emotions. Finally, Shannon broke the potent spell when she defensively asked, "Are you saying that you're a Rebel?" Was he trying to entrap her? she wondered. Did that explain the black mask he had donned? Had he also sneaked inside for some reason, perhaps a criminal one? "What are you doing here? If you've come to harm the President, I'll try to stop you," she vowed.

He replied mirthfully, "This is my bedroom while I'm here on business. You can't disturb the President in the middle of the night, and I might not allow you to see him at all." Blane was confused by her earlier behavior when he was kissing her. Just how desperate or foolish was she? he asked himself. After hearing her sad story, he had decided he wouldn't take advantage of her, but he did want to understand her. If she truly had been frightened, then why hadn't she screamed? She wasn't acting like a normal female at all. Lord, she had guts and a desirability he yearned to explore. His gaze engulfed her with

28

longing. "Since you're running out of money, I might be persuaded to let you share my room while I decide if your problem is real and worth his time."

Shannon bristled at his intimate suggestion and high-handed manner. "Don't be absurd, you vulgar rake! I have a hotel room, and I can work to support myself if necessary. After all I've been through, I've earned the right to see him! Besides, who are you to prevent me from speaking with President Lincoln?"

"I'm the man who can send you over to Old Capitol Prison if you rile me. Either you can stay here until morning or you can return to your hotel and wait to hear from me. Whatever you decide, you aren't seeing him tonight. After I check around about you, I'll be in touch with my answer. Be honest, or be gone before tomorrow afternoon. If you're lying, I'll treat you like a blood-thirsty Comanche."

His last two statements baffled Shannon. "Who are you? What are you?" she questioned. He certainly had a fierce hatred and contempt for Comanches! She wondered why. Without a doubt, she knew that he and Hawke wouldn't get along. "How can I trust a wicked stranger? Just give me five minutes with Lincoln. Just five minutes," she stressed.

"I'm a good friend of Lincoln's. You have no idea what war is like, or you wouldn't be here. The Old South has vanished forever, Shannon. Lands have been neglected. Towns and plantations have been looted or burned or abandoned. Bridges are down and rail lines have been severed. Rebs who thought this war would be fast and fun are functioning on sheer ego and obstinacy, existing on blind pride. That whole area reeks of disillusionment and bitterness and dissension. A lack of supplies and heavy casualties have inspired staggering numbers of deserters, and they make dangerous men. You don't want to witness such tragedy. It's grim and depressing." He paused for effect. "Still want to play heroine?"

"I have no choice," she replied sadly, realizing that if it was that bad in the South, Corry and Greenleaf needed her more than she imagined.

He recalled a point of hers. "You said you couldn't return to Boston. Why? I want some answers, woman, or I call the guards."

Shannon inhaled and exhaled deeply. The closer she stayed to honesty, the better her chances were of winning over this nettling creature who was too wary and enticing. She was vexed by the fact that her words, looks, and charms were being ignored. How dare he question her word and breeding! How dare he treat her with such disrespect and indifference! "I was . . . having problems with the man my father left me with there. Since he knew that none of my family might survive, he began pressing me to marry him. It seems father signed some paper that gave Mister Simon Travers control over Papa's business until either he or one of my brothers returned. I should have been left in charge, not that vile beast. Travers refused to give me money or help me locate my brother. I took cash from my father's office and left Boston. I'm positive he's chasing me. If I don't hurry, he'll find me and stop me. I wouldn't marry him if I were destitute and alone."

"He can't force you to return to Boston, or to marry him."

Shannon frowned in dismay. "He said he could prove my family was a nest of Southern spies. He threatened to get me into trouble if I continued to refuse him. I told you, he has control of my finances."

"Tell me, are you really trying to get to your brother, or just fleeing this man? I want to know more about this Travers," he demanded.

"Simon Travers. He's a cotton factor. He and my father were partners. He's thirty-eight and a mean and

30

ugly scoundrel. He's detemined to get me and all of my family's holdings. Please help me," she urged.

Blane sighed heavily and stroked his smooth jawline. "Somehow you don't seem as helpless as you try to sound. Why is that, Shannon?"

Shannon blushed at his barely veiled insult. "You've never met Simon Travers! He's despicable. I wouldn't marry him if he were the only survivor of this ridiculous, bloody war. I can't help it if my father reared a spirited filly. But I know my limitations." Shannon tried to avoid Blane's probing gaze. "Darn you!" she exploded. "Travers has a paper that declares him my guardian. I know it's a fraud. Papa wouldn't have dared sign me over to any man. In fact, I suspect those business papers are forgeries as well. I won't allow him to get away with these deeds. I have to get to Danville. And even if Travers manages to steal all we own, I must help my brother."

"I see," Blane murmured, knowing what that particular driving force was like and feeling a curious empathy with her. "Now you're making sense. Still, you are a purebred Southerner, and I'm not convinced that you're an honest one. You'd never turn over crucial information about the Rebs. So what would I get for all my time and trouble?" he asked, thinking that if she remained in Washington, she would be available during his visits. He found her to be a fascinating creature, one whose unusual traits and wild spirit appealed to the part of him that thrived on adventure and challenge.

"I have no money or jewels to offer you for your services," she answered, waiting to see if he would name another source of payment. She was relieved when he did not make the kind of wanton suggestion that would have forced her to terminate their relationship instantly. To save Corry's life, she would close her eyes and surrender to the repulsive Travers before yielding for the same reason to this man who seemed to inflame her very soul.

"I can't permit you to enter enemy territory, Shannon, for any reason," he informed her. "You could get plenty of good men killed trying to assist you or protect you. Death and pillage roam the South like greedy scavengers ravaging a decaying corpse. The best thing you can do is to find a job here until this conflict is over. If your brother is anything like you, he'll survive. I'm certain President Lincoln will offer you his protection from this Travers. And if you'll give me some facts, the next time I head south I'll see what I can learn about your brother and your home. Now let's get you back to your hotel. I'll speak with you later." She was too bewitching, he thought uncomfortably. He would have to get her out of his room.

Shannon stared at the handsome man before her as she speculated about his words. Then she told him, "You have no right to stop me from going home to Georgia, nor from trying to help my brother. If Lincoln and the Union won't help me, I'll do it alone. Good night, sir."

When Blane didn't release her, she glowered at him as she ordered her brain to think fast. "You said I couldn't see him, so I'm leaving. Unhand me, or I'll wake the entire house," she threatened cleverly.

"I'll see you back to your room. It's late and dangerous outside." Blane grasped her arm and began pulling her toward the hall door.

"No," she protested. Shannon's keen mind had conceived a daring plan that would defeat her smug captor and enable her to see Lincoln. She put her ploy in motion. "If those guards see us leaving together this time of night, you know what they'll think. My reputation would be tarnished. I'll go down the tree and sneak back to the hotel. My shoes are behind the bushes. Where's my hat?"

"It's a long walk, Shannon. You aren't going alone," he insisted.

"All right," she deceptively conceded when his chin and gaze revealed his obstinacy. She would teach him a lesson or two! "Let me climb down the tree and you can join me outside. But if you don't contact me tomorrow, I'll be back. I'm not a quitter or a coward."

Blane knew that he could lock the window after her exit and that she would never reach the ground before he was beneath the tree. He grinned, assuming that if he let her have her way, she might mellow a little, or a lot. "Fine. Just be careful. Oh yes, I'm Blane Stevens." He released her, scooped up her hat and handed it to her, then approached the window.

Shannon twisted her long hair and stuffed it under the hat. Joining him at the window, she declared, "I'm not being cocky or rash. Will you at least think about what I said?" she inquired, tugging at his arm. "Please, Blane." She would show him who was smarter and quicker!

Blane glanced down at her upturned face. Moonlight gleamed in her blue eyes and illuminated her ivory complexion, which still bore streaks of soot. Her features had been artfully sculptured. He felt his body warm and his respiration quicken. His hand reached out to caress her cheek and to capture the single tear rolling down its smooth surface. She certainly had a way of appealing to a man, emotionally and physically. Before Blane gave it another thought, he pulled Shannon into his comforting arms and his lips seared hers in an exceptionally tender kiss.

Shannon dismissed any guilt over her actions as she swayed against him and returned the pervasive kiss. He had mentioned going south . . . She would use every feminine skill she possessed to entice Blane to take her with him. Were conditions as bad as he had described? she wondered. Until she learned what she was facing, she could use Blane Stevens and his expertise.

The contact between them held a surprise for her.

Shannon's head began to spin and her body flamed at his touch. Yes, she decided, this masterful rogue could defend her against any peril. There was something so intriguing and enchanting about him. He was a man, a real man, just like her brothers and Hawke.

Blane's embrace tightened. His mouth fused to hers and his tongue slipped between her parted lips. He felt Shannon tremble and press closer to him. He comprehended her warring emotions—the awakening of passion—and for a moment, he didn't want to end this madness. He knew Shannon had lost sight of her mission to ensnare him with innocent flirtation. Regretfully, he pushed her away and remarked hoarsely, "Let's get you out of here before I test the height of your desperation and the depth of my control. You are a very tempting witch, Blue Eyes." Blane wondered briefly if the attraction between them might become so overwhelming that he could mindlessly seduce her. But he instinctively knew it would be a mistake this soon. Despite her audacity, she was a well-bred lady.

Shannon was bewildered by his effect on her. She lowered her face as its heat warned of an annoying blush. Damn him! she cursed inwardly. He couldn't be persuaded to take her south. He was a man accustomed to controlling himself in any situation and was probably one of those domineering males who believed a woman's place was under her father's or husband's thumb. When Blane lifted her chin, she quickly lowered her lashes to hide her accusatory glare. "If you grab the limb and hold it steady, I'll meet you below," she stated raggedly.

"Make sure you stay put at the hotel until I contact you. The next man you beg for help might demand a high price for it. I think I'll give you a tour of Capitol Prison tomorrow to show you why you don't want to become a spy. Get those naïve ideas about gallantry toward female spies out of your head, Shannon. A spy is a spy. If you

34

attempt to charm information or assistance from the wrong man, you could find yourself in deep trouble. Men who are about to face death get crazy feelings and ideas. Soldiers away from home and family forget manners and conscience. Men without women can be blinded by someone who looks like you. Don't try to cross enemy lines alone or you might find yourself confronting one of those ruffians who doesn't recall he's a Southern gentleman," he stressed to scare her.

Shannon decided to test her assumptions about him. She entreated, "Can't you help me, Blane? I'll find some way to repay you. I can't remain here, and I have no money to go elsewhere. Travers will use anything to get at me. What if I were your mother or sister or wife? Wouldn't you want someone to help her locate and rescue you? I could pretend to be a nurse or a singer. All I need is a little kindness."

Blane knew his answer must be no, but decided it was too late at night to argue. This woman was intoxicating and he wanted to know more about her. He would be in Washington for a few days longer. In that time, Shannon could offer him delightful company. He needed a diversion from this war, which couldn't last much longer. He needed to feel alive and fresh. This malicious conflict was as bad as—if not worse than—the Indian slaughter he had left behind. If not for a matter of honor and revenge, he wouldn't be here now. And so far, he hadn't tasted either. "How about we discuss your troubles over dinner tomorrow? By then, I'll have had time to give them study. I'll figure out something for Travers." He didn't like men who ravished or beguiled naïve girls.

Shannon noticed a tinge of rage in Blane's voice when he mentioned Simon's name—or had it been bitterness? Though she might be innocent in some ways, she knew she had captured Blane's eye and attention. Still, he

35

wasn't taking her seriously. He didn't want to help her rescue Corry; he wanted to bed her! She doubted he would discuss her troubles with the President, and he definitely wouldn't take her along on his next journey. Again she wondered how she could disarm Blane and get to Lincoln for five minutes . . .

Shannon exhaled loudly. Then she looked at Blane and smiled. "I guess we have to do things your way—for now," she specified, taking another tack. "Dinner sounds marvelous. You wait and see, Blane; I'll convince you to help me," she hinted coquettishly.

Deceived, Blane grinned roguishly and nodded. He leaned out the window, grasped the limb securely, and pulled it toward him. Before he could tell Shannon he was ready, she seized his ankles and flipped him over the sill. His grip held around the limb, although it swayed and groaned ominously. Fury surged through him as Shannon closed the window and locked it. Blane lifted his legs and wrapped them around the limb. Slowly and cautiously, he edged toward the trunk, vowing that the deceitful little creature would regret her actions. She was a clever and daring vixen, a superb actress, and Blane realized he might have been tricked in more than one way. What if she were an assassin? he wondered disconcertedly. Berating himself, he hurried to prevent her from making a lethal error.

Shannon raced down the stairs and began to check each room for the President. When she decided she had located it, she boldly entered and hesitated inside the doorway. She called his name twice. When a deep voice asked who was there, Shannon replied, "Sir, it's Shannon Greenleaf of Savannah. I must see you on an urgent matter. It can't wait. I'm unarmed, Mister President; you can search me."

"Give me a moment, Miss Greenleaf, and I'll join you." The sleepy man knew she could have slain him in

36

his sleep if she had been an enemy. He believed that since this woman had had the courage and wits to get inside the White House and into his bedroom, she should be heard. He tossed aside the covers, stood, and slipped into his robe. Without lighting a lamp, he moved to join Shannon at the shadowy doorway.

"Sir, I locked out a Mister Blane Stevens when he tried to stop me from seeing you. I expect that he will rush up here and arrest me at any moment. Please, if I could have only five minutes of your time and attention, I'm sure you'll help me," she hurriedly informed him.

The sound of chuckling drifted to her ears from the dark room. He queried in amazement, "You took Blane off guard? That's a first. Come along, Miss Greenleaf; I most assuredly must hear both intriguing tales."

Blane covered the steps two or three at a time and seized a startled Shannon. Yanking her toward him and confining her within his unbreakable hold, Blane said antagonistically, "You tricky vixen, I'm placing you under arrest. I can't wait to see how you try to worm your way out of prison. I don't fool easily, my little chameleon."

"Let her go, Blane, and settle down. This young lady and I have some talking to do," the other man stated patiently and kindly.

"Sir, this is a cunning Rebel spy. She climbed the tree outside my room and sneaked inside. She's shrewd and dangerous, and handed me a devious tale as big as Texas." He would fix this temptress for making a fool of him! She would be sorry her mission had placed her within his grasp tonight and for the next few days! A tiny female had done what no foe had done before—outwitted him.

"I am not a spy, and I'm not dangerous," Shannon protested.

"Not dangerous? You pushed me out a third-story

window," Blane revealed, shaking her roughly. "I could have been killed or injured."

"Served you right! You refused to let me see President Lincoln."

"In the middle of the night? Disguised as a man and sooted up for concealment?" Blane snapped in rising vexation.

"That's the only way I could get to him, you brute!"

"It's impossible for you to see President Lincoln tonight. I told you I would handle matters and contact you tomorrow."

"For dinner," she scoffed. "You didn't believe me, and you weren't going to help me! I'm running out of money, and I don't have time to be toyed with by a charmer like you, Blane Stevens. With or without anyone's aid or permission, I'm going to Danville, Virginia."

The older man was amused by the interaction between Shannon and Blane, and by the ebony smudges on both. He watched as the angry girl struggled to turn in Blane's arms, but he held her fast against his chest. Shannon could only glare into Blane's challenging eyes as she repeated her claims and offers. The older man was intrigued by her suggestions and touched by her suffering.

Blane declared, "Where you're going is Old Capitol Prison, you little wildcat. Only a loyal Reb would pull a stunt like this."

She spoke to the man behind her instead of to Blane. "I owe the Confederacy nothing, Mister President. Rebels killed my father and my brother Temple; they imprisoned my brother Corry. Regardless of the dangers, I will do whatever is necessary to defend my family and my home. Mister Stevens underestimates women. They can be just as patriotic as men—just as brave and clever. I have a duty and desire to aid my country, to save lives,

38

to help end this war quickly. I searched my heart and mind for weeks before coming here. I know I'm doing the right thing. Please give me a chance to prove myself. At least help me get home to Greenleaf near Savannah."

The man's mirthful words halted their dispute. "Let's go downstairs and run this matter around calmly. Such a brave and cunning lady deserves to be heard, even at midnight."

"President Lincoln wouldn't like this, Mister Manning. If he were here tonight, he would order her imprisoned and interrogated."

Shannon twisted in Blane's grasp and stared at the silver-haired man with her penetrating, slate blue eyes. He was not Abraham Lincoln!

At her reaction, the man smiled genially and introduced himself. "I'm Silas Manning, Miss Greenleaf. You could say I'm Abe's confidant, his aide, his loyal minion, his factor. If you have business with him, it goes through me first. Anyway, he isn't home tonight. Let's talk and see how serious and honest you are. Bring her along gently, son."

Blane's mind whirled with the staggering facts she revealed in her last outburst. His suspicion about Shannon multiplied. She was a Greenleaf from Savannah with a brother named Corry . . . It had to be the same family! But why would she tell him her real name, he wondered, unless she didn't know about her brother's wicked deeds and his own vengeful pursuit of her brother . . . unless she didn't realize he was the man who was after her brother's life. So, Corry Greenleaf had gotten himself captured and was sitting in Danville Prison, helpless. *Danville Prison?* his sharp mind echoed. That was a Confederate prison for Yankees. What would Corry be doing in a Yankee prison—an insidious Rebel spy pretending to be a captive to obtain critical information from other prisoners?

Blane and Shannon exchanged challenging glares in the shadowy hall of the White House. The simmering Texan held her wrist firmly as the three descended the stairs and walked into the library to talk.

Blane knew he must reevaluate the situation quickly and with a clear head, for surely this she-cat had something devious in mind. He had visited Greenleaf on three occasions in his hunt for that marked-for-death brother of hers. Blane had disguised himself as a Rebel agent named Major Steven James, and the overseer had told him, "All the Greenleafs are off fighting this war, Major James. I don't know where they'd be nowadays. You can leave a message. I'll pass it along if any of 'em returns soon. Ain't no family braver or more loyal to the cause. I was left in charge of their home and lands till this war ends."

Was the whole family "a nest of Southern spies" as Simon Travers had accused? Did this Bostonian have proof? Was that why she was fleeing from Travers, or was that claim a lie, too?

Blane stole a glance at Shannon. What a dainty puzzle! Undeniably the vixen was meddlesome, but so tempestuous—as wild and unpredictable as a violent thunderstorm over the plains. She was utterly and potently appealing, but was she honest and trustworthy? He grudgingly admitted to himself that he could be allowing her humiliating trick and her identity to color his opinions and emotions. Was it possible that she was an innocent, and that this lecherous Travers was using her family's crimes to coerce her into marriage? He couldn't imagine this feisty minx permitting or enduring such a repulsive defeat. From past experience, he knew it was bad when feelings got in the way of judgments and actions. A man had to ignore them and do what he must. That was why he was so damn good at his job. He could be cold and unfeeling—unreachable. One

40

thing he didn't like to be was wrong; another was weak.

Blane had been searching for Corbett Greenleaf since the young man had left Texas in December of 1860. Shannon had provided Blane with his first clue to his quarry's location. And yet that fact wouldn't help if Corry were a Rebel spy using another name. Blane realized he might need Shannon to identify Corry for him. Then another aggravating point stabbed home. Considering her present age and her tender one in '60, he had to admit that she could be unaware of Corry's actions. If that were the case and if she weren't a hazardous spy, he would be using her to help destroy her brother—her last family member.

Was that an honorable road to justice, he asked himself, or merely the path to brutal vengeance? Blane shook his tawny head to dismiss any twinges of guilt or reluctance. Shannon Greenleaf was an audacious stranger, a stunning temptress. He would not put her needs or demands above those of the Union and his beloved Ellie. As they reached the library, he pushed aside those rankling thoughts.

Chapter Two

After Shannon related her story, Lincoln's assistant leaned back in his chair and studied her. Ideas flooded Silas's keen mind. Ending this awesome war was President Lincoln's main concern, even if this was an election year and McClellan was chasing him frantically toward the polls. War was a grisly, oppressive affair that tarnished any administration. Lincoln had dealt with many burdens—the staggering Union defeats and those draft riots last year. For emotional and political support, the President needed substantial victories from Grant, Sheridan, and Sherman. Could this clever, young daring woman help his friend and superior? He looked over at Blane and Shannon, observing their silent confrontation.

When the redhead glanced at the manly rogue sitting near her, she discovered Blane's penetrating gaze on her face. He was sitting like a coiled viper ready and eager to strike at her. His hazel eyes were as cold and hard as a canning jar filled with snow. Could she blame him? She had duped and embarrassed him. What if she needed his help later? Shannon surprised both of them when she stated abruptly, "I'm sorry about tossing you out the window, Mister Stevens. I hope you weren't injured."

Her blue eyes quickly examined his face and frame before she relaxed and returned her attention to Lincoln's aide.

Out of respect for the older man and from smoldering fury, Blane held his silence. He assumed Silas would politely hear out the persistent female, then gently dismiss her. Then, he would handle this little she-devil. She would be only too eager to earn his mercy!

"Blane was right when he told you it was dangerous to head south, Miss Greenleaf. Both sides are tired of the fighting and killing. Loyalty and spirit are running low. A war that wouldn't last a month has been going on for years. Families and friends have split. Homes and lands have been burned. People are starving and dying. It isn't a pretty sight, young lady. People are robbing to stay alive. Many of the wounded go without medicines. Some of the soldiers have no weapons, or tents for shelter, or proper garments. Raiders roam the countryside, looting and terrorizing. The Union is mounting a tougher offensive all over the South. The Rebels are fighting just as desperately to hang on until we withdraw, but we can't. It's no place for you."

"No disrespect, sir, but I would be there now if my father hadn't sided with the Union and moved us to Boston until this conflict was resolved. There are plenty of women in the South, many of whom are spies or loyalists. I know I can do something to help my brother and perhaps the Union. I want this war over so I can go home to Greenleaf. I'll be safe. I know many people from my travels with my father and brothers. I can sing and play the piano, so I could pretend to be an entertainer. The war hasn't stopped that pleasure. I know about herbs and medicines, so I could nurse. Wounded men might share vital secrets, or their pockets might contain them. I've been courted by a newspaper man and a photographer, and each taught me something about his profession. I can ride and fight and shoot and handle

43

a knife."

When neither man spoke, Shannon brazenly vowed, "The only way you can keep me from heading south is to imprison me. I don't think you can find adequate charges for such an action, and I doubt President Lincoln would allow you to drum up false ones. Just put me in touch with loyal Unionists or undercover agents who can help me."

"Don't trust her, sir," Blane advised gravely. Was that her scheme, he wondered, to worm her way into the Yankee spy system and destroy it?

Shannon rashly sneered, "Because I outsmarted you? If I hadn't been concerned about making noise, I would have proven to you I can defend myself. Where is the President? I'm certain he would help me."

Silas rose from his chair and stretched. "Blane, you escort Miss Greenleaf back to her hotel. Shannon—if I may call you that—I'll send for you at three tomorrow, after I've conferred with the President. I have the impression you can be of service to your country, and I'm sure Abe will agree. We'll discuss matters after a good night's sleep. Blane, I want you at that meeting, but see me first at two."

Lincoln's minion was cognizant of how many Northerners had opposed and still opposed this grim war. He knew the emancipation policy had birthed many outspoken Copperheads against his cherished leader. Morgan's raiding in the Great Lakes had created panic, as had Lee's bold intrusion into Pennsylvania and the advance toward Washington. With luck, Admiral Farragut's conquest of Mobile would appease some fears, for it would sever vital enemy supply lines. If only the Southerners wouldn't remain so dedicated to this divisive, futile cause. Aloud, Manning explained, "All I need is a little time and a lot of effort to make a few plans. Good night, Miss Shannon Greenleaf. Good night, Blane."

Shannon beamed with pleasure and relief. "Thank you, sir."

Blane couldn't believe what he was hearing. He queried incredulously, "You believe her, sir? You're going along with this wild scheme?"

"You will too when I explain everything tomorrow," Silas Manning said, then grinned broadly at the stunned Texan. As was true with Lincoln, he knew most of Blane's troubles and traits from soulful talks before a cheerless blaze on lonely winter nights over the years this man had worked for them. He hoped that this extraordinary woman might purge and heal Blane's emotional wounds. It wasn't good for a man to hate, to seek revenge, for so long. Silas was positive Lincoln would agree.

After the President's agent left, Blane and Shannon exchanged wary looks. "Don't be mean, Blane. I won't intrude on your territory or life. I have to do what I know is right for me and my family. I'm not a Rebel, and I'll prove it to you in less than a month. Will you check with President Lincoln in four weeks, then make your judgment?"

Blane's eyes moved over Shannon's face and figure. How could their meeting be a simple coincidence? Was she working for the Rebs, for Corry, or neither? "Something tells me I'm going to regret meeting you tonight," he muttered, then grinned wryly. There was more than one way to obtain the truth from a deceitful woman . . .

Shannon laughed. "I could say the same, but I won't." Her eyes drifted over his towering frame. His shoulders were broad and well muscled. If he carried any extra weight, it didn't show through his snug garments. She noted that his whiskey-colored hair was mussed, and she found herself wanting to run her fingers through it like a comb. His jaw was set in angry lines, which only served to increase his masterful image. Noticing the gun and knife belted at his waist, she smiled again.

45

Blane followed Shannon to where she had concealed her shoes, then she sat on the ground and pulled on the dusty boots. As they headed across a moonlit lawn toward the street, Blane grabbed Shannon from behind as he asked, "If I were a villainous Reb bent on ravishing you, how would you protect yourself, sly vixen?"

Shannon's right foot entangled his as she seized his neck and flipped him to the hard ground. Taken unawares, Blane found himself straddled by Shannon with his own knife at his throat. "One false move, villainous Reb, and I'll pierce your jugular. Like I said, Blane, I can defend myself. I didn't want our fighting to draw attention to my presence before I could get to see President Lincoln. Contrary to your current opinion, you might eventually discover I'm not a helpless ninny."

Shannon underestimated Blane's strength and wits. She suddenly found herself pinned beneath him and the knife wrestled from her grip. She couldn't move. Shannon smiled and remarked, "Mister Manning's right; you are one of the best. I can't believe how you moved without a sound upstairs. Since my antics have taught you to be more careful, would you teach me that move? I might have use of it one day soon."

Blane chuckled. Either she was superior at her job or she was one amazing female. "How about this move?" he teased, kissing her.

"You're one of the best in that area, too," she confessed merrily when their lips parted. Blane had released her hands and they slipped around his neck. She drew his head back to hers and returned his playful kiss. She had the feeling she should make friends with this man who could move as rapidly and potently as lightning. If he had any influence over Lincoln and his aide Silas, she wanted him to use it to her advantage. Besides, she didn't want him resentful of her, or repulsed by her.

46

Blane's hands moved to either side of her head as he kissed her deeply and hungrily. He was stimulated and surprised by her eager response. As his tongue darted skillfully into her mouth, he discovered hers feverishly dancing with it. He felt her arms tighten around his neck and sensed her arousal by the way she lifted her body toward his.

He didn't halt his enticing actions until a guard called out, "Anything wrong, Major Stevens?"

Blane replied, "Nothing, Tom," then pulled Shannon to her feet. For a moment, he had forgotten their location and his intention. He would have to watch her magnetic allure.

"Major Blane Stevens," she murmured, visibly impressed. He was a rare specimen of manhood. "I see no end to your accomplishments and skills. We don't have to be enemies. After tomorrow, we won't ever see each other again. This will be nothing more than an amusing story to relieve the boredom of a wintery night." A curious pang struck Shannon as she spoke these words. To cover it, she asked, "Where did you come from, Blane?"

"My mother," he quipped, then laughed.

"Very funny," she chided. "You sound Southern."

"Texas, Ma'am," he replied. "Like you, I had to git when everyone sided with the Rebs. Besides, I was tired of Cavalry life and scouting. Would you like to know how many Comanches this boy's peeled?" He wanted to probe her reaction to killings. When Shannon grimaced and shook her head, Blane ordered, "Make sure you stay put in your room until I or one of Lincoln's guards comes for you. You might be sorry you met Silas Manning. To him, winning is everything."

"What do you think he has in mind?" she questioned eagerly.

47

"I don't know," Blane admitted worriedly. Lord, he wished he knew if this treasure were genuine. Of all the women in this land for him to meet and desire, why did it have to be this gal who had been born Greenleaf's sister? He forced himself to remember Ellie and the past. He wouldn't be surprised if this unique vixen sought revenge after he confronted her brother. It was crazy to get tangled with her! Explaining an affair with this beauty to Ellie would be as easy as winning and retaining Shannon if she learned the truth, especially after he killed Corry. Perhaps he should convince Manning to refuse her wishes.

They walked in silence for a time. When they reached her room, Blane unlocked the door and handed her the key. He had always been a keen judge of character, but she mystified him. He stared at her strangely before cuffing her chin, pulling the door closed, and leaving.

Shannon locked her door and readied herself for bed. She was in a state of mingled depression and elation. Blane's face kept entering her mind. To date, she hadn't met a real man—one who was brave, intelligent, and well bred. Those she had met previously were too similar, too dull, too awkward—except for her three brothers.

She had yearned to meet a unique man, one who displayed all of the traits that she admired. Blane was everything a woman could want. No, she reflected, perhaps he was too handsome, too virile, too disarming! No doubt he was an adventurer, a taker, a user. Yet his charms were irresistible. Her lips and body still tingled from his kisses and embraces. Yes, she was powerfully attracted to the devilish rogue!

As Blane returned to the White House, thoughts of Shannon filled his mind. He had to respect her wits and courage, her resolve and cunning. She was dangerously enticing, and he craved her. He was accustomed to women pursuing him, but Shannon had behaved as if he were nothing special. Her kisses had been playful, almost childlike. Yes, he told himself, that lady was as perilous as a Texas blue norther and as highly skilled as a Comanche warrior!

At two the next day, loner and special agent Major Blane Stevens was gaping in disbelief as Silas Manning revealed his plan and confirmed Lincoln's agreement. "It will work, Blane. Traveling as a family, you two could get in and out of places other agents couldn't. With her acquaintances and talents, she'll be an asset to you. Who would suspect a husband and wife, or a brother and sister? If you use that blind or lame act again, she could be your helper. She knows important people, Blane; she's valuable to us. She's quick, smart, and alert, son. With those looks and charms, in one day she could get facts it might take you weeks to obtain."

"It's dangerous to take her along, sir. If I'm busy protecting or teaching her, how can I get my work done? What if we're captured? You know they would go hard on her. Worse, they could try to use her to get at me. She might not be as tough as she acts or as loyal as she pretends. Besides, she wouldn't take orders from me. She's bullheaded and spoiled and conceited. Mark my words, sir; facing blood and guts, her mettle would vanish. In less than a week, I'd have a helpless female or crybaby on my hands. It won't work."

"Shannon's smarter than you realize, Blane. I daresay she'll get you out of a few scrapes. She knows how to handle danger. I read something very special in her." He didn't want to tell Blane he had seen the tussle on the front lawn the night before. Those two would make an exceptional team. "Why don't we tell her you're going along as Rebel agent Major Steven James, as her protector and assistant? That way, if you're captured, she couldn't expose your real secret identity, The Blade. If you recall, she didn't lose her wits when you captured her and intimidated her last night."

Blane didn't care if she discovered his Steven James role, for many people knew about it. But few knew he was the legendary Union agent, the Blade. Shaking his head, Blane declared, "No way, sir. She would be unbearable if she believed she was my boss."

"How about becoming partners? I'll tell her she must follow your lead during a crisis, since you're the more experienced one."

Blane resisted Silas's plan. "I don't like this, sir. She could get us both killed. Steven James has plenty of helpers, but the Blade always works alone. She doesn't know what she'll be facing soon."

Silas coaxed, "Will you try it for a month? If it doesn't work out, you can leave her in a safe place or bring her back to Washington. Do this for Abe and the Union, Blane. We can use Shannon's help, even if it's only as a protective cover for Major Steven James. And in case you haven't considered another point, we need to learn if her brother is a captive at Danville and if he's there working covertly for the Rebels. You haven't forgotten that Abe and I know about you and Corry Greenleaf?" the silver-haired man hinted pointedly. "You'll need her to identify him. If you are right about her motives, what safer place for a clever spy than under your eye and control? Think of the challenge, Blane—unmasking a bewitching spy or proving her innocent. Surely you aren't afraid of her allure? I had believed you capable of handling any person or event," he cunningly goaded. "I suppose I could assign another agent to Shannon. It might not be wise to pair you two, since your personal feelings are involved; that could hamper your actions and decisions. It could make matters worse for both of you when you discover she's for real. I just wish our other agents were as superior as you are."

Blane paced the length of the room. He reflected that besides the danger to their lives, there was the danger to his emotions. Shannon, with her big blue eyes and flaming hair, was far too tempting. What if she were guilty? What if she were blameless? What if she refused to follow orders? What if she were injured? What about their nights together?

Just after Blane related his decision, there was a knock on the door and Shannon was invited into the President's study. Blane stood with his back to her, pretending to stare out the window, his fingertips jammed into his back pockets. Silas explained his ideas to Shannon. "President Lincoln agrees with my decision, but we can't promise to get your brother out of prison," he concluded.

Shannon glanced at Blane's back. He hadn't moved or spoken. "Blane disagrees with you, doesn't he, sir?" When Silas glanced away and Blane stiffened, she frowned. Why did Blane continue to doubt her words and talents? It was becoming a challenge to Shannon. Why couldn't he take her along, the selfish brute? "I thought as much. Why?" she asked aloud. So much for her promise not to intrude on his life or see him again! she mused inwardly. Was that why he was annoyed? She was determined to change his mind.

Blane let Silas express his feelings and doubts. "A month, Shannon, that's all you have to prove you won't be a hindrance or danger. Our main concern is the survival of the Union. Is that agreeable?"

Shannon directed her reply to Blane in the form of a question. "If I promise to follow orders and stay out of trouble, will you give me a fair chance? If it doesn't work out, you can drop me anywhere."

Blane turned and looked at her. "You tricked me last night. Today, I'm supposed to take your word without question or delay? You're one of the few people who can

51

successfully hide the truth from me. At times, my life could be in your hands. Another tumble out a window doesn't appeal to me. If we were captured or detained, one slip from you and the Union could suffer. What if you were injured and I had to leave you some place? Would you betray me for revenge? Women can be rash or spiteful creatures. Both sides are fighting in the South. What happens when you see Southerners or friends slain or captured? What happens when you have to deceive them? This is talk; that's reality. Would you turn against the Union? Against me? Why should I trust you?"

Shannon rose and walked over to him. She gazed up into his skeptical expression. She sensed that his feelings had been aroused by more than just her or last night. "Please, Blane, I won't deceive you again. I'll do whatever you say—immediately. Take me. You won't be sorry."

Blane wondered if she realized how her words sounded to him, especially when she used that stirring tone? He would like nothing better than to take her—right to his room to make love to her! As surely as her eyes were blue, this assignment would be trouble. Whatever happened, there would be no personal victory possible for him. But why not yield to Lincoln's and Silas's wishes? Shannon wouldn't last a week on the trail. Maybe that was the best solution to this predicament.

Blane shrugged and responded flippantly, "If I don't let you tag along, you'll only head out by yourself and get into trouble. I'm warning you now, woman. Stay close, keep your mouth shut, and obey orders. If you don't, I'll drop you faster than a hot branding iron."

Instead of insulting him or arguing, Shannon impulsively hugged him and thanked him. Blane eyed her anxiously. Trouble and temptation! "Shannon, there's one other thing. If you're lying to us and you turn traitor, woman or not, I'll slay you where you stand. Understood?" He witnessed Shannon's astonished look, then her nod of comprehension.

The Texan escorted her to the hotel and left her at the door, reminding her of their dinner appointment to discuss their imminent journey. Shannon entered the building to be told that a man named Simon Travers and two soldiers were looking for her. Shannon's face paled. She told the clerk she would be staying at the White House. If anyone wanted or needed her, she could be contacted through her friend and host, President Lincoln. Shannon prayed that that news would stall Travers.

Shannon quickly packed selected items in a carpet bag. She paid the hotel clerk to have her other cases sent over to the White House before dinner. Shannon immediately went to speak with Silas before Travers could return. If he dared to come to the White House, the President's assistant might help her avoid or thwart him. With luck, she and Blane could be gone before Travers found the courage to seek her there.

Upon her arrival, Shannon was taken to a private study. When Silas Manning joined her, she inquired, "I know this is presumptuous, sir, but can I stay here until Blane and I leave? There's a man from Boston named Simon Travers following me, and I'd like to avoid him if possible."

"No one would harm a woman under the protection of the President. What has this Simon Travers done?" When he saw Shannon's reaction to his query, he smiled and remarked, "Blane told me about him. There's more to this matter with Travers than a romantic and financial pursuit, isn't there? Blane told me that every time his name was mentioned, you went pale and shaky, as you did just then. I know you have mettle and wits, Shannon. Why does he terrify you?"

Lincoln's minion was a gentle and wise man, and

Shannon felt she could trust him and depend on him. "Simon Travers . . . tried to force himself on me several times, but I have no proof. When my maid tried to stop him the last time, he had her arrested for theft. He's wicked and powerful, sir. The local authorities refused to defy him. They said I had to remain with him. The day I ran away, he had removed the lock on my bedroom door and I overheard him giving the servants the night off. I knew what he was planning. I knocked him out, bound him, and locked him in a closet. I took some of my money and escaped. I traveled westward for two days to throw him off my trail. Then I disguised myself as a man and came to seek President Lincoln's help to find Corry. Travers would never challenge my brother." She stopped before telling him about Hawke and his role in her life. For now, that information was too private and complex to expose.

"You are a spunky, ingenious woman," he complimented her. "Until that paper can be proven a forgery and your charges against him true, Abe would have no choice but to return you to his custody. It's a shame you'll have vanished before he can hear Travers's claims and carry out the law," he hinted, then laughed roughly as he winked at Shannon.

Shannon smiled. "Thank you, sir. I'm sorry about Sally being jailed because of me, but I couldn't help her. Can President Lincoln send word demanding her release, or a full investigation? I know I'm asking many favors, but a woman alone during these times falls prey to evil men like Simon Travers. I'm sure he's convinced the soldiers he's with that I stole money from him, just as he's probably shown them that false guardianship paper. If he gets his hands on me again, everything will be lost."

"Relax, Miss Shannon Greenleaf, for you have three strong, smart men on your side. We won't let him catch you. From now on, you're our responsibility. If this

Travers shows up, I'll send him over to Mrs. Lucy's. She'll detain him for a spell to give you a chance to get away. I'll see to a few matters while you get disguised."

"Does that mean you're still letting me go with Blane? When?"

"Right now, Shannon. You did say you could ride?"

"Like a champion," she responded happily and proudly.

He chuckled at her expression. "Then how about slipping into pants, boots, and a shirt? I have a feeling this Travers is a persistent fellow. Let's get you out of here quickly and safely. From now on, you're the Flame, a notorious Union spy," he mirthfully informed her.

Silas left while Shannon hurriedly switched garments. She folded her gown and placed it inside the bag that she had brought with her. She exchanged her slippers for riding boots, and after braiding her hair, she donned her felt hat to conceal it. She wouldn't be able to wait for her valises to arrive. When the jovial Silas returned, she announced eagerly, "Ready, sir."

He scanned her appearance. "Perfect. Only one problem," he murmured. "I can't locate your partner. I'm sending you out of town with one of the soldiers. He knows where to stop and wait for Blane. When he joins you, you two will ride close to the Potomac River until just before Fredericksburg. Then you'll head for Richmond. If you two get separated for any reason, Shannon, try to make it to Miss Elizabeth Van Lew's. She's on our side. Take these."

Shannon looked at the small gun and knife he was handing her. She smiled as she placed the weapons' belt around her waist. "I'll be careful, sir, and I won't let you and the President down."

Within ten minutes, Shannon was following a soldier's horse as they galloped out of town. They rode hard and fast for an hour, then halted and concealed themselves.

For a time, all Shannon could think about was escaping Travers and finding Corry. As two hours passed and darkness surrounded them, her thoughts shifted to the unpredictable and mysterious Blane Stevens. Her mind traveled to Hawke, with his sparkling mahogany eyes and dark sable hair, so different in looks yet so similar in prowess and character to that hazel-eyed blond.

Around ten o'clock, Shannon tried to persuade the soldier to return to town, insisting, "Either something's happened to Major Stevens or he's on his way. I'll be fine. If something's wrong, you can return to warn me. I'll wait here until dawn, then follow Mister Manning's instructions. I was told where to meet Major Stevens if we got separated or if we met with trouble." The soldier refused to leave her.

At midnight, Shannon encouraged his departure again. He hesitated. He was hungry, weary, and nervous. Major Stevens was to bring the supplies, and the soldier was confident that Stevens was invincible. Surely he would be along shortly. If not, who would know? He didn't like hanging around this ravishing beauty who was under Lincoln's protection, and who inspired severe hunger pains in his groin. And that rich widow he was seeing could become annoyed at his tardiness and drop him. He didn't want to risk losing any of her favors—in or out of bed.

Shannon was delighted when the soldier mounted and left. Now she felt she could relax while she waited for Blane. She didn't require a bodyguard, especially one who kept rubbing his protruding crotch whenever he thought she didn't notice. She wondered if most men were consumed by the urgency to bed any available woman whenever they were afflicted by uncontrollable swellings and pains in that private region. She knew her brothers had often assuaged such desires, for she had secretly witnessed a few of those wanton encounters and startling pleasures, but she had never been tempted to experience them—at least she hadn't until Blane!

Shannon yanked her mind from such forbidden thoughts. She was concealed, and she had a gun and a knife. And she was certain that the soldier had been anxious to depart. As another hour passed, Shannon fretted over Blane's delay. Traveling and working with him was going to be stimulating, if he ever arrived. She wondered if this were some sort of test of her courage and obedience. Perhaps he was observing her at this very minute.

Shannon leaned back against a tree and closed her eyes to rest them. Rising early this morning had added to her lack of sleep the night before and her weariness was beginning to reveal itself. She listened to the night sounds and began to doze.

Suddenly a stirring sensation flooded her as Blane's lips nibbled at hers before he kissed her soundly. She yielded to his arms and mouth, then a peaceful sigh escaped her lips as she nestled her head against his shoulder. "I was worried about you, Blane," she said unknowingly.

"I can tell you were," he teased, shaking her to arouse her. He didn't know why he had felt compelled to kiss her, but he had enjoyed it. "What the hell are you doing here alone? Where's your escort? I'll have him hanged for desertion. And why are you sleeping, woman? Enemy scouts could be working in this area." Blane wondered if she had forced her escort to leave her alone for some devious reason. He still hadn't decided which approach to take with her tonight or in the future.

Shannon was awake by then. She explained her solitude and fatigue. "Where have you been? I've been waiting for hours."

"I didn't know you were missing until I went to the hotel to fetch you for dinner. When I got to the White

57

House, Silas was in a meeting. The man he left on duty to inform me of the change in plans had an accident. By the time I learned what was happening, it was late. I packed and here I am. You shouldn't have been left alone. You're my responsibility, woman."

Blane realized how easily those words had left his mouth. He did feel a curious possessiveness, he rationalized. She owed him! Until he finished with her, he wasn't about to let any man take Shannon Greenleaf, especially not the slimy-fingered Travers. It disturbed him to know she had been honest about this, for he knew about Travers's visits to the hotel and White House, and he knew about Shannon's explanation to Silas this afternoon. He had viewed the papers in Travers's possession; he had heard Travers's allegations and claims. More vexingly, he had observed the predatory gleam in that devil's eyes. Lord, what would he do if he discovered she was being totally honest?

"We're too close to town to camp here. Travers is putting on the pressure to locate you. Your little ruse in Boston really annoyed him. It's my guess he's out for blood, if he can't have you." When she looked alarmed, he caressed her cheek and coaxed, "Don't worry about him. If he shows up again, I'll take good care of Simon Travers for you. Demons and charmers rile my temper and boil my blood."

Shannon recognized the intimidating tone in his voice and the look on his face. Was he being serious? Would he be her bodyguard? Maybe she had judged him too harshly, too rapidly. She smiled. "With you, Silas, and the President on my side, I'm not worried." She stretched and yawned.

Blane eyed her. He knew she would need time to adjust to the demands of the trail. Should he allow it? If he hadn't met Travers today . . .

"You'll ride with me for a few hours and get some

sleep," announced Blane. "You're no good to either of us in this condition," he added somewhat harshly to hide his rankling feelings. He would find another place to deposit this bag of fluff, out of Travers's reach.

Shannon scowled at him. "When are you going to realize I can take care of myself? Am I not sitting here safe and sound?" Ride with him! her mind screamed. Touching him? Should she?

Now that they were alone, was she afraid of him? Blane wondered. Did she know who he was, to her brother, to the Union? Was she afraid of herself? "I'm the boss, remember?" he said aloud. "You agreed to follow orders. Come along, Flame," he commanded sternly, pulling her to her feet.

Blane mounted, then lifted Shannon and placed her sideways across his muscular thighs. Her left side nestled against his firm body. "Sleep, woman. We've got some hard riding to do." He pressed her cheek to his shoulder, seized the reins of her horse, then kneed his mount into a steady pace. He was relieved when she didn't argue or rebel.

Shannon placed her left arm around his back and the right one over his waist, then locked her fingers at his left side. She closed her eyes. For now, she would play the vulnerable female and, in truth, she relished the feel of Blane's arms and body. His manly scent teased her nose, and his strength and confidence gave her courage and comfort. She snuggled closer to him. When his embrace tightened, she smiled and went to sleep.

Blane felt Shannon's body slowly go limp. He decreased his pace to allow a smoother ride and was puzzled by his concern. He rationalized that as long as they were moving, they were putting miles between them and Washington. He didn't want Travers to interfere with his schedule, or with his plans for Shannon. He cuddled her shapely figure snuggly to his body and, for a time, he rested his cheek atop her head.

Shortly before dawn, Blane guided the horses into a tree-sheltered area that would conceal them from the eyes of anyone passing by. He dropped the reins to the ground and eased off his steed's back without arousing Shannon. Catching a blanket between his fingers, he headed for a grassy spot. He balanced the sleeping girl on one leg while he spread the blanket with his free hand. Very gently and carefully, he placed Shannon on it.

Blane watched her curl to her side, pleased that her slumber had been undisturbed by his fluid movements. He unsaddled the horses and allowed them to graze and water at a nearby creek. Then he flexed his tense muscles. Though he was accustomed to going without sleep when the situation demanded it, he could also sleep with one eye and ear open, which was his intention now as he stretched out beside Shannon. Almost immediately, she turned and snuggled against him, as if his warmth or scent had drawn her to his body.

Blane smiled as his arms encircled her. Maybe Silas was right about one thing: she could be a big help to him. At least this trip wouldn't be dull. No, dull wasn't the right word. Distraction was what she could offer, and perhaps pleasure. If she was lying, then he owed her nothing and could freely take what he pleased. Maybe ruining a woman so special to Corbett Greenleaf would provide ample and perfect punishment for Corry's crimes against Ellie . . .

Blane was shocked by what he was thinking. Could he do such things? Lord, how he wished this war would end before he lost all touch with morals and reality. In a couple of hours they would eat and head for Dixie. To face what? These were his last thoughts as he drifted into a light sleep.

Shannon opened her eyes to find herself lying beside Blane. She didn't want to disturb him, so she remained

60

very still. This man was so contradictory. He could be so warm or so cold. He could be so gentle or so tough. He could be so enticing or so repelling. But what a man he was—virile, handsome, charming; so self-assured. How lucky she was to have him as her escort, her partner. Maybe . . .

Blane's hazel eyes opened and locked with Shannon's, and she quickly averted her probing gaze. "When did we camp?" she asked uneasily.

"Two hours ago," he replied, then stood and stretched to loosen his stiff body. He glanced at Shannon and teased, "I wanted to sleep longer, but you have a potent stare, Blue Eyes."

"I beg your pardon?" she asked in confusion.

"I'm a light sleeper, and I could feel you looking at me. Why?"

Shannon's cheeks filled with color. "I was trying not to awaken you. Did you get enough sleep?" she inquired, changing the subject.

"When I'm on the move, I require little sleep. There's a creek over there if you want to freshen up before we eat. We can't risk a fire, so it's cold biscuits and salt pork."

Shannon's nose wrinkled, but she didn't respond. Blane chuckled. "You'd best get used to trail food. I told you this trip wouldn't be easy."

"I'll be just fine, Major Stevens," she retorted sassily.

He instantly scolded, "Drop that name, Shannon. It's dangerous where we're heading. Until I tell you different, you're Shannon James, wife of Steven James. Most of the Federal officers know me. But if anyone else asks questions, I'm a shipper from New Orleans who sided with the Union. When the fighting increased in that area, I brought you along for your safety. You'll play the obedient wife who doesn't defy her husband's words or actions. Understand?"

"Why wife? Why not sister?" she pressed nervously.

61

He replied almost sullenly, "There might be times when we have to move out swiftly and secretly. A man doesn't keep his sister at his side at all hours. And I won't have to worry about love-struck Rebs chasing an unattached sister. When we cross the Rebel lines, we'll appear to be traveling around to obtain supplies and information for President Davis."

"I see," she murmured, questioning this perilous arrangement. An arduous journey would be nothing compared to danger of spending so much time in the company of this fascinating man! "What about this naked finger?" she hinted, holding up her left hand and wiggling the digit in question.

Blane didn't want to tell her to claim she had donated it to the Confederacy to buy arms and supplies. He wanted his ownership to be vividly seen. He searched his pockets and finally withdrew a gold band. "Make sure you protect it and return it later. It was my mother's," he lied defensively. Then he reached for her hand and slipped the ring on her finger. "Any more questions?" he asked in a tender voice. For the time being, he knew gentleness would be more apt to ensure her cooperation.

She lowered her head to shield her turbulent gaze and to conceal her revealing expression. She was vexed by his low opinion of her intelligence and perception. To pass off a new ring as his mother's, he would have to think her brainless! Was he wed, or planning to marry? Her pride would not allow her to ask. "None. Blane—I mean Steven—when can we head for Danville to check on Corry?"

"First comes Richmond. That's where Tredegar Iron Works is located. The South is short on powder mills and iron works. Most of their big guns are made at Tredegar. I need to find out how many guns are being made, how quickly, and where they're being sent. It'll reveal their strength and area of attack. The South is outmanned and

62

outarmed; she can't stand much longer. Until she falls, those guns will claim more lives. You said you knew Johnston, so he's our second target. If we can't link up with him, we'll track another one of your acquaintances." He knew those plans would be the fastest ways to test her loyalty and worth. He refused to admit to himself that they would keep her around him longer as well.

"But what about Corry?" she protested.

"Johnston and Bragg should be operating in the general area of Danville. First the missions, Shannon; then we solve personal problems. How valuable would your services be once you attempted to free a Yankee soldier? I don't mean to sound cold and heartless, but the war and the Union come first. The sooner it's over, the sooner prisoners will be released. Corry's freedom won't inspire peace, and he's only one fighting soldier. If you disagree, we part here. Well?"

"We do it your way," Shannon acquiesced after pensive thought.

"Sometimes your intelligence and mettle surprise me," he stated with a mischievous grin. He passed her a biscuit with salted pork. "Eat up, wife, and let's get out of here."

Shannon rode beside Blane for hours. Her aching body let her know it had been a long time since she had strained it this much. When they halted for a break, Shannon wondered if she could dismount, yet she was careful not to complain or show weakness. She walked around to relieve her stiffness and bent over as she flexed her back and shoulders. Suddenly Blane's hands were massaging them. It felt too good to feign strength and stamina. What a mercurial man he was!

"Been a while since you rode like this, if ever, right?"

"If you think I'll play the martyr or the fool, you're wrong. That feels like sheer bliss. If memory serves me, this soreness will decrease each day. I won't be a hindrance for long."

"Actually, you haven't been one yet," he commented, then tickled her playfully. "At least I have an honest woman on my hands."

Shannon peeked over her shoulder and grinned. "Thanks for the trust and special treatment. I have a feeling I'll earn them."

"Most assuredly, Mrs. James. Ready?" He winked at her.

"Ready." Shannon stretched one last time and mounted.

During the afternoon, they began to encounter signs of past battles and the other horrors of war. They passed burned homes and buildings, devastated landscapes, numerous graves, deserted huts, old campsites, dusty and shabby people, bone-tired, spirit-weary soldiers, all of which transmitted an aura of decay and misery. The people whom they encountered, civilian and military alike, wore looks of desolation. Clearly many were hungry; most were in rags. Children lacked smiles and healthy flesh. Elderly people could barely move along the dry roads beneath the stifling sun. The soldiers' uniforms were tattered and soiled, and their rusty weapons were as scarred as their souls. Bandages tied around foreheads, arms, or legs were gray with filth. Most seemed to be traveling without purpose or direction, as if movement represented a continuation of life or a promise of hope.

Shannon read varying degrees of suffering in those faces and she yearned to help. Blane guided his horse beside hers when a few of the wanderers crowded around her and begged for food or money. She was baffled by the hatred in the eyes of those who scanned her healthy mount and body and she was about to ask Blane to share their food when he seized her bridle and raced away.

After he reined in miles down the road, she demanded, "Why did you do that? They were starving. Many were wounded. Women, children, old folks. You are cold and heartless, Blane Stevens!"

Blane grabbed her collar and yanked her face close to his, nearly ripping her from her saddle. "I told you, there's a war going on—a bloody, cruel war. We'll be confronting people like that nearly every day. How can we survive to carry out our missions if we give away our food and money and horses? Then we would have to steal or beg. Sharing isn't the best thing you can do for them; helping me and the Union end this nightmare is! Listen to me, Shannon," he urged, softening his tone. "You've got to close your eyes and heart to such sights. I know how hard that is, but you must. If you don't, you'll be so confused you won't know which side to take. Starving people can be dangrous. They'll steal all you have or they'll betray you for food. Look what you're willing to endure to help your brother. Just imagine what mothers or fathers would do to save their children and homes. If you can't handle or stomach those sights, what about crossing a battlefield strewn with mutilated bodies?"

Blane released his grip on Shannon, but she remained near him. Her eyes were wide and lucid, and they drew him without mercy. "Shannon, Shannon," he mumbled wearily. "Do you realize what you'll confront in camp hospitals if you play nurse? Do you realize what you'll witness in enemy prison camps? You'll break or flee, woman."

Shannon sensed how upset Blane was about her conduct. He liked appearing tough and cool, yet he could be so gentle and sensitive. "I'm sorry. It's just that it was such a shock. You're right; war was only a word to me until today. I won't go soft on you again."

"You sure you want to continue? It'll get worse. We'll

be in Alexandria soon. You can get back to Washington from there."

To lighten their moods, she speculated blithely, "Would you desert your wife in the midst of enemy territory, Mister James? Why, I haven't even gotten adjusted to wearing this ring yet." Shannon boldly caressed his cheek, running her finger over the knife scar. "How did you get this?" she asked in curiosity.

"Some dreary night, I might tell you how you almost lost me to Comanches before we had a chance to meet. I want to make town before dark. Do hot food and a soft bed sound tempting?" Maybe they would be enough to convince her to stay in town, after the sights she had seen today.

Shannon beamed with pleasure. "What are we waiting for, sir?"

There was a Union encampment near Alexandria, where soldiers were awaiting orders from General Grant. Shannon remained with the horses while Blane reported to the officer on duty, using the password to guard their safety. He was smiling when he joined her. Shannon wisely refrained from asking any questions until they were inside their room.

Dropping their belongings on the floor, he told her, "You can relax now. This is a safe house for guests. Things sound pretty bad south of here. We'll have to cross Union and Rebel lines to reach Richmond." Blane removed his shirt and tossed it on the bed. He poured water into a basin and splashed his face. "I told them you were tired, so you wouldn't be joining us for dinner. That accent of yours might make them a bit nervous. You can eat and rest here."

Shannon was relieved that she wouldn't have to share dinner or small talk with rough soldiers in a tent. She was smiling faintly when Blane turned to study her reaction to his words. "I'm an obedient wife and partner who

66

follows orders, sir. Besides, I'm too tired and hungry to argue. You'll probably learn more over a few sips of whiskey without my distracting presence."

As he was drying his face, Blane eyed her over the cloth. His softened eyes reminded her of warmed brandy. "You're learning fast, Mrs. James. While I'm gone, keep this door locked. Hopefully I won't be kept out too late. We'll have a long ride tomorrow."

"Any chance of a bath? No telling when my next one will come."

"Nope. We've gotta keep attention to us at a minimum. It's an inconvenience of trail life, unless you're brave enough to bathe in rivers and streams." Blane wondered how long it would take her to show her colors.

Shannon tried to pull her gaze from his bronzed torso with its rippling muscles. Blane aided her by pulling on a fresh shirt. As he was combing his sun-kissed hair, he hesitated for a moment to observe her in the mirror. Shannon looked away, feeling strangely warm and edgy and heard him slipping out the door.

She paced the large room until Blane returned with a hot meal and placed it on the table. "You're going to spoil me," she teased.

"How so? You're already spoiled. See you later, Shannon."

She closed the door and locked it. Seating herself at the small table, she savored the vegetables and cured ham, letting each bite linger on her tongue. She inhaled the aroma of the freshly baked bread before each bite. The coffee tasted bitter to her without sugar, and she pushed it aside, though not without thinking of the starving people she had seen today and feeling guilty over this feast she was enjoying. Blane was right; they needed their strength and health to play their parts in ending this horrible war. She was surprised to find that Blane had included a glass of red wine, and she sipped it slowly. Realizing this might be her last good meal for a long time, Shannon consumed the remainder snailishly.

Later, she used the basin and tepid water to bathe as best she could. Then, assuming Blane wouldn't return tonight, she donned a summer nightgown taken from her carpet bag, brushed her hair, and lowered the lamp flame. After checking the window to make sure it was inaccessible to intruders, she climbed into bed. As she wiggled into the softness, she sighed in pleasure and, within moments, she was fast asleep.

Blane's dinner and the conversation that followed had taken longer than he had imagined or intended. He knew the flaming haired beauty would probably be asleep by now. Perhaps the trusting, inexperienced woman had left the key in the lock. If so, it would be a simple task to slide a paper beneath the door and dislodge the key with his small knife, allowing it to fall to the paper. He could then carefully pull the paper under the door, retrieve the key, unlock the door, and slip inside to join her. Shannon had indeed overlooked the key, and Blane discovered her error with mixed emotions: relief and annoyance. He would warn her about removing the key from the lock.

Once Blane was inside the room, he moved silently to the bed. She was sleeping peacefully and deeply. He noticed her empty food tray and grinned. Then Blane stripped off his shirt, boots, and pants, and was about to join her in the bed. Looking down at Shannon's slumbering figure, he felt his loins stir to life, and he realized the dangers such a move would pose.

This wasn't the time or place to test his self-control. If Shannon snuggled up with him again, he would be lost, and so would her purity—if a creature so ravishing and impulsive could still be in possession of her innocence. He was willing to bet all he owned that Shannon was up to something, that she was withholding facts about herself and her intentions.

Blane sighed irritably. Then he unrolled his sleeping bag and doused the lamp before stripping naked to combat the August heat. He reclined on the thin bedroll, aware of the hard floor beneath him. This mission was going to test more than his wits and courage, even more than his patience! Shannon Greenleaf was a mystery, and a smart man didn't unravel an enigma like her without caution and time. He remembered the way she had nestled against him and the way she had responded to his kisses. Perhaps this mission wouldn't be all work . . .

Chapter Three

September 1, 1864

Shannon awoke to the sound of splashing water mixed with audible sighs of resignation and pleasure. She glanced to her right to find Blane washing his face and hands as he cleared his groggy senses. She wondered how a man could shave before he was fully awake, for she noted that his jawline had been cleared of what had been surprisingly dark stubble for someone with his hair coloring. He was wearing black pants that would supply just enough room for his splendid lower half if his weight remained the same. His tawny hair had not been combed or brushed, and she saw that droplets of water had fallen to his smooth chest and now ran downward over his bronze torso in glistening rivulets.

Pale gray light peeking through the curtains told her it was still early. "How did you get in here? Did you learn anything? Where did you sleep?" She fired the questions at him in a rush as she unthinkingly sat up and turned to him for answers. "What's wrong, Blane?"

Blane was staring at her. He shook his head to recover mastery of his rebellious senses. Lord, she was radiant in the morning. Her future husband would never roll out of

70

bed to get chores started on time! Flaming hair tumbled riotously over ivory shoulders. Firm breasts teased against her thin nightgown, as if wickedly determined to snare his attention. Sleepy blue eyes settled on his face and tantalized him with their sultry glow. Didn't she comprehend her enormous desirability? Was she playing feminine games with him?

Shannon was too busy watching Blane to realize how he was watching her. His body was lithe and smooth, inviting hands to roam slowly and sensuously over it. He looked as if his skin would retain much of its glowing bronze color all year. His shoulders were broad and his waist narrow. Her father and brothers had had very hairy chests, but Blane's was bare like Hawke's. His nakedness accentuated each strong bulge, each flat plane, each attractive curve. She found it strange that she intensely enjoyed just looking at him. She wondered how many women he had known intimately, for surely his list of conquests was lengthy.

A horrible thought struck her. She had not asked if he had a wife or sweetheart back home. What if he did? Would that stop her from thinking about him, from desiring him?

"You left the key in the lock," he informed her, then explained how he had used certain acquired skills to obtain the key and get inside the room. "It's a simple trick, one I'll have to teach you later. Be glad I was your midnight caller, but don't forget about the key again," he warned gravely, then laughingly added, "But I sure was glad you were careless last night. I was exhausted." He returned to the task of drying his face, hands, and torso, while she observed him intently.

"Where did you sleep?" she inquired again, recalling how he had made camp and slept with her the night before without awakening her.

"There," he informed her, pointing to the rumpled

71

bedroll. He twisted from side to side at the waist. "And I feel every minute of it. A hard floor doesn't yield like the earth." Tossing the damp cloth on the washstand, he informed her, "I didn't want to startle you by sneaking into bed so late. For appearances, I'll have to stay with you at night. But a screaming wife after midnight would have been difficult to explain."

They had slept together once, and he had seemed a man of integrity. He hadn't made any attempts to force his attentions on her, other than at their first meeting when he had been trying to frighten her into a confession. It was selfish to force him to sleep on a hard floor while she slept in a soft bed. And, she rationalized that a casual attitude should throw him off balance. "We're both adults, Blane. We could have shared the bed. It's big. I'm not a silly child, or a weakling."

Blane walked to the bed and pulled Shannon to her knees on its edge. "That's the problem, Flame. We're both adults. You're a very tempting woman. In the future, can I trust you to stay on your side—if we're lucky enough to find another soft bed?"

Shannon laughed. "I'll try my best, partner." At the sudden roar of a nearby cannon, Shannon pressed herself tightly against him. "What was that?" she asked without moving away from him. Was this town under siege? Would they be trapped amidst a bloody battle?

"A warning to approaching Rebs. There's a lot of fighting going on east and west of here. It's going to be rough and dangerous riding."

When Shannon shivered in dread and uncertainty, Blane shifted his hands from her bare shoulders to beneath her heavy hair. He grasped her neck just under her chin and tilted her head. With the height of the bed, Shannon's eyes and lips were invitingly close and arresting. Their bodies touched. Her hands came to rest on his shoulders. Blane had wanted to tease her or test her, but he changed his mind.

Shannon felt warm and calm, as if the world and its troubles were far away. This man drew her to him as if he were a potent and undeniable force of life and strength. His contact and gaze made her feel giddy, weak. He caused her heart to pound and her respiration to become labored. She enjoyed the touch of his hands, the gaze of his entreating eyes, the feel of his lips on hers. They were in the midst of war, and they could be killed at any time. Her brothers had explained and unknowingly demonstrated the physical side of sex, but the emotional facets still confused her. Perhaps selfish destiny wouldn't allow her time to find true love and experience blissful lovemaking. It was indeed possible that this war could destroy her entire family, including herself.

Blane knew it was past time to halt this heady contact. He chuckled as his left arm embraced her and his right forefinger caressed her parted lips. "You didn't do your best when we were camped," he teased. "You know a woman has to be the stronger of the two sexes because men have no self-control around beauties like you."

"Well, I am your wife," she rashly retorted.

"You are, aren't you?" he replied, his lips stealing over hers.

Shannon and Blane clung together as their mouths shared a wild and breathless kiss. A persistent knocking on the door separated them abruptly. Blane answered it to find a woman holding a tray with their breakfast, compliments of Colonel Greyson. Blane thanked the woman and carried the tray inside. He glanced at Shannon and shrugged nonchalantly.

"This could be our last good fare for ages, woman. Eat up," he advised, trying to douse the wildfire in his body while he pulled on his boots. He hurriedly combed his hair and slipped into a shirt.

Shannon freed her legs from the tangling covers and

73

left the bed. After washing up, she slipped on her shirt and fastened two buttons over her breast area. Having been reared around three handsome and playful brothers, she had lost a certain amount of her modesty. It had not been unusual for her brothers to help her with petticoats and gowns when she was rushed or when servants were busy. Sometimes one would sit or lie on her bed late at night or early in the morning to chat or share secrets. Now, having spent so much time alone with Blane, Shannon unconsciously lessened her restraint, which was easy to do when he was in this genial mood.

She joined Blane at the small table to consume scrambled eggs, fried potatoes, coffee, and biscuits. "When do we leave?" she asked after her last bite.

"As soon as you're dressed," he replied stonily, avoiding her gaze. He was curious about her lack of inhibition, worried about it. "I'm going to get the horses ready. I'll return for you in thirty minutes."

Shannon watched him rise and leave. His mood changes annoyed her, but she decided that whatever was bothering him today was his problem. She quickly slipped into clean pants and a shirt, then brushed her hair and braided it. Since the people here knew she was female, there was no need for her to conceal the long and heavy plait. She stuffed her gown and dirty garments into her bag and sat down to wait for Blane.

When she responded to the knock on the door, she confronted a rosy-cheeked soldier who seemed about the same age as she. He stared at her creamy face, blue eyes, and red hair for so long that Shannon finally prodded, "Yes?"

"Yore husband . . . He's waiting downstairs, Ma'am. I was sent to . . . fetch ya." He almost babbled as he gaped at her.

74

"Thank you. I'll be right along," Shannon replied politely.

"Kin I carry yore bag fur ya?" he offered, grinning broadly.

"Yes, please." Shannon followed the gawky male to where Blane was standing beside their horses. The blue-clad officer with him boldly eyed Shannon, then smiled appreciatively. She nodded her head in greeting, wondering what he thought about their situation.

Blane helped her mount, then tied her bag behind her saddle. He agilely stepped into a stirrup and gracefully passed his sinewy leg over the horse's back. He glanced at her, smiling affectionately for their audience. Then, they headed toward Fredericksburg.

For the next few days, the riding seemed one endless blur of contradictory scenery and aching muscles. They passed through or near grounds of past or future battles, and Shannon was astounded and distressed by the damage she viewed. Blane had described conditions and sights accurately. War was such a devastating force, as injurious as unleashed nature on the rampage. Suddenly she understood words that before had held little meaning: "Brother against brother," "friend against friend." And she understood, too, that she would have to become a traitor to her beloved South if she aided the Union.

As if possessing some keen extra sense, Blane managed to keep them away from other people, if indeed any had survived in the area. At times, she could hear the distant roar of cannons and numerous guns. She wondered how many lost lives each sound represented; how many homes and businesses were gone forever; how much property was being scarred beyond use for years. What a terrible waste of life and land, she mused sadly.

When they halted to eat, Shannon forced herself to

75

consume whatever Blane placed within her hands. When they stopped for the night, she was so exhausted that she was asleep within minutes. She was even too tired and depressed to worry about her dusty, sweaty body. It was a time for existing, nothing more.

At one rest stop, Shannon asked, "When will we reach this Fredericksburg? We've been traveling for days."

"It's behind us, Shannon. We're going straight for Richmond. We have to pass through this area while Lee and Grant are battling elsewhere and Sherman has your friend Johnston on the move. It looks as if the Rebel supply lines are about to be cut in half. It can't last much longer. There's little food and money left in the South to use or to confiscate. If we can prevent foreign governments from sending aid, the Christmas star might shine over a united land once more."

The evening they reached the outskirts of Richmond, Shannon was about ready to collapse in her saddle. He led her to a large mansion that was situated on one of the city's most prestigious hills. While Shannon remained on her horse, Blane chatted with the lady who answered the door. The spinster smiled at Blane and nodded several times. Finally, Blane joined Shannon and helped her dismount.

"This is Miss Elizabeth Van Lew's home. You'll be staying with her. Lizzie's known as a Union sympathizer, but few people take her seriously. You'll discover she's very loud and assertive. She'll fill you in on as much as possible. Stay put until I return."

Was he abandoning her? "What about you?" Shannon asked, her eyes and voice exposing her fatigue and worry.

"I'll be around. Watch what you say and do," he warned. If Shannon wasn't who and what she claimed, she might expose herself here.

After he delivered her bag to the front porch and bid the prim yellowish blonde farewell, he approached

76

Shannon. Maybe he was a fool, but he was getting used to having her around and wanted to continue the stimulating arrangement. He was vexed to find himself wavering in his decision to leave her behind. "Keep your head on your shoulders, partner. This town is full of hungry men, Rebel rogues starving for beauty and attention. I don't want you tempted to stay here surrounded by comfort and admirers when I'm ready to leave."

Shannon laughed. "Why, sir, you insult my honor. I'm a married woman," she stated thickly. "Or am I?" she queried.

"Here, you're Shannon Greenleaf of Savannah. Since you'll doubtlessly be seeing people who know you, you'd best use your real name to prevent suspicion. My identity stays the same—Steven James. However, I might have to court you as a means of getting to see you."

"Court me?" she teased. "Have you forgotten there's a war going on? What if one or both sides tries to draft you by force?"

"Don't worry about me, Flame. See you in a few days."

As he started to leave, Shannon caught his arm and tugged on it. When he looked at her, she smiled and coaxed, "Be careful. I've gotten rather attached and adjusted to my current partner. I would hate to train another one to overlook my rankling flaws. As you've discovered, I'm not known for my patience or easy-going nature. You've been more than fair and considerate, Blane, and I'm deeply grateful."

Their gazes met and searched, as if both had something to say but couldn't find the words or courage. Shannon handed him the gold wedding band. "Just in case we get separated, you had better take this."

Blane's hand closed around the ring still warm from her body heat. "If there's trouble, don't forget you know both presidents."

"Get moving before someone sees you," she warned.

Shannon joined Elizabeth on the porch. Both watched

Blane's departure. The woman next to Shannon appeared to be in her early forties. Her eyes were bright blue and piercing and her bone structure was sharp and prominent. Like Shannon, Elizabeth was small in height and weight, and it was obvious that she was well bred and intelligent.

"Don't worry about your sweetheart. He'll be safe. I might as well confess right now, the townfolk think I'm daft and foolish. Of course that image helps me carry out my work for General Grant and the Union. They don't realize how cunning and daring we Southern women can be. Mind you, I'm not a Yankee, but I do hold to the Union. We'll get you settled, then have hot tea and cakes."

Elizabeth showed a weary Shannon to a guest room on the second floor. While the woman went to fetch water for her, Shannon stripped off her trail clothes and pulled on a robe from the bed. She couldn't resist stretching out across the entreating surface to relax her stiff body. Before Elizabeth returned, Shannon was asleep.

The Virginian was touched by the beauty, gentility, and fatigue of her guest. She lowered the lamp light and left Shannon to rest.

That following morning, Shannon slept late. When she awoke, she was embarrassed by her laziness. She found her hostess in the parlor and smiled sheepishly as she said, "I must have been exhausted."

"You needed the rest. Come and sit down. I'll get you something to eat. Do you prefer tea or coffee?" she inquired graciously.

"Tea, if you please. It's very kind of you to take me in, Miss Van Lew. I do hope I'm not imposing during these terrible days."

"Of course not. But please call me Lizzie. I'll return shortly."

Soon, Shannon was devouring a delicious meal and

78

sipping hot tea. She asked Elizabeth numerous questions about the war and her activities. The woman seemed only too happy and proud to share her adventures. "Is it very dangerous to be a Union spy in the South?"

"Rarely, my dear. They don't take female spies too seriously, unless we're caught in the act. They threaten us every so often, but we laugh it off. Whenever I pick up valuable news, it's fairly simple to send it to the nearest Federal officer. People have such lax tongues and wits. Did you know that President Davis stays here?"

When the younger woman gave her her full attention, Elizabeth stated, "It's a marvelous place for a spy, Shannon. So much news passes by here through careless lips. The Confederate Signal Corps works out of Richmond. Cabinet meetings are held nearby. Generals come to plan strategy with Davis. A woman in my social position can entertain and visit as she pleases. But tell me how you came to be here, and traveling with that handsome, mysterious Yankee."

Shannon related her personal story to the sympathetic woman and admitted to her lack of knowledge about her dashing companion. Shannon leaned back in her chair and murmured despondently, "I really don't know what I can do for the Union or my brother."

"Why don't you start by visiting President Davis? You would be surprised what you can learn during a simple chat."

Shannon was astonished and dismayed by the bold suggestion. What would her father have said and felt about her duping his old friend, a national hero during the Mexican War and now a president? What about morals and scruples? How far was a spy supposed to go in the line of duty? "Steven told me to stay here until his return."

"That's nonsense. Don't waste such a priceless opportunity. You'll be in no danger. I can pass along any information you glean over there. Men think we're helpless children. Surely you didn't come this far merely to decorate the arm of Steven James?"

Shannon knew Blane would be upset with her for disobeying orders, but Elizabeth's idea did sound logical and important. Besides, she and Blane were supposed to be partners. Perhaps she could prove her value by obtaining vital facts while he was gone.

"Tell me what to do and say," she encouraged the older woman.

By three o'clock, Shannon's hair and body were scrubbed and dried. She dressed in one of Elizabeth's best day gowns, the sapphire color of which enhanced her appearance. Following Elizabeth's directions, she called on President Jefferson Davis in the "gray house" on Clay Street.

"Miss Greenleaf," he addressed her as he opened the door to his study. "What are you doing so far from home? How's Andrew?"

Shannon revealed the deaths of her father and older brother and the imprisonment of Corry, but she let him believe they had died as brave Rebels. She quelled the bitter remorse that rose within her. Deceiving this particular person offended her deeply. She was hardpressed not to break down and confess her guilt, but she knew that doing so would endanger many lives, including Blane's. She reminded herself that her despicable actions might help end the war, and to achieve this goal she would have to bear the cost of betraying this man.

She explained how she had been forced to flee her father's northern partner, noticing his wary look when she told him where she was staying. "My father knew Mister Van Lew, so I imposed on Miss Elizabeth when I managed to get this far South. She kindly took me in, fed me, and loaned me clothing. Can you give me a pass to get home, sir? I must see if Greenleaf has survived this war.

Then I'll find some way to locate Corry and free him. When I heard you were here, I thought you would want to know about Father and Temple."

"The people are becoming bitter, Miss Shannon. Either the South will soon know glorious victory or tragic defeat. When President Buchanan said he would not hold the Southern states in the Union by force, we believed him. It sounded so simple and quick years ago. Now the land runs red with Confederate blood. Suspicions and wild charges abound. We've lost too many good men like Andrew and Temple Greenleaf. I fear the weight of this office grows heavier each day. At this moment, Union troops are moving closer to Richmond. Some have taunting picnics at my beloved Briarfield. We need food, supplies, guns, medicines, horses. We need money and hope, Miss Shannon."

"I have none of those things to give you, sir. Simon Travers controls the Greenleaf business and fortune, if he hasn't stolen them by now. I hoped and prayed I would be safer among friends. I never expected to find such utter destruction, so much death and misery. Is there no way to establish a truce, sir?"

They were interrupted by a messenger. Shannon felt wicked as she eavesdropped on the conversation outside the study door. Horror filled her. She hurried back to her seat and waited for Davis's return.

When he again entered the room, Davis was distracted and dismayed over the news he had received. Shannon told him she would return to Miss Van Lew's and leave him to his work. She smiled when he said he would have a pass prepared and sent over to her.

"Well, what did you learn?" Elizabeth probed eagerly as she sat with Shannon in the parlor.

"Sheridan is having large victories to the west; he's

81

trying to drive Anderson out of the Shenandoah Valley. Grant is keeping Lee on the move. They're not far from here, slightly southeast. Sherman has been ordered to head south out of Tennessee to sever the supply lines through Georgia, then turn northeastward. They intend to trap the leading Confederate officers and men between them. They plan to keep squeezing and squeezing until they conquer Richmond."

"But that's all good news for our side, deary. What about the Rebs?" Her blond ringlets danced up and down as she moved her head.

"That's the point, Lizzie. They know all about the Union's plans. How could those newspapers be so foolish? They've been printing battle strategies! The Rebels sneak in the papers and learn our moves, then make a strong defense line. No wonder this war is endless. There is some bad news for our side. There have been numerous casualties during the last few months, and they plan to make the South pay. Davis said Sheridan planned to leave nothing in the Shenandoah Valley—nothing, Lizzie."

The older woman patted her hand, then cooed like a dove, "Now, now, deary, enemies can't fight without supplies. It's one of those evil necessities of war, weakening and discouraging your enemies."

"But there are women, children, and old people living there. What about winter? Can such atrocities be committed in the name of victory? For peace? Did you know that Lee tried to attack Washington last month? Now, Sherman's been given the same orders to leave nothing behind for the Rebels' use. Not just businesses, railroads, and armories! Everything, Lizzie: food, shelter, medicines, crops. Between Sheridan and Sherman, half of the South will be destroyed. When the war's over, the suffering will continue for years."

"Then let's do our best to help end the war before more

destruction is carried out," Elizabeth suggested calmly.

"How can we get the Confederacy to fold?" she asked skeptically.

"Shannon, don't turn against us," she beseeched worriedly. "You must remember whose side we're on, who's in the right. The South initiated the hostilities. Your brother is languishing in a Rebel prison, not a Federal one. War is a costly, grim business."

"Do you know where Steve was going?"

"He didn't say, deary."

"When did he say he would return for me?"

Elizabeth replied shockingly, "In a week or so."

Shannon stared at her. Blane had told her a few days. How dare he take off without telling her anything, especially the truth! "I'm heading for Danville as soon as President Davis sends my pass. If and when Steven returns, tell him I couldn't wait a week or so."

"You can't get inside a prison. It's too risky, Shannon."

"I have to get going before my path is cut off, Lizzie. I got from Boston to Washington alone. I'll tell them I'm a nurse. I'm going."

"Then don't carry any papers except your pass. Whatever you see or hear, commit it to memory. I'll give you some names of friends. And I'll see if I can prepare you a medical bag for deception."

Shannon smiled. "Thanks, Lizzie. I'll do whatever I can."

Shannon's pass arrived the next morning, giving her safe conduct across Confederate lines. If she were caught by Yankees, she could say she had tricked the Rebels into giving her the pass. As Elizabeth said, if she wasn't carrying any incriminating papers, what could they do to her?

She packed the garments Elizabeth offered for her disguise and tried to rest before her departure at dawn.

83

Shannon was drowsing when Blane's voice rent the silence of her room and thoughts.

"What's this nonsense about your leaving in the morning?"

"Not nonsense, Steven James, but fact. I didn't come all this way to sit in a comfortable house while you do all the work. I have a pass."

"I know. It was crazy to go see Davis. You agreed to follow my orders, not Lizzie's or others'. But you did achieve a small victory. Your information gave me the idea of planting false news in the Northern papers to mislead the Rebs. Sometimes your impulsiveness outweighs your brains, woman. I can't believe you were leaving in the morning."

Just to provoke him, Shannon remarked seductively, "Actually, I was coming to look for you. After spending so many days and nights with you, I was missing my errant partner. You grow on a person, Mr. James."

Blane seized her shoulders and yanked her into his arms. He challenged, "Then show me how much you missed me." His mouth closed over hers fiercely as he lowered himself and her to the bed.

At first, Shannon wanted to fight him. The emotional battle lines had been drawn, and she knew he smugly believed he could conquer her. It was to him a matter of pride and subtle punishment. Yet she quelled her resistance and surrendered to his kisses and caresses. She wanted them and took delight in them, even if she did mistrust him. She had an uneasy feeling she was being manipulated and deluded by this beguiling rogue.

Turning her head to the side, Shannon gasped out, "I'm your partner, remember? We share the mission or we go our separate ways. Stop being so bossy and overprotective."

"What did you tell Davis yesterday?" he asked. Damn this female for stealing his peace of mind and rigid self-control. He constantly had to tread gingerly on this unfamiliar ground. He hadn't been able to stop thinking about her. Why was she tempting and taunting him? Didn't she realize he wasn't made of stone? Was she trying to enchant him into carrying out her wishes before the Union's? Or was she using him to unmask Yankee spies and their linking system? She hadn't related any unknown facts to Elizabeth, but she had gotten a travel pass quickly and easily. Had she hoped to leave before his return—leave with the names and locations of Union sympathizers? How could she look and sound so innocent? He needed to probe her story promptly and there was only one place and one person who could supply the truth.

Shannon retorted, "Tell me where you've been and what you've done, then I'll answer. Some partner you are, keeping secrets and vanishing for days. What if I had needed you?"

Blane stiffened in anger and vexation when she questioned him. Should he trust her? Could she be genuine? He pulled free of Shannon and stood up beside the bed. His fists were clenched, as were his teeth. His voice and expression warned Shannon of his fury and tension. "I'm heading for Lynchburg at dawn. It's about fifty miles north of Danville. I have to go to both places. There's a field hospital at Lynchburg; you could work there until I return with news from Danville Prison. It's too risky for you to waltz into a holding pen and have Corry blow our covers when he spots you. I'll find a way to get a look at the prison roll. You'll be of more use at the hospital anyway. Wounded men talk to a pretty face and gentle hands. If you want to tag along under my terms, fine; if not, good luck on your own."

As Blane was stalking to the door, Shannon called out, "Wait. I'm coming with you." Inwardly she mused that Blane possessed the strength and charm to seduce her,

85

yet he had stopped and waxed so antagonistic. What was the matter with him? He treated her like a dread disease, one he had rashly but willingly contracted, then fearfully battled. Why did Blane keep enticing her, then pushing her away? Did it have to do with a woman left behind in Texas? With the new wedding band he carried? Was he using her to test his love and commitment to another female, or was Blane simply misleading her because he wanted to bed her?

"Meet me out back at six," he said over his shoulder, then left.

Bittersweet longing filled her. She was becoming too involved. She wanted to know the truth about the ring and the man, but she was afraid to ask about either. As long as she didn't know his marital status, she could respond to him. If he was merely betrothed and she didn't know that fact, she could justify her shameless enticement. Would it change anything if she learned he was unhappily wed? she wondered. Yes, married was married. Why did Blane have to give her such a difficult time? Couldn't he tell she was willing to make love to him? Damn him for teasing her and taunting her!

They had traveled for four days when they came upon a Rebel encampment near the small town of Farmville. They had been walking the horses for a breather, and Shannon had been asking him questions that had cost him his attention. Before Blane perceived their danger, they were surrounded by three scruffy sentries. He pulled Shannon close to him and glared at the hostile soldiers in tattered gray uniforms.

"I want to speak with your camp commander," Blane stated smugly. "I'm Steven James of New Orleans. I work for President Davis."

"Why ain't you in uniform fighting like the rest of

us?" one asked.

"Yeh, riding around all clean and fed like some dandy Yank."

"Even got his own woman. I ain't had me no woman for . . . I can't recall how long," the third asserted sullenly.

"We have vital business in this area. This is my wife, so kindly treat her with respect. Take us to your camp," Blane demanded.

"No man ain't got no wife like this. Ain't she pretty, Jed?"

"I'm Shannon Greenleaf James, daughter of the late Andrew Greenleaf of Savannah. I have a travel pass from President Davis himself. Let us continue, or you'll be sorry," Shannon inserted angrily.

"She's got a tongue on 'er," the second man teased merrily.

"She could be speaking this side of the truth, Henry."

"Let me see your special pass," John ordered, ribbing his friend.

"I'll show it to your camp commander," Shannon replied, her anger increasing her courage and determination.

A captain rode up and questioned the curious situation. Blane related the problem. The officer reprimanded the three soldiers, then escorted Blane and Shannon to camp. The commanding officer insisted on seeing them immediately.

"Major Benjamin Clifford," he introduced himself.

Blane repeated his and Shannon's false identities. "I have some matters to scout for President Davis near Appomattox and Lynchburg. Word is Sheridan is heading this way and Sherman's footing it toward Georgia. And that ain't the end of it. Grant's trying his damnedest to move in from the east. Looks like this whole area might be surrounded by Yanks within the month, so

87

Davis wants to see if and how we can set up a defense line. My wife is a nurse; she plans to work in the hospital in Lynchburg until I complete my scouting."

Clifford glanced up from the papers in his hands. "Seems you two have clearances to go where you please. Why'd you bring her along?"

"The Yanks burned our home, and I haven't found a safe place for her to stay. Every town we visit has just been attacked or is about to be attacked. She's a brave and smart filly. She's as safe with me as anywhere. I thought she could help and rest while I get this assignment done quickly. I need to report back to Davis in Richmond in two weeks."

The officer glanced at Shannon as if mildly charmed by her, his brown eyes lingering a moment on her fiery hair, then on her blue eyes. "We can sure use another nurse in our field hospital here. We get wounded from all four directions. Besides, ain't no use to take your wife to Lynchburg; they moved that hospital to Danville a few weeks past. Since you got to pass this way again, I can find a place for Mrs. James to stay until you return. She'll be under my protection. I'll show her around myself tomorrow."

Blane was relieved when Shannon didn't openly react to the news about Danville. "Thank you, Major Clifford. Time's precious right now."

"Captain Smith, show Mister James that new map we prepared. Holders of territory change everyday. We don't want you walking into no den of Yanks. Your wife can wait here and have a cup of tea. Smith, get the Jameses a few supplies. It's nearing supper time."

A curious feeling washed over Blane. He couldn't refuse the Major's suggestions and assistance without appearing suspicious and he hoped Shannon knew what to say to protect their lives. He followed Smith to a nearby tent. He studied the map, noting several errors.

Were they intentional? Entrapping? He glanced toward the vanishing sun. Five o'clock—too early to sneak away. They would have to stand and bluff.

The captain who had shown them to camp escorted them to a small house that had been taken from Yankee sympathizers. Smith placed a few supplies on the table, tipped his cap, and left.

Blane looked at Shannon. "I don't like this, Flame."

"Like what?" she inquired, focusing innocent blue eyes on him.

"Leaving you here with these scruffy Rebs. You will be careful?" He had waited for Shannon to insist on going with him, especially to Danville. Now that she knew the hospital had been moved there, it surprised him that she didn't. She seemed willing to remain behind in this Rebel camp. A refined Southern lady should be appalled to stay here alone, he reflected. She had been furious the last time he had left her behind. Why relent so soon? Did she have plans to sneak off to Danville the moment he was gone?

Shannon was waiting for Blane to suggest or insist she go along with him. Maybe he wanted to check out the Danville area before taking her there. Maybe he wanted and needed some breathing distance from her. The physical attraction between them did seem to alarm him. She knew she mustn't press him or aggravate him. He had promised to help with Corry, and he had gotten her this close without trouble. His concern was touching. "You worry too much. We've done just fine so far. How long do you think your trip will take?"

"I hope less than ten days. Have you ever done any nursing?"

Shannon chuckled. "As the only female in a family with four active males? Hours and hours of nursing, Mister James. These Rebs would suspect Davis of treachery before casting curious eyes on me."

89

"What did the major have to say while I was studying his maps?" Blane wondered if he was mistaken about the Rebel's reaction to her. Had the officer recognized her? Maybe he was being too wary, too sensitive where she was concerned. Yet he didn't tell her that the maps were false or even hint at Clifford's strange manner.

"You're lucky I've been to New Orleans several times, since you claimed it as our home. I covered for us very nicely, thank you. He did seem intrigued that my maiden name is on my travel pass. I explained about President Davis's friendship with my father, and I told him Mister Davis still considered me Andrew's little girl. By the way, I told him we've been married since June tenth of '62. The name of your firm is James Shipping, Limited. We have no children."

"Anything else?" he probed anxiously.

"I didn't give him time. I asked about his family and home."

"Smart girl," he murmured, flashing her a stirring smile.

Shannon and Blane worked together to prepare their meal. They ate it in near silence, each contemplating the other. When the dishes were washed, Blane drew bucket after bucket of water for her from the well near the back door. Shannon heated enough water to take a refreshing bath with scented soap and to wash her hair.

Blane stood in the shadows of the small house and scrubbed his hair and body, rinsing with a bucket of cool water. Afterward, he strolled around, allowing Shannon time to complete her task. He hadn't missed her remark about *"four"* active males." Who was the fourth man? If there was another brother, why had she kept it a secret? A lover? A huband? That carelessly dropped clue added another suspicion about her motives. Perhaps it wasn't Corry sitting in Danville Prison . . .

At nine-thirty, Major Clifford joined him. "Glad

you're still up and around, James. I have a small unit heading for Appomattox under the cover of darkness. If you ain't got any objections, it would be safer for you to travel with them. They plan to head out around ten."

When Blane entered the house and locked the door, he found Shannon curled on the bed, dozing. Her damp hair had been braided to avoid tangles during the night. She had rolled to one side and had tossed back the cover in an inviting manner. Blane came forward and sat down. It was perilous to look at her or to speak with her in the light. He doused the lantern and lay beside her. For a time, he listened to her breathing, which revealed her deepening slumber. He couldn't take off without telling her, but he had to go. What if he didn't make it back into her life again? What was the truth about Shannon Greenleaf?

He gently shook the lovely creature beside him. "Shannon . . ."

Shannon turned and snuggled up to him, her left hand falling gently across his bare chest. When he murmured her name again, she sighed dreamily and mumbled a few unintelligible words and one he was able to decipher— "Hawke."

The name seared through his mind. Rage mounted swiftly within his taut body. Time was short, too short. He placed his lips at her ear and whispered softly, "Where's Hawke, love?"

"Gone . . . I'll find . . . him. Save him," she muttered dreamily as images of Hawke and Corry flickered in her groggy head.

Blane shook her almost roughly, calling sharply, "Shannon! Wake up! I have to leave in a few minutes."

"Leave?" she echoed, trying to arouse herself.

Blane related the details of Clifford's visit. "I have to go or it will look suspicious."

"You can't leave tonight," she argued in panic.

He turned his head and asked, "What do you mean?"

"Nothing," she replied softly. Was he blind or naïve? And how could Andrew Greenleaf's daughter lie here in bed with a near stranger and even consider making love to him! It was crazy! It was wanton! Let him go! she told herself. Maybe he would miss her, learn to appreciate her!

"Would you come a little closer," he asked, "I can't hear you."

Shannon grimaced in the darkness, chiding herself. She shifted her body until their sides touched. "How's that, Mister James?"

"How's this, Mrs. James?" he countered, turning and pulling her into his arms. His lips brushed her hair, her cheek, then her mouth.

Shannon nestled against him and returned the kiss. What if he didn't return? What if he were killed or taken prisoner? "Blane, is there a special woman in your life?" she asked nervously, uncontrollably.

"Just my partner," he responded, then kissed her again, thinking only of how much he wanted to rip off her gown and make passionate love to her.

His hand tentatively cupped a breast. He waited for Shannon to stop him. When she didn't, his mouth fused hungrily to hers. His fingertips circled the swiftly rising peak and he was thrilled and encouraged by its eagerness. His body felt as if someone had placed a torch to it. Lord, she was an irresistible temptress. She was driving him wild with her feverish responses. Damn Fate for intruding tonight!

When he knew his control and wits were slipping away rapidly, he told her between gasps for air, "I want you, Shannon, but there isn't time tonight. We'll have to wait for the right place and moment." He knew there was enough time for him to thrust into her urgently and sate his carnal desires, but not enough time to make love to her as he wanted it to be during their first time together. For some inexplicable and irrational reason, he couldn't bring himself to use her merely for physical release. No, he wanted to take her leisurely, sensuously, tenderly, thoroughly, and without interruption. He wanted to see, feel, taste, hear, smell, and enjoy the entire, lengthy experience. He was certain that when he possessed this woman, it would be a staggering, unforgettable experience. "If you feel otherwise, tell me right now, and when I return, I'll know to keep my distance."

"I want you too, Blane," she stated simply and truthfully.

Chapter Four

Shannon had difficulty getting to sleep after Blane's departure, which came immediately after her wanton admission. She silently prayed for his safe and hasty return. She also prayed the sensual extraction of her confession had not been a cruel ruse or an impulsive action during a moment of torrid weakness. She would have to learn to control her wild craving for him until she was certain he was free and felt the same way about her. What could be worse than falling in love with a man who belonged to another woman, or falling in love with a man only to lose him to death or to his fear of surrender, unless it was falling prey to a devious charmer who wanted nothing more than sex!

That couldn't be true of Blane, she reasoned, for he could have taken her plenty of times. His rigid control and reluctance baffled her. Maybe he didn't care deeply about her and knew it would be wrong to claim her falsely. Maybe she was doing or saying something to repel him. Maybe he didn't like inexperienced virgins or feared they offered trouble and strings. Maybe there was something in his past that plagued and halted him. So many "maybes" plagued her mind that she couldn't sleep. How she wished this war weren't going on so she could get to know him. Her body warmed anew as she recalled their parting moments.

The following morning, Shannon dressed, took her medical bag, and reported to the doctor on duty. She talked until her throat felt parched. She bathed faces and hands until she was weary. She changed bandages until she wanted to scream or retch. She fed men too weak to help themselves. She listened to heartrending tales of death and destruction. She remained ever alert for the names of friends.

It didn't take long for her to realize that medical supplies were as low as military and food supplies. She knew the doctors were using her as a distraction for a lack of proper anesthesia. Most men were too proud to show pain before this angel tending them. As the day passed, Shannon noticed many four-wheeled ambulances arriving and camping nearby, though few of their folding bunks held wounded men.

Almost too exhausted to eat, she snacked quickly, bathed, and went to bed. She didn't care if Major Benjamin Clifford had requested her presence for dinner. All she needed and wanted was sleep.

When Shannon reached the field hospital the second morning, she discovered a curious and distressing fact; the ambulances were loading the injured soldiers to transport them to the newly established Confederate hospital near Danville. They would leave within two hours, and Shannon had been ordered to accompany them.

Shannon hurriedly sought the major and anxiously questioned him. "When we arrived, sir, we were not told you would be dismantling the camp and leaving today. What's going on?"

Clifford removed his hat. "The Yankees are advancing

on us, Ma'am. Surely you realize we cannot leave you behind. To capture a beauty like you would give the Yanks a priceless war trophy." When Shannon glared at him, he halted his curious words and tried to mask his devouring look. Frowning, he insisted, "Only a joke, ma'am. If you'll excuse me, I am rather busy. You're to ride in one of the wagons with the doctors. I suggest you get packed and ready to leave," he advised sternly.

"This is so sudden. What about my husband? You'll have to send word to him. Where are the Yankees now?" she inquired in dread.

A satanic gleam filled his eyes as he calmly informed her, "I'm afraid Mister James is heading straight for their line. Unfortunately the Yanks shifted their route after he studied our maps. Hopefully he and my men will have enough sense to be on the alert and escape. He can catch up with you in Danville. I'll see you get shelter, food, and safety."

Shannon looked at the grisly soldier before her. Today his uniform was dirty and rumpled. He smelled of black coffee, dust, and malodorous cigars. His brown hair hadn't been combed or washed. Thick brows rested like fuzzy caterpillars over his dingy green eyes and this morning's stubble hadn't been removed from his face.

As if anticipating her doubts, Clifford watched her intently. Shannon had the impression she couldn't trust this man. Far worse, she had the alarming feeling that he had sent Blane in that perilous direction on purpose. She sensed that if she tried to flee, the major would have her pursued and returned. She had no idea where Blane had gone. Danville was her only choice, and not a bad one. She absently toyed with the gold band on her finger.

Clifford patted her shoulder and said, "Don't worry, ma'am. He seems like a smart 'n' brave man, and he shore has reason to return."

The large hand on her shoulder was clammy and

offensive, as was the man's tone. Shannon wondered at the strange look in Clifford's eye and his curious air of smugness. Surely she was safe; she was surrounded by men. She dismissed her qualms and returned to work.

The journey to Danville required seven days. Shannon was anxious for even a few hours' privacy and quiet. She had written countless letters for ailing men, letters she knew would never be delivered but that gave dying or ailing men hope and joy. She heard cries of pain and moans of misery. After sleeping on one of the ambulance bunks for six nights, she wondered how severely wounded men could survive such a terrible ordeal. She learned that some did not. Occasionally on the bumpy trail, they had been forced to halt for emergency surgery or to ease the agony of the men being bounced around in the wagons. By the last day, her nerves were taut and her body was pleading for relief. Everyone was delighted to reach Danville.

Upon her arrival, Shannon was kept busy until midnight helping the doctors and other nurses to get the new patients settled and tended. When she was shown to a makeshift sleeping quarters, she didn't argue. She merely fell on the bunk and went to sleep, without eating.

For two days Shannon prayed for Blane's arrival. If he had made it back to Farmville, then he knew where to look for her. What if his mission had taken him elsewhere? What if they wouldn't see each other again? What if he were glad to be rid of the responsibility of her? What if Major Clifford continued to observe her so closely and frequently?

Shannon discovered the location of Danville Prison for Federal soldiers. She heard that local Union sympathizers carried food and clothing to the soldiers. To make contact with them could expose her, and she knew she would have to find a clever way to get to the prison. It thrilled her soul to think that Corry was so close. Yet she found herself praying he wouldn't be in that awful "stink hole" a few miles away.

Corbett Greenleaf . . . Shannon closed her eyes and called forth his image: Standing five feet eleven, Corry had a well-developed frame covered with light golden flesh. His chestnut brown hair was usually brushed back over his ears to reveal short sideburns. It fell into a natural part just slightly off center and curled impishly at the nape of his neck. His upper lip was thin, but the lower one was full, giving him what the girls called a "kissable mouth." When he smiled, which was most of the time, deep creases appeared from his nose to a little below the corners of his mouth and tiny creases could also be seen near his slate blue eyes. Corry's eyes were large and expressive like hers; they sparkled and danced with *joie de vivre*. The dark brows over them were long and nearly touched above his nose, which was perfect. He was an extremely handsome man with a smile that warmed the soul and a personality that appealed to everyone he met. He could make anyone and everyone laugh. He brightened any room with his sunny spirits . . .

A short time later, one of the doctors unknowingly aided her when he told Shannon he was going to check on the prisoners' health and living conditions. She instantly asked to accompany him. When he tried to refuse her, Shannon lowered her head as if in shame and told him, "Sir, I fear one of my brothers was persuaded to fight with the Yankees. I was told he's being held in prison here. If I could just go along and make sure he's all right, I'll be very grateful."

The doctor had seen many such cases of divided loyalties. He knew how hard this beautiful and gentle woman had labored with the Rebel wounded. She carried a letter of protection from President Davis himself. Why

98

should he doubt her word or loyalty?

"I would appreciate it if you don't mention this to the others, sir. With so much suffering and killing, they might not understand or accept my position. Major Clifford is already behaving strangely toward me," she stated candidly. "He makes me uncomfortable."

Doctor Harrison Cooper gazed at the delicate female. He was charmed and deceived by her soft manner. He, too, had thought the major's behavior strange after this woman's arrival. "Come along. We'll find your brother, if he's here. I'll tell Major Clifford it was my idea to take you along," he remarked, smiling broadly at her.

Danville Prison was situated on twenty acres of meadow land, the grassy covering of which had long ago been worn down to bare earth. It was enclosed by a stockade fence of sturdy saplings such as those protecting Western forts. The commandant's office and residence had been built nearby, as had huts and tents for the guards. The doctor headed in that direction to acquire permission from Lieutenant Colonel Robert Smith to enter the prison. The commandant was unavailable.

Captain William Hood was astonished by the beautiful woman who entered his office with the intention of helping Doctor Cooper examine the Yankee soldiers. He was far more astounded when she told him she was seeking Corbett Greenleaf of Savannah. Shannon was delighted by Doctor Cooper's help in this matter. In fact, he had suggested the lie she was about to relate, having assumed her brother would be only too glad to say anything to get out of the filthy prison.

"You see, Captain Hood, a terrible mistake was made after the battle. Corry had been dressed as a Yankee to penetrate their lines and get information for the Confederacy. He was captured and sent here. I received word of this monstrous error and came as quickly as

99

possible to correct it. You must allow me to see my brother," she insisted.

Captain Hood asked for the roll-call register. His gaze slipped over it twice. "No Greenleaf listed here, ma'am."

"Maybe he gave a false name to protect the honor of his family, sir. I received a letter from a friend who witnessed the entire affair. I must go inside and look for him. Please, sir. I need your help." She used every feminine wile she knew to disarm him. Smiling demurely, she reasoned, "How could you doubt my safety when you and your men will be there to protect me?" She dabbed at false tears with a handkerchief the captain had rushed to give her. "Surely such a kind and honorable officer wouldn't deny my urgent request? It is such a tiny and simple one." She artfully fluttered her lashes and smiled again. "Why, Captain Hood, if you believe I'm dangerous, you can bind my hands and hold one of those naughty guns on me," she teased, then giggled. "I'm sure Papa would find some way to reward you later."

Utterly charmed, he sighed heavily. "I guess it won't hurt nothing. Let me fetch some guards. These Yanks are quick and sly."

Inside the compound, Shannon dismissed his last words with contempt. These men didn't have enough energy to be "quick and sly." Far to the left, a section of the wall overlapped a stream used for fresh water. Ragged tents and rickety shanties filled the enclosed area. Fires burned here and there where food was being prepared. She could tell from the men's shrunken bodies that food was normally scarce or of low quality.

As some of the men were too weak to move from certain areas, Shannon and Doctor Cooper walked around with the guards and Captain Hood. Every ten feet or so, Hood would call out Corry's name. "If you're about, Greenleaf, answer up. Your sister's here to see you."

The prisoners watched Shannon with keen interest. Hood asked, "What unit was your brother with, ma'am?"

Shannon knew she couldn't tell him, so she replied fretfully, "I don't know, sir. A woman pays little heed to such information. I do know it was after the Battle of Chancellorsville in May of last year. I was told that those captives were sent here to be confined."

The mention of that particular battle gave Hood a chance to boast before the Yankee prisoners. He grinned and declared, "Yep, Chancellorsville was a bloody battle, but a victory for our side. Old Lee whipped Hooker even though he was outnumbered and outgunned. Between Lee and Jackson, they had Hooker running like a dog with his tail twixt his legs. Lee and Grant've been dancing up and down the countryside ever since. 'Course, Lee's smart; he always keeps his troops between Grant and Richmond. From what I been hearing, Grant's trying his best to take Petersburg. You people best be glad you got outta that area afore Grant and Lee stomped all over it."

Shannon appeared distressed by her failure to locate Corbett. If the guards and officer hadn't been so close to her, she would have tried to question some of the men. Finally she turned to those men forming a small crowd behind her. She had prepared for such an event. Slipping her fingers between the buttons of her dress, she pulled out a small Union flag and unfolded it. Glancing at the men to make certain they had noticed it, she carefully pushed it back into its hiding place. She asked, "Did any of you fight at Chancellorsville? Do any of you know Corry, Corbett Greenleaf? You have mothers or sisters or wives who are just as worried about you; please help me. I need to locate him for the President. The war will be over soon, so why does it matter?"

"Miss?" one of the soldiers called out faintly, comprehending her clues.

Shannon headed toward him. Hood grabbed her arm. "You can't go over there, ma'am. These men are nasty and dangerous. Ira, bring that Yank over here," he ordered, seeing her distress.

The man was led to her. She smiled and coaxed, "If you know anything about Corry, please tell me."

"The camp got too crowded early this year. Some of the prisoners were transferred to a new one in Georgia called Andersonville. If he hasn't been freed or escaped, this Corbett could be there."

Shannon went white and trembled. "But that's the one all the papers say is so horrible. Surely they wouldn't send Corry there?" she hinted, trying to pick out the clues in his words.

"I hope not, miss," the prisoner agreed. "It isn't fit for any man, Union or Confederate. I heard lots of 'em escaped on the trail."

Shannon smiled and thanked him. When Doctor Cooper completed his look around, they returned to the hospital. She worked at his side until eight that evening, when he insisted she quit for the night and go to the small room that had been assigned to her.

Another two days passed and Shannon became more and more aware of Clifford's constant observation. His gaze became so strong and frequent that she could sense it before sighting him. She had not done anything wrong, so he couldn't harm her, could he? Shannon couldn't help but recall how Simon Travers had drummed up false charges against her maid, charges that had been accepted by the law. She had to admit that law and justice were not always right or fair. What if someone in Washington or along the trail had betrayed her? What if someone had discovered the truth about Blane or Corry, which would implicate her as an enemy? Something was brewing.

Corbett wasn't here. Blane might never arrive. She wanted to get away from Danville and Major Clifford, but she needed a plan and an opportunity.

Before another day passed, Shannon knew something was very wrong. Every time she turned around, Major Clifford was there, watching her with a predatory gleam in his eye. As much as she wanted to learn any facts she could, she was careful not to ask the incoming wounded any suspicious questions. Shannon tried to behave normally, but the major was getting on her nerves. Had he discovered the truth? She decided that no matter how dangerous it might be, she would have to get away tonight!

As she did each day, Shannon went to the corral and tended her horse. It was her way of making certain he remained within her reach. Shortly after noon, she took a break for a nap, knowing she would have to ride hard and fast all night. Later she gathered food and a canteen and concealed them in her medical bag. After she was packed, she had nothing to do but wait for darkness.

A soldier knocked on her door and called her name. Shannon trembled. She reluctantly responded to his summons. "Yes?"

"Major Clifford wants to see you, ma'am," he informed her.

Shannon cringed in alarm. "It's late, sir, and I'm very tired. Please tell the major I will see him in the morning."

When she tried to close the door, his hand grasped its edge and prevented her action. "I'm sorry, ma'am, but he said it's urgent."

"Urgent? I've done my duty today, sir. If there are more incoming wounded, someone else will have to see to them. I'm exhausted. How can I be of help to anyone if I collapse from fatigue or illness?"

"If necessary, ma'am, I'm to bring you by force," he insisted.

Qualms filled Shannon. She allowed her shock and displeasure to show. She must call his bluff. "I beg your pardon? I'm a private citizen, under President Davis's protection. How dare your major order me about like one of his soldiers! This is unforgivable conduct. I shall not tolerate it. You will remind the major of such facts, sir."

The soldier flushed red and shifted nervously. "I'm under orders. You must come along. The major has news of your husband."

Shannon's blue eyes brightened. "Why didn't you say so?" she chided him. Blane—at least there was news of Blane. Instantly she knew that his statement had been a lie. Still, she would be forced to see Clifford. "Give me a moment, sir," she asked, then closed her door. She concealed the gun and knife beneath her clothing, smoothed her dress and hair, then left with the private.

Shannon was taken to a house that Clifford had confiscated by force from an unfortunate family who proclaimed themselves Union sympathizers. He motioned for Shannon to enter and be seated. After dismissing the private, he tried to lock the door without her noticing. Shannon instantly became alert. "Yes, Major? It's late, and I'm exhausted. Did you want something?"

He walked to a sideboard and lifted a decanter. "Wine?" he offered. When Shannon refused it, he poured one glass and sat down.

"Sir, I'm very distressed over this offensive treatment tonight. Your private said you had news of Steven," she continued, wanting to get this confrontation started and finished.

The man crossed his leg casually and smiled—a smile that was more a leer. "Relax, Miss Greenleaf. We need to talk. I want this meeting to be pleasant and mighty interestin'. Yesiree, me and you needs to talk," Clifford murmured in a provocative manner.

"About what, sir?" she asked, exposing her vexation.

"You, Miss Greenleaf," he responded. "You see, I have some Georgia boys who joined up with me after their troop was scattered. One of them knows you. He told me you Greenleafs sided with the Yanks. Then I was told you went to Danville seeking a Federal captive. What do you think I should make of all this?" he inquired cockily.

"That someone is either mistaken or telling lies. If that is all, sir, I shall return to my room. I find your conduct rude and insulting."

"After you and your *husband* arrived in my camp, I thought your story seemed a bit wild. While I kept your man busy, I sent one of my men to Richmond to do some checking. Seems one of our agents in Washington came up with a curious story about a flaming redhead who's a good friend of Lincoln's. Seems this beauty vanished with a Major Blane Stevens, one of the Union's best agents. It also seems that a Simon Travers from Boston has great interest in retrieving this ravishing woman, and the law's on his side. I ain't too smart, ma'am, but I can add up these many clues. What are you and Stevens really after?"

"I don't know what you mean, sir. I am not the only woman with red hair. You have no right or evidence to make such ridiculous charges. In fact, sir, I believe you are a liar. No soldier has had time to cover such a distance. Are you trying to deceive or intimidate me?"

"Are you forgetting about the train between Lynchburg and Richmond? After my man returned, I thought you and me should have a private chat. You know, spies don't fare well in Dixie, ma'am."

"Spy? You're accusing me of spying? You're absurd! Ask the doctors, nurses, and wounded if I have tried to procure any information from them. If you dare, search my room and belongings. Question Doctor Cooper about our visit to Danville Prison. Bring my accuser to confront me—this Georgia boy you mentioned. Have your agent from Washington come here and swear upon a Bible that I am the redhead he mentioned. You have no proof because there is none. I shall have you reported and punished for this outrage. You overstep your authority, sir."

Chilling laugher from Clifford's grinning lips filled the room. "You're saying you didn't come from Washington? Straight from the White House? You're saying you don't know Blane Stevens, that he ain't Steven James? You're saying you didn't visit with Elizabeth Van Lew in Richmond, a known Yankee spy? You're saying you didn't flash no Yankee flag as a sign to them prisoners?" he challenged insolently.

"I will not relate my personal comings and goings to you. But for your information, President Davis knows I was staying with Miss Lizzie; that's where he sent my travel pass. My father did business with Mister Van Lew before the war. As for the prison incident, it was a trick to obtain news of my brother. I have nothing to hide, sir, but I will not be interrogated or harassed by the likes of you."

Clifford drilled his gaze into hers. "If that's true, then you won't mind if we capture and shoot Major Blane Stevens? And you won't mind Simon Travers arriving and taking a look at you tomorrow?"

Shannon couldn't stop the color from draining from her face. "Why would a Boston Yankee come here? Have you forgotten I know President Davis, that I carry a personal letter of protection from him?"

"I'm sure he'll be delighted I've caught the spy witch who made a fool of him and weaseled his help. A woman like you don't go running around the country without good reason. I ain't no bloody fool or idiot. I can prove

106

my charges, and I can hold you before 'n' after I do."

"Who is this Georgia boy?" Shannon continued her flimsy bluff.

"Captain James Thornton of Savannah. Know him?"

Yes, she recalled that beast. She remembered how she had rebuffed him on countless occasions and twice refused his proposal. The last time she had seen James, he had been beaten soundly by Hawke. "Surely you can't accept the word of a scorned suitor?" she scoffed.

"I have a compromise for you, Miss Greenleaf," he began.

"A compromise?" she repeated when he fell silent. Shannon rose and went to the fireplace to put distance between them. This predicament did not look good at all. Clifford was stretching the truth.

"If you stay here and forget about being a traitor to the South, I'll forget what I've learned about you. By now, Stevens should be dead or captured. When Travers arrives, I'll tell him you escaped and send him on to Georgia. If'n you compromise."

Shannon did not require clarification of "compromise" and "stay here." This villain could cause her trouble and peril. He was a threat to Blane. But pay for his silence and protection with her body . . .

Clifford followed her to the fireplace. As one hand cupped a breast, he added, "You'll live here with me until the danger's passed."

"Take your hands off me," she demanded in outrage.

"If I'm forced to arrest you, you'll be sent to Danville. There ain't no hotel for women over there. I wonder how long you'll be healthy confined with all those sex-hungry, diseased men. When they get you inside that filthy pen, they won't care if'n yore Rebel or Yank. While they got you, they'll forget they don't have no food 'r shelter—till they use you up. I might have to toss 'em another traitor's tail to keep 'em settled down. Starving prisoners can get awfully rowdy and dangerous."

"You wouldn't dare commit such an offense!" she shrieked. "I am a woman, a Southerner. Many of the highest ranking officers in the Confederate Army know me and my family. You wouldn't dare."

He chuckled wickedly. "I can do whatever I want to a Union spy. I can hand you over to the three men who captured you and Stevens. They deserve some reward, don't you think? There's plenty of woods around here. Wouldn't nobody see or hear nothing. After I finish with you, they'd be glad to help you *disappear*. When I say you left, no one would dare doubt me or miss you. You should be glad I'm being so kind and generous to a spy 'n' traitor."

Shannon gaped at the evil man. War had twisted his mind. But would he commit such a crime? His expression said yes. Shannon knew there was no way she could get out of this predicament unless she rendered Clifford helpless for hours. She watched the man's gaze shift to her bosom. His face became flushed and he licked his lips. If she screamed, no one would help her or believe her. Clifford took her silence for defeat and tried to unbutton her dress.

Shannon caught his hands to halt them. She sighed heavily, setting her ruse into motion. "All right, Major Clifford. I'm not a criminal, but I doubt I could prove my word against yours. I'll have to accept your offer. But I won't be rolled on the floor or handled like some cheap harlot. This deal will be our secret, is that not so?"

He smiled, thinking he had won. "As long as you live here with me and follow my orders, no one will be the wiser."

"How do I know I can trust you?" Shannon probed.

"The same way I'll have to trust you," he retorted. "We got something valuable to trade: I need me a real woman, and you need my help." When he attempted to unbutton her dress again, Shannon tried to stop him. He slapped her hands away and warned, "You got to learn to share everything, girl. I want me a peek at these beauts. I been thinking about how they'd look and taste for days. You're real scared of this Simon Travers, ain't you? Why'd you become a spy?"

Shannon did her best to appear vulnerable and afraid, but she wanted to claw out his eyes and evil heart. There was no available weapon, and it was futile to pit her meager strength against his. She had no choice but to allow his gropings until she got the upper hand. "I'm not a spy, sir, but I know I can't prove it. I was in Washington and I did meet Lincoln and Stevens. I merely told them I would aid their cause in return for their help with locating my brother. I had to get away from Simon; he was forcing me to marry him. You've been watching me. You know I've done nothing to hurt the Confederacy. I don't want to be placed inside Danville Prison or turned over to those men. I have no choice but to do as you command. I only wanted to find Corry and get home to Savannah." Tears eased down her cheeks.

Clifford's evil lust prevented any remorse or sympathy. "You need me to take care of you, Shannon. I'll be real good to you," he mumbled hoarsely, his glazed eyes fastened to her exposed breasts. He was becoming crazed by them. "By damn, they's beauts, real beauts! Was you diddling Stevens?" he questioned abruptly.

Shannon inhaled and panted, "Certainly not! He's a Yankee." Where was Blane when she needed him? Was he alive? Free? God help her, she wanted to kill this vile man! *Patience*, she warned herself.

"It's time we go to bed," he announced ominously as he continued to fondle a breast with each grimy hand.

"I'll need privacy, sir. I've never . . ." Shannon chose her words carefully and cleverly. "Please give me a few minutes."

Clifford's mouth curled into an eager smile. "You're a virgin?" he asked excitedly. When Shannon nodded and blushed, he licked his lips once more. His wide eyes roamed her shapely body.

"You won't hurt me?" she entreated as if terrified and subdued.

"'Course not. You get in there and get undressed. I'll join you soon. You try to escape and I'll have my men take turns with you while I watch. Behave yourself, 'cause I don't want to share you."

"Please don't call your men, sir, and don't hand me over to Simon. He's mean and evil. I'll do whatever you say. Just be patient and gentle. I understand my position." Shannon knew the man was so consumed with lust that he would never suspect her thoughts and actions. The wicked devil assumed she was petrified and defeated. Well, he didn't know Shannon Greenleaf at all!

"Then get in bed and be ready for me," he ordered sternly.

Shannon entered the room he had pointed out to her. Working swiftly, she doused the lantern so that only moonlight filtered into the darkness. She removed her dress and shoes and dropped them in full view beside the bed. Stuffing pillows beneath the cover, she formed a bodylike shape. Then she searched for a weapon and, finding a heavy candlestick, she quickly concealed it as she awaited his arrival. She would be given only one chance for freedom. Heaven help her if she bungled it. *Oh, Blane, where are you, my love?*

She could hear the glass and decanter clinking

110

together as the repulsive major took another drink or two. The door stood ajar. Shannon was poised for attack, then remembered how tall he was. If she missed her target . . . She hurried to the bed, tossed the pillows aside, and snuggled beneath the cover, wondering what was keeping him so long.

Finally the door squeaked and a shadow fell across the floor. Clifford's eyes spotted the discarded clothing and the hump under the covers. He grinned. This had been easier than he imagined. He had scared her silly with his threats. He was glad Simon Travers wouldn't arrive for three days to pay plenty to ransom this pretty tart. It was too bad that greedy Yank wouldn't get a virgin bride— one victory more for the South. Yep, this was going to be a nice little treat. He couldn't wait to get inside of her helpless virgin body. He looked down at his large, rigid manhood, then lovingly fondled it. His baby had the size and power to give lots of pain or pleasure, depending on which hunger he was in the mood to feed and enjoy. His teeth almost itched to chew on her nipples. Sometimes giving pain was as good as sating himself inside a woman. He glanced at the belt in his other hand. That fun could come later, after he got her broken in.

"It's gonna be real good for us, Shannon." He chuckled lewdly, then walked to the bed, nudging her clothes aside with his toe. "If you don't want me to take this belt to your backside, girl, hand over the rest of your clothes," he ordered with a laugh as he popped the pillow with the weapon. He laughed again when she jumped uncontrollably and squealed. In every town he had entered, there had been some female he could intimidate or trick. "I know how to use this belt on women that don't mind me. You know you don't want me tearing off them underclothes, and I can't get to you through 'em. Shuck 'em, girl. I got a real nice gift for you. You don't

111

want me getting mad and rough."

Shannon detected the smugness and evil in this man. And when she considered the differences in their sizes, she realized she could never overpower him. She would have to wait until he was close enough and dazed enough to strike with the heavy candlestick. She wiggled out of her undergarments, grateful for the darkness and covers. Tossing them to Clifford, she slipped her hand beneath the pillow to grasp her weapon securely. She was ready and eager to do battle with this villain.

Clifford sniffed the garments and laughed before he dropped them and the belt to the floor. Flinging aside the covers, he seized her by the ankles. Then he roughly jerked her body sideways on the bed, placing himself between her spread thighs. Gripping her hipbones, he prepared to yank her toward him as he stated excitedly, "It's best for you and me if this first plunge is fast and hard." His shaft was poised to thrust forcefully and brutally into her exposed womanhood.

As his body fell forward on hers, Shannon struck him time and time again with the heavy weapon. At first, Clifford groaned and thrashed as he tried to avoid her unexpected attack. Even after he went limp, Shannon hit him again, almost hoping she had killed the vile beast. Realizing there was no time to waste, she shoved him from her naked body, then sat up breathing rapidly.

When her racing heart and respiration slowed, she glanced at the form beside her. He had lied to her. He had intended to rape her savagely. What other lies had he told? Knowing she had to leave quickly, she struggled to her feet, seized Clifford by the ankles, and pulled and heaved until he dropped to the floor. Revulsion flooded her as her gaze traveled over his loathsome body. Light from the adjoining room fell across his frame. Even in a flaccid state, his manhood was enormous. Surely it would have ripped her apart if he had impaled her with it.

112

She yanked the sheet from the bed and tore sturdy lengths from it. She bound his feet twice, then did the same with his hands behind his back. Taking a wider piece, she wrapped it around his head numerous times to gag his mouth. Next, she blindfolded him. As her roaming gaze checked her progress, it landed on his "gift" for her. She tore another narrow strip from the sheet. Trying not to touch the disgusting member, she tied a "ribbon" tightly around the base of his shaft. With luck, he would never be able to use it again, she mused angrily—at least not to violate and torture an innocent woman! She wished she had slain him. During a moment of battle, it would have been justified, but planning it and carrying it out with a clear head would have been nothing less than premeditated murder.

She searched for a root cellar and was delighted when she located one in the kitchen pantry. She labored until she had Clifford's body near it. Without guilt, her foot shoved him into the black hole. She pondered her emotions and the smile that teased her lips when she heard a loud thud below her. Closing the cellar door, she pushed heavy items over it, then propped a chair under the door handle to the pantry. That should keep Major Clifford busy long enough for me to be long gone! she told herself.

Shannon washed his blood and grime from her nude body, then pulled on her clothes. Noticing blood on the floor and bed, she hurriedly covered the bed with a quilt and mopped away the bloody smears, then glanced around to make sure no clues to her attack were visible.

Without delay, Shannon returned to the hospital and stole into her room. After gathering her belongings, she left unseen. No one was around the corral to prevent her from saddling her horse and walking him away from the enclosure. At a safe distance, she mounted and rode into the shadows.

Shannon had ridden only a mile from camp when a soldier stopped her flight. "Halt! Give your name and business or I'll open fire," the masculine voice shouted from the impenetrable darkness.

Shannon reined her horse and called out, "It's Shannon Greenleaf. I'm heading for Georgia. I have permission to pass through, sir."

"Permission from who?" the man called back, stepping into the moonlight. "Where you riding off to so fast, Shannon?"

"James Thornton, you beast! How dare you tell Major Clifford such lies about me and my family. Just wait until I see your father and mother. Your daddy'll take you to the barn and thrash you soundly for shaming him like this," she warned, trying to sound brave and furious.

"Don't sling foul lies on me, Shannon Greenleaf. We both know your whole family're bloody traitors. It didn't surprise me you took up with some Yankee devil. You always did take to rogues, didn't you, you hot-blooded slut? I should have taken care of you and your Yankee stud myself, instead of exposing you to the major. You ain't going nowhere. Clifford's promised me a piece of your ransom from Travers. And I might even git a piece of your tail if there's anything left when the major finishes. He's got an ornery reputation with women. It shore won't be like it was with that Yank—or your precious Hawke."

"You knew Clifford was planning to rape me and blackmail me? Whatever has happened to you, James Thornton? This crime is beneath even you. Why did you betray me?" she inquired, wondering how to overcome this new obstacle. If he took her back to camp . . .

"You've had it coming for years, you shameless bitch. I wasn't good enough for you, but old Hawke was. Where is that black-eyed savage? Why ain't he sniffing your tail like always? Don't tell me you dropped him for a Yankee

114

stud. Hawke was never the sharing kind."

"You're disgusting, James Thornton! You'll be sorry for this."

"I'm just sorry I told the major about you before I took my revenge. I heard your papa and Temple got themselves killed. I also heard my good friend Corry's a Rebel prisoner. Now, Clifford's gonna get you bad, and it serves you Greenleafs right for turning on us. That only leaves Hawke. Where is he, Shannon? Me and him got a score to settle. I wonder if he'll come running back when they put you on trial and hang you, if you survive tonight. Let's get you back to the major."

Shannon was thinking swiftly in desperation. "Listen to me, James. It's not what you think; it never was. Hawke left right after the war began. I don't know where he is. I'm only trying to locate Corry and get him home. If you'll let me pass, I'll marry you when the war ends. I give you my word of honor," she lied shamelessly.

James laughed wildly, then sneered contemptuously, "A Thornton marry Hawke's leavings? And what about this Yankee stud you been traveling with? Ain't no telling how many beds you've warmed. I wouldn't even piss on you, woman."

"James Thornton, you're the vilest, lowest form of man or beast. I have never slept with any man. Do you hear? Any man! But when I do, it won't be one like you or Clifford. I would die first."

"I hope Major Clifford beats you black and blue before he sells you to that Yank from Boston. You're going back to camp, one way or another."

"I don't think so," a deep voice argued from behind James. "Drop your weapon, if you want to live another day, Reb."

James whirled to shoot the intruder, but as he did, a gun butt slammed into his jaw, breaking it and rendering him unconscious. James was thrown backward by the forceful blow and landed roughly. He didn't move.

Shannon wondered if she were dreaming. "Blane? Is that you?" she whispered, afraid to trust her eyes and ears.

Blane responded crisply, "Yep, it's me, Shannon." He bent over James's body to make sure he was out cold.

Shannon slipped off her horse and raced to the handsome blond. When he stood, she flung herself into his arms and shrieked, "Blane, I'm so glad to see you. Clifford said he sent you into a trap. He said you were dead. How did you find me?" she babbled excitedly.

Blane grasped her wrists and set her away from him. "Thanks to Major Clifford, three more men are dead. How did he know about me?" he asked, wanting to know why Clifford had acted so strangely at their arrival, even before this Rebel betrayed them. As he awaited her reply, he removed James's shirt and belt, bound the man's hands and feet and, pulling a large handkerchief from the Rebel's pocket, he gagged the man and rolled him into the bushes.

Shannon stared at Blane. Was there a hint of accusation in his voice? She didn't like his mood or his question. She wondered how much of her quarrel with James he had overheard. "If Clifford's still alive, ask him. I left him knocked out, tied up, and locked in the root cellar. I'm riding before another sentry arrives." She stalked angrily to her horse, then mounted.

Blane was beside the animal instantly. He grabbed Shannon and yanked her into his arms.

Struggling, Shannon yelled, "I've been through hell during these last two weeks, and I survived on my own! So don't show up and start ordering me about like your slave. Put me down, you brute," she commanded.

"Answer me first," he stated in refusal. "And be quiet!"

Shannon stiffened in rage but complied. "Satisfied?"

116

she asked. "I didn't expose any of your secrets. I suppose you think I am to blame for revealing your identity to Clifford. Is that what you wanted me to admit?" she asked sarcastically. "Put me down. I'm getting out of here."

"What did you mean 'if he's still alive'?" Blane probed, having witnessed the entire confrontation between her and James.

Shannon glared into his face as he held her in his arms like a child being carried to bed. "He tried to rape me. I beat him senseless with a candlestick. For all I know and care, he might be dead. If not, he won't see the light of day or crave another woman for a long time." Shannon revealed her meaning as she related the incident in detail.

Blane stared at her this time. Suddenly he laughed.

"It isn't funny, Major Stevens. I thought you were my partner, my bodyguard. You're never around when I need help or advice. I seem to do better on my own." After her irritation and fears were vented on him, she described her visit to the prison. "You see, I don't need you at all."

Blane grinned as he lowered her feet to the ground and released her. Playfully he teased, "It didn't look or sound that way earlier."

"If you mean that yellow-bellied snake," she sneered, nodding at James, "I could have handled him. He's the villain who betrayed me—rather us—to Major Clifford." With one agile movement, Shannon hiked her skirt with her left hand and, with her right, withdrew the knife from the sheath strapped to her thigh and placed the point at Blane's heart. "This, Mister Stevens, was my path to freedom. That, Mister Stevens, is James Thaddaus Thornton of the Savannah Thorntons, a spurned suitor. His family was close to mine. I didn't want to kill him. I was merely waiting for him to get close enough to attack."

117

"You're mighty generous with your enemies, Shannon."

"Tell that to Major Clifford when you see him again—which we will if we don't get moving, sir. I would hate to imagine what he'll do to us if we're captured, especially to me."

"Let's get moving, partner. Raleigh is a long ride."

"Raleigh? North Carolina? Why go there?"

"Actually, we're heading for Wilmington on the coast, by way of Raleigh and Fayetteville. I'll explain later, partner. Let's get some miles between us and your numerous thwarted suitors. I thought you told me Rebels were gentlemen who didn't harm ladies," he reminded her.

Shannon clenched her teeth. "They were before this war changed them into beasts. Do you want me to admit that you're right again?"

"No need, just so you know it," he teased, cuffing her chin.

"What about Corry, Blane? Surely you've heard what Andersonville is like? Remember, he is a Federal soldier."

He replied, "Remember, Major Clifford and Simon Travers will be looking for you in that direction. Corry will have to wait."

"He has a spy in Danville Prison. We should warn them."

"There isn't time, Shannon. Let's mount up and ride."

Blane lifted her and sat her in her saddle. She followed him to where he had left his horse. As he mounted, Shannon asked again, "How did you find me? Your timing was perfect—too perfect."

"Tell you later," he tossed over his shoulder, then rode away.

Shannon watched his retreating back in the moonlight. She was tempted to head in the other direction. He

118

could be so infuriating. She had never needed and wanted the comfort of his strong arms as she did at this moment. A picture of Clifford poised nude and ready to ram her body with his large male weapon flashed across her mind and she shuddered. She clicked her reins and kneed her horse into a pursuit of Blane's. Racing behind him, she vowed to hear an explanation the moment they halted for rest. He owed her one!

Chapter Five

Blane pushed Shannon until she was too exhausted to question him when they halted. He was not ready or willing to discuss anything with her tonight, or rather this morning. In Blane's mind it seemed that every day more and more entangling vines of doubt surrounded her and tried to pull her from her pedestal of rarity and perfection. Yet she always managed to find a clever way to retain her balance and position.

Everything about this temptress of destiny was complicated. Just as he was on the verge of believing that his dark opinions were wrong, she or someone would do or say things to convince him he was right to mistrust her and resist her. She could readily create and pour on honeyed lies and beguiling charm when the situation demanded it. Having heard her argument with Thornton, he couldn't determine which words or actions to accept as truth. How did he or James know if Clifford had truly tried to attack her? And even if he had, perhaps Clifford hadn't known her secret role, or it hadn't mattered during his bout of frenzied lust. If anybody knew how Shannon could incite a man to mindless passion, he did. As all these thoughts whirled through Blane's mind, he refused to acknowledge that it was this mysterious

120

Hawke and her silence about him that incited his fury and his doubts.

After a short sleep and a quick meal, Blane had her up and moving again. Because each was waiting for the other to make truce, this swift and silent pattern stubbornly continued until they were five miles north of Raleigh. Blane ordered Shannon to conceal herself until he made certain the house they approached was still a safe house. He warned her to stay awake and alert.

She watched him ride away, then sat on the ground. In ten minutes, she jumped up and paced, fearing she would fall into mindless slumber. She kept eyeing the large house she saw in the distance. If Blane hadn't met with danger, what was taking so long? Should she ride in or stay put as he had ordered? What had she done wrong to annoy him? Forty-three minutes passed. Then she saw him standing on the porch, waving her forward. She mounted and obeyed.

As she dismounted, Shannon stared openly at the pretty brunette who stood beside Blane. In comparison, she felt tiny and dirty. She noticed the way the woman's gaze roamed over her, then over Blane. The brunette, who appeared to be about thirty, smiled and invited Shannon into her home. Shannon glanced at Blane and frowned, then followed the woman. Miffed for some inexplicable reason, Shannon remained quiet and alert.

After serving them a hot meal of roasted venison and potatoes, the woman asked Shannon if she would like a bath. Shannon blushed but quickly replied, "Yes, if you don't mind the trouble."

"Blane, would you fetch the water?" Catherine Delany asked sweetly, her gaze passing over his body with obvious appreciation.

"Sure, Cathy. Where's the tub?"

"I'll put it in the second bedroom. Then Shannon can turn in after her bath. I'm sure she's exhausted, aren't

121

you, Miss Greenleaf?"

Shannon realized this woman was not a stranger to Blane. She had caught the undercurrents between them. As she watched Blane prove that he knew his way around the house, she fumed inwardly at his present behavior and that of the last few days. He had been staring at her and treating her like . . . like that intolerable disease again! Let him, she mentally decided. She was tired of trying to understand him. She was ashamed of mooning over and chasing after a man who obviously didn't want to be admired or loved. She dismissed thoughts of that passionate night in Farmville, as he had evidently done.

"Yes, I am very tired. I'm sure you and Blane would like to visit privately. A bath and a good night's sleep would be sheer heaven."

From her emotionless tone of voice and expression, Blane couldn't interpret her remarks. As if she were a child, he teased, "Come along, Shannon. I'll show you where to bathe and sleep."

Shannon sighed and stretched, intentionally trying to draw his gaze to her supple and shapely figure. "If you don't mind, I'll finish my coffee while you fill the tub. Do you need any help, sir?"

Blane grinned roguishly and replied, "I've filled tubs for ladies before." He stripped off his shirt and tossed it over a chair.

"I'm sure you have—plenty of them," she responded flippantly, as if she had forgotten that the last one he had filled had been for her.

While Catherine observed the bare-chested man, Blane drew the water and deposited it in a large tin tub in a small bedroom at the back of the house. "Your bath is ready, Miss Greenleaf," Catherine informed Shannon, as if eager to have her out of the way.

"Do you live here alone, Catherine?" she asked innocently.

122

"For now," the woman answered. "My husband and brother are off fighting this futile war. That should teach them to join the strongest side next time. The fools should know the South is doomed. With luck, neither one of them will return to trouble me."

Shannon gaped at the cold-hearted woman. "Your family is fighting for the South, but you're aiding the North?" she pressed.

"Does that surprise you?" Catherine asked indifferently. "A woman does what she must to survive. Around here, the Yankees rule—at least most of the time. Anyway, the South will lose, and I'll be handsomely rewarded for choosing the right side. At this moment, Grant is eating away at Petersburg and Richmond. Sherman is chewing his way toward Georgia, and Sheridan is burping West Virginia. The Rebels don't stand a chance against such forces."

"How do you know such things?" Shannon inquired.

The brown-haired woman grinned and whispered shamelessly, "I sleep with the right men. It's amazing what a man will reveal when his head's next to yours on a pillow."

Shannon's first thought was, what a perfect mate for Major Clifford. "Aren't you afraid the Rebels will unmask you and kill you?"

"Surely you're teasing? Most of my information comes from loose Rebel lips and lusty appetites. What about you, Shannon? How long have you been with Blane? How do you extract your information?"

Shannon didn't miss the use of her first name. Was the woman deceiving her or perhaps trying to embarrass her? Was she attempting to withdraw information? How could she, or any woman, whore for information? Shannon concluded that she didn't and couldn't trust Catherine Delany. "I don't," she replied.

Catherine's skeptical gaze swept over Shannon as she

probed brazenly. "You don't what? Don't use your body and feminine talents to entice information from Rebels and Yanks? Or you don't try to get any facts for Blane and the Union?"

Shannon tried not to show her disgust. She prevented herself from scolding or teasing the woman, for she knew that Catherine might be telling the truth. "I don't go seeking information, but I do pass along anything I overhear. Ask Blane to fill you in on my job. I need to bathe and rest, Mrs. Delany. It's been a long and dirty ride from Richmond." If the woman knew she had lied about coming from Richmond, it didn't show.

Shannon was pleased when Catherine finally left the room. Blane should have told her who this woman was and what to say to her! she mused angrily. After scrubbing her hair, she reached for the bucket to rinse it. As the tepid water suddenly splashed over her head, she thanked Catherine for helping her, though she was perturbed by the woman's intrusion and brazen rush.

"You're welcome," Blane murmured, then chuckled as she flung her long hair over her head to her back and glowered at him. Now that he had Shannon safely out of danger, he could relax and think clearly. He had been troubled over his recent behavior and conflicting emotions. What if there had been another man in her past? Was that so unexpected, so shocking, so unacceptable? He had been sending her some awfully confusing signals. Was he jealous? Afraid of her and these wild feelings? Afraid of learning the truth about her? Afraid of how his secrets would affect her? Did he want her? Yes, yes, yes . . .

Shannon hiked her knees, then ineffectually attempted to cover her breasts. "Don't tell me you're speaking to me again. Am I still alive? What are you doing in here? Where's your . . . friend?"

A playful smile relaxed his features. "Gone to hide our

124

horses and tend them. Don't take Cathy so seriously. She's selfish and a bit outspoken, but she can be trusted. I owe you an apology for being so distant and harsh these last few days. I had some unpleasant matters to sort out and discard. I'm sorry I wasn't around when you needed me, Shannon. I'm responsible for you, and I failed you back there. As you've seen, I don't take kindly to defeats, even little ones."

He hadn't replaced his shirt, and Shannon's eyes drifted over his golden torso. Her gaze lifted to his tousled hair, then lowered to his face. His brows were not heavy or bushy like many men; they barely arched, seeming to curve very gently past his eyes. Those hazel eyes were small, but expressive. The ends dipped downward without appearing to droop. When he was intensely alert, they seemed more brown, but when he was calm and playful, as he was now, they appeared a rich, tawny green. A bump on his nose told her it had been broken in the past. As her gaze roamed, she saw that his face and frame exuded strength of mind and body. Again, she wondered about the scar on his jawline.

Shannon wanted to stroke his amber hair with its sunny streaks, to caress his tawny body of satiny hardness, to snuggle into his protective arms. She wanted to reach out and pull those full lips to hers and kiss him thoroughly. She wanted to discover him fully. But he had spoiled things with his mercurial personality and contradictory treatment. He had made her wary of him and her feelings. When the emotion-heavy silence interrupted her reverie, she tried to clear her wits. "Forget it, Blane. I'm not your responsibility, or your problem, or your failure. If you had been around, both of us would have been in deeper trouble. As for your friend, the way she was pressing me for information makes me wonder if she is trustworthy. She certainly has a vulgar mouth. You should have prepared me for meeting this woman to avoid my making any mistakes. Is there something between you two?" Shannon asked boldly.

"You are," he murmured, hunkering down to stop towering over her. "Just to be safe, keep your mouth shut and your eyes open. I wouldn't want trouble because you two think you're rivals."

Rivals, she mentally echoed. Was he telling her something about him and Cathy? Was he enticing or discouraging her? "Papa used to tell me one couldn't see a smile in the dark, so an enemy didn't know it existed. Tell Cathy it doesn't. That should prevent any feline attacks on me. I'm tired. Would you mind giving me a little privacy, Major Stevens?"

"You sure I can't help with your bath?" he offered, moving the back of his fingers up and down her arm. He remembered what it was like to kiss her and hold her. He wanted to enjoy those experiences again. With her hair soaked, it had become an even darker red. Her ivory face was flushed from the heat of the day and from his nearness. But it was her mesmeric blue eyes that held his attention. As if magnetized, they drew him deeper and deeper under their spell. He wanted to hold her and caress every inch of her body. He yearned to steal her breath with kisses, to make love to her. His smoldering, provocative gaze exposed his passionate thoughts and feelings.

Shannon was astonished by the heat in his eyes. If Catherine had not been nearby, she might have been tempted to warm herself with it. "Not this time," she murmured coyly to tease him, as his mood and look seemed to tease her. "We'll have to wait for the right place and moment." She was echoing the words he had spoken on that bewitching night in Farmville, before he had left only to return to shun her. "This isn't it," she informed him.

Blane's hazel gaze locked on her blue one. When they

were alone and close at times like this, it seemed as if nothing and no one existed or mattered to either of them. If only he could keep all past and current realities from assailing them until—

A noise captured his ear and his attention. He turned his head sideways and listened. His eyes narrowed; his jawline tensed. "See you later," he stated, then left.

Taking a hint from his actions, Shannon hurriedly completed her bath. Before she could dry and dress, Blane rushed into the room. He grabbed a coverlet from the bed, yanked Shannon to her feet, then wrapped the cover around her wet body. He scooped her into his arms. When she struggled, he muttered anxiously, "Rebels coming. We've got to hide. Clifford's probably got an alert out on us by now. No one could mistake your description, my flaming-haired witch. Besides, they know our names and ranks. That means your letter from Davis isn't worth a single bean."

Shannon let him take command. He carried her to the hearth where Catherine was removing the decorative fire board, then he let her down. "Sorry, Flame, but get inside," he commanded.

Shannon looked at the sooty, oversized hole and balked. She had just taken her first bath in days! Maybe he was overreacting.

"Get inside, woman! There's no time to argue! They could draft me or arrest us! Damnit, that could be Clifford or Travers!" With those words, he practically crammed her into the large area and told her to stand up and make room for him.

Shannon pressed into one corner of the chimney as Blane worked his way in beside her. "Keep still and quiet, Shannon," he warned.

Catherine tossed Shannon's carpet bag and dirty clothes at their feet. Next came Blane's shirt and weapons. She put the fire board into place and twisted the catches. A spinning wheel and other objects were placed on the raised hearth before the hand-painted summer closure. Catherine quickly checked for revealing soot. Then she hurried around the house, removing all signs of their presence. She dipped her head into Shannon's tub, then dampened her skin. With a cloth wrapped around her wet hair, she answered the knock on her door.

"Sorry to disturb you, ma'am, but we need to use your well and yard for the night. Do you mind?" the lieutenant inquired.

"Certainly not," Catherine told him with a bright smile.

"We also need to search your house and grounds," he added, removing his hat and watching her closely.

"Why?" Catherine asked, focusing sky blue eyes on him.

"Deserters, runaway slaves, Union spies," he answered calmly.

Catherine half turned and informed him, "As you can see, sir, I'm quite alone." Her eyes lingered on the dusty gray uniform, which didn't always reveal the truth about its wearer's loyalties.

"Then you won't mind if I make sure?" he persisted.

"If you must." She opened the door and moved aside. "You will be careful with my things. My husband was slain at Shiloh, and I have little of value left. If you promise to be careful with my belongings during your search, I'll share my evening meal with you, sir."

"It smells mighty good in here," he stated, sniffing the air.

"Venison. I shot the deer myself. Perhaps I should serve you outside. It might not look proper for you to join me alone. We wouldn't want your troops repeating such gossip to your wife."

The unwed Lieutenant Paul Barclay introduced himself to Catherine, then told his men he would conduct

128

the search of her home. He ordered them to look around outside and to set up camp for the night. Afterward, he followed Catherine around the house, searching here and there in the obvious hiding places as the coy woman distracted him.

Shannon was frightened. She leaned toward Blane and whispered, "What about the horses? What if they find us?"

Blane held her head between his hands and whispered in her ear, "If you stay still and quiet, they won't. Relax, Flame. I don't bite."

Shannon glanced upward at the light above them. She could see Blane's laughing features. She stuck her tongue out at him. How could he be so calm and playful at a time like this? She wished she weren't facing frontward with him facing backward. Their right sides touched with an unsettling intimacy, for his shirt was missing and she was too aware of her nudity beneath the coverlet. As she clutched the quilt with both hands, she eyed the soot on her freshly scrubbed body and hair and frowned in dismay. It was hot and cramped inside the dirty chimney, despite its larger-than-normal size. Trapped with him, she was glad she had bathed and now smelled of wildflowers. It would serve him right to be driven wild with temptation!

She almost held her breath as the search went on and on. She kept her gaze lowered, wondering if this ploy would work. Every so often, she would hear laughter between Catherine and the Rebel officer. She prayed those were the only sounds she would be forced to overhear tonight! When she finally looked up at Blane, he was leaning against the front corner, watching her and grinning. Shannon averted her gaze.

After two hours, Shannon was leaning against her corner. She was tiring and her hands were cramping. She dared not shift her weight for fear of striking the items at her feet or the fire board. She prayed no crawly creature would touch her, especially a spider, for she knew she might scream. She hated those multilegged things, almost as much as she hated the thought of being discovered and captured like this.

The heat increased inside the blackened confines of the chimney. If Catherine invited the Rebel officer into her bed, Shannon realized, she and Blane would be stuck here until morning, or whenever. How could her stiff and weary body remain thus all night or longer? She wondered if her partner considered her responsible for their precarious situation.

She looked at Blane once more. He didn't appear the slightest bit uncomfortable or upset. She wondered how he felt about Catherine, about her current actions? She leaned her head against the stone wall and looked at the darkening sky. Perspiration trickled down her temples and between her breasts; it beaded on her nose and upper lip, and made her arms and body clammy. When she wiped at her face, she smeared black streaks over it. As Blane struggled to contain his mirth, Shannon looked at her hand and guessed what had happened. She scowled at him.

As delicious aromas teased at her nose, she was glad they had eaten an afternoon meal. She was so thirsty, and her fatigue was increasing. Her eyelids were becoming very heavy. Even her shoulders wanted to droop and her knees wanted to buckle. With her head against the stones, she feared to close her eyes and lose her scant control.

By midnight, the moon was in view above them. Shannon felt it was safe to assume the search had been completed unsuccessfully. She also felt it was safe to assume that Catherine was not sleeping alone, for surely she would have released them otherwise for a breather and water. The overpowering odor and snugness of her surroundings worked unmercifully on Shannon's nerves. She would have liked nothing more than to have kicked down the fire board and screamed for ten minutes.

Perceiving her tension and exhaustion, Blane shifted slightly, drawing her attention. He whispered into her ear, "Lay your head on my chest and get some sleep, love. I won't let you fall or move. Don't be pigheaded; you're about to faint and that would be noisy."

Shannon's gaze tried to pierce the shadows to see his expression. The angle of his head and the meager light did not allow it. He placed his hands beneath her arms and lifted her cautiously, settling her snuggly between his body and the back wall. His legs imprisoned hers to prevent any movement, and his left arm rested around her shoulders. His right hand pressed her damp face to his moist chest, then held her head in place. Finally, he laid his cheek atop her fragrant head.

After a few minutes, he whispered, "Could you move your fists out of my chest? That cover isn't going anywhere, love."

Shannon realized her balled hands were hurting her chest as well as his. She relaxed them, flattening her palms on his body. She was nestled tightly and securely against him and, suppressing a peaceful sigh, she closed her eyes. This time, only his manly scent filled her nostrils.

Blane felt her body go limp. Knowing Shannon felt safe and calm enough to go to sleep in his embrace made him smile. Time passed. He commanded his fingers not to caress her silky flesh and awaken her. His control was sorely strained when her head rolled to his arm, causing the moonlight to expose her face. Her lips were parted. He wanted to close his mouth over them. In slumber, she looked so fragile, so innocent. He grinned at the smears of soot on her face that gave her a mischievous-child image. She was so mysterious, so appealing.

Overcome with desire for Shannon, he shifted just enough to allow the quilt to slide to their feet. As she snuggled against him, his bare chest met her exposed breasts. A tingle of excitement surged through him. His loins flamed. He realized that his impulsive action had been a mistake. His hands itched to caress her. He was tempted to arouse her and make love to her right there in Catherine's chimney but decided it wasn't the time or place for their first union. Besides, it was possible she would reject him, considering his recent treatment and Clifford's attempted rape.

Blane knew that Shannon found him attractive, but he wasn't certain she would want him to make love to her. In Farmville that night, she had confessed desire and willingness. Who was this Hawke? Why was she keeping quiet about him? Where had he gone, and why? Was she really seeking Corry, or Hawke? That spurned Rebel suitor of hers had made it sound as if she and Hawke had been lovers—mismatched lovers. At least she hadn't been willing to bed Clifford for information or freedom. If he ever saw that bastard, he would kill him! The same was true for Simon Travers. In fact, he should have slit Thornton's throat for betraying her. If Shannon hadn't been standing there watching, he would have!

Blane realized his teeth were clenched and his body was taut. He forcibly relaxed both. At least his rage had cooled his passion. He leaned his head against the stone wall, afraid to look at her again. He tried to forget that night in the house when she had said, "I want you too, Blane." But did she want Blane, or the Blade and his help? Did she want Blane, or someone to replace Hawke? The sooner he discovered those answers, the better for both of them, though he needed to obtain them on his own. To press or probe her might be a mistake.

Blane dozed off and on during the night. Never once did he release his hold on Shannon. He was glad she was so exhausted that she could sleep in this uncomfortable position. Eventually, he noticed the gradual brightening of the sky overhead. Soon, with luck, the Rebels would leave.

Blane heard the door close behind the Confederate officer, then he heard him call out to his men to prepare to leave. At first, Blane decided to let Shannon sleep until the soldiers were gone. Grinning devilishly, he changed his mind. After a difficult night like this one, he could use a little amusement and comfort this morning.

Leisurely and sensuously, Blane pressed kisses over Shannon's face. When she began to shift and sigh dreamily, his mouth closed over hers. Shannon tried to pull away, then recognized the dank setting and the man who was pinning her to his body. He whispered in her ear, "You were making noises. I had to quiet you down. They're getting ready to move out. Won't be much longer now."

Shannon whispered, "You make a marvelous bed, partner."

With his head bent, he turned his head and smiled. His movement brought their faces close and his lips moved over hers once again.

Shannon lifted her arms and put her hands behind his head, wiggling her fingers into his damp hair. She returned his kiss and his embrace, savoring this wild moment confined with him.

Blane's hands cupped her head as his mouth urgently meshed against hers. They moved to her back and pressed her intimately to his fiery body. His lips moved down her throat and nibbled at her shoulders. How he wished he could bend lower. His right hand drifted down her side and gently grasped her buttock to press her to him.

Shannon inhaled and stiffened as she realized the quilt was missing. Glancing downward, she found that her breasts were practically glued to his torso. With her palm

133

on his forehead, she shoved his head upward and sent him an admonishing glare. There was no way she could retrieve the coverlet. Her face, neck, and chest went red.

Blane whispered, "When you wiggled, it slipped, love. I can't reach it. You want me to close my eyes?" he jested.

"You did that on purpose. Get away from me, you lecherous snake," she mouthed angrily. Immediately she held tightly to him, knowing his view would be better if they separated. "Don't you dare. Stay still," she commanded. What was she going to do?

Blane passed his hand over the stone wall, then wiped soot over her chest and shoulders. "That should hide your naked beauty from me. Want me to cover all of you with a black coat?"

Shannon repeated his action on his chest, then rubbed soot over his grinning face. She fought to control her giggles, for all she could see were white teeth and eyeballs. She didn't know—as Blane did—that the Rebels had ridden off during her mischief. When he seized her wrists and pinned them high above her head to assail her lips with his, she dared not resist him or verbally berate him.

Catherine knocked on the fire board. "You two still alive in there? I'll free you in a minute or two," she called to them.

"A timely rescue, Miss Greenleaf," he remarked huskily.

"You are a deceitful devil, Blane Stevens," she accused.

When the fire board was moved aside, Catherine saw the dirty quilt tangled around their legs. The woman removed their belongings, then said, "You can come out now." She didn't try to conceal her laughter at Shannon's predicament.

"I'm first, Blane Stevens, and you shut your

eyes!" Shannon warned him. "And stop laughing! It isn't funny." The last two remarks were for Catherine, for the woman's laughter grated on her nerves.

Blane wickedly put his dirty hands over his eyes. "Take off," he ordered merrily. "I won't peek. Just hurry. I'm hungry and thirsty."

Shannon wiggled into a sitting position, then inched off the hearth. She snatched up the quilt and covered herself. "Ready." As Blane nimbly removed his body from the chimney, Shannon noted her sooty handprints on his face and body. She glanced down to find his black prints boldly displayed on her own flesh. She started to scold him but saw the way the brunette was eyeing the revealing marks.

Catherine's laughter had ceased. "I hope you two weren't too hot or cramped in there. The lieutenant was sleeping on the porch," she lied for Shannon's benefit, knowing she couldn't fool Blane.

"Actually, Blane makes a most comfortable bed. There wasn't a problem until he let my cover slip to the floor."

"Shannon, you disappoint me. Surely you wouldn't get angry over a silly accident?" the woman chided coolly.

"Of course not. But that's when it got too hot and cramped," Shannon replied, her audacious gaze almost daring Blane to speak. Shannon's meaning was clear to everyone. "I need another bath. Would you mind drawing more water, Blane?" she asked sweetly.

"A quick bath, my fiery Flame, then we're off," he informed her, astonished and amused by her immodest conduct. "I think we both need one. Can you fetch the horses, Cathy, while my partner and I clean up? Your new admirer, Paul Barclay, might return later."

"I'll help you get things ready," Catherine offered, unwilling to leave them alone. What they did in the woods couldn't be prevented, but she would not allow them to make love in her house. She had wanted to plant doubt and insecurity in Shannon's mind this morning about her relationship with Blane and about Shannon's greenness with men and the subject of sex. Clearly Blane was working his charms on the redhead, but she would give Shannon plenty of reasons to resist him. She had vowed to herself this would be the handsome rogue's last chance to bed her and guarantee her loyalty. "You'll need to eat before you leave."

"Thanks, Cathy, but we've got to rush." Blane left the house to begin drawing and hauling the water for Shannon's second bath.

Catherine joined him at the well as he was preparing to wash the chimney's deposits from his virile frame. Oddly, he had a surge of modesty and hesitation about stripping and bathing in front of this promiscuous woman. She reached to pull the cloth and soap from his grasp, wheedling seductively about helping him. When she began rubbing her body against his and stroking where a lady shouldn't under these circumstances, Blane's vexation mounted, though his passion and shaft did not. He read a matching and hazardous vexation in Cathy's eyes.

A rash idea came to mind and he foolishly used it to put an end to her annoying scene. "This ain't how I planned for this visit to go, Cathy. I got stuck with that haughty bitch from Georgia. I can't let her see us getting too close. She's actually a Rebel spy. My mission is to unmask her and her contacts, but she's a tough one. I'm trying to disarm her with my masculine charm, but I can't move in on her too fast. She'll get suspicious or jittery. As soon as I pull some facts from her, I'll dispose of her and come back here for a proper visit—one we'll both enjoy. Now get along before she sees us and you spoil all the progress I made last night. It won't take long."

While Blane scrubbed by the well and Shannon

136

scrubbed in the bedroom, Catherine headed for the concealed cave halfway up a nearby hill. The cave went deep into the hillside, with a fresh spring at its rear. She had staked the horses there to feed on hay and to rest, and she knew it would require at least twenty minutes to saddle and fetch them.

Blane entered the bedroom and asked Shannon to wash the soot from his back. "Sorry, love, but I can't reach it. Do you mind?"

"Kneel beside the tub and don't turn around," Shannon told him. When he did, she moved to her knees to reach him. She soaped the cloth and washed until all traces of black were gone. Holding the cloth over her chest and sitting down, Shannon asked, "Would you please check my hair, then return the favor, partner?"

"Delighted, Miss Greenleaf." Blane continued to move the lathery cloth over her back and shoulders long after they were clean.

Finally Shannon asked, "Am I that dirty? Isn't it coming off?"

"It's gone, love. I was enjoying the exercise and view."

Shannon glanced over her shoulder. "You are a devilish beast."

He leaned over and kissed her lightly. "I know, love." He left Shannon smiling and shaking her head.

Taking a jar from the kitchen, Blane went to the yard, and caught a hen. Cutting off its head, he drained its blood into the glass container. Afterward, he concealed the jar and the dead hen from both women.

Shannon completed her task and dressed in men's clothes. She looked at the filthy water in the tub, then grinned. She would let Catherine empty it later. That would use up some of her excess energy!

"Shannon, you coming?" Blane's voice called out.

"Shortly," she responded as she braided her hair.

Blane glanced at Catherine. "Don't mention what you

told me. With her being from Georgia, it would cause her to worry too much. I want to keep her real calm, so I can finish this business with her. I can't believe he would burn Atlanta." Blane shook his head in frustration.

"Captain Barclay said he was destroying everything in his path. He plans to reach Savannah within two months; that'll cut off another major port. Paul admitted that the Shenandoah Valley's a lost cause, and Grant's winning the Wilderness Campaign by leaps and bounds. Those foolish Rebs keep fighting and dreaming and dying. If the South doesn't yield soon, there won't be anything left to conquer or rebuild."

A lengthy silence passed between them. "Blane, can't you stay longer? We could sneak visits to the cave to tend the horses. I want you. Just another day or two?" the brunette entreated.

Blane responded, "Sorry, Cathy. Shannon and I have to be in Charlotte by Thursday; then we're to head for Richmond. After I make those two stops, I won't need her help anymore. I'll file my report and hightail it back to you."

Shannon paused in the doorway, wondering if she should interrupt. She bumped the door aside to announce her entrance. Both people looked over at her. Blane smiled. Catherine grimaced.

They ate quickly and silently. Shannon thanked Catherine for her hospitality, then dismissed herself to wait with the horses while Blane said his farewell in private. He jointed her and mounted. Catherine wished them success in Charlotte, then, as she watched their departure, they vanished into the trees, heading westward.

After riding for an hour, Shannon asked Blane, "Where are we going? The sun's to our left, not at our backs."

"South to Fayetteville. If you're wondering about

138

Cathy's words, I did tell her we were heading west to Charlotte. She concealed us, but I have a curious feeling that she's playing both sides these days. I caught her going through your bag when you left it on the table."

Shannon expressed surprise. "There's nothing in there but some clothes. And I didn't tell her anything," she added proudly. "She gave me a bad feeling from the start. You think she'll send them after us?"

"Without a doubt, especially after she discovers I played her for a fool this morning," he remarked, then described his confrontation with Cathy. "You know what they say about a scorned woman. She'll guess the truth eventually, when I don't return. Let's hope I can spread the word in time for others to avoid her, just in case she's willing to hurt someone to spite me. Besides, she'll want to punish you. If the price is suitable—which it will be if Travers gets to her—she'll sell us out."

"She had better hope it isn't Major Clifford. He has this lust for whipping. He'll make her sorry she works for either side—if the bastard is still alive." Shannon blushed and frowned. "I don't know what's come over me. I'm getting as cold and cruel as they are."

"Either it's the war, or the company," he murmured.

"Probably the bad company," she announced with a touch of renewed humor.

When they halted shortly thereafter near an old, dilapidated hut, Blane told Shannon to splint and bind his right leg.

"Why?" she asked curiously.

"We're nearing heavy Rebel lines. I've got to appear wounded or they'll never let us pass. Until we reach Fayetteville, we say we're heading for home south of town. Then we tell everyone we're heading for home near Wilmington. Now, let's get our disguises on."

Shannon watched Blane rip his pants leg, then pour blood from a jar over the ragged area. He took his knife

139

and hacked free two boards from the hut to use as splints. He placed one on each side of his right leg. "Ready, love."

Shannon was staring at the blood, which either rolled down his leg and pants or stuck in clots along the way. Blane shook her. She looked at him and swallowed hard. The blood smelled, and the sight of it turned her stomach. She couldn't understand why, not after being a nurse recently under terrible conditions. "Where did you get blood?"

"From Cathy's hen house. But I made sure she didn't catch me. You all right?" Blane asked, noting her pale face and trembling form.

Shannon forced a tight smile. She wrapped the leg as Blane had requested, then watched him dribble more swiftly coagulating blood on it. She was baffled when he lay down and rolled in the dust. When he stood, he made tears in his garments, then dirtied his face and hands.

"Now to disguise a beautiful, flaming-haired temptress. We'll have a little more time to use your pass before news gets around about us. If Clifford made it out of that cellar, he might be reluctant to say how and why he got put there. It's my guess he wouldn't involve the army. I'd bet he'd wait for Travers, then put that scum on our trail. And if Travers didn't bring his own cohorts, Clifford would probably loan him those three who met us at the entrance to the camp. I wouldn't be surprised if Thornton joined them. And now we have Cathy craving our blood as well. We do have this way of making lots of enemies, don't we?"

Bewildered and alarmed, Shannon couldn't move as he made rips in her shirt and pants. He shoved her to the ground and rolled her in the dust. Using his hands, he made certain her pale face and neck were almost as dark as his tanned complexion. When he poured blood on her left arm above the elbow, she yanked free and shouted,

"What the blazes are you doing, Blane? Have you gone mad? I'm filthy."

He chuckled as he bandaged her arm, then dampened the white cloth with bright red liquid. "If we didn't fool 'em into searching in the wrong direction, Blue Eyes, they could be closing in on us right now. We can't be certain Clifford didn't report us. If they make it to Cathy's, she'll blow it for us. Thing is, they'll be seeking a handsome rogue and a beautiful enchantress. Who would recognize us now, love? Except for this flaming hair." He lifted his knife and seized her braid.

Shannon whirled on her seat, placed her feet on his abdomen, and kicked him with all her might. The action sent Blane toppling backward as she screamed at him. "Oh, no, you won't! Touch my hair and I'll cut off your hand, you crazy bastard!" Shannon had come to her knees. She was breathing rapidly as she glared at him with fiery blue eyes.

Blane rubbed his stomach and declared, "You pack a mean blow, Flame. I was only kidding. You can hide it under your hat. Just don't let it down to fly in the wind. It's as enchanting as you are."

Blane dirtied and bloodied another bandage, then tied it around his head.

Shannon stared at the man sitting on the ground, then at herself. "Look at me, Blane. I'm a mess again. How could you?" she wailed hoarsely as unshed tears stung her eyes.

Blane had to admit she looked pathetic. "It's to save our lives, Shannon. You can rest and bathe in Wilmington."

"Wilmington?" she echoed incredulously.

"We have to stay in these disguises until we reach the next safe house. Wilmington is where many of the blockade runners operate. That's where they sneak in supplies and weapons. That's where foreign money gets

141

in to prolong this stupid war. We have work there, so stop complaining. If you don't like my methods, choose your own." Eleanor's gold band on Shannon's finger reflected the brilliant sunlight and harshly reminded him of painful demands. "Why should I worry about you? I'm sure a Greenleaf can safely charm her way through the gates of hell."

Blane stood and hobbled over to his horse. Using brute strength, he lifted himself into his saddle. "I don't plan to get ensnared or delayed by your troubles with Clifford or Thornton or Travers. We've got a war to fight, Blue Eyes. You coming or not?" he asked coldly.

Shannon didn't know what to make of his quicksilver moods. She gathered the medical supplies and stored them. She wouldn't argue. Considering her recent luck, he was probably right again! She packed her things and mounted. "Anything else, sir?" she inquired sullenly.

"From here on, I'm Corry Greenleaf, your newly found brother. I was fighting with General Lee northeast of Petersburg when I was wounded. You were nursing in the hospital in Fredericksburg where I was taken. Since my injury won't heal any time soon, we decided to head home to check on our parents and plantation. You got that?"

"What if we meet someone who knows my family or Corry? Anyway, you're more like Temple." She wondered if Blane was getting peeved by her determination to locate Corry, for he had spoken her brother's name so coldly and sarcastically. She had been patient and cooperative. She was not solely responsible for their troubles!

"Keep your eyes and ears open. If you recognize someone, call me Steven; then we'll use our husband/wife routine. Understand?"

No, she did not. "How can we ask about Corry if you're pretending to be him?" she persisted in concern.

142

"Didn't you tell me he was at Andersonville Prison?"

"I said that a man told me he might be. He also hinted about an escape. Why are you being so hateful this morning?"

"Andersonville is several hundred miles from here, so forget about Corry for now. If he escaped, it's possible we'll locate him along the way. Nothing would suit me better. As for my behavior and mood, they were inspired by a childish brat who should have learned some lessons about precaution and danger by now. If you didn't sleep well last night, blame your lecherous Rebel friends of genteel birth."

"Go to hell, Stevens! I'm tired of you picking on me all the time! It's not my fault if you got stuck with me. If you have a just grievance against me, then get it out in the open so we can settle it. If not, then stop plaguing me, or complain to Lincoln, but leave me alone! From my viewpoint, you're the only childish brat around. You aren't the only one who'll be enormously delighted to end our disagreeable association! I have enough on my mind without being harassed by you at least five times a day. What makes you the authority and expert on every matter? It seems to me that I've proven my mettle and wits by now. If you have a different opinion, that's too bad! Forget it! You aren't worth the time and effort it takes to try to please you!"

Shannon gritted her teeth, then snapped her reins over her horse's flank. The animal raced off at a rapid gallop. She heard Blane shouting after her, but she ignored him. She knew why he was calling her; the sun was at her back. She didn't care. She had to get away from the temperamental rogue who was causing havoc with her emotions—emotions that had been in a state of turbulence for too long without the tranquil break her sanity demanded.

Shannon kneed the animal to run faster. Suddenly a

shot thundered nearby. Her horse cried out loudly, then stumbled. Another shot was fired and pain filled her head. The animal staggered and his forelegs buckled. One more shot ran in the silence. Her horse fell sideways to send her rolling from his back. She was gasping for breath as she touched her forehead, then brought red-tipped fingers before her eyes. This time, she knew it was her own blood. Two names streaked across her mind: Travers and Clifford. Her gun was missing. She tried to reach for the knife in her boot, but her head was spinning like a whirlwind. Her vision gradually blackened as she went limp on the dry grass.

Chapter Six

"Dadburn you, Pete! You dun shot tha hoss too!"

"Hellfire, Horace! Me gunsight is off agin. Let's see whut he's a'carryin'. Leastwise some vittles er weapons."

After hearing three gunshots, Blane halted his pursuit and listened intently, knowing that if he rashly charged into a blind situation, he might get both of them killed or captured. He told himself to be quick yet careful and silent. Fear and panic shot through him as forcefully and swiftly as currents of lightning.

As the two men headed for the fallen body to rob it, Blane dismounted and left Dan, his horse, a safe distance away. He gingerly crept toward the sounds of the gunshots and voices, his movements hampered by the false splint. He dared not rush blindly to Shannon's aid, but his nerves were taut with dread. When he peered through the bushes to see two shabbily clad ruffians approaching Shannon's motionless figure, his rage nearly cost him his rigid control. His disguise would be of no use to him now. He jerked his knife from its sheath and sliced through the carefully wrapped bandage; then, tossing aside the splints, he quickly surveyed the situation.

When Pete snatched off Shannon's hat and rolled her

over, he gasped in shock. "We dun shot a gal, Horace. Look, a purty'un."

Horace dropped to his knees by Shannon's waist. His gaze raced over her face and figure. "Hell, Pete! We's in big trouble. Is she dead?"

Pete placed his ear to her chest, then flashed his friend a smile that revealed the absence of several teeth. He shoved stringy, grimy hair from his face. "Nope. What'cha think we oughtta do with her?"

"Look at this hair, red as a sunset. Skin white as milk."

Horace and Pete laid aside their guns to examine their victim closely, and as they did, the Texan sprang from his hiding place. His pistol butt came down heavily on Pete's head. As Horace turned his body, Blane's foot kicked upward, sending a forceful blow to the man's chin. When Horace struck the ground, Blane lunged over him and began punching his face. Blane didn't halt until the man's head was bloody and his own knuckles throbbed. He looked at Pete, dissatisfied with his one blow. With his booted toe, he kicked the downed man twice.

Blane grabbed Pete's arm and flung him away from Shannon. He seized Horace's limp body and did the same. He picked up the two rifles and tossed them into the woods, sorry he had not broken them first. Moving to Shannon's side, he checked her condition. The bullet had grazed her temple, but the wound wasn't serious. He examined her from head to toe for other injuries and, finding none, he exhaled loudly in relief and joy. His temper had almost cost her her life. He would have to learn to control it during those moments when the past seized him.

Blane ripped the bandage from his head and cast it away. He found the clean fillet in her medical bag, then tended her gently. He was distressed. How could he explain his obligations? To her they wouldn't sound just, or even true. Why had he kept silent this long? Because

146

he had wanted to spend time with her! Because he wanted her! The moment she discovered the truth, she would leave him, with bitterness and hatred and mistrust in her heart. It was too late and too dangerous to reveal his intentions. And he wasn't even certain any longer just what those intentions were. He had to decide how the past and future would affect Shannon and Eleanor. Damnation, he had to kill Corbett Greenleaf; he had promised revenge for Corry's violation of Ellie. Lord, his indecisiveness was tormenting both of them.

With only one horse, they would have to ride double and pray they weren't sighted and chased. He walked his mount to where Shannon was lying. He wanted this woman, and by damn, he would try to keep her if there were any way possible! He went through her belongings to see what could be left behind to lessen the weight on his horse. He was grateful Shannon weighed so little. He stuffed her brush, slippers, and a set of undergarments into his saddlebags. Spreading out his sleeping roll, he placed one dress, a clean shirt, and a pair of pants on it; then he rolled the clothing inside to prevent stains and wrinkles.

Everything else would have to be discarded. He noticed that Shannon hadn't worn or brought along any jewelry. But he did feel two metal plates that she had attempted to conceal in a slit in the lining of her carpet bag. He wiggled his fingers until he captured the thin plates between them and was able to withdraw the pictures. The first one revealed the four-member Greenleaf family. Shannon appeared around sixteen in it. Lord, even then she had been an unforgettable vision!

He stared at the two younger men, who were attired in Federal uniforms, and decided Corbett was the one with the laughing eyes and disarming smile. Both were good looking and muscular, as was their father, Andrew. Since the plates were in black and white, there was no way

Blane could determine coloring. The expressions of all three exuded confidence and excitement; their bearings, wealth and breeding. Shannon's look was guarded, with a hint of worry and sadness. The date of the photograph was apparent; it had been taken at the beginning of the war, just before the younger Greenleafs had left home. Two of the men were dead now, and he was the appointed executioner of the last one.

Blane expected the next plate to be a photograph of Shannon's mother. Instead, it was a picture of Shannon and a handsome man with very dark hair and eyes. The photograph had been taken in a garden, in the summer from the looks of the scenery and her clothing. The rugged male was standing almost behind her, with the top of her flaming head teasing just above his strong chin. That would make him a shade over six feet. As she posed within an encircling embrace, their arms and hands were overlapped. Their skin tones contrasted visibly. The man's right cheek was nestled against her left temple. The couple on the metal plate looked so happy that day long ago, so perfect together. There was a glow in her eyes and a serenity in her expression that couldn't be ignored; this was true of the man's features as well. Their expressions and position riled Blane, for he knew this had to be the mysterious Hawke.

Hazel eyes drilled into the striking features of Shannon's companion, features that were strong and appealing, features that would be hard for most men to match or best. No wonder Thornton had lost out to this earthy male he had called a "rogue," whatever his lineage. He held himself like a man on constant alert. Blane could perceive strength of will and body from the image. This was a man who feared nothing and no one. This was a man with keen instincts and considerable prowess. This was a man who knew how to survive, who was no coward or weakling. This was an awesome rival for any suitor!

The love and rapport between this Hawke and Shannon was obvious. He eyed the beautiful woman, trying to guess her age and date the photograph. It could have been taken a few years past, or a few months past. He wished Hawke's hand hadn't been covering her left one. Yet Thornton hadn't sounded as if he had been referring to a husband. Where was Hawke? Why had he left her? Was he alive?

Blane cocked his arm to fling the rankling photographs into the woods, but he hesitated, then changed his mind. He might have use of these pictures, especially the one of Corry. He stood and went to his horse, concealing the thin plates in a special pocket beneath his saddle. To prevent her attackers from obtaining anything valuable, he sliced the bag and remaining items beyond use. He even cut through the stirrups and bridles to ruin the saddle.

Blane tied the sleeping roll to his saddle and replaced his saddlebags. When all was ready, he gathered Shannon in his arms. Seizing the horn and placing his foot in the stirrup, he mounted. He laid her across his thighs and held her securely with his right arm. "Let's go, Dan," he murmured to his well-trained animal.

Within an hour, Shannon was stirring. Blane continued their steady pace, his gaze defensively locked on the view ahead. It took a while for her to fully regain her senses. At first, she was confused.

"Blane? Why am I riding with you? What happened to my head?"

Without looking down at her, he stated crisply, "It's obstinacy and impulsiveness that got you attacked and nearly killed. That was a stupid move. You were lucky those varmits couldn't shoot straight."

Shannon tried to remember what had happened, but her mind was fuzzy. "How bad is the injury?" she inquired, aware of his irritation with her.

"You'll live. Too bad I can't say the same for your horse."

"My horse?" Shannon peered around his arm. "Where is he?"

"Dead," he answered tersely. To prevent a lengthy discussion, he went on to relate the details of the frightful event. His mood and tone silenced her.

Shannon rested her aching head against his brawny shoulder. She wished she hadn't behaved so childishly. From his point of view, she was probably nothing more than a nuisance. He was used to traveling and working alone. No doubt she cramped his style and movements. She was always needing help or a rescue. She recalled how little sleep or rest he had gotten lately, especially last night. Reluctantly and ruefully, she murmured, "I'm sorry about the horse and all the trouble. Sometimes you just antagonize me beyond thinking or acting clearly."

"The feeling is mutual," he retorted harshly. "If you don't learn to follow orders by Wilmington, I'm leaving you there. Understand?"

"What happened to your splint?" she inquired curiously.

"I had to cut it off to save your miserable hide. When I find a safe place, I'll let you make me a new one."

Shannon stiffened in his arms. "You don't have to be so hateful. I apologized. At least I have a real wound to display now!" she snapped.

"If we're chased, you'll wish you had a horse instead."

Shannon crossed her arms and sank into silence. She secretly wished he would make a mistake in judgment so she could rescue him. Then they would be even. No, it would require several on his part! she realized. Why did he have to be so smart and fearless—so right all the time?

Blane halted their journey in midafternoon to rest and water his horse. He had avoided farmhouses, small settlements, and people. The woods were thick along the riverbank, offering them coverage. He unsaddled Dan and rubbed him with a dripping cloth for a short time. As Dan drank, grazed, and moved around, Blane joined Shannon.

"Here," he offered, holding out jerky and a cold biscuit.

Shannon looked at the brown roll of dried beef. "No thanks."

"How can you maintain strength if you don't eat?"

"Give me something decent and I will," she replied tensely. "That stuff stinks and it makes my teeth sore. Hand me the biscuit."

Blane watched her nibble daintily on the bread and stare across the water. If she would be honest with him, he wouldn't be so tough on her. Why was Hawke such a big secret? What if he were more of a barrier between them than Corry? "Shannon, where do you get your size and coloring? They're unusual. I'm curious."

She turned her head and looked at him quizzically. From a bloody quarrel to a serene chat? "My mother was Irish. She had red hair, blue eyes, and fair skin. I take after her and her family, the O'Shannons of Kerry County, Ireland. They supplied my name and looks."

"Your mother must have been very beautiful," he remarked.

Shannon glanced his way again. "She was," she admitted without sounding vain. "It was her family tradition to select names to flaunt the family's roots and ties. She was named Kerry, and I got the Shannon. It's also a major river there. She died when I was nine. That's how I became such a tomboy, being raised by two brothers. My father traveled a lot with his business. I did tell you he was a cotton factor as well as a grower?" she asked, then watched him nod and smile.

"For a few years I spent most of my time tagging after

151

Temple and Corry. Sometimes I wonder how those days passed so quickly. But Temple and Corry discovered girls, so I was left to study all those girlish things. Then . . ." Shannon placed her fingers to her forehead and lowered her head. She massaged the spot as if her head pained her.

Shannon remembered how most people had viewed and treated Hawke because of his half-blooded Indian birth. Of course it had been worse in his lands than in the South. Despite his bloodline to chiefs, he had been forced to earn his honor and position among his people. When he moved to Georgia, Hawke's relationship with the family had been kept a secret. It seemed easier to explain the startling and somewhat suspicious adoption of a "half-savage woodscolt" than to expose Hawke as Andrew Greenleaf's bastard son. She didn't want to justify Hawke or her father's rash actions to this mercurial stranger who had revealed a fierce hatred and contempt for Comanches. Too, such an explanation would uncover so many painful, complex, and intensely personal experiences and emotions, and might inspire many questions and doubts. Her father's wanton behavior and his cruel rejection of Hawke could give Blane a terrible opinion of her and her family. After that incident with Clifford, she felt Blane might think her guilty of some wrong—like father like daughter. "What about your home and family?" she asked.

"Like I said, I'm from Texas, from a large family. There were seven of us kids, five boys and two girls. My family had a ranch near Fort Worth until October of '60, called the Rocking *S*. We raised cattle and horses, and sometimes a lot of mischief. My parents and two of my brothers, Kirby and Daniel, were slain during a Comanche raid in '51. I was eighteen, trapped in the middle of the pack, and burning for adventure and revenge. Besides, a ranch doesn't need three brothers all trying to be boss. I suppose I always was a restless youth who didn't care for raising cattle or busting my rear breaking mustangs. I didn't want to give orders or follow 'em. Becoming an Indian scout got me off the ranch and taught me plenty about life and people. You could say it made a man of me, or tried its damnedest," he jested, then sent her a winning smile. "I've probably killed more Comanches than you've got red hairs. I made those devils sorry they attacked the Stevens's ranch. This was a gift from them," he remarked dryly, pointing to the scar on his jawline.

"Clayton and Jory worked the ranch while I tried to clear Texas of renegades. Then the Cavalry got involved and convinced me to roam half the West, taking on any devil with red skin. That kind of existence gets stale, Shannon. When the talk got hot about war, I figured I'd try my hand at battling a different kind of enemy. I joined the Union forces the day war was declared. Jory stayed behind with his wife, Martha, and Clayton's got Sue Anne. They're taking care of a pack of kids and the new ranch near Houston. My older sister, Lucille, is married to a cavalryman named Edward Connor; they're living at a fort in the Dakota Territory with two sons."

Shannon was glad he was finally relating facts about himself. Thank goodness she had not mentioned Hawke or Comanches! Blane had not revealed a woman in his life, present or past. Whose ring was she wearing? Why had it been in his pocket? She dared not be nosy. Too many questions, especially about the ring, might silence him. *Let him open up at his own speed. Be polite and charming. Don't panic him*, she told herself. "What about Major Blane Stevens, now that he's a man?"

He joined her laughter, then answered jokingly, "As for Major Blane Stevens, he plans to return home as soon as Lincoln finishes with him. Funny how a war changes a person. Ranching doesn't look so bad to him anymore.

How's the head?" he probed.

She noted how he had changed the subject. Her fingertips gingerly felt the sensitive area. "Fine. Probably just a flesh wound."

"We're both lucky," he replied, his voice chilly. "Let's ride."

As she swatted a fly on her bloody sleeve, she crinkled her nose and asked, "Can I wash up and change shirts?"

"No. You're safer dressed like that. But drop your braid into sight. I don't want any more varmints mistaking you for a man. I'll get two branches and you can wrap my leg again." In his turbulent state of mind, he had forgotten about his disguise.

Shannon glanced toward his saddle on the ground. Her eyes widened. "Where are my things?" she shrieked in alarm.

"I had to leave most of them behind. Two people and a few supplies are more than enough for Dan to carry."

"You threw away my clothes and . . ." Shannon went pale and quiet. Anguish filled her eyes as they darted about in thought.

Blane knew she was more upset about the loss of the photographs than her garments. He told her what he had spared, except for the pictures. "I figured you might need a dress and slippers along the way."

Shannon stood and paced. "We have to go back, Blane. I had something valuable hidden in my bag."

"Money? Jewels?" he inquired with feigned innocence.

"No," she finally responded. "Family pictures."

"I'm sorry, Shannon, but we can't turn back. It's too dangerous."

"Please," she beseeched him, her eyes teary and her voice strained.

Blane was relieved she hadn't lied to him. He sensed her pain, but he couldn't lessen it. He needed the photograph of Corry more than she did. And he couldn't return the one without the other. Later he would, but for now he told her, "No."

"Damn you! You had no right to throw away my belongings! I'm going back," she stated defiantly.

"We've been riding for hours, Shannon. You wouldn't know where to look, and I'm not going to tell you. A picture isn't worth risking our lives. I said I was sorry." Blane quelled his guilt. "Listen to me, Flame. By now, we could have Rebels on our heels. What if soldiers found those two men? How would they know who attacked whom? I won't let you charge into danger. You're injured, woman. We can't make good time sharing a horse, so stop acting like a baby. You've only yourself to blame for riding off like that."

Shannon whirled away from him. "Damn you for always being right! I'll admit the incident was my fault. Everything that happens seems to be my fault, or you think it is. I suppose I should be grateful you didn't discard all of my things." She lowered her head and inhaled raggedly. "Those photographs were so precious to me, Blane. They were my only link to family and home—sometimes my only link to sanity. As long as I had the photographs, I didn't have to face the truth. If I could look at their faces, I could believe they were alive and real. It gave me hope. I hate this war, and sometimes I hate you. I want to go home. I want my family. I want . . ."

Blane had been walking toward her, touched by her anguish. He had been about to pull her into his arms and comfort her. Shannon's half-finished statement halted him, for he assumed it was Hawke she wanted. Blane was mistaken. Shannon had almost said, "I want you."

Blane seized her shoulders and roughly pulled her around to face him. He shook her, commanding, "Get hold of yourself, Flame."

155

Shannon burst into tears. She dropped her face to his chest and clung to his waist. Blane didn't know what to do or say. He couldn't push her away. His arms closed around her shoulders. He decided he was being too rough on her. Maybe she had a good reason for lying to him. She couldn't help who or what she was. Under these circumstances, her mistakes were understandable. Yes, he was blaming her unjustly and treating her unfairly. Actually, she was doing extremely well. She had shown courage, daring, cunning, and stamina.

What did it matter if she were reaching out to him to soothe or to replace another loss? And what if she were using him for her own purposes? Wasn't he doing the same with her, using her as a cover, using her to obtain information, using her to get to Corry? Why did it trouble him that she loved or had loved another man? Maybe Hawke was dead. Maybe Corry was dead. Maybe her home was lost. Maybe she had no one and nothing left. In view of recent happenings, he couldn't fault her for being afraid, for crying. After all, she was a woman.

"Don't cry, Shannon. I know I'm being a selfish, hard-nosed brute. I'm just trying to keep us alive and safe. I'm used to traveling and working alone. I don't take delays or defeats well. You scared me this morning. When I saw you lying in that grass, bloody and out cold, I went wild. I nearly beat those Rebs to death. I get impatient and angry when people do reckless things. No matter what you think, I don't want you harmed, and I don't blame you for our misfortunes. You've been a good partner, and I hate seeing you this miserable. I'm sorry about your things, but we have to keep moving ahead."

Shannon lifted her head and looked into his eyes. They were soft and yellowy green. His expression was serious, compassionate. A breeze was ruffling his tawny hair and teasing wisps of it against his forehead. His face was dirty.

156

Her heart increased its pace and her skin tingled. She swallowed and snuffled. "I know taking off like that was a stupid thing. I deserved getting shot. I don't mean to be so impetuous and pigheaded. Get the things and I'll bandage your leg."

Blane smiled at her as he wiped away her tears. "You can also be very brave and smart, Shannon Greenleaf." He kissed the tip of her nose. Then, after fetching the necessary items, he sat down.

Shannon pushed up his torn pants leg and placed a splint on either side. "Hold this," she instructed, then began to wind the cloth around his leg. She noticed how brown and muscular his calf was and felt slightly wicked touching him. He handed her several bloody strips, which he had saved from this morning. She tied those around the clean cloth. Then she removed her arm bandage and placed it on his left arm. She eyed him and smiled. "Two head wounds might look suspicious. And with an injured leg and arm, you couldn't be expected to fight."

Shannon packed up while Blane saddled Dan. He lifted himself into place, then extended his hand to her. Shannon grasped it, but to her surprise, Blane sat her before him and proceeded to kiss her passionately and urgently. Then, without a word, he lifted her again and swung her around behind him. Drawing her arms about his waist, he kneed Dan into a steady gallop.

Shannon pondered his strange action. What an unpredictable man! She could feel his muscles working beneath his shirt. It felt wonderful to be riding so close to Blane, she reflected as she rested her face against him.

They encountered two groups of soldiers, both heading north. Neither questioned, nor appeared to doubt, their story or wounds. They learned that Davis and Lee had requested that all available men head their way to help defeat the ever-advancing Yankees. The dejection and disillusionment could be read in the soldiers' faces and their postures. It seemed that everyone was ready for this war to end, but no one knew how to accomplish that feat with pride and without enormous losses.

Blane wearily told the first group, "It's bad east and south of Richmond. It's looking bad for us everywhere. Hood's being run ragged in Tennessee. If we don't get more supplies and money from somewhere, them Yanks are gonna lick us. President Davis told me to get my sister away from Fredericksburg. He's expecting another attack there. How's it look down home way near Charleston?"

The gray-clad officer replied, "As far as I know, son, we're still holding both Carolina coasts. I been hearing rumors them Yanks are gonna strike out at South Carolina and Georgia; they're Confederate strongholds. You and your sister be mighty careful riding that way."

Just before they met the next group of Rebels, Shannon asked, "Why did you say Charleston? You changed our story. I could have made a mistake."

"We've lost time, Flame. If anybody's trailing us, I hope they take my bait and head away from Wilmington. You did just fine."

During their second encounter with Rebel troops, the colonel in charge asked Blane sternly, "Why ain't you with your unit, Greenleaf?"

"A man can't fight with a cracked leg and sliced arm, sir. I have orders from President Davis to take Shannon home. She's been nursing our men for two years, and she's been wounded twice. The President said I could mend while getting her away from the battleground." Blane showed the vexed officer Shannon's letter. He claimed his orders had been stolen along with most of their possessions when they were attacked by Rebel deserters. "They shot her horse right from under her."

The balding colonel studied the pale, dirty woman. He

reached over and yanked the bandage from her head, startling her and Blane. The man stared at the wound as if surprised it was there.

Blane snatched the bloody cloth from the colonel's hand. "Sir, if I were not injured and this were not war, I would be forced to challenge you in defense of my family honor. Rest assured, our President will learn of this outrageous offense. Touch my sister again, and I shall forget you are a high-ranking officer of the Confederacy."

Blane shifted her from behind him to before him. He tenderly replaced the bandage and inquired about her condition. Shannon told him she was fine. She focused fiery blue eyes on the colonel. "You are a dishonor to your rank and country, sir, a dishonor to your name and family. I can promise you this matter will be reported the moment we reach Charleston. I shall request that President Davis strip you of your rank. If the distance between us did not prevent it, I would slap your miserable face. Were my father alive, you would pay dearly for this insult. My family has fought valiantly and unselfishly during this war. How dare you question a Greenleaf's word or honor!"

Shannon called out to his men, "Hear me, proud Confederate soldiers. Beware of a leader of such low stature, a man who attacks injured women, who doubts the word of our noble President. Beware of a leader who wastes time assailing wounded Southerners when our side is swiftly losing this wretched conflict. A man without honor is a dangerous man. You, sir, make me feel ill. Let's go home, Corry, and waste no more time and strength on this beast."

The flustered colonel watched the two ride away, berating himself for his foolish behavior. Shannon's wound had convinced him of their honesty. He glanced at the soldiers nearby, who were looking at him with

159

contempt and disrespect in their eyes. He shouted at them, "I suspected them to be Yankee spies. You men forget this silly affair."

Miles down the road, Shannon exhaled loudly. "That was close. Maybe my recklessness this morning saved our lives."

Blane chuckled, then concurred, "Perhaps destiny compelled you to take off like that. You were great back there, sister."

Shannon leaned away from his chest and smiled at him. "I'm glad I can finally do something right, brother. Have I earned a pardon?"

"You've also earned this." Blane bent forward and kissed her.

When their lips parted, Shannon laughed. "What if we had met another band of Rebels? How would you have explained such behavior?"

He nuzzled her cheek and sighed dreamily. Tapping her ring finger, he said, "I quickly would have used our husband/wife story."

"Always a crafty answer for everything," she teased. "Your intelligence and alertness astound me. I couldn't have a better partner."

Blane smiled. "I'm glad you appreciate me, Mrs. James."

"I appreciate you, and you appreciate me, and we both appreciate the Union. Does that make us even for awhile?" She laughed, suddenly feeling cheerful and serene.

Blane observed her sunny mood. "I suppose it does."

Shannon didn't ask to ride behind him. And when she nestled against his chest, he didn't suggest it. Instead, he dropped a kiss atop her head, briefly tightening his embrace. Lord, she fit nicely in his arms, he reflected, admiring the way the sun on her head brought her hair to fiery life. He was inordinately pleased that she seemed so totally relaxed.

Just before dusk, Blane left the road and entered the trees to their right. He guided Dan along until he found a spot that appealed to him. "I want you to hide in those bushes over there. I need to scout around to make sure we won't be camping near any Rebels."

As Shannon slid to the ground, she coaxed, "Be careful."

Once she was hidden, he rode into the trees. In less than an hour he returned, smiling and reporting that the area around them was clear.

Blane handed her two apples, then grinned at her surprise. "I found a tree on an old farm. Everything else had been burned or stolen. You might like this better," he hinted, offering her salted ham that had been fried and stuffed inside a cold biscuit.

Shannon laughed. "You were hiding this," she softly accused.

"Yep. I thought it would be better for supper. I considered hunting for a rabbit or deer, but the smell of roasting would carry too far. This'll have to do for now, Flame. When we reach Fayetteville, I'll get you a proper meal if I have to steal it."

Shannon laughed again. "Your honesty astounds me, sir. You had best take this, brother," she suggested, handing him the ring.

They consumed the meager meal slowly. Then Blane spread the blanket and told her to get some sleep. Shannon stretched out and flexed her body as she gazed at the stars and the clear sky overhead. She felt calm and safe with Blane, and strangely closer to him. Her eyelids began to droop, and soon she was asleep.

Blane joined her, feeling it was safe to do so. His actions were almost an imitation of hers. After watching her for a time, he turned his back, knowing it was the only way he would ever get to sleep.

When morning came, they breakfasted on more apples and biscuits washed down with water. Shannon didn't complain, and soon they were on their way again. They rode for hours, passing stragglers every so often. So many people had lost so much that they didn't know where to go; they just seemed to have a need to move on in search of peace and safety.

In what seemed a stroke of good luck, they met a generous Rebel colonel who provided Blane and Shannon with a hot meal. The officer was eager for information from any area of fighting. He found Shannon's beauty and conversation pleasurable, and delayed his journey to enjoy them.

When Shannon and Blane were asked to spend the night in his camp, Blane accepted for Shannon's benefit. He knew she could use some rest and good food. To repay the officer's kindness, Shannon talked and visited in his tent until she could hardly keep her eyes open.

Blane finally put his arm around her and said, "It's time for you to turn in, Shanny. Thank you for your hospitality, sir. My sister and I deeply appreciate it. This trip home has been hard on her. And I ain't much use all busted up like this."

In the tent to which they were assigned, Shannon slept on her bedroll and Blane slept on his. The end flap had to be left open for fresh air, for the early October nights were still warm.

Afraid of being overheard, they talked little, though at one point Shannon whispered across the short distance between them, "Are you ever scared? I mean, really scared? Scared you won't survive this war, at least uninjured? Scared you might lose everyone and everything you love?"

"Give me your hand, Shannon," he ordered softly, reaching out for it. When she extended her arm toward him, he gently grasped her hand and squeezed it. He rested their clasped hands on the ground, then coaxed, "You have me to protect you. You won't ever be alone; and you can have me as long as you need me. But don't stop being afraid, Shannon; it makes a person more careful and alert. There's nothing wrong with being afraid, just with being a coward—with being too scared or too hurt to pick up the pieces and start over again. Don't ever let that happen to you. Go to sleep. I'll be right here guarding you."

Shannon was troubled and bewildered by his words. She had perceived the anguish that surrounded his statements, and his pain touched her deeply. She wanted to roll into his arms and comfort him. Yet, she instinctively knew not to press him tonight. She briefly tightened her fingers over his hand. As if deciding his hand might be heavy, he shifted his grasp to place his on the bottom against the dirt. His thumb rhythmically stroked the back of her hand. It was amazing how wonderful and stirring that simple contact felt. Shannon confessed quietly, "Sometimes I'm afraid of you, but I'm never afraid with you."

Blane lifted his head and looked over at her, noting that her respiration pattern had altered. She didn't turn his way, but continued to stare above her as he whispered, "Then we're almost even. Sometimes I'm afraid for you . . . and of you. Go to sleep. It's dangerous to talk here."

When noises awakened her, she sat up to find Blane missing. As she moved to stand beside the tent and look around for him, she spoke politely and genially with soldiers passing by. The commanding officer walked over, smiled, and offered her a morning meal.

"Where is my brother, sir?" she asked, trying not to show fear.

"He went hunting with several of my men. Insisted on paying for your food and care somehow. Said he didn't

163

need a healthy leg to shoot. You got yourself a good brother, Miss Greenleaf. Makes me proud and happy to see a fellow take such good care of his family."

When Shannon told him about the offensive incident on the road yesterday, the man puffed up with anger. She continued, "If you have a doctor or medical officer, I would like him to look at the wound. I'm sure it isn't anything serious, but one never knows about infection."

When their meal was over, the Confederate colonel sent for a private who knew a great deal about doctoring. The young man was only too pleased to check her injury. His smile faded when he heard how she had received it, as did the commanding officer's.

"Keep it clean and covered, miss. Try to change the bandage every five or six days. It should heal nicely, but you might have a tiny scar there. You think I should look at your brother's leg?"

"He was checked recently. The doctor told him to leave it be for another three or four weeks." When the private left, she turned to the officer in charge and said, "Thank you for your help and concern, Colonel Smith." She sent him one of her most radiant and innocent smiles.

Blane and the others returned from a successful hunt to find Shannon laughing and chatting privately with Smith. They had acquired enough meat to provide strength and to fill bellies. Blane accepted a bundle of food for their next meal, along with the name of a family who would give them shelter during their stop in Fayetteville. The officer also gave Shannon a blanket to ward off the chilly nights, which he said were approaching fast. For the first time she felt guilty, for she knew many soldiers were in need of such items.

They were also given a letter of protection from Colonel William Smith, which they soon had to use when they met a doubting Southern officer. The man read both letters, eyed the young couple, then allowed them to pass. Blane could feel the man's sharp eyes piercing their backs. He scolded himself for not questioning or suspecting a curious mark that he had noticed at the top of the page. Was it a code? he wondered. Prepared to be chased, he didn't relax for ten miles.

In Fayetteville, Blane didn't go to the house suggested by Smith. Instead, he made his way east of the town to a small plantation, then dismounted near a gradually collapsing shed. As he cut off the false splint to facilitate his movement, Blane told Shannon, "Stay here with Dan and wait for my return. I need to look around before we approach the house. If you hear any gunshots or shouts, you mount up and ride like hell out of here. Understand?"

Yes, she understood clearly. It seemed to her she was always telling him to be careful, but she did so again. She feared that one day soon he would be cautious, but that it wouldn't matter. At present, they were in the heart of the Confederacy, and she didn't feel at home. She despised what was happening to her beloved country and people. As usual, she watched and waited in dread. She tried not to think about other dangers, such as nocturnal wild animals or snakes. Darkness surrounded her, for only a thin slice of moon hung in the sky.

Blane eventually made his way around the area that enclosed the house and barns. Sighting or hearing no indication of another's presence, he walked to the house, knocked, and was invited inside.

He came back for her over an hour later. Blane was amused and warmed when Shannon hugged him fiercely. "By the way," he told her, "at this stop you're my new wife. Just play along with whatever I say." He caught her left hand and pushed the gold wedding band in place.

Shannon followed Blane and Dan to the back porch, where an older man and woman were standing with a candle. The amber-haired Texan passed Dan's reins to the man and smiled at the woman. He captured Shannon's hand in his and drew her close. She pondered his mellow gaze and gentle behavior and questioned his impending deceit. Every time he slipped that ring on her finger, she wondered if some jealous ghost were going to strike her dead. How long would it be before he liked and trusted her enough to explain it? If she were lucky, maybe he hadn't used it yet. And if she could manage it, she wanted it to belong to her one day! She carefully observed all three people in the flickering candlelight.

Blane's smooth voice asserted calmly, "Mrs. Thomas, Joseph, this is my wife, Shannon. I just captured her. Believe me, it was long and hard work winning this beauty away from countless admirers. Things are so bad all over. Too many soldiers and dangers. I couldn't leave the new Mrs. Blane Stevens behind. I guess you can see why," he remarked proudly, clasping Shannon to his chest and kissing her forehead to conceal her look of astonishment at the name he had used.

"Shannon, this is Mary and Joseph Thomas, my good friends. They make sure the Rebs don't find me when I'm working this area. They'll feed us and hide us for the night. You have them to thank for keeping me alive plenty of times," Blane informed her.

Shannon smiled and greeted the two people cordially. "I hope you don't mind our sudden arrival, Mr. and Mrs. Thomas. I know this work is dangerous for you."

"Joseph, you get Blane's horse tended while I take these tired folks inside and feed 'em proper," the woman said, taking command. "You look like you both could use a warm bath, hot food, and lots of sleep," the woman who appeared to be in her fifties surmised.

"They all sound marvelous," Shannon replied. "Thank you."

"We best get crackin'. Those Rebels have a way of

showing up unexpectedly. I can't tell you how many times they've searched the house and barns. Knowing you, Blane, you've already scouted the area."

He grinned and nodded. "It's clear for now."

"What if they come around during the night?" Shannon asked. "How will you explain us? What if they try to confiscate Dan and enlist Blane?"

The woman laughed merrily. "Not to fear, child. No evil can harm you under our roof. God protects us and our cause."

Shannon watched the woman closely. She was short and plump and seemed filled with energy and excitement. Her dark, wrinkled skin indicated that she spent hours outdoors. Her light blue eyes sparkled with vitality and expectancy. She drew Shannon closer to say, "We have this secret room beneath the house. Joseph built it all by himself from our root cellar. You two will be safe there. Come along before any gray pants see us."

Blane unsaddled Dan and Joseph led the loyal beast away. Hoisting the saddle over his left shoulder, Blane followed Mary inside and dropped it near a cupboard in the kitchen.

"Don't you have any workers, Mrs. Thomas? Who helps you and your husband manage and protect your property?" she inquired.

"None left, child. They all went off to fight the war. We didn't have slaves, just hired laborers. We don't believe in buying human flesh and forcing their labor. It don't matter. Joseph says our good earth can use the rest. We have a small garden to keep us busy and to prevent suspicion about our food supply."

Shannon lowered her thick lashes, feeling guilty again. This time, she worried over taking food from these old people and placing them in peril. "I wish there were some way we could pay you."

"Don't be silly, child. We knew this war would be long

and hard. We stored up canned foods and cured meats. All over the house there are hidden spaces filled with tin cans and jars. We have fruits, vegetables, stews, soups, salmon, boiled beef, sardines, and even oysters. There's cured hams and bacon slabs. We have tea and spices and flour hidden. Me and Joseph have plenty to share with our friends. Them Union officers aren't the only ones who can afford canned foods. My Joseph used to ship them back and forth between here and Europe—mainly England and France. I'll give you and Blane a few to carry along. Can't risk getting caught with too many on you."

The woman showed Blane to a bathing closet on the side porch. "You fill this tub for your little woman while I show her around."

Mary walked to a staircase to the second floor. She reached under the bottom step and wiggled her fingers. The three lower steps rose as a unit, displaying another set of stairs going down into a dark space. Mary took a lantern and told the younger woman to follow her. At the bottom, Mary turned and smiled to Shannon. "See?"

Shannon's gaze roamed the shelves of glass jars and tin cans. It flickered over sacks of flour, corn meal, and sugar. Tins of coffee, tea, and spices were also on display. Above her hung cured hams, salted flanks of venison, and slabs of bacon. Shannon was stunned by the abundance and variety of food, especially when so many people within a few miles of them were literally starving. To be fair, Shannon rationalized that the supplies were being used for a vital cause.

"Me and Joseph prepared well for this war. God told us it was coming. During those first two years, we sneaked more supplies into Wilmington, then here. But the Rebs started watching and searching every ship and wagon. You have to watch them devils; they're greedy and sly and wicked. That's why we can't pass out food to poorfolk. Them devils would hear about it and they'd

168

come here and take everything."

Mary pointed to the corner. "We got weapons only for hunting and protection. 'Least those guns won't kill none of God's children."

The woman had spoken accurately. Their collection appeared to be a small arsenal. Nearby, Shannon also noticed extra blankets, several canteens, leather pouches, and assorted pieces of clothing.

Seeing Shannon's interest, Mary beamed proudly as she informed her, "Whenever I can get clothes or supplies for my friends, I keep 'em here until someone needs them. Those Rebs steal everything loose when they search the house. Satan has them blinded; they follow him like dumb sheep. One week, they came nearly every morning, trying to catch us off guard. Well, we'd best get you fed, bathed, and tucked in. No telling when them fools will show up again."

When they returned to the kitchen, Joseph had their meal ready. He had set out slices of ham, peas, carrots, corn muffins, peaches, and tea. While water heated, Shannon and Blane feasted on the delicious meal. Weary and hungry and aware of possible danger, they ate quickly and quietly.

"I know this will be difficult, Shannon, but hurry with your bath," Blane instructed.

As Shannon scrubbed in the bathing closet, Mary cleared away their dishes and food remains. She placed the empty tin cans in the hidden pantry beneath the stairs, then prepared the room where Blane and Shannon would hide and sleep tonight.

As Blane scrubbed in the darkness near the well, the sixty-year-old Joseph strolled around the yards to make certain no one was approaching. He felt tense tonight. He wanted this couple to rush and conceal themselves. An agent like Major Blane Stevens was a great risk to aid, and he feared becoming a Union martyr. Sometimes he wondered if he and Mary were doing the right thing. His wife was a stubborn, determined woman. Maybe he feared her disapproval more than God's or the Confederacy's! He scratched his head of thinning hair as his brown eyes darted from one shadowy area to another. He was beginning to doubt that either side was totally right or wrong. His large nose itched, then his bushy brows. He kenw it was from anxiety. He sighed with relief when Blane whistled completion of his chore.

"Need any help, child?" the woman inquired as she entered.

Shannon had dried off but was standing with the bath sheet wrapped around her. "Could you ask Blane to send me a clean shirt and pants," she asked modestly, mutely chiding her oversight.

Mary smiled warmly. "You don't need to stay dressed and ready to leave. No one can find you in our secret room."

"Blane and I were attacked and robbed on the road. Besides one dress and a pair of slippers, pants and a shirt were all we could save."

"You wait right here, child." The woman left hurriedly to return soon with a cotton nightgown. "This will be a mite roomy, but cooler and more comfy. Please use it, child."

Shannon knew she couldn't refuse the woman's kindness without inspiring doubt, and she wished Blane hadn't lied about their being married. Shannon accepted the gown and thanked her. She slipped into it.

Mary gathered her dirty clothes. "I'll wash these and Blane's. By morning they should be dry. There, now, don't you feel better?"

"Much better. You're very kind and generous. Thank you."

Mary looked into the kitchen to make sure the men weren't there. She led Shannon to the cupboard, which had been shoved away to expose another staircase. Mary laughed and commented, "They always search attics and closets or look under rugs and furniture for secret doors. You'll be perfectly safe down there, child."

Shannon looked down the steps in surprise, for she had expected to be sheltered in the hidden pantry. A lantern was hanging from a long peg at the base. She could make out a door, which led beneath the house. The woman bid her good night and told her to go along and get settled. Shannon moved slowly down the stairs and entered the room. Her eyes widened in disbelief. She found herself in a small bedroom without windows.

Shannon moved into the room and looked around her. The walls were planked and painted. A double bed that looked enormously soft and inviting was situated in one corner. She saw a table nearby that held a pitcher of water and a basin. Beneath it on a shelf, there were cloths and several cups. Above it was a small, round mirror with candle holders attached to the wall on either side of the shiny surface. She noticed one chair beside a smaller table that held an oil lantern with flowers painted on it. A Bible had been placed beside the lantern. The right wall near the door revealed pegs for hanging garments, if the guest was fortunate enough to have any. The left wall beside the door exposed a curtained-off-area. When she peeked inside, she blushed, for the small area contained only a chamber pot, white trimmed in red.

Shannon smiled and relaxed. While descending those steps, she had feared she would find herself in a dim room with walls of moist dirt and corners that enticed those crawly things she hated. Though she did notice the floors were hard-packed earth, there was a small rug by the bed, a wash stand, and a chair. Crocheted and embroidered pieces decorated the tables and a floral coverlet brightened the bed with the same fabric that had been used for the curtain to the private area.

She heard Blane's boots on the stairs. Carrying his saddle, he entered the secluded room, then lowered his leather burden to the ground right of the door. "Isn't this wonderful?" she asked.

Blane grinned. "They're something, aren't they? Now do you see why I told them we're married?" He turned and put out the lantern behind him, then closed and locked the door.

Shannon's gaze slipped over his damp hair and clean garments. He had even shaved! "No, I don't," she replied. "They sounded and behaved like good friends, people you could trust. Why mislead them?"

"They are good people, God-fearing folk who wouldn't hold to our sharing this room—not with you age and looks," he added roguishly. "They think the Lord's going to reach out soon and strike down these Rebels. They consider what they do their God-ordered duty. I'm selfish, woman. I didn't want to sleep with Dan, or risk being caught here. If they found me, the Thomases and Shannon Greenleaf would be in danger. Besides, it's exhausting to stay alert twenty-four hours a day for days on end. I need to have complete rest for a change."

"I understand, Blane. I'm glad you're staying here with me. I wouldn't sleep a wink if I had to worry about you and our safety."

Blane captured the material of her gown between his fingers and asked, "What's this? You been losing weight?" He chuckled.

"Seems you discarded my only nightgown, Mister Stevens. When Mary insisted on loaning Mrs. Stevens one of hers, I couldn't think of a logical reason to refuse. It is 'a mite roomy, but cooler and more comfy,'" she stated, quoting Mary, then clasped her hand over her giggling mouth. "May I have my brush before this hair tangles beyond fixing?"

172

Blane chuckled as he went to his saddlebag and retrieved it for her. "Do I need to use my sleeping roll, Miss Greenleaf, or can I trust you to keep on your side of the bed and behave yourself?"

"As I recall, we've spent many nights together, and I haven't ravished you yet. I suppose I can control myself another night or two. If I can't, you've only yourself to blame for being too irresistible." Shannon pulled aside the covers and sat on the bed. "You don't see any spiders, do you?" she asked worriedly as she worked her tangles free.

Blane could tell she was serious, so he didn't laugh or joke. "Mary keeps it too clean down here. No spider would dare build its web in this room. But I sleep with one eye and ear open, remember?"

"You don't plan to do so tonight," she reminded him. "Will you leaven the lantern on?" she entreated softly. "It would be so dark and scary in here without some light."

"Can't, Flame. I don't have a nightshirt, and these clothes will be too hot and confining to sleep in. Sorry, love."

Shannon halted her movements to stare at him. "You can't sleep without any clothes," she informed him nervously.

"The light will be out and I'll stay on my side with my back to you. I promise not to ravish you, Flame, no matter how tempting you are. Haven't I been good so far? Just think of me as brother Blane." His twinkling hazel eyes drifted over her pink cheeks.

"What about Dan? Will he be safe in the barn?"

"They have an old shed with vines growing over the cracks. Joseph hid Dan there with plenty of hay and water. It looks so awful, the Rebs don't even search it anymore. They don't know about the one clean stall at the rear. Even if they found Dan, they couldn't find us down here. Calm yourself, Flame. I warned you in Washington and along the trail that the spy business isn't an exciting game."

"I'm beginning to discover that fact." She braided her hair and placed the brush on the wash stand, then she slipped into bed.

Blane put out the two candles beside the mirror and started to lower the lantern. "Are you sure all the lights have to be put out?" she asked again, eyeing their shadowy surroundings.

Blane hesitated as he glanced over at her pale face. He lowered the light as much as possible, then placed the lantern on the floor. Only a dim glow flickered in the room. "How's that?"

"Thanks, Blane," she murmured in gratitude.

"Turn over and settle yourself," he advised. When she followed his order, he stripped and joined her.

Shannon felt the bed sway beneath his weight. She stiffened her body to keep from rolling against his and watched the eerie movements of light as they danced on the wall before her. Without it, she mused silently, this room would feel like a pit. Shannon realized she was shaking.

Blane listened to her erratic breathing for a time; it revealed her tension and fear. "If this arrangement makes you too uncomfortable, Shannon, I can sleep on the floor," he offered, propping himself up on his side toward her.

"I guess I'm overly tired and scared tonight. I feel like we're trapped in here. What if the Rebels came and found us? There's no way we could escape. What if they burned the house over us?"

"Both doors to this room bolt from the inside, Shannon. If anyone tried to move aside the cupboard, it wouldn't budge. The Thomases claim it's nailed to the wall to keep it from falling over and breaking their dishes.

174

We're sealed in safely, love. Don't be afraid."

"I'm sorry, Blane. I'm not accustomed to living in fear, or to being attacked by men like Major Clifford or those two ruffians on the road, or running and hiding in chimneys and holes in the ground, or staying filthy for days. I've never been hungry before. I've never seen such misery, so much destruction and hatred and killing, so much lying and deceiving. I never imagined this journey would be so terrifying or difficult. I'm embarrassed to be such a weakling and a coward." She shuddered. "I just want to go home. I want my father and brothers. I want to feel safe and happy again. Will this war ever end?"

Blane rolled to his stomach, then pulled Shannon to her back. He gazed into her face and caressed her cheek. "I know it's been hard on you, Flame. If I could change things, I would. All I can promise is to protect you with my life."

"Would you hold me? I feel so safe in your arms."

Blane knew the danger of their contact, yet he complied, embracing her tightly and possessively. He wished she hadn't become involved in this hazardous conflict, but he was glad she was snuggled against him at this moment. He brushed kisses over her forehead, her cheeks, the tip of her nose, and her chin. His face caressed hers, his hands stroked her back and arms, and as he inhaled her sweet smell, his body grew warm.

As if she had been a kitten, Shannon nestled against him and silently encouraged more stroking with her reactions. Her fingertips teased over his shoulders and back and she sighed peacefully. His skin felt so cool and silky above its hard interior. He smelled as fresh as a spring breeze. She closed her eyes and let her senses absorb the stirring sensations within her. As her head rolled to his pillow, their lips touched lightly.

Blane nibbled at her mouth, dropping a brief kiss on it

every so often. One of his hands moved around her body to move lightly and sensuously over her throat and shoulder. Savoring the feel of her flesh, he moved his fingers over her face and down her neck to journey over her arm. His hand found hers and brought it to his lips. He kissed each finger, then her palm, then worked his way over her wrist and up her arm. When his mouth claimed hers with its first searing kiss, she moaned softly, arched her body against his, and clung to him.

Their surroundings were forgotten. The war was forgotten. All reasons not to make passionate love were forgotten . . .

Chapter Seven

Blane's tongue parted her lips and wandered inside her mouth. His body was smoldering with need for hers. Her responses kindled his desires. He had waited so long for this moment, had craved her so fiercely. His quivering fingers unbuttoned her gown to allow his hand to fondle a breast. His mouth left hers to trail kisses down her throat to the creamy mound, and his tongue circled its protruding point before he captured it with his mouth. His hand roamed down her side and worked her gown above her hips. It fondled a firm buttock and stroked her thigh. Slowly and gently his hand searched for a fuzzy covering and another taut peak. Ever so skillfully and gently, his finger moved up and down its satiny surface, though it had come to life even before his encouraging strokes.

Shannon derived great pleasure and stimulation from his actions, and she wanted them to continue. Her stomach briefly tightened as he deftly worked his skills on her body, but she refused to think about anything or anyone except Blane and this rapture he was inspiring. Her hands roamed his powerful shoulders as she dreamily floated on romantic clouds, her senses alive and her body aflame.

Blane wanted and needed to feel her flesh against his. He pushed the gown higher until it wadded beneath her arms, exposing her ivory skin to his gaze and touch. His mouth took hers almost savagely as he clasped her to him. When Shannon said and did nothing to halt him, he moved atop her. Tenderly he parted her thighs and prepared to enter her, cautioning himself to be gentle. As his mouth and hands provocatively distracted her, he tentatively pressed his manhood against her stubborn entrance. Finally, he thrust within her.

Shannon's outcry was muffled by his mouth. She struggled to push him away. When Blane's lips left hers, she accused in panic, "You're hurting me. We shouldn't be doing this."

Blane hesitated. He was already within her and his shaft was burning with desire. He wondered if he was too large for her small body. "I'm sorry, love," he whispered against her lips.

His warm breath and tenderness stirred Shannon, for the pain was fleeing swiftly. She kissed him and hugged him tightly but didn't know what else to do. She didn't want him to withdraw from her. A curious warmth had begun consuming her heart and body. She would wait a while longer to see if the pain returned.

Blane sensed her indecision. His mouth skillfully worked on hers, then at her breasts. He caressed her, hoping her passion would return. Soon, she was clinging to him and responding again. He moved gingerly until he was assured he wasn't hurting her. Then he set a seductive pattern, entering and withdrawing as he inflamed the nerves inside her womanhood. "I've wanted you since that night you sneaked into my room, Shannon. You've been driving me wild with hunger. Surely I've died and gone to heaven."

Blane was right. The movements were sheer bliss. She relaxed and allowed him free rein over her body and passions. The flames built until Shannon was positive they would be consumed by them. Never had anything felt so wonderful in her life. She arched her body to meet his thrusts. Her arms held him possessively. Now she understood the yearning that had chewed at her every time she looked at him.

Shannon's surrender was straining Blane's control and his body shuddered from the stress on it. He worked feverishly on her release, fearing his own would come too soon. When she began to writhe and moan beneath him, he knew she was racing up passion's spiral. He increased his pace, teasing and tantalizing her beyond defeat. His lips went to her ear to entreat hoarsely, "Come to me, Shannon. Yield to me, love."

Ecstasy burst within Shannon. Tiny fingers of exquisite pleasure stroked her womanhood. Her head thrashed on his pillow as her body demanded to experience every tingling sensation he was creating.

Blane dismissed his guard and pounded hungrily into her receptive body. His potent release stunned him. He almost cried aloud as the staggering spasms overwhelmed his body and mind, as if sending shocks through them. He found he was gasping for air and felt sweat beading on his face and frame. He labored lovingly until he had nothing left to give. Then he rolled to his side, carrying Shannon with him. He was exhausted but utterly content. His arms encircled her as he placed kisses over her face. He wanted her near him, touching him, a part of him.

Neither spoke or moved. They merely felt and savored. Gradually both fell asleep, locked in each other's arms.

When Blane awoke, he watched the woman beside him and he was filled with curious emotions. He had never enjoyed lovemaking more than he had last night. He felt as if Shannon belonged to him. He arose, careful not to disturb her. She needed her rest, for they would have an arduous few days ahead of them. He went to the basin and washed quietly. Then he dressed and silently unbolted the door. Placing the lantern on the table, he brightened its glow so she would awaken with plenty of light to chase away any lingering fears. He closed the door behind him, then noiselessly mounted the steps.

He greeted Mary and Joseph cheerfully. "That's the best night I've had in ages. I think I'll have a look around. I'll return shortly."

Mary handed him a cup of coffee to drink during his stroll. When Shannon didn't appear soon, Mary wondered if she had fallen asleep again. She went downstairs and peeked into the room. "Mrs. Stevens? You'd best rise and dress, child. Breakfast will be ready shortly."

Shannon stirred and sighed, then glanced toward the door at the smiling woman. "Good morning. I'll be ready in a little while."

After the woman closed the door, Shannon tossed aside the cover. The borrowed gown was wrinkled terribly. Shannon removed it and started to bathe. She noticed the dried blood washing off her skin onto the cloth, and knew its meaning. Had she been crazy to make love to a man she hardly knew? What was Blane thinking about her this morning? No doubt he was panicked at the idea of what an entangling situation this could be. Would he be sorry? Would he behave differently?

She dressed in her pants and shirt, then pulled on her boots. She unbraided her hair, brushed it, and braided it again neatly. As she went to straighten the bed, bloodstains caught her eye. She flushed red and seized the basin, soap, and a cloth. She had to wash away the evidence of their wanton union.

The door opened and Blane entered. He stared at Shannon in confusion. Walking over to her, he asked,

"What are you doing, love?"

Shannon had been concentrating so hard that she hadn't heard his boots on the steps. At the sound of his voice, her left hand covered the stain. "Nothing," she replied modestly.

Blane looked down at her bowed head and rigid body as she knelt by the bed. Women didn't pray with soapy cloths in their hands and basins of water at their feet. Noticing the wetness of the sheet beneath her hand, he grasped it and lifted it.

Shannon stiffened her arm in an attempt to prevent his action as she shrieked, "No! Don't, Blane. I'll be there soon. Wait for me upstairs."

Blane's bewildered gaze went from the bloodstains to Shannon's head. Although he was still holding her wrist captive, she didn't look up at him or yank it free. All of the clues settled in and alerted Blane to the severity of the situation and to her embarrassment. He should have guessed last night she was a virgin! The difficulty hadn't come from his size or the length of time since she had made love to a man. A flurry of questions and emotions filled him. What about Hawke? What about Thornton's charges and insults? He was baffled, pleased, and dismayed all at the same time, and exceedingly thankful that Clifford had failed! He would have to reassess his thoughts, feelings, and actions now.

Shannon murmured softly, "I was trying to wash the sheet. You know what they'll think when they see this. They'll know we lied."

Recalling his jest to the Thomases earlier, he chuckled. "They'll think we spent our first night together in this room. Don't worry about the sheet," he coaxed, pulling her to her feet. "It isn't important. Except to prove you belong to me now." He kissed her feverishly.

"You aren't upset about this?" she asked uncertainly.

"No, love. Unless it's for not waking you up and

making love to you again this morning. I've never known a woman like you."

"Is that good or bad?" she inquired, relaxing slightly.

"So far, a little of both," he replied honestly. "If you're of a mind to, you can make it all good for me from now on."

"Me? You're the one who's always waxing good and bad, hot and cold. I never know what mood or behavior to expect from you."

"I can be mulish at times, can't I?" he said beguilingly, extricating himself from her entrapping question. "But sometimes you're to blame."

"Sometimes you're absolutely right. Aren't they waiting for us to join them for breakfast?" she hinted, becoming too warm in his arms.

He laughed. "I think I'm being slyly rejected or dismissed."

"I think you're absolutely right again," she teased.

Their eyes met and spoke. Blane's palm moved over her hair, exploring its silkiness. When she tried to lower her head, he caught her braid and pulled on it, lifting her chin. He was grinning when their gazes fused. "You can't get away from me, Shannon."

Just before his mouth closed over hers, she whispered, "I'm not sure I want to." Her arms rose and went around his neck.

Blane's arms overlapped her back. He lifted her light body from the floor and locked her snugly against him as he kissed her urgently. He refused to release her until Mary called down the steps to ask if they were ready to eat. Blane smiled into Shannon's face as he replied, "Ready. Be there momentarily." To Shannon, he whispered, "But I wish the food were different to match my appetite. Yep, I was crazy to let you sleep late, Mrs. Stevens."

Shannon boldly inquired, "Why did you?"

"Fear. I was afraid you'd be too . . . uncomfortable this soon after . . . last night. Did I hurt you? I wanted you so much I had trouble restraining myself."

"You were absolutely wonderful, Mister Stevens. I'm glad it was you here with me last night. Don't worry about me. I'm fine."

After breakfast, Shannon and Blane expressed their thanks and said their good-byes. Mary Thomas prepared them a light snack for midday, then gave Blane a bundle that held two cans of mixed vegetables for soup. She told him the soup could be warmed right in the can over a campfire. Adding a few more items, the woman smiled and wished them success.

Once on the trail, Blane told Shannon, "Mary gave me the names of two safe houses along the way. The password is *Armageddon.* If you can sing or play the piano, she said there's a music hall in Wilmington where you can rest and work while I check out the ports for blockade runners. She said rumor has it that Rose Greenhow, the famous Rebel spy, will be returning soon from London with money for the Confederacy. I surely would love to prevent any new flow of money and supplies from filtering in. Joseph told me the runner boats come in around Cape Fear River. Would it be all right for me to leave you there for a week or so?" he asked surprisingly.

"I've heard of Rose. She published a book last year about her experiences. To hear her tell it, she's single-handedly supplying the South with all the information they need to win this war. They've imprisoned her on several occasions. She implicated some powerful men. Is it true that Queen Victoria received her when she docked in England?"

"From what I've heard, yes. Of course, a woman of such daring and courage would impress another woman in power. She also met Napolean the Third. They've been treating her like a heroine over there. No wonder she finds spying so stimulating and believes her own reputation."

"Why would the British and French behave so badly? Don't they realize the North is the strongest power over here?"

"They need cotton and tobacco, and they're Southern crops. They've loaned the South money against future crops, and that'll hurt the South once this war ends. Did you know Rose lived only a few blocks from the White House on Sixteenth Street? Too bad she wasn't around for you to worm you way into her confidence. We could use knowledge of her operation and agents."

"Was she really as powerful and devious as the papers said?"

"President Buchanan used to call on her frequently, as did many cabinet members, judges, and congressmen. She's always been very political. Rose has a knack for enticing information."

"Is she beautiful?" Shannon inquired curiously.

"She has a look of elegance and refinement. She's dark eyed and dark haired like a Spaniard. She's friendly and charming. I believe she's nearly forty-five now. She's learned how to wrap men around her finger with those smiles and airs of hers. And Rose is smart. She makes certain she doesn't get caught with anything damaging on her. The man who became her nemesis is Allan Pinkerton, the famous detective. He was determined not to give her a moment's peace. But even in prison, she ruled the drab setting like a banished queen."

Shannon listened to Blane's voice and laughter. Other than the talk by the river about his family, this was the most conversing he had done with her since they had been thrown together. She liked this genial facet of his personality. "Have you ever met Colonel John Mosby?" she asked.

"That so-called raider. He and his band are nothing but renegades. The Rebels see him as a hero, but he's cold and cruel and calculating. I'd like to put him and his unit out of business."

"Did you ever meet him?" she pressed again.

"Once. I'll never forget him. He's a lanky man with thin lips and piercing eyes. He terrorizes the countryside and nibbles at Union flanks. He's one of those people who believes it's all right to win the war any way possible or necessary. I'll give him his due; he does command loyalty and seems fearless. Lincoln got word Mosby's Rangers were terrorizing the Union captives at Andersonville Prison. Captain Wirz, that blood-thirsty Swiss, finally let some of the inmates capture and slay several of the raiders. That broke their power hold. Sometimes it's bad inside those camps. Men fight or kill over food or a blanket. It's the animal instinct for survival. They say Wirz is in constant pain from an old wound and that's why he's so savage and unfeeling."

Seeing Shannon's pained look, Blane comprehended his mistake. He wished he hadn't mentioned prisons, especially Andersonville. "I suppose Lincoln's working hard right now just to get re-elected. Sherman's victories should help him." Instantly Blane knew he had introduced another bad topic. "You didn't answer me earlier. Can you sing and play music?"

Shannon was aware of his sudden changes in subjects. She let him have his way. "Yes, I can do both. I'll be fine in Wilmington."

"Is there anything you can't do?" he teased, reaching back to tickle her. She wriggled away but didn't laugh. He grimaced.

"I can't find my brother and help him escape."

"Don't worry, Shannon. I promise you I'll find Corry Greenleaf."

Shannon didn't notice his frosty tone of voice as she

185

hugged him. "Have you ever met the mysterious spy called the Blade?"

"No one who meets the Blade ever knows it. He's smart. How do you know about him?" Blane asked, placing his hand over hers.

"I read about him in the papers, and people talked about him at most gatherings. I wonder who he is and why he remains so secretive."

"Obviously to save his life and to get information more easily. I could do more if my face and name weren't so well known. Same goes for you, Flame," he asserted, then chuckled strangely.

"What do you mean?"

"By now, every area we've passed through has heard of the beautiful and daring Union spy called the Flame. If we don't keep moving, that reputation will catch up to and entangle us."

"You're teasing me," she accused merrily.

"Not much. Be careful and don't expose yourself to the wrong people. We know Clifford and Travers are dogging you. I would guess that Cathy's let your new identity slip to someone. News travels fast on spy lines. Within a month or two, you'll be as legendary as the Blade."

"Don't be silly. I haven't done anything to earn fame or infamy."

"You're wrong, love. When questions start being asked, every man who's met you will add more color and detail to those encounters. Since they couldn't capture you, they'll have to make up some wild story about your clever deception and escape. Don't you see, love? In times like these, people need heroines and heroes; others need someone to blame for their errors and weaknesses. They enjoy creating legends, polishing them, making them special, unconquerable, infallible. Who better than a beautiful, unselfish angel who courts death and danger

186

to help them? Myths like Flame and Blade inspire hope and courage."

"Doesn't that place our lives in more danger? Isn't it hard to carry off secret missions when people know who and what you are?" she fretted aloud. "No wonder the Blade keeps himself unknown."

Blane smiled. "Myths provide a feeling of excitement and romance, a stimulating aura of mystery, a distraction from bloody reality. That's why the Blade appeals to so many people. He's said to be clever, mysterious, powerful, fearless. They think he's someone to respect, to admire, to envy, to hate."

"Do you envy him, Blane?"

Blane was quiet for a moment before replying, "No, I don't. He has to remain a loner. Being a legend is an awesome responsibility."

"Do you respect and admire him?" she continued, intrigued.

"Sometimes I don't and sometimes I do. Sometimes he's forced to do things for the Union that hurt innocent people. Sometimes he does or says anything necessary for the success of his mission. Sometimes he gets blame or credit that he doesn't earn. On the whole, he's an honorable man. But sometimes his personal honor gets all tangled up with love and loyalty for his country."

"Has he hurt you or used you?" she probed at his odd tone.

"Yes, he's made me do something that might be wrong."

"Might be wrong? How could he make you do anything against your will? You're the most fearless and powerful man I know. From your remarks, I thought you hadn't met him."

"He's a complicated man; I really don't know him at all, not anymore. Maybe the war's changed him. All I know is I promised Lincoln I would do whatever needed

187

to be done to help end this war."

"I don't think I would like this Blade. I'm not sure I agree that to use any means necessary to obtain victory is just. An honorable man has to know where to draw the line between right and wrong, even in war."

"That's the trouble during war, Shannon. How does one truly know the difference between right and wrong, between good and evil? Take our loyalties and assignments. We do some things that are bad and wrong, in the name of helping good and right. What if we're forced to kill a Rebel officer to steal information or to save our lives? Would that theft or murder be justified? If a town or home is attacked and destroyed because of the information we provide, is that wrong or our way of fighting evil? In war, the lines are fuzzy and distorted, and justice isn't black and white. Where do we draw our line, Flame?"

"I don't know. I suppose each incident has to be judged when it arises. Before the war, I would have sworn I couldn't slay a man for any reason. I would never have stolen or deceived decent folk. There are many things I wouldn't have done if this war hadn't started. It's so hard to know what's right and wrong these days."

They had talked through their noon meal and during most of their ride. By keeping off the road and away from settlements and homes, they had encountered very few people. On occasion and at a distance, they had seen camps where homeless families or wounded soldiers were awaiting their fates. Shortly before sundown, Blane found a promising spot for them to camp for the night.

Dan was left to graze and drink near a creek. "You stay here while I take a look around," Blane ordered as usual.

When he returned, he teased, "Why isn't my supper ready?"

"You didn't give me permission to build a fire, sir."

"Good girl," he complimented her intelligence. "We'll

188

have to eat cold food tonight. I could make out a large camp not too far away."

"Which side?" she questioned anxiously.

"Rebs. Don't worry. We'll eat and nap, then sneak around them before daylight. We're beyond their sentries' range."

Shannon didn't want to eat cold vegetables from a can, but she was hungry. "Let's save the soup for a fire," she coaxed.

"That leaves carrots, peaches, and green beans to share."

Shannon wrinkled her nose and brow. "Do the honors, sir."

When Shannon could stomach no more of their meal, she went to the creek to wash her hands and face. Blane joined her, squatting and splashing water on his face and neck. Sitting on the bedroll, Shannon unbraided her hair and began brushing it.

Blane suggested, "Tell me about your family and home."

Shannon ceased her chore and stared ahead thoughtfully. She was glad he wanted to know about her, "Andrew Greenleaf was an unusual man to come from genteel aristocratic stock. He didn't think or behave like most Southern landowners who possessed wealth and a matchless bloodline. In a way, he was selfish and rebellious. You Texans would call him a maverick or a renegade, but he was a clever and subtle one. I don't think Papa ever realized that his wishes came first. There were times when I wondered if I knew him or understood him at all. He was one of those dreamers who felt that if people didn't know certain things, they couldn't be hurt or influenced by them. And yet, family honor and name were very important to him, sometimes too important," she murmured, pushing aside those painful memories.

"Papa could be tough, even merciless, if necessary.

Most of the time, he was a good man, a strong one with a compelling personality. After Mama died, he was restless. That's when he got mixed up with Simon Travers; he wanted someone to help him run the factor business. With memories of Mama haunting him at Greenleaf, he needed to get away from the plantation for long spells. He never believed in slavery, so we employed workers for the fields and in our home. Papa traveled up and down the coast and to Misssissippi and Louisiana, buying or bargaining for cotton crops. Until '56, he spent a lot of time in your Texas. He had made . . . special friends there during the Mexican War. Then he began staying home more, letting Simon handle most of the firm's affairs. I was hoping he would meet another special woman, but he never remarried. Losing his love was extremely hard on him—too hard."

Shannon began brushing her hair again as she talked. "Papa believed that a man was responsible for his own fate and good fortune. And he didn't think a woman should have any say-so about business or politics. I was glad he took those trips so I could do whatever I pleased. When Papa was around, I had to be the perfect lady. I had to entertain neighbors like the Thorntons and their offensive son, James. For awhile I was terrified old man Thornton was going to convince Papa to hand me over to that snake. I would have run away from home before marrying him."

Blane chuckled but held silent. Shannon grinned. "When Papa was away, Temple looked after the plantation and family. He was the strong, quiet type, like you. He was a caring person. He was sensitive and gentle. Everybody liked Temple and enjoyed his company. He never wanted or tried to hurt anyone. The other men knew they could trust him. But he could be very sly. He and Papa teased each other pointedly, but they never argued. Temple would listen to Papa's orders and pretend

190

to obey them. As soon as Papa left home, Temple did what he knew was best for the family and our lands. If Papa ever caught on to Temple's deceit, he never corrected it. My brother was special, full of life and love. He used to talk to me for hours about anything and everything. If I had a problem, Temple always had time and answers for me."

Shannon was quiet for a time. "I'm not sure I believe he and Papa are dead. It's as if they're away on a trip. I keep thinking and feeling I'll see them again soon. Papa could be a hard man, but I loved him dearly. I remember him with Mama. I think he loved her more than life itself. Papa could be as gentle as Temple but as rascally as Corry. I couldn't understand him after her death. He was as happy and content as when Mama had been alive. By accident, I learned why he had spent so much time in Texas, and why he stopped going. It took me a long time to understand how someone could love two people at the same time." Shannon had decided to slowly start dropping hints about her past. Perhaps soon she would be able to relate everything.

Blane didn't take her statement as she had hoped. He argued, "No, Shannon, it isn't possible to love two people at the same time, not in the way you mean. A man can be fascinated and charmed by his mistress, but he would never marry her. Desire and love are not the same. They can be partners, but desire can work alone. Perhaps your father used love to excuse his behavior to himself and his family. If he truly loved your mother, there would have been no room in his heart for another woman. If he loved the other woman, he couldn't have been happy with your mother. You must accept it for what it was—a weakness, a flaw. Love is all consuming, Shannon; there isn't enough of yourself left to share with another person." He paused. "Tell me about your home."

Shannon didn't refuse his words. She needed to give

him more time to know her before adding Hawke to her father's list of flaws and weaknesses. Would a bastard half-brother color his opinion of her? She let him change the subject. "Wait until you see Greenleaf, Blane. It's beautiful. The entrance is half a mile from the house. There's a five-feet high wall the color of sand and you have to ride under a huge arch. On either side of the arch, there is a hand-painted branch of magnolia leaves and over the top it says Greenleaf. Once you pass under the arch, the road is shaded by two rows of live oaks. Their branches bow and meet overhead to form a green tunnel, and gray moss hangs from them and sways in the breeze." She closed her eyes and envisioned the sight. "Our yards are filled with magnolias, live oaks, roses, camellias, dogwoods, and countless azaleas. You should see it in the spring. It's breathtaking. There's a gazebo in the garden. I used to go there every morning to read or study. The house is huge, with four towering columns across the front. I won't tell you any more; you'll have to see it for yourself when we get there."

Blane couldn't tell her that he had seen it several times before. She was right; it was elegant and beautiful. He had known after hearing her name that she was rich and polished. If not for the war, she could have had her choice of husbands, just as wealthy and refined. Why Hawke? Why Blane Stevens? Thornton had been mistaken; it wasn't because she was a spoiled, molten-blooded vixen who craved "rogues." "What about Corry?" Blane ventured. "You forgot him."

"Corry . . . How does one describe Corbett Greenleaf?" she asked herself mirthfully. "He's a charmer, Blane. He's funny and bright, but carefree and impulsive—like someone you might know," she jested, then laughed. "As you might imagine, he and Papa came to verbal blows many times. He couldn't stay quiet like Temple. No, Corry always shouted out his opinions. Papa used to take Corry with him on certain trips and make him work along the way. He thought it would take some of the wildness out of him. Papa never understood Corry. He had such a zest for life and adventure. He was a lot like you've described yourself. Maybe the Cavalry was what he needed. He has a smile that would warm the coldest day. You know, those kinds of smiles that use everything: eyes, lips, face, bearing. He's irresistible. Every woman who meets him wants him and chases him."

Shannon looked over at Blane, who was paying close attention to her words. She was warmed and delighted by his interest, and she continued. "Corry is nothing like Papa or Temple. I think he has wanderlust in his blood. I wouldn't be surprised if he became a sailor. He loves to travel. He loves a challenge. Papa used to say he couldn't sit still long enough for a fly to land on him. At social gatherings, Corry was always the center of attention. Both men and women liked him. Despite his ego and restive nature, Corry was a vulnerable person, and easygoing. But I doubt he revealed his true self to many people. That's why he and I got along so well; he could be himself with me, and I could do the same with him. We used to hunt and fish and ride together. The autumn before the war started, Corry changed. He started pulling into himself. I know it had something to do with what happened on his last trip west with Papa."

"What happened on the trip?" Blane asked.

"I don't know. Corry and . . . Papa wouldn't tell me. When they got home, they were hardly speaking. It wasn't like Corry to keep secrets from me and Temple. Something was eating at him. If the war hadn't begun, I think Corry would have left home that spring. If I hadn't lost my bag, I would show you their pictures."

"Being a female, didn't you ever scold Corry about his many conquests? Think of all the hearts he must have broken."

Shannon stared at him. "Corry never made promises to women. It wasn't his fault if they chased him and wooed him. Do you hold yourself responsible for the broken hearts you've left behind?"

Blane chuckled. "I try not to break any hearts," he asserted.

"Corry didn't do so deliberately. Women found him appealing. They practically battled to see who would be on his arm at the next event. He went out with many girls, and he never misled them."

"How do you know what was said or done in private?" he teased.

"I know Corry, and he never would have been cruel intentionally. But can you blame a man for accepting a woman who throws herself at him?"

Blane laughed devilishly when Shannon turned red at her words. "Don't laugh, or I'll smack you," she warned. "You men have the upper hand. You can do or say whatever you please, but women can't. It isn't fair for you to have so much freedom and fun. If a woman wants to do the same, she either has to pay the price or resist such impulses."

"Neither of your brothers married? How old are they?" he asked.

"Temple . . . died when he was twenty-three. He was going to be wed in May of '61. When the Greenleafs sided with the Union in April, Mister Jamison canceled the wedding. Temple and Clarissa had planned to elope as soon as the conflicts were settled. What could Mister Jamison have done after the fact? I wrote her about Temple's . . . death, but I don't know for sure if she received my letter. I suppose I should call on her when we reach Savannah."

194

"And Corry?" he hinted quizzically.

"Like me, he's never met anyone who suited him. He was waiting for that one special person who comes along unexpectedly and steals your breath and thoughts. Besides, he was only twenty when the war started. That's hardly a confirmed bachelor."

"Let's see . . . That would make Corry twenty-three now. A nice age for getting married and settling down with a wife and child. Any woman should enjoy going to live at your Greenleaf. Corry is the heir now." He paused. "What are you looking for in a man, Shannon?"

"One who has all of the best qualities of my father and brothers, with none of their weaknesses or flaws. I like the strong, silent type who knows when to be gentle and funny. I want him to be brave and clever. I want him to be rich and famous and powerful. I want him to be perfect," she jested, then winked at him. Thinking she was flattering him too much, she mischievously added, "And I do love dark eyes and hair against tawny skin, and white teeth. To be enchanting and appealing, he must be handsome and virile and utterly charming."

"What about whiskey-eyed wheat-heads?" he wailed playfully, annoyed by her words. Why must she remind him of Hawke! Damn her, she belonged to him! She couldn't love and have both of them!

"They'll do, if I have no other choice," she replied, laughing. She assumed Blane understood how she felt about him and knew she was teasing. When she noticed he wasn't smiling, she ventured, "Take Blane Stevens for example; there's a man who could enchant any woman. Who could resist those hazel eyes, that tawny hair, bronzed skin, and abundant charm? He's fairly close to being perfect, if he would stop being so bossy and overprotective."

"I thought women liked men who took command of situations, who protected them from all harm, who knew

195

how to please them. Have I been using the wrong approach and talents on you?"

"I told you, Major Stevens, you're almost perfect. Tell me more about you and your family," she encouraged. "What about your other sister, besides Lucille? Where's the new ranch?"

"Eleanor Stevens met one of those charmers like Corry. He convinced her he was in love with her, seduced her, got her pregnant, then left. She hasn't heard from him since. When I left for the war, Ellie was still praying for his return. That's why I took this job for Lincoln, to travel around helping the Union while I search for the bastard who ruined my sister. When I locate him, I plan to kill him."

"Has she tried to contact him? What if there was a reason why he couldn't return. If I were you, Blane, I would give him a chance to talk before I shot him. Sometimes there are very good reasons why two people can't marry. Don't be impulsive, or you may regret it. Are you so sure Ellie's wrong about him returning?"

"Yes, Shannon, I am. As of January of '61, the charming rogue left my sister with a bastard son to make sure she remembers him. He's never tried to reach her or to accept his responsibilities. Clayton and Jory contacted him twice, but the son-of-a-bitch denied even knowing her. When Jory warned him I was coming after him to haul him back to Texas to marry Ellie, he wrote back and insisted I try to do just that. He claimed he wasn't to blame and Ellie would have to find someone else to force into marriage. By the time I located his home, he had taken off. I still haven't found him. When I do, he'll wish he had married her. I promised myself and my family I would keep him from ruining another girl's life."

"That was years ago, Blane. What if he's changed? What if he loves her and wants to marry her? He could have returned to Texas after you left. Please talk before

196

you kill him."

"I got word from home while I was in Washington, meeting you of all people. Fate sometimes amazes me. When this war is over and I return home, I plan to find Ellie a good husband, one who deserves her and . . . her son. That ring you're wearing, I bought it for her. A mother looks better wearing a wedding ring, doesn't she?"

She advised him, "Don't push her, Blane. Love comes along rarely. A woman can't accept just any man in her life. Let her find the right man to replace him," she urged. "Maybe you can't love two people at the same time, but you can find new love, can't you?"

Blane studied Shannon's expression. Her words struck him oddly. Maybe . . . Blane shook his head. Even if Hawke wasn't between them, Corry was. How could he be so cruel to Ellie as to bring the sister of her traitorous lover into the family? How could Shannon deal with living with Ellie and little Corry? How could she deal with the truth about her brother? "How does a son replace a father, Shannon? There is no acceptable reason on earth for a man to deny his son his rightful name, to tag him a bastard. If you give life to a son, you owe him. What kind of man could reject his son, could be so cruel to him? Such a snake deserves to die." He stared off at the horizon to break the somberness of his mood. "I'm tired. How about you?"

"Exhausted, partner." She yawned and reclined. Heaven help her, how could she ever explain Hawke after what Blane had told her?

"I'll check around before turning in. You go to sleep. Tomorrow's another long, dusty day." Blane vanished into the darkness. When he returned, Shannon was asleep, as he had hoped.

He gazed down at her, praying silently, *Lord, help me if I'm wrong about Shannon and me and this situation.* Blane decided that the woman asleep before him couldn't be a good enough actress to have hidden her knowledge of Corry's treacherous actions during the spring of '60 or her fear at hearing him vow lethal revenge. No, Corry hadn't confided that secret. But could Shannon's brother be persuaded to do the right thing by Ellie? From Shannon's talk, it didn't sound as if Corry had any reason not to marry his sister. If he could solve Ellie's problem and restore her honor without killing Corry Greenleaf, he could have Shannon.

Chapter Eight

That next morning, it had been easy for them to sneak around the Rebel encampment. But as they traveled during the next two days, Shannon became aware of Blane's curious mood. Since the night they had camped after leaving the Thomases, he had been quiet and unresponsive. At times, he had even been edgy and terse. Throughout their lengthy rides, she had felt the tautness in his body. Whenever they had halted for breaks or sleep, he had avoided unnecessary contact and conversation. She could tell something was troubling him, but it seemed a different kind of mental turmoil than that which he had undergone before their intimacy.

Was it she or he? Were fears of their getting too close worrying him? Shannon was annoyed and dismayed by his distance. The nights were getting cooler, and she craved his body heat and the comfort of his arms. Had she disappointed him the night they had made love? Perhaps their familiarity or intimacy threatened him. She remembered Corry telling her that men got nervous and sometimes nasty when a girl either started meaning too much to him or started getting too possessive. If that was the problem, she needed to be patient and understanding. But for how long?

Another difficult day on the trail passed. Shannon was exhausted and irritated when they halted at dusk, for they hadn't gone unnoticed all day. Around two, Blane had been forced to fight two men who had tried to steal their horse and supplies. He had fussed and resisted when she had wrapped his bruised and bloodied knuckles, perhaps because she had been the one to get the drop on the two men and deter them. Since the nettling incident, they had spoken little.

Blane made camp near a deep gully through which ran a narrow stream. The banks were over five feet high and the water was only eight or nine inches deep. Blane felt it was safe to build a campfire.

Shannon refrained from questioning him in his present foul mood. She watched him open the tin cans and warm the soup, but didn't so much as glance at her. After handing her one, he swiftly consumed the other, then told her he would be gone for about an hour.

Shannon watched him vanish into the woods, then sighed heavily. She walked to the edge of the bank and gazed down at the water. She smiled. If Blane had chosen this spot, then it would be safe, she assumed. Since he would be gone for awhile, why couldn't she bathe quickly? Shannon made her way down the steep incline, then yanked off her clothes. Chilly air swept over her skin. She hurriedly wet her body, lathered herself, then rinsed off. She had no choice but to dry off with her dirty shirt. With the blanket wrapped around her, she washed her pants and shirt as thoroughly as possible. She flinched when she heard Blane's laughter. "Stay where you are!" she shouted at him.

"I can't see anything. It's dark, and the bank's too high," he said, going to sit cross-legged by the fire. He was wondering how to apologize for his broodiness. "I knew what you were up to when I saw bubbles floating downstream. Do you know the risk you're taking?"

"Risk? It's too cold for snakes and too early for chest colds. Surely my devoted partner wouldn't attack me, even if he is as mad as a soaked hen because I saved his stupid life. I can't help it if I'm selfish and want to keep him around a little longer."

"That isn't why I was mad," he argued. "I was angry at myself for letting those men sneak up on us. I don't know where my head is these days. Since you and I became partners, all I think about is you or protecting you. I've been too distracted and too restrained; that's worse than no control or caution. I've got to stop worrying about you, Blue Eyes. From the way you handled yourself in Danville and today, I'm certain you can take care of yourself. I guess I just wanted to be the one to do it. You know, male pride and ego? I don't like being careless and putting your life in danger. Some protector I am. As to risks, Flame, I was referring to intruders, not me."

"I knew this place was safe; otherwise you wouldn't have camped here or left me alone. You're too hard and demanding on yourself, Blane. What kind of partner would I be if I didn't help out once in a while? Besides, most of the dangers result from my tagging along. You would be fine if I didn't concern you. Catch these clothes, please."

He came to the edge of the bank and grabbed the clothes that she tossed up to him. Extending his hand, he pulled her up the bank. He eyed the blanket encasing her body and grinned. "Have you forgotten how hazardous such garb can be?" he teased.

Shannon sent him a coy smile. "Is that so, Mister Stevens?" She took the wet clothes and spread them over bushes, knowing it was too chilly for them to dry during the night. When she shuddered, she asked, "Do you realize it will be getting cold soon?"

Blane smiled happily. "Good. 'Cause Nature doesn't seem to realize it's mid-October."

"Well, I certainly do." Shannon noticed his wet head and bare chest, then recalled his remarks. "You took a bath downstream?"

He sat by the fire without donning his shirt. "I was hot and sticky, and mad. I was going to stand guard for you when I returned. I see it isn't necessary. Always the impulsive and impatient vixen."

As darkness closed in on them, she queried, "Aren't you ever satisfied? You don't want me to act childish or spoiled, but you get riled when I show spunk or daring. What do you want from me, Blane?"

"I want you, Shannon," he answered simply and unexpectedly.

Shannon watched him tease the fire with a large twig. He hadn't looked at her as he spoke. Her heart drummed wildly. Why was he so wary? Why couldn't he reach out to her? It almost seemed as if there were some invisible barrier between them. He wanted her, but did he want to want her? He was constantly attracting and repelling her. What a befuddling man!

"You are so contradictory, Blane Stevens. I wish I understood you. I wish I understood myself," she added in a muffled tone.

Blane's gaze lifted to fuse with hers. "I wish I could help you to understand me and yourself, Shannon; I can't."

"Blane, I . . . I'm going to sleep." Shannon walked to where he had unrolled the sleeping mat. She reached for her clean shirt and pants.

Blane stepped up behind her and his hand covered hers. "Don't," he entreated. "I can keep you warm tonight." When Shannon didn't move or speak, Blane nervously chatted, "It's a good thing summer is running late this year and we're so near the coast. We could be freezing in the mountains. It was generous of the Thomases to give us each a coat. We'll be needing them

202

soon. You're shivering," he remarked, moving hands up and down her arms. Grasping her shoulders, he turned her to face him. As his thumb moved over her lips, he asked, "What am I going to do about you? Do you know how you affect me, Shannon?"

Shannon comprehended his meaning. Without releasing his gaze, she replied, "Hopefully the same way you affect me. I want you badly, and that scares me. More so, it scares me to think I can't have you."

Blane nodded agreement. His eyes roamed her face leisurely. Then his hands drifted upward into her hair, enjoying how it felt against his fingers. As if he could wait no longer to have her in his arms, he drew her to him. He didn't talk or try to rush the moment. For now, all he needed and wanted was to hold her, to feel her heart beating next to his body, to know she was there willingly . . . and trustingly. He closed his eyes and absorbed each sensation and emotion. Was he crazy to get so deeply involved before destroying the wall between them?

With Blane so close and intoxicating, Shannon couldn't think of anything but her desire for him and his for her. Love and commitment were frightening things. They could be as perilous as war, if one-sided. Shannon snuggled close to him and inhaled his special scent. His virile torso was deeply tanned, the flesh cottony soft, and the interior stony hard. His entire frame was lithe and strong. The knife scar on his jawline appeared to be the only flaw on the magnificant male.

Shannon dreamily moved her hands over broad shoulders and down a hairless chest where muscles protruded slightly before flattening into a taut stomach. Her respiration quickened, and her insides seemed to be quivering with anticipation. A smoldering glow warmed her skin. His arms were always so enticing, so stimulating. She looked up into his face. Handsome could not adequately describe him, for he possessed more than exceptional looks. It was the way his hazel eyes, tawny complexion, sun-kissed hair, and appealing features worked together to create an unforgettable and matchless allure. He drew her to him with more force than her blood drew her toward her family.

Wanting to feel her flesh against his, Blane moved his fingers to loosen the blanket and let it fall to the ground. He groaned as the staggering sensation flooded his mind and inflamed his body. He nibbled at her ears and shoulders. His hands stroked her back and hair. His lips found hers and possessed them urgently. His embrace tightened so forcefully that she lost her wind. His mouth was exploring and stirring desire within her and he claimed her senses with determination and skill.

Blane lifted Shannon and placed her on the bedroll. He covered her neck with kisses as he rid himself of his pants and boots. His hands and movements grew bolder as they labored to increase her passion. His warm breath caused her to tremble, to cling to him. As his mouth seared over her breasts, her fingers played wildly in his hair.

Shannon's senses were alive and alert. He was controlling and intoxicating the very essence of her being. Her body was sensitive to his every action. Every inch of her burned and pleaded for his touch, his talented caresses. She wanted him to invade her very soul and claim it as his own. The first time they had united their bodies, it had been wonderful. But tonight, it was sheer rapture.

His hand provocatively traveled down her stomach and teased along her thighs with long, sweeping strokes. He sought out her secret place and immediately heightened his passion as well as hers. Surely this was blissful torment. Blane called on all he knew about lovemaking and women to give her the most fulfilling experience possible. He wanted this blending of bodies and spirits to last for hours. It couldn't, he knew, for they needed to sleep and rise early to continue their perilous trek. When they reached Wilmington, they would have privacy and comfort and safety. The war would have to wait while he spent two days with her, two glorious days that could be their last ones together. His hands and tongue prepared her to take him greedily and uninhibitedly.

A flood of sensations washed over Shannon, sensations that caused her to relax and to tense simultaneously, sensations that created ecstasy and torment, sensations that fed some needs and inspired others. She allowed him to do as he pleased, for whatever he did pleased her. She had yearned for this moment for days. "Oh, Blane, what are you doing to me?"

Blane shifted his hips between her thighs and gently entered her with his torrid shaft. This contact was more staggering to his senses and control than the touching of their naked bodies. Lord, she played havoc with his self-control and sensual talents! He wanted tonight to be especially meaningful to her, for perhaps she hadn't known full pleasure and contentment that first time.

Shannon's hands roved along the rippling muscles of his back as he tenderly moved in and out of her compelling body. She lifted her hips to receive each entry, then moaned at each withdrawal. She crossed her legs over his and held him snugly. Her mouth meshed feverishly with his as their tongues performed their own mating dance.

Shannon's behavior told Blane when she was ready to challenge and conquer ecstasy's peak. He increased his lunging pace to a gentle savageness. "Ride with me, Shannon. Be mine alone. Come to me, my fiery enchantress, come to me," he entreated raggedly in her ear.

His words and actions sent Shannon over the crest of

hesitation. Her cry of release was muffled against his shoulder, and as she began her downward spiral after victory, Blane's body shuddered with the force of an equally blissful climax. His mouth seized hers and he kissed her ravenously until every spasm ceased.

Blane shifted to his back, holding Shannon in place. Her cheek rested on his thudding, damp chest. His fingers were interlaced behind her back and his face turned skyward as he searched for normal respiration. As he gradually discovered it, one hand went behind her head and clasped her head closer to him. Shortly, he rolled her to her back, placing him half atop her, and stared into her large blue eyes.

Blane couldn't pull his gaze from Shannon's face. She looked so beautiful lying there naked in the moonlight, glistening from her exertions. The flush of passion still brightened her cheeks; the glow of appeasement softened her potent gaze. She was so innocent to be so sensual and bewitching. He couldn't ignore her or resist her. He couldn't keep his hands or mind from her. But could he have her if he carried out his revenge? No, she would despise him. On the other hand, could he forget his duty and vengenace to win Shannon? They were endangered by war; perhaps he wouldn't survive to face such a difficult decision. If only Shannon weren't so entrancing, so giving, so damn trusting! If only she weren't . . . It was useless to avoid reality; she was Shannon Greenleaf, and he couldn't ignore or discard the past.

Shannon observed him curiously, for his mood confused her. His gaze was such a puzzling mixture of emotional turmoil. She observed several contradictory feelings: pleasure, contentment, affection, possessiveness, astonishment, and remorse and anguish as well. She wondered what was troubling him so deeply. Those were far too many emotions to be attacking him at once, especially now. "Blane, is something wrong?"

"We're in perilous country, Shannon. One wrong move and we could both be destroyed. We've got some hard and painful times ahead of us. There are things I'll have to do that no one will understand. I wish it could be different, Flame. Whatever happens from now on, take care of yourself. You're as rare as a white buffalo, and just as special."

Shannon mentally questioned his odd expression and tone. It didn't sound as if he had been referring to the war. His remarks sounded personal and tormenting, as if sliced from his soul before they could be spoken aloud. Was he going to desert her in the next town? "When we get to Wilmington, I'll follow orders; you needn't worry, Blane."

He assumed and hoped she had misunderstood him, for he had spoken rashly. Her comment misled him. "Wilmington is the chief port for Confederate supplies. It's still in Rebel hands, Shannon. We might sound Southern, but we can't afford any slipups. There could be other Thorntons and Cliffords and Traverses around. Watch yourself carefully."

Shannon smiled and caressed his cheek. "I'll be good, sir."

His forefinger stroked her eyebrow. "Charleston and Savannah are the same, Blue Eyes. The Rebs control those major ports too." He didn't confide that Savannah was the goal of Sherman's present offensive. If the man continued the strategy that had been used for destroying Atlanta, Shannon might not have a home left after he reached her lovely town. "As major supply points for the South, they are major targets for Yankee ships and inland assaults. Stay clear of the docks, understand? I don't want to leave you behind anywhere, Shannon, but there'll be times when I must. Promise me you won't take foolish risks."

She smiled lovingly into his face. "I promise. Wherever you leave me, I'll be waiting there when you return. Promise me you'll stay safe and return as quickly as possible. I'm so alone without you."

"There's only one thing that can keep me away from you, Blue Eyes, and I plan to overcome it." His mouth closed over hers, and once more he made love to her before allowing slumber to claim them.

When Blane and Shannon were only a day from their destination, trouble struck. Blane left Shannon with Dan while he crept forward to locate the source of the noises reaching his keen ears. Her head having become sore from wearing the heavy plait for many days and nights, Shannon unbraided her hair, retrieved her brush, and sat down to wait for Blane. As her mind relieved their last few nights of passionate lovemaking, she ran her fingers through her hair to separate the strands.

Meanwhile, Blane had discovered a large Rebel encampment being set up for the night. He was astounded by the number of men and weapons before his line of vision. He noticed several cannons and caissons. He edged into a better position to view and count the number of supply wagons and to ascertain their contents. Clearly this unit was preparing for a large assault. But where and when? He eyed the camp through his field glasses. Blane felt he must seek that information to pass along at their next stop. Their next stop . . . Wilmington . . . and Shannon. His body flamed as he envisioned those impending days and nights in her arms. Lovemaking on the trail was hazardous. He was always under a strain to keep his wits sharp while she was driving him wild with hunger and pleasure. To be able to relax completely and place all of his concentration on . . .

He didn't get a chance to move closer. A shout to his

left seized his attention, "Hold there! Present yourself or be shot!"

When the man sent forth a horn blast to summon other guards, Blane tensed. He cursed himself for allowing his attention to stray. Knowing he couldn't bluff free of this situation, he also cursed his recklessness. Rebels would be swarming all over him soon. A flurry of frantic thoughts raced through his astute mind. He and Shannon couldn't escape riding double. Even if he tried running in the other direction, they would search this entire area for hidden missives after his capture or escape. If he left her behind, she would be found and interrogated. Confused and frightened, she might convict herself.

There was only one thing to do. Blane ran toward Shannon's hiding place. Bullets whistled past his head and body. He darted right and left to avoid them. He didn't have much time. He tossed his saddlebags into the thick underbrush to his left. He knew the mingling of their clothes and possessions would inspire doubts. He grabbed the piece of rope dangling over his gun and snatched Shannon around to bind her hands. As he worked, he whispered, "Too many Rebs to fight or flee, love. Pretend you're my hostage. I can get away later. Don't panic and reveal the truth. Meet me in Wilmington."

"This is Sergeant Clayton Phillips of the Confederate Army. Give it up, Yank," a stern voice called through the bushes as they surrounded the couple. "You ain't leaving here alive and free."

Blane backed against a tree and pinned Shannon against him. He placed a knife near her throat and called out, "Keep your distance or this Rebel temptress will die before me! I got me a lady hostage. Let me ride out, and I'll drop her down the road," he offered.

The brawny sergeant commanded, "Let me see her."

"Get an eyeful, 'cause she's dead if you rush me."

A head of black hair and a shoulder clad in gray peered around a large tree. Blane caught her hair and yanked her head backward. Taken by surprise, Shannon squealed and jerked. Blane chuckled wickedly. "Pretty little witch, isn't she? You wanna trade?"

"Who is she?" the man inquired, aware of her beauty and her dangerous position. Enormous blue eyes snared his attention first, then a head of flaming red hair that settled wildly around her shoulders.

"One of your Rebel daughters I captured on the road last night. She wouldn't tell me her name. She's a fiesty little bundle. Didn't know you Rebs grew 'em so pretty and tough. Answer the nice Reb," he commanded, jerking on her hair again.

Shannon cried out before she could prevent it, but she knew what Blane wanted from her. As if petrified, she hurriedly answered, "I'm Shannon Greenleaf. I lived near Wilmington. For months, I've been nursing near Fredericksburg, but President Davis ordered me to come home. It's really bad in that area. Grant and Sheridan are closing in fast on Richmond. I was traveling with three wounded soldiers when we were attacked by thieves or deserters. I got away, but I don't know what happened to the injured men. I kept running, until last night. While I was sleeping, this beast found me and took me prisoner. He stole my horse and he won't release me. Please, you must—"

Blane shouted, "I didn't say give us your life story! She makes for real good protection. She could make for more if I had the time," he alleged, capturing her chin and crushing his mouth down on hers.

Before making contact, Shannon heard him whisper, "Fight me."

She obeyed, struggling fiercely and futilely in his grasp. When his lips left hers, she sneered, "You animal!

My father and brothers will hunt you down and slay you for this offense! Have you no honor or manners, sir? You will die in Dixie, you repulsive rogue!"

"This is war, ma'am; we soldiers gotta take pleasure when and where we find it. Well? You Rebs wanna take this vixen off my hands? Or do I open her gullet and empty it?"

The sergeant licked his dry lips. He didn't know what to do. "I'll have to confer with General Moore. Give me a few minutes." Turning to a soldier next to him, he ordered, "Private Toliver, go explain matters to the general. Bring me his answer quickly." He glanced at Lieutenant Pike and frowned when the younger officer shook his head and scowled.

The private rushed off to carry out his assignment. None of the men doubted that General Richard Moore would allow this ruffian to go free in order to save this beauty's life and to avenge her honor. In less than ten minutes, the private returned with a pale face and wide eyes. He relayed the general's dismaying message.

To Shannon, those minutes were excruciatingly long. She trembled in suspense and dread. One or both of them could die today. She had so much living to do, so much loving. Behind her was the man of her dreams and heart. How could she help them escape?

Blane already knew the climax of this fateful drama, yet he would play along just to keep Shannon close to him a while longer. He was acquainted with the reputation and feelings of General Moore. Realizing what Blane had witnessed, the general would feel there was too much at stake to compromise. Phillips had known the general's answer, too, but wanted the responsibility of Shannon's fate taken out of his hands. Blane wished it might have ended differently for him and Shannon. Dying was a fact of life, especially during war, he knew, but why now, when he had found the right woman? Whatever happened to him, he had to think of Shannon first. He cursed his blunder today. But hadn't he known from the beginning that if he was ever shot or captured, it would have had to do with protecting his partner!

Sergeant Phillips called out ruefully, "I'm sorry, Miss Greenleaf, but we cannot make such a trade. We must not allow this Yankee to get away and endanger our assignment. He's seen too much. I hope you understand this is war, and I must defend the Confederacy and my men before one life. I fear, sir, I must call your bluff."

Shannon's face lost its remaining color. Blane was going to be captured and killed. "You would allow him to slay me before your eyes?" she asked. "I am under the protection of President Davis himself!"

"I am truly sorry, miss, but he must not escape and warn the Yankees. President Davis will understand our dilemma and choice. Sir, if you possess any morals or mercy, release her," Phillips coaxed, wanting it to appear he had done all he could to save the lovely creature.

Shannon was alarmed. How could she live after Blane was shot? "He is a beast, sir. You cannot allow this injustice! Has this war destroyed all honor and conscience? We are the Confederacy, sir."

Blane couldn't afford any perilous interference from Shannon when he surrendered. He whirled her toward him and mumbled, "Shut up so I can think, woman." He landed a stunning blow in just the right place to avoid damage but to render her unconscious. Blane noted the fury on many faces that was prompted by his action. Shannon would be safe. No doubt many soldiers would argue over who was going to escort her into town. At least she knew where to go for help. For the first time, Blane doubted his own survival and prowess.

He locked his impenetrable gaze on Sergeant Phillips. "She spoke accurately; what man or men of honor and breeding would allow such an injustice? Union soldiers are not slayers or violators of innocent women. I will surrender her life and my weapon to the Lieutenant."

Pike stared at him in astonishment and confusion. "Why me, sir?"

"Because your eyes tell me you would be a man of honor and courage if you were in charge. I shall not yield to weaklings or cowards. I request that you be my executioner. Are these terms acceptable?"

Sergeant Phillips fused a dark scarlet at the insult, but wanting this offensive matter settled promptly, he agreed. "Do your duty, Lieutenant Pike." After all, he mused, this bastard would be in his care soon!

Pike walked to where Blane was standing. He held out his hand for the weapon. Blane drilled his gaze into Pike's, then smiled. He passed the knife to the Rebel officer, then shifted his precious burden into the other man's arms. Blane raised his hands and waited.

Sergeant Phillips ordered three men to take Blane into custody. "General Moore will want to question him. Lieutenant, you see to Miss Greenleaf. Perhaps the doctor should examine her injuries."

"I'll see to it, sir." Pike lifted Shannon's limp form in his arms and headed for camp. He had trouble keeping his eyes off her face. He could understand why no man could slay this enchantress.

Shannon awoke to find herself on a cot in a tent. She studied her surroundings, trying to ascertain her situation. The man nearby turned to find her staring at his back. He smiled warmly and came forward.

"I see you're awake, Miss Greenleaf. How do you feel?" the middle-aged man with heavy whiskers inquired kindly.

"What happened?" Shannon probed curiously, rubbing her jaw.

"To our surprise and pleasure, the Yankee surrendered."

Shannon's gaze widened. "He surrendered!" she declared, her astonishment concealing her distress. Of course, what else could he do? If not for her, he could have gotten away. He had been right in Washington; she was a danger and hindrance, and a distraction. She had to find a way to help him!

"He turned you and himself over to Lieutenant Pike. He even requested, or rather demanded, for Pike to carry out his execution."

"Execution!" she echoed. "Surely the general would not hang a man who spared my life when my own side was willing to sacrifice it?"

"Calm yourself, Miss Greenleaf. He will be taken to prison after he's questioned. I noticed a wound still healing on your temple," he stated pointedly to change the unsettling topic.

"When we were attacked on the road, I was shot. It doesn't hurt anymore. I kept it bandaged until I ran out of clean cloths. Will it leave a scar?" she asked, trying to sound feminine and vulnerable.

"Perhaps a very tiny one. Your curls will cover it most of the time. Your jaw will be sore for a few days. You're lucky. No bones or teeth were broken. I cannot imagine a man striking a woman."

"Why not? General Moore ordered my life to be sacrificed. A blow is nothing compared to death, sir," she haughtily informed him.

"I'm sure the general will explain everything. He wishes to see you as soon as you've recovered yourself. Do you feel like talking?"

"I would like to freshen up first. Where's Dan and my belongings?"

"Dan?" the doctor probed.

"My horse. What few clothes I managed to save after

214

our attack are rolled inside my sleeping mat. While traveling, I've been dressing like a man to avoid attention and assault, which failed to help me on two occasions. I would love to bathe and change, if you will kindly help me, sir," she asked, focusing appealing blue eyes on him.

A mellow voice replied from her left, "I will be honored to assist you in any way, Miss Greenleaf. I'm Lieutenant Zachary Pike."

Shannon's attention was drawn to the ruggedly handsome man poised in the opening. His hair was thick and silky, like a mink's pelt. His eyes were golden brown, as warm and soft as fresh taffy. Although not as dark as Blane's, his flesh was tanned. A neat mustache covered the area between compelling lips and a nicely shaped nose. He exuded an air and look of gentility. At last, here was a true Southern gentleman, she mused, as she smiled and thanked him.

"I will fetch your bedroll immediately. I'll have Private Toliver tend your Dan. I'm delighted to find you well and smiling."

"From what I understand, sir, I have you to thank for both conditions. Miss Shannon Greenleaf is in your debt, kind sir."

A charming smile curled one corner of Zachary's mouth and his sherry eyes glowed with fascination and admiration. "When you're ready, Miss Greenleaf, I'll escort you to General Moore's tent. He wishes you to join him for supper and a talk."

Shannon's smile faded. She lifted her chin proudly and defiantly. Tossing her tangled curls over her shoulder, she responded, "Only if you can join us, sir. Otherwise I must refuse the invitations of the man who calmly ordered my demise. After Dan and I have rested, I plan to continue my journey to Wilmington. I would be there now if that Yankee scoundrel hadn't captured me and headed north for Union lines. I daresay, sir, it is frightful to be used as a hostage."

After Zachary delivered her bedroll and fresh water to the tent, he closed the flaps to give her privacy. Shannon placed the bundle on the cot and unrolled it. She was delighted she had put her clean undergarments with her dress. She wished she had been as thoughtful about her slippers and brush, as she couldn't ask Pike to search for the saddlebags. She eyed the sealed tent flaps before hurriedly stripping and washing. After donning the blue gown that Elizabeth Van Lew had given her, Shannon rolled her dirty garments inside the mat.

Taking the wet cloth, she wiped off her boots. When her things were gathered and the tent was straightened, she unlaced the bindings and pushed aside the flaps. Unaware of how sensual and earthy she had appeared when dirty and mussed, she had assumed it would be to her best advantage to assail these men's senses with her femininity and charms. As she noticed the way Zachary's gaze widened and boldly roamed over her face and figure, her confidence and excitement returned.

"You look ravishing, Miss Greenleaf," he complimented her.

Shannon fluttered her lashes and smiled coquettishly. "You are far too kind, sir. I have neither brush nor slippers to complete my grooming. I shall be eternally grateful to return home. Papa warned me that nursing would be perilous and demanding. I fear I was too stubborn to listen and too naïve to understand. I felt it was my duty to aid the Confederacy with my meager talents, however or wherever they were needed." As Zachary took her by the elbow to escort her to General Moore's tent, she asked, "Have you ever met President Davis, sir?"

"I have not had the honor, ma'am. Have you met him?"

Shannon smiled and nodded at the men they met. "I

216

had that pleasure while I was still a child, sir. He and my father fought in the Mexican War together. He was a great hero during that conflict, as he is in this one. He visited our home on several occasions. He used to tug my braids and tease me about these freckles."

Zachary's eyes went to her nose and cheeks. He grinned. "You have very few left, and they are most becoming."

"I visited the President just before I left Richmond to come home. He did not realize his personal letter would not provide the protection and respect that he desired and I needed. But the President is worried these days. The Union forces grow stronger and bolder with each sunrise. They have ample supplies and weapons, while our side barely has enough for defense. More of our men are deserting or changing sides after each battle. I fear the days ahead are dark and deadly, sir."

"Don't worry your pretty head, Miss Greenleaf. We're massing troops and supplies now for a strike at Grant's flank. Once he's caught and squashed between us and Lee, the Union will retreat long enough for us to rest and resupply our units. Our blockade runners are getting through nearly every week now. We've got sympathizers in the North and in Europe. They recognize the injustice of this war. They're sending weapons, food, supplies, and gold to help us."

Shannon beamed falsely. "Oh, sir, that's wonderful. I wish I could sail to England and France to carry out such a valiant mission. How exciting and heroic. Papa would simply die of vexation and fear."

"Where do you live in Wilmington?" he asked politely.

"I don't actually live there, sir," she responded cautiously, just in case he knew the people and area. "Our plantation is just below Atlanta, but President Davis said it was too dangerous to head there. He said

217

Wilmington was one of our safest and strongest ports. He told me to stay with old friends of his, Major Timothy and Annabelle Marlowe. Did you know that Union troops are ravaging the entire area between Nashville and Atlanta? President Davis said those villains are laying waste to anything they cannot carry with them."

"Once we join forces with Lee and finish off Grant, we'll challenge those scoundrels to a battle they'll never forget," he vowed confidently. "Do you have other family?"

Shannon lowered her gaze and inhaled sadly. "I lost a brother at Shiloh, and I have no idea where my other one is. My father is with General Bragg, or was the last time I heard anything. I fear this bloody war will cost us many fathers and brothers. Why couldn't the Northerners leave us alone? President Buchanan said we could secede."

Lieutenant Pike squeezed her arm and encouraged, "It will be over soon, one way or another. Pray for our victory, Miss Greenleaf, or the North will crush us under their boots in defeat."

They arrived at General Moore's tent. Zachary stepped aside for Shannon to enter. She was surprised to find a table set and ready. She looked at the tall man in a clean gray uniform. His probing gaze and controlled expression unnerved her, but it didn't show.

"Miss Greenleaf," he stated, coming forward to greet her. "I'm pleased you could join me for dinner. Pleasures are rare between battles. I was hoping to see you and make amends for your distress."

Shannon held her shoulders stiff and her chin high as she glued her challenging gaze to his piercing one. "I find your treatment of Southern women insulting, sir. Rest assured my family and President Davis will learn of this outrage unless your motives are beyond question."

218

"Rest assured, they are," he countered without flinching.

Shannon's gaze took in his clean-shaven face and wiry physique. His graying hair and wrinkles suggested he was nearing fifty. His lips were thin and his nose was long and straight. His cheekbones stood out prominently above noticeable hollows that met his sharp jawline. He did not appear the least troubled by his lethal order. Nor did his invitation to dinner seem to be an apology for it. His action came from an ingrained habit of showing Southern hospitality.

"Than I shall be forced to accept your word on the matter, sir," she responded, wisely resisting the impulse to demand an explanation. "After all, I am safe, and he was bluffed into a capture. Evidently you know your strategy well and do not hesitate to follow it."

Oddly, General Moore smiled. Her breeding and intelligence pleased and relaxed him, as did her lack of a demand for answers. "I'm sure such an experience was difficult and frightening for you."

Shannon shuddered and sighed dramatically. "Yes, it was, sir."

"Please, be seated," he offered, pulling out a chair for her.

Shannon tucked her skirt and obeyed. "Can you spare one of your men to escort me into Wilmington? I am most anxious to end my journey safely and quickly. I would be most appreciative."

"I'll have Lieutenant Pike do so in the morning," he conceded. As they were served stew and bread and wine, he asked, "Where was this Yankee heading, Miss Greenleaf?"

"I presume for the Union lines, sir. When he seized me and Dan, he mumbled something about us getting him through Fayetteville and Raleigh without any trouble.

219

He didn't talk much, except to tell me to be quiet whenever I pleaded for release." She sipped the red wine. "He was most rude along the way. I daresay his family forgot to teach him any manners or to give him a sense of right and wrong."

"Did he keep you bound all the time?" Zachary inquired angrily.

Her fork halted in midair between bites. Lowering it to her tin plate, Shannon answered, "No, he said that it would look suspicious to anyone we met. He threatened to shoot me or anyone necessary if I shouted a warning. I dared not defy him." Just as she lifted her fork again, she brightened as if recalling a fact. "He did say something about Wilmington being too hot for him, whatever that means. I'm sorry, sir. After that other attack, I was so scared I didn't pay much attention. I didn't realize travel was so hazardous. It would have been less dangerous to continue nursing in Fredericksburg."

Moore chuckled. "That's all right, Miss Greenleaf. Your survival is all that matters." The general watched her for a moment.

Shannon bit her lower lip to hold back her surly retort. She ate quietly and eagerly. "I don't wish to appear ill-mannered by eating so swiftly, sir, but I am literally ravenous." She hoped that would halt his questions for awhile, or perhaps end them all together.

"Then enjoy your meal, and we'll chat later."

"General Moore?" a voice summoned the commander. Moore called out, "Enter."

Private Toliver appeared before the tent and said, "Sir, I need to see you privately. It's urgent." He glanced sheepishly at the redhead who had turned to gaze at him.

Moore's brow furrowed in annoyance, but he rose and joined Toliver outside. Muffled voices mingled excitedly. Within minutes, Moore turned and ordered sternly, "Lieutenant Pike, come along with me. Private Toliver, you stand guard here." To Shannon, he stated crisply, "We'll return shortly. Please continue while the food is warm."

When the two officers were out of sight, Shannon went to Toliver and inquired anxiously, "What's wrong?"

The man shifted nervously and stammered, "The . . . general will handle . . . it, ma'am. You go on and eat."

"Please," Shannon entreated, smiling provocatively at him. "I heard you mention the prisoner. What about him, Private Toliver?"

Though charmed by this beauty and wanting to please her, he eyed the direction Moore and Pike had taken before replying, "Major Phillips has gone wild over there. He was questioning the prisoner. When the Yank refused to talk, Major Phillips started beating him. I knew the general wouldn't be pleased. He don't torture captives before he hangs 'em. Boy, that Yank's a tough one."

Anguish and terror filled Shannon. "What do you mean, before he hangs him? Won't he be sent to prison?"

"Usually we send captured Yanks to holding camps. But we're heading for Petersburg as soon as the other two regiments join us, so we ain't got time or escorts to spare. Moore said he'll have to hang this one. If word got out about our plans, them Yanks would head south and stop us. Phillips wants him to spill his guts afore he swings in the morning. Phillips is real mad 'cause that Yank shamed him. That Yank is something. I've seen his kind before. He won't talk."

Shannon could read respect in Toliver's tone and gaze for Blane's courage. "It's a shame he's a Yankee," she asserted.

"Yes'm, it shore is. We could shore use men like that."

So can I, Shannon agreed in mounting fear. She returned to her seat and completed her meal without appetite. Her mind was spinning with reckless plans. She envisioned Blane's handsome face and virile body all bruised and bloodied. In a camp this size, she couldn't do anything to help Blane. She didn't know her way around or know where her love was being held and beaten. Her love . . . Yes, she did love Major Blane Stevens. What could she say or do to obtain his freedom, or at least ensure his survival? If only Moore would send him to a prison camp; he might stand a chance to escape or to survive there. If only she could persuade one of the men to help her release him. There wasn't enough time to enchant and blindly enslave any of these men. Moore was totally unreachable. Phillips was crazy. Toliver was too weak. That left Pike. What could she offer him for Blane's life?

Chapter Nine

General Moore and Lieutenant Pike returned to the tent to find Shannon finishing her wine. Private Toliver was dismissed and the two Confederate officers joined her at the table. Both seemed to have no trouble with lost appetites or with consuming the remainder of their chilled meals. Neither offered an explanation for their hasty departures.

Shannon decided that feminine curiosity might prompt her to ask, "Is there a problem, sir? We aren't in any danger, are we?"

Moore smiled indulgently and replied, "Nothing to concern yourself about, Miss Greenleaf. Lieutenant Pike, why don't you take Miss Greenleaf for a stroll, then show her to her tent. I'm certain she's exhausted after her rough ordeal. Tomorrow morning you may escort her to Wilmington, but please return promptly."

"Thank you, sir. Your assistance is most generous," Shannon told him, leveling a charming smile on both men. "If I do not see you again, General Moore, God speed the victory to end this war."

"Your family will be proud of your courage and help. I only wish it were safe enough for us to carry along such a brave and lovely nurse."

Shannon smiled and nodded her gratitude. "When I get home, I will do my best to be of service to those in need there. If you meet Andrew or Corbett Greenleaf, please let them know of my location and state of health. Surely they are as worried about me as I am about them. It is so hard for women to remain behind, ignorant of their loved ones' fates. Yet, as I have learned recently, it can be just as difficult to go forth and help them or others. I shall look forward to nights without the sounds of death and destruction tearing into my sleep, and days of not viewing the suffering of our courageous soldiers."

When neither man picked up the conversation, Shannon murmured dispiritedly, "Now I understand what President Davis meant about carrying a heavy burden. It must be an enormous responsibility to order men into battle, knowing so many will never return. Sometimes I wonder if my family will survive this terrible conflict. So many women will be left to face the future alone. It makes one feel so helpless." She dabbed at the false tears she had managed to create.

"Now, now, don't distress yourself, Miss Greenleaf. God willing, victory will soon be ours," the general said to comfort her.

"What if He is not willing, sir?" she inquired dejectedly. "The President seemed so worried, so doubtful, when I saw him. People are losing hope; some are changing sides. The Northern citizens and Union Army have so much, and we have so little."

Moore patted her hand on the table. "You must not lose heart. Our men are brave and daring, determined to win this war."

"Soldiers cannot eat, ride, or shoot courage and determination, sir. If you had seen the misery I have witnessed, you would feel the same. But I am a woman, and a woman is unaccustomed to fighting and killing and sacrificing. Perhaps it strikes me so deeply because I had

224

never viewed or experienced such evils before this war."

"Come, let me clear your mind and soothe your fears with a stroll," Pike entreated. "You are too young to be so unhappy."

Shannon rose as he pulled her chair away. "Good night, sir."

General Moore stood in the opening of his tent, smoking a cigar and watching Shannon depart on Pike's arm. Dusk was approaching swiftly, but that flaming hair and sapphire gown stood out brilliantly against the dry landscape and gray uniforms. After a private cleared his table, he returned to it to make notes about the captured Yankee and the exquisite Southern belle whose fates had clashed briefly. In three days, he would head north with his regiment to challenge his own fate.

As the Rebels prepared for the night, they halted their tasks to admire the beautiful young woman on Lieutenant Pike's arm. News of her recue had worked its way around the camp within minutes. News of Major Phillips's brutal treatment of her captor had also sped around the large area. Some men agreed with his punishment and savage interrogation; others found the harsh actions cruel and unnecessary. What man, Yankee or Rebel, could resist such a tempting treasure found alone on the road? By the same token, what man could slay her to earn his freedom or revenge? After all, it hadn't been proven that the man with a Southern accent was a Yankee spy. They could merely assume that his silence meant guilt.

Shannon appeared to be giving smiles of encouragement and respect to the soldiers, but she was scrutinizing the camp. She mentally tallied the number of cannons and caissons. She tried to count the number of soldiers. She surreptitiously examined the quantity and quality of their supplies and gear. She also studied their mood.

"Tell me, Lieutenant Pike, where do you live?"

225

she coaxed.

"Near Charlotte, ma'am. I come from a large family."

She looked up at him and smiled. "Are you always this short of words, sir?" she playfully teased him. "If you have other matters to attend, I shall understand. You may escort me to my lodgings."

The bewitched soldier quickly assured her he was not bored or needed. As Zachary Pike spoke of his home and family, Shannon tried to look attentive. Yet, she listened only closely enough to obtain facts to continue the conversation, but not enough to distract her from her observation. It was a talent most Southern girls learned early, to display interest in the man at her side during a party while cleverly scouting all available men and the feminine competition in the room. Each time the lieutenant finished a topic, she encouraged him to begin another. She carefully avoided talk about war, the encampment, and their impending assignment. She behaved as if he were a marvelous diversion from their depressing surroundings and the reality of war.

As they approached a tent where a guard was posted, Shannon realized it might be where Blane was being held until morning. She made certain her face and voice did not betray her anguish and fear. As casually as possible, she asked what she felt was not a suspicious or unreasonable question. "What happened to the man who abducted me? Was he a Rebel deserter or a Yankee? Why did he injure me?"

"He is quite harmless now, Miss Greenleaf. Would you care to see for yourself? He will be punished for his vile abuse of you," he remarked coldly, touching the sensitive area on her jaw where a vivid bruise was gradually forming. "No man should mar such beauty."

Shannon flinched and shrieked, "Ouch! It's very sore. Does it look awful?" she questioned as she fingered it lightly.

226

Zachary stopped and turned her to face him. His eyes roamed her face, then settled on the injured area. "You couldn't look awful in any condition or garments. I shall personally make sure that Yank suffers more than you do. Here, see how brave and dangerous he is now." Pike directed her attention to the tent at his right.

In the dim light, Shannon could make out a figure bound to a post. She lifted her chin and strutted into the tent. She halted to Blane's right and glared at him. His face revealed several bruises and cuts. Blood had dried around several injures; two were still moist with red liquid. One eye would surely turn blackish blue by dawn. His lower lip was split and swollen at the left corner. His nose didn't appear broken, but it had bled profusely at one point. That beast Phillips had allowed the blood to flow over Blane's mouth, down his chin, then drop to his shirt and chest. Shannon was appalled.

"I see you've made a start on his punishment," she remarked as if unmoved by her foe's pain and condition. "Before I became a nurse, such a sight would have sickened and distressed me. But I have seen men without eyes or arms or legs, men whose blood flowed redder and swifter than this despicable brute's, men who were not guilty of his evil deeds. I hope you make certain he cannot harm another woman."

Shannon had prepared for such an opportunity. While she was alone in Moore's tent, she had removed her knife from her boot sheath and had slipped it into her dress pocket. She mentally thanked Elizabeth for the deep pockets and Hawke for the knife sheath and the Rebs for not searching her and Blane for discarding her slippers. She recalled Hawke saying that one never knew when a hidden weapon would come in handy.

She stepped closer to scoff in Blane's face, "I told you you would be sorry for mistreating me and trying to steal my horse." As she removed the knife from her pocket

227

and carefully placed it in the correct position in Blane's hands, she punched him in the stomach to obscure her action and declared, "That's for striking me in the face! I would return your blow in kind, but I do not wish to have your blood on my hands and gown. Were my father here, he would thrash you soundly. Next time, perhaps you will think twice before kidnapping and abusing a lady."

Blane's fingers wrapped securely around the handle of the knife she had passed to him. He glared at Shannon with narrowed eyes, causing the creases near them to deepen. His hair was tousled from the forceful blows to his face, and his ribs ached from those delivered to that unprotected area. On one hand, he was furious with her for taking such risks; on the other hand, he was pleased by her conduct. "If I ever meet a Southern *lady*, I'll try to recall your warning, Miss Greenleaf, wasn't it? I should have taught you some manners while I had you, seeing as your family failed to do so. Next time, perhaps you will think twice before running around the countryside alone, enticing defenseless men. You're the one who needs a good thrashing. I was a fool to give in and release you. Your pretty hide isn't worth mine." His hazel eyes swept over Shannon's face and body insultingly, then relaxed into appreciative lines. He grinned devilishly with some effort, ignoring the pain from his injuries. "Maybe I should have taken the time to toss you on your back; then I wouldn't be here right now. Or at least I'd have died a happy man."

"O-o-o-oh," Shannon spit out angrily, delighted for the first time to feel a hot blush flooding her cheeks. "You are a vile beast, sir, and I hope they beat you morning, noon, and night!" She whirled in a huff and stalked outside. "Which way is my tent, Zachary?" she asked hastily to prevent the man from lingering with Blane. "Clearly this brute has not learned a lesson. Yanks are so crude and arrogant."

Pike joined her promptly and Shannon immediately asked about Dan. Even though Pike assured her the animal was fine, she insisted on seeing for herself. "I've had him since I was sixteen. General Moore wouldn't confiscate Dan, would he?" she asked worriedly, cleverly lacing her voice with deep affection for the sleek animal.

"Certainly not. You'll need him to get to Wilmington. I hope that disgusting Yank didn't offend you. I should not have allowed you to see him. I never imagined he would behave so crudely."

"During the past two years, I've seen and met all kinds of men, Lieutenant Pike. Usually I don't allow their words and behavior to bother me. I suppose seeing a man who has treated me so wickedly is different. I shouldn't have punched him or exchanged insults with him. To conduct oneself in such a manner lowers one to the same level. I must apologize for my childish behavior. He just made me so angry."

Dan was familiar with Shannon's voice and touch, and he responded to them as she stroked his neck and spoke affectionately to him. She smiled at the guard and her escort. "I can see he's fine. Thanks." As they turned to leave, Shannon noticed Blane's saddle nearby.

Pike walked her to the tent to which she had been assigned. Then he squeezed her hand and told her he would see her in the morning. She could tell he was delighted by the prospect of escorting her into town. When Shannon was inside the tent, she sank to the cot and sighed heavily. At least Blane had a chance for escape, if no one discovered the knife before he could sever his bonds. If someone did, she would be in terrible trouble. If Blane got free, surely he would come here and let her know before he fled camp, if he could find her.

Without undressing, Shannon stretched out on the cot. Time passed. The tent was stuffy, and she was restless. Where were the cool October breezes? By midnight, the camp was still and silent. She couldn't relax or fall asleep. What if Blane had dropped the knife? What if he was injured badly? What if he couldn't get to or past the guard? What if she had exposed herself? She recalled the words about having no time to transfer or keep prisoners. Hanged . . .

Shannon knew her way around the camp. Blane might need her to lead him to Dan. Besides, she was concerned about staying here after his escape. She jumped up and paced the small, dim area. Impulsively, she crept outside and headed toward the tent where Blane was being held prisoner. Her eyes darted around as she stealthily made progress. She knew which areas to avoid from her stroll with Pike. As a twig snapped beneath her boot, she halted and removed them, leaving them behind. She was glad her steps were not hindered by multiple petticoats, but she wished she had thought to change into her pants and shirt. She dared not return to the tent, for her courage was gradually diminishing as time went on. Aware of every sound, she almost held her breath. She was thankful her dress and hair blended into the shadows, and she wisely avoided open, moonlit spaces as much as possible.

As she reached the prisoner tent, she noticed there was no guard posted. Her heart raced wildly and frantically. His absence could mean only one thing: Blane had escaped. What to do? She was near the center of camp, between her tent and the beckoning corral. She couldn't risk retrieving her boots and clothes, nor could she chance returning to her tent, then playing the innocent in the morning when Blane's escape was discovered.

An arm banded her body and a hand clamped over her mouth, stifling her instinctive scream. As she shifted her eyes to their corners, she noticed a gray sleeve. She had been caught, exposed as Blane's accomplice instead of his victim. There was no use in struggling or protesting. The

230

moment the alert was sounded, escape would be impossible. But if she could work her charms on this Rebel, at least Blane might have a chance to get away. Surely the Confederates wouldn't hang a nineteen-year-old woman. Undoubtedly her new captor was Zachary Pike! Perhaps she would be forced to pay for Blane's life after all . . .

Blane's voice whispered in her ear, "It's me, Flame. Relax."

Shannon nearly fainted from relief and tension.

He warned, "Be quiet until we're out of here."

Taking her by the hand, he started moving off to their left. Shannon shook their clasped hands to get his attention. When he bent forward, she whispered in his ear, "The corral is to the right. Dan and your saddle are there. Guards are posted at every corner. Follow me," she suggested, hoping he wouldn't mind her lead and advice.

At the last tree before reaching the corral, Shannon halted and motioned to where the nearest guard would be standing. Blane told her to stay hidden while he disposed of the sentry. When all was clear, he would give the bird whistle he had taught her during their journey. As Shannon grabbed his arm and stared at him in panic, he reminded her of his stolen uniform, which would dupe the guards until it was too late for action. He cuffed her chin and smiled.

Shannon watched Blane swagger across the moonlit area between the tents and the large corral. She leaned against the tree and prayed for his swift success. Ten minutes crept by as her nerves tingled with apprehension. Shannon had closed her eyes to say another prayer, when the signal from Blane sounded in her ear. She smiled and straightened.

"You shouldn't be out here alone, Miss Greenleaf," Pike's voice gently scolded her. "It's a mite chilly and you don't have a wrap."

Shannon cringed in alarm, then quickly found her wits. She smiled at him and stretched her limbs sensuously. "I couldn't sleep. Too much excitement today and tension tonight. I went to visit with Dan again; he makes me feel close to home. It's so muggy and uncomfortable. Do you think it's going to rain? Storms always make me restless."

"I think it has to do with being near so many swampy areas. Of course, it does rain here about a fourth to a third of the year. It's late. Why don't I walk you back to your tent?" he offered.

"The breeze is so nice out here; I'd like to enjoy it a while longer. Your camp is well guarded, so I'm perfectly safe, Lieutenant. I'm not doing anything wrong by being here, am I?"

"No, but it isn't truly safe for a woman so beautiful to be left unattended around so many susceptible men. Does your jaw hurt?"

Shannon forced herself not to flinch when he gently caressed the bruised area. "You are a very kind and sensitive man, Lieutenant."

"From the first moment I saw you being held captive in that man's arms, you warmed my heart and soul, Miss Greenleaf. I wish there was more time for us to become acquainted. Perhaps after the war has ended, I might call on you?" he inquired hopefully.

"I would consider it an honor, sir." Shannon did not want to appear edgy or forward, but she didn't know how to handle this situation. This was not the time or place to be coy or aloof. She thought it best to observe his behavior, then respond instinctively.

Bewitched by Shannon, Lieutenant Pike was not about to leave her standing there alone. His body was inflamed by desire. It was war, and perhaps he would never see her again. If only he could taste her compelling lips and

232

embrace her just once. As she watched him with her hypnotic eyes, Pike was drawn to her. He slowly leaned forward, fearing she would reject him, hoping she would not. His mouth brushed hers tentatively. When she did not pull away, his arms eased around her and his lips claimed hers fully. He kissed her eyes, her nose, her cheeks. He murmured before taking her lips again, "Shannon, my angel, you tempt a man to sheer folly. What must I offer for your promise of marriage?" he inquired shockingly.

Shannon wasn't certain if she should yield briefly to distract Pike during Blane's escape or allow Pike's captivation to increase to aid her protection once Blane's flight was uncovered. Whatever happened, she could use Pike's assistance and support. Shannon returned the kiss and leaned against Pike's chest. She heard him moan softly and felt his embrace tighten. As his kisses waxed feverish and his caresses became bold, she responded deceitfully even as she panicked.

A thud and a grunt sounded in her ears just as Pike fell against her. As he was lowered to the ground, Shannon saw Blane's scowling face behind him. She was not given time to react. Blane hurriedly bound and gagged Pike with items of his clothing. Shannon prayed the lieutenant wasn't injured.

Blane seized her hand and yanked her ear to his mouth. "I hate to interrupt, but let's get the hell out of here. Keep quiet. Walk leisurely in case someone notices us. Maybe I'll pass for your admirer."

Shannon followed Blane to where two horses were saddled and waiting. Besides a second horse and saddle, he had stolen two Confederate haversacks, blankets, two bedrolls, two jackets, and several weapons. He helped her mount before swinging agilely into his saddle. Shannon tucked her skirt beneath her and followed Blane's lead.

They walked the horses a short distance from camp.

Blane held up his hand to halt their movements and Shannon tensed. Blane motioned for her to wait there. He dismounted and slipped into the trees. Shannon trembled, recalling the last time she had been left behind to wait. She heard voices; the guards were talking and laughing while on duty! That's what had caught Blane's keen ear. He would overcome them easily and quickly. Surely fate would be on their side tonight.

The noises ceased. Soon, a grinning Blane returned and mounted. "All clear," he whispered smugly. "But stay alert," he added.

When Blane felt they were a safe distance from camp, he nudged Dan into a swift gallop. Shannon did the same with her mount. They traveled rapidly for hours, having no choice but to remain on the road because of the heavy underbrush and marshy landscape. Just before dawn, Blane took a side road. They traveled another hour, then halted at an abandoned home, the elegance of which had suffered from a lack of attention and heavy looting.

"No time to explain. Wait here. I'll return soon," Blane called over his shoulder, then headed into the woods.

Shannon did as she was ordered but mentally questioned his actions. She glanced around, dismayed by the spoiled beauty of this setting. Paint was cracking or missing on the walls of the two-story mansion. Windows were filthy or broken, and doors were falling off their hinges. From what she could see, drapes and furniture had been removed, probably stolen or sold. A small balcony over the front entrance hung perilously in a futile attempt to retain its grip on the house. Faded shutters swagged at haphazard angles. This house, which had surely known grand and happy times, was a pathetic sight today.

The yards were cluttered with weeds and overgrowth. Untrimmed bushes sprouted limbs in every direction.

Rose and camellia bushes were being slowly strangled. One barn had been burned—long ago from its appearance. Other structures exposed the same kind of disrepair and abandonment as the house. She wondered what evil had befallen the owners of the house to drive them away and to keep them away.

She could see or hear nothing that indicated human or animal life nearby, and she wondered why they were stopping here. Surely their escape had been discovered by now. Right this minute, a furious unit of Rebel soldiers would be tracking them. Why was Blane wasting such valuable time here? This dilapidated place depressed her.

Blane appeared with another man at his side, carrying a shovel. They joined Shannon. Without words, the two men hurriedly unsaddled the horses. Blane went to the end of the porch and began digging up several bushes. When they were set aside, he pulled on the latticed covering at the base of the porch and removed it. He lifted the saddles one at a time, ducked, entered the opening, and returned empty-handed. The other man drew a bucket of water from the well and handed it to Blane. Shannon watched in confusion and silence, not wishing to slow or distract them.

"Get in, Flame," he commanded, pointing to the opening.

"In there? With spiders and Lord knows what else?" she argued.

"We don't have much time! Do as I say, woman!" he shouted harshly and impatiently. "Those Rebs will be tearing this country apart looking for us. We've got to stay hidden until they pull out."

Shannon turned to look at the other man. Blane grabbed her arm and nearly flung her beneath the porch. He ignored her squeal of protest and surprise. "You know what to do, Jeremy." With those words, Blane joined her in the shadowy area and sat down.

The man called Jeremy nailed the latticed section in place, then replanted the bushes. He carefully removed all signs of disturbance. He called out, "Good luck, sir," then vanished with the horses.

Shannon listened as the trotting of hooves gradually subsided and all was quiet outside. As her eyes steadily adjusted to the amount of light present, she became frightened of being trapped here, by soldiers and time. She anxiously glanced around, astonished to find the dirt area clean. The saddles, weapons, and gear had been placed near the middle of this raked section. The wall beneath the house was solid brick. Under the porch section, decorative lattice work separated solid wood portions. There were just enough openings in the crisscrossed design to allow sufficient air and light to enter their new refuge. The abundance of overgrowth around the porch concealed their location without denying the needed air. The area under the steps had been boarded, sealing them in securely. Shannon could smell damp earth, but the odor was not offensive. "Wouldn't it have been better to keep riding? We had a good lead. How long must we stay here?" she asked nervously.

Blane was sitting Indian-style on an oilcloth groundsheet. His expression told her he wasn't in the least worried about their safety or predicament. He took two swigs from a stolen bottle of whiskey, then grinned at her. "This is the last move they'd expect us to make. Might as well relax, Flame. We'll stay here at least four, five, or six days. We can use the rest while they run themselves ragged. Want a sip to warm your bones?" He held out the bottle. Knowing how frightened she probably was, he was attempting to sound light and casual.

Shannon stared at him, then wrinkled her nose.

"Whiskey at nine in the morning? No thanks." She scanned their surroundings once more. "What about food and water? And spiders," she murmured.

"Look over there," he instructed, pointing to a stack of cans and the bucket of fresh water. "Jeremy steals things and leaves them here for such occasions. He's taking the horses miles down the road and hiding them in an old barn. Even if they're found, no one will think to search here. To be on the safe side, Jeremy won't come around until the Rebel camp is dismantled and they move northward. Just don't panic if those Rebs come snooping around," he commanded, his words sounding like deep growls in his throat.

Shannon wondered if Blane was as confident as he tried to sound and look. He had recently faced death and a beating; surely that had to affect a man, even someone as powerful and dauntless as Blane Stevens. Sitting on folded legs with her buttocks resting on her feet, she looked at the dirty gown and at her scuffed hands. She brushed them off against each other, then fluffed the dress. She eyed the ceiling and realized its height would allow her to stand and move around without slumping. Moreover, if there were spider webs there, she would be a comforting distance from them. The idea of being cooped up like this for days with this arresting yet often exasperating man was both unsettling and stimulating. He hadn't even hugged her or kissed her or thanked her!

Blane watched her and chuckled. He was intrigued by this complex vixen. "Are you really this afraid of fuzzy creatures with long legs?" he teased, taking another drink from the bottle. His body was stiff and achy, and he didn't want her to realize how much he hurt.

"I can't help it. Snakes and bugs don't bother me at all, just spiders. I suppose you aren't afraid of anything," she scoffed.

"I suppose you're right," he mirthfully agreed.

"'Course I don't care too much for brutal lickings or dying. Or fickle women."

Shannon grasped his meaning. "What else was I supposed to do, raise a commotion by slapping his face or shrieking insults at him? Since he had me cornered, I figured the least I could do was distract him while my partner escaped, or generously returned to rescue me—for which I deeply thank you, sir. Would you mind explaining what happened after you clobbered me for no logical reason? I didn't want to be too inquisitive with my gracious hosts. By the way, thanks for not breaking my jaw or teeth. I hope that tap was intentionally light."

Blane laughed, and the sound was mellow and rich. He had washed the blood from his face, but bruises and swelling were visible. He removed his boots and jacket, then unfastened several of his shirt buttons. He pulled his saddle over, stretched out, and propped his head on it. After he calmly related the details of the grueling episode, he told her, "I think I'll catch a nap. Didn't get much sleep last night. If you're still restless, why don't you entertain yourself by going through those haversacks and saddlebags. Might be something useful in them." He flexed his lithe body and closed his eyes.

"I need to doctor your injuries. They must be hurting. I'll look for some medical supplies. You can stay awake a while longer."

"I've had worse, and they can wait. I'll need my energy and strength when Lieutenant Pike comes charging after you. The way you stirred his blood, it won't settle down until he finds you. That was some show you put on in the prisoner tent. I wonder if Pike realized you were flirting outrageously with your handsome captor?"

Sometimes he was the most infuriating, arrogant male she had ever met. "Don't make fun of me, you beast. I've proven my courage and obedience. You were the one who

238

put on a show in the tent. How could you make such naughty remarks? I was mortified. If I hadn't been afraid they would be suspicious of me after your escape, I would have been tempted to stay behind to be rid of you and your overbearing manner. If you don't want help, just go to sleep and leave me alone."

She moved over to where Blane had dropped everything. Lifting one haversack, she dumped the contents into her lap. She turned her head and frowned at him when he said, "There's a shirt and pants in one of those bags. Before I stripped him, I noticed that the sentry looked about your size. Might be more comfortable than that billowy gown. What happened to your boots and slippers?" His position didn't change, nor did his eyes open.

Did the man notice everything? "I thought it might look somewhat odd to be carrying my bedroll around during a stroll, so I left it in the tent. As for my boots, they were making too much noise while I was sneaking over to see if you needed any help, so I removed them. I doubted anyone I met along the way would realize I was barefoot."

"Me too. They would be too busy staring at that ravishing face and body. You didn't waste any time twisting Pike around your finger. He'll be twice as mad about your treachery and guile. I bet he's stalking you right now." Blane chuckled softly.

"Since I helped you avoid a hanging this morning, surely I can depend on you to make certain he doesn't get his eager hands on me," she retorted. "Now be quiet and go to sleep before I punch you again."

"That was real effective, but it smarts on broken ribs. To get such punishment, I must have upset those Rebs by treating you so roughly."

Shannon corrected, "What upset the Rebs, or more accurately Major Phillips, was your spying on their camp

239

and refusing to give him information. It didn't help any that you humiliated him during your capture. Are you sure you're all right, Blane? I am sorry if I hurt you, but I had to do something to get close to you."

"I thought you didn't ask any questions. How did you obtain so many facts?" he queried, rolling to his stomach and looking at her.

"Men have a way of carelessly dropping information when their thoughts are on other matters. Perhaps you should remember that when you share a pillow with a woman. Need I remind you, there is a nice way to ask me what I learned back there. Just because you were forced to surrender to save my life, you don't have to take it out on me."

"Flame, would you kindly tell me what you saw and heard while I was being tortured?" he asked in an almost caressing tone.

Shannon flashed him an annoyed smirk, but she related all she could remember. "Why didn't you get away when they spotted you?" she asked.

Blane was amazed by her sharp wits and keen memory. "I was surrounded. It seemed wisest to surrender until my clever partner could think of some way to get us out of our predicament."

"What if they hadn't fallen for your little ruse? What if I had been placed under guard? You could have been killed." Shannon knew Blane was hiding the truth; he could have fled without helping her. Why hadn't he? He had warned on several occasions that he would leave her behind if she became a threat or hindrance.

"I knew they would be stunned by your looks and charms. I had no doubt you would be safe. But in all honesty, I was surprised you took such a risk to save my hide. Frankly, our escape was almost too simple," he murmured retrospectively. Shannon did have a curious way of getting into and out of peril. Had he been allowed to escape? Had Shannon been open and honest with him? She couldn't possibly be a Rebel spy with him as her assignment, could she? No, Fate had merely been on their side.

"Simple?" she echoed skeptically. "At any moment we could have been seen and shot." Borrowing his strangely voiced words, she stated, "I was surprised you took such a risk to return for me when Pike blocked my departure. I would imagine you are exasperated with me by now."

"I owed you, Flame, just like you owed me. Now we're even."

Shannon glanced at him. She was puzzled by his tone and look. "Are we?" she probed. No, he was still miffed at her. Why?

"What's in the bags?" he asked, noticeably altering their trains of thought and conversation.

Shannon fingered the items in the first haversack. "A razor, whetstone, cloth, soap, comb, jackknife, sewing kit, Bible, change purse with seventy cents, matches, writing supplies, a mess kit, and two bank notes for ten dollars each. The second one has much the same," she continued, having seen such belongings in the possession of most soldiers she had encountered. The essential needs were always a mess kit with cup, plate, fork, knife, spoon, and the sewing kit with buttons, needles, and thread. "He was carrying a pipe and tobacco if you care for a smoke. Let's see," she murmured, holding up one item after another. "A match safe, candle holder and candle, a mirror—oh . . . and a pen and ink and fancy writing paper. He must have a sweetheart somewhere. Ah, yes, here she is. A pretty thing," she remarked, holding up the small portrait.

Blane laughed heartily. "If that's his woman, no wonder he went off to war. I'd rather face a gun than marriage to her any day."

"That's mean, Blane Stevens." Shannon lifted the

cartridge box and peeked inside. The tin insert was filled with bullets. She examined the weapons. "At least we can defend ourselves," she commented.

"Those are two reasons why Georgia is so important to the Rebs. That rifle is made in Athens by the Cook & Brother Company. It's one of the finest rifles in use now. Take that pistol; it's made of iron rather than steel, since the South is lacking in that commodity. It comes from Spiller & Burr in Macon. The breech is covered with a brass frame to prevent the barrel from splitting when it's fired."

When Blane continued to watch her, she began trembling with longing. She looked at the item in her hand. "This sounds awful, Blane, but what keeps a bayonet in place when it's driven into a man's body and withdrawn?" she asked, eyeing the long, sharp weapon.

"It attaches securely to the end of a .58-caliber rifle. Once it's shoved into place on the barrel, normal flesh doesn't dislodge it."

She shuddered in revulsion and slipped the bayonet into its scabbard. He had plenty of cartridges and two large knives. She recalled the one he had placed at her throat during their first meeting. She looked inside the saddlebags. She found two shirts, a pair of pants, socks, a "butternut" jacket, long underwear, and a vest. She knew they would come in handy, as winter wasn't far away.

"Blane, what will we do when winter comes?" she inquired. When he didn't answer, she looked over at him. His eyes were closed and he was breathing evenly. Shannon observed the fascinating man. She was so glad he was alive and with her at this moment. Could she ever make him care deeply for her? For now, he was enduring her presence and making use of her. But what about later, when the war ended. She thought about the times they had made love and wondered how he viewed them. Had

242

he felt more than simple enjoyment?

She quietly replaced the items and weapons. Taking an extra blanket, she spread it out and lay down. There was nothing else to do, and she was tired. A surge of loneliness and anguish shot through her. Grief joined those plaguing emotions. She had tried to close out thoughts of her family and home. But this location had brought them all back. She remembered hiding beneath the porch with Hawke long ago. Now he was gone, and her father was gone, and Temple was gone, and perhaps Corry was gone. Why? This wasn't their war, their problems.

Shannon did not realize she was weeping softly until Blane pulled her into his arms and asked tenderly, "What's wrong, Blue Eyes?"

"Will it ever be over, Blane? What will happen to us?" she asked, crying against his chest.

"The past is never over, love; it always controls or influences the present and future," he told her, hugging her tightly to him. "But if we're lucky, we'll survive and be able to start over again. Get some sleep. You'll feel better afterward." Blane wanted to make love to her, but he knew they both needed rest. Their minds and bodies were exhausted. He was damn lucky Phillips hadn't broken anything, but he was stiff and sore. "You saved my life, Shannon, and I'm grateful. Don't blame yourself for me getting injured back there."

That was the problem; Shannon did blame herself. "If we get out of this alive, Blane, and reach Wilmington, I think we should part company," she unthinkingly suggested.

Blane lifted his head and gazed down at her. "Why?"

Watery blue eyes focused on him. Her solemn gaze scanned his injuries. His lower lip was swollen, with a reddish blue split near one corner. One eye was darkened, with another small cut beside it. Several

243

bruises were visible on his cheekbones, which would discolor even more with time. His nose was still slightly red. She cleared her throat and speculated, "Next time, I could get you killed. I'm too inexperienced and unskilled, Blane. We both know I'm a danger to you and your missions. Without me hanging around your neck, you could move around more quickly and safely. I know you turned yourself in yesterday to protect me. And if you weren't so damn stubborn and proud, you would admit it. Look at your face. Phillips could have killed you. Did they tell you they were planning to hang you this morning?"

He was moved by Shannon's concern and anguish. Maybe he was crazy to keep her around, but not for the reason she was suggesting. He was being selfish, placing her life in constant peril. He had used up most of the excuses for keeping her with him, all except one. The fact hadn't changed that if he left her somewhere, anywhere, her life would still be in danger. By now, too many Rebels knew about the Flame.

As he caressed her cheek, Blane asked himself if he was falling in love with her. There was no doubt he possessed enormous desire for her, deep affection, and respect; and he didn't mind her infringing on his time and privacy. She was invigorating, charming, comforting—and yes, distracting and endangering. He couldn't bear the thought of anything happening to Shannon. Blane pulled her tightly against him as he stroked her hair and back. He recalled telling Ellie that it was impossible to fall in love with someone so quickly after their first meeting. He had tried to convince Ellie that her feelings for Corry were simply physical desire. Could Shannon beguile him and desert him, as her brother had done to Ellie? If not for the war and her perilous situation, would she have looked at him twice? Would she be sharing passion with him right now? Could he hold her loyalty and affection if the war ended today? If Hawke suddenly returned?

During his silent reverie, Shannon had regained control of herself. Now she entreated, "You know I'm right, Blane. This was a crazy idea from the start. I don't belong here. It didn't seem this dangerous and hard when I was planning it. I can see why you battled Silas and President Lincoln about my coming along; you knew I couldn't succeed. You knew I'd be a threat to you and the Union. All of those times when we got into trouble, you could have extricated yourself in a flicker if I hadn't been weighing you down. The best thing I can do is go home."

"All right, we'll separate in Wilmington," Blane agreed, noticing the crushing effect his words had on Shannon. He continued, "Until I complete my assignment. Then we head for Charleston as planned. I've gotten used to having you around, Blue Eyes. You've saved my life two times, and you constantly save my sanity." He pushed straying curls from her pale face and smiled. "Don't be so hard on yourself. You're learning fast. What happened to all that spunk and determination?"

"I lost them when I saw you sacrificing your life for mine."

"You worry too much. I've gotten out of worse predicaments. Don't you see, Flame; Fate put you there to rescue me. Are you sorry you came along? Sorry you're stuck with me as a partner?" he teased, tugging on a lock of coppery hair.

"Never. But you should feel that way," she declared sincerely.

"Why should I? I kind of enjoy the extra benefits of having you as my partner. Lincoln could never reward me as you do. I wouldn't want you anywhere but right here. I'll grant you a few weeks' rest from me in Wilmington, but that's all. This war has been long and hard. It drains a man. I need you to keep me living and feeling. I need you to keep me going and pushing." He nuzzled her neck and made her laugh. "Make love to me, Flame," he coaxed, suddenly needing her fiercely. He wanted to see, feel, and experience her total surrender. He wanted her to think of nothing and no one but him. He needed to read a matching desire in her eyes, to witness her utter abandon in his arms, to prove his hold over her emotions.

Shannon lifted her head and gazed into his greenish brown eyes. "Here?" she questioned, glancing around them. "What if the soldiers come? Or Jeremy returns? Or another agent arrives?" She glanced at the many small openings in the latticework. "We have no privacy," she argued, even as her heart began to beat wildly and her body warmed.

"I'll keep one eye and ear open for intruders. I want you, Shannon. I need to feel you next to me, as close as possible. Life can end so swiftly. I need to know you're mine. Let's prove we're still alive, prove we're together and nothing else matters."

"But you're hurt, Blane," she reminded him hoarsely. She tentatively touched his cheek and mouth. "I'm to blame for this."

He captured her hand and kissed each fingertip. He guided it to his swollen manhood. "This is the only thing you're to blame for, love, and it hurts far more than a few cuts and bruises. Right now, you're the only thing that matters to me. I need to be held tightly in your arms. I need to be a part of you, Shannon, a part that no one else has known. I need you to feel the same way."

"I do feel the same way, Blane," she confessed shamelessly.

Blane smiled and kissed her nose. He rose to a hunched position, reached for the oilcloth, and withdrew his knife. He made several holes along one side, then suspended it from nails along a center porch beam. "If anyone does peek in, they won't see anything. This area is too long, and that dark backdrop will prevent any silhouettes from showing against the light at the far end." Blane didn't say that making love on an oilcloth could be noisy. He spread two blankets on the ground and made certain everything was out of their reach, that there was nothing to touch that could make alerting sounds if intruders arrived. Blane expected they would sometime today. Having taken all of the precautions he could, he stripped off his pants and lay down. Rolling to his side and propping his jaw on a balled fist, he looked at Shannon.

The morning sun had vanished behind swiftly gathering storm clouds, concealing much of their light. Between the suspended oilcloth and the heavy foliage around their end of the porch, the area was very dim, but not enough so that he could not see her face. She was sitting on the edge of the blanket with her legs folded beneath her. She looked apprehensive, shy, afraid. To her, this setting was intimidating rather than romantic. "Are you all right, Shannon? If this bothers—"

Shannon bent forward and lightly placed her hand over his mouth to silence him. Making love in a secret place where they could be discovered and entrapped by enemies at any moment was frightening. But although she had not yet become adjusted to this kind of total intimacy between them, she craved him fiercely, so she battled her apprehensions.

Blane understood her insecurities and fears. He gently pulled her hand from his lips. "If this troubles you, Shannon, we don't have to make love here and now." He sat up and pulled her head to his chest, wanting to show her that his feelings went deeper than mere physical desire. He dropped kisses on her forehead and hair. "I want to make love, Shannon, but I won't be angry if you don't feel the same."

Shannon lifted her head and peered into the ever-increasing dimness to meet his sensitive gaze. Her fingertips gently brushed over his bronzed face with its bold display of concern for her. She had almost lost him forever. He was so perceptive and understanding.

Leisurely and unknowingly, her fingers began to drift over his shoulders and arms. She pressed him to his back on the blankets. Her palms sensuously wandered over his chest and shoulders, as she relished the feel of his skin and inhaled his manly scent. The light had diminished even more during the last few moments, but she didn't need sight to enjoy his splendid physique. She opened her mind and pores to pure sensation. To think of making carefree love beneath this dark porch while numerous enemies were frantically searching for them now seemed exciting and tantalizing. It was like showing contempt for danger and death. It provided her with a heady sense of power and stimulation. It made her feel erotic and earthy. Amid countless perils, they were halting to fuse their bodies and spirits savagely and blissfully. They were encased in their own private haven where they could do or say whatever they pleased. Her body tingled. Was this impetuous? Daring? Audacious? Yes!

Shannon leaned back and unbuttoned her dress. She was aware of Blane's intense gaze and erratic breathing as she slipped it over her shoulders and dropped it beside the blanket. She unlaced her chemise and removed it, then her bloomers. She tossed them on the discarded gown. She unbraided her hair and shook it free, allowing it to settle in carefree abandon over her ivory shoulders and supple breasts. Then she bent forward and kissed the right side of his mouth. Her tongue carefully roamed his lips and danced wildly with his. "The only thing I feel, Blane, is desire for you. I want you with every part of me."

248

Blane rolled Shannon to her back. Her hair fanned out around her head, enticing Blane's fingers to rush into it and savor its silky texture. He tried to kiss every spot on her face. His mouth took hers hungrily and he ignored the discomfort of his lower lip. Then his mouth roamed down her creamy neck, assailing every inch of it. She squirmed and giggled when he playfully ravished her ears, his warm breath and rich laughter inflaming her. His mouth captured one breast point and greedily tormented it with kisses and gentle bites. His tongue flickered over it and around it, mischievously teasing its taut peak, then moving to the other to repeat his stirring actions.

Shannon writhed on the blanket, closing her eyes and opening her senses to experience exquisite pleasure and rapturous torment. Blane's lips played over her ribs and attacked her navel. There, his tongue tickled her and caused her to squirm and laugh. His mouth fastened to her breast as his hand stroked over her abdomen and entered a red patch of fuzzy hair. When his finger made contact with the throbbing peak, she moaned and grasped his head to pull it closer to her entreating breast. He stimulated the aching bud until it burst into full bloom and she was quivering and thrashing with unsuppressed need.

Blane moved between her thighs and looked down into her flushed face, which was barely visible in the waning light. He savored the look in her blue eyes and the way her body arched upward, pleading for his. He smiled roguishly and lowered his mouth to hers, sealing their lips tightly. His hard shaft tenderly plunged into her receptive womanhood. With slow deliberation, he thrust back and forth and from side to side with blissful expertise. He entered her deeply, until their groins touched, then he softly and seductively ground himself against her, tantalizing the susceptible bud once more.

Shannon moaned and writhed as she was engulfed by passion's flames.

A thundering noise seized their attention. Both knew it was not a warning from the impending storm. A gasp of fear and panic left her lips as her head jerked toward the latticework section to her left. Blane read sheer terror in Shannon's eyes. When her pale face turned upward, her probing gaze seemed to be questioning their fate. Then Blane's palms covered her ears to block out all reality as he continued to make love to her.

Chapter Ten

It had taken Zachary Pike several hours to revive after Blane's attack, to study this rankling development, to make plans to rescue the Southern beauty and to recapture the daring prisoner, and to ride off after them. Without disturbing General Moore's slumber, Pike had ordered squads of three men each to search east, west, and north of their camp. He had led his seven-man unit southward, feeling certain that it was the right direction. Pike had hoped to overtake them within an hour or two, for he had not expected the fleeing man to travel rapidly with a delicate female, whether she was his prisoner or not.

Pike wanted answers to some very distressing questions. Had the mysterious man whom they had captured yesterday kidnapped Shannon again? Or had the handsome rogue beguiled that delicate lady into aiding him? Pike could understand if Shannon was confused and angered, even enchanted. The Confederate soldiers had been willing to sacrifice her to take her abductor captive. Yet her captor had surrendered to his enemies rather than slay her or endanger her life. Shannon had observed the brutal treatment that chivalrous man had received, and perhaps she considered herself partly to

251

blame. After all, Moore had not explained either the man's beating or his willingness to let her be killed.

Just as perturbing to Pike was the mystery surrounding that valiant captive. Perhaps the blue-eyed temptress had a good reason for assisting the man's escape. The man was definitely a Southerner. But if he was not a Unionist, why had he remained silent? Was he a Confederate deserter, afraid of arrest and lethal punishment? Was he a criminal? Could he be Shannon's brother or sweetheart, and she was simply defending him? The man was surely concealing something crucial. But was that ravishing redhead a part of it? Pike wanted to believe that she was not.

The hoofprints on the main road revealed nothing more than that several people had traveled it recently. Pike concluded that the prisoner would expect them to think he would gallop hard and fast for Union lines; but being clever, the man might ride toward Wilmington. Along the way to town, he and his men would have to search every possible place of concealment.

As he came to a side road, he noted that several people had ridden along it within the last day. Pike's hopes soared as they reached the abandoned mansion. For him to halt and hide here would be cunning and daring! Pike was most respectful and envious of the man's ingenuity.

The troops dismounted and tied their reins to bushes near the porch, within a few feet of the two they sought. Pike ordered his men to scour the house, sheds, barns, and yard. "Look under, around, in, behind, and over everything. Even if it doesn't look big enough to conceal a dog, search it! Check out the trees and under those large bushes. Two of you men make sure those old haystacks aren't being used and inspect the corn crib and loft. Jeb, you ferret through that overgrown garden and under that pile of trash and old lumber. You men searching the house, check for footprints in the floor dust before you disturb it. Don't leave a closet or cabinet untouched, and move any furniture left. Examine every large piece."

Pike ran his fingers through his mussed sable hair. His sherry-colored eyes sparkled with determination and ancitipation. "Tim, you look around in the attic, and see if there's a cellar. If there's any way to get on the roof, check it too. Leave nothing untouched. This man is a master of guile. If you have to, shoot him. But don't harm the girl."

"What if she's on his side and shoots at us, Lieutenant Pike?"

"Don't be a fool, Jeb!" Pike ranted as his tension mounted. "If she were his accomplice, would she have left camp without her shoes and belongings? She rode out barefoot because that infernal Yank abducted her after he knocked me out. Probably forced her to remove them to prevent noise." From their placement, Pike knew that was not true.

"How do you think he got untied, sir?"

Pike played with his dark brown mustache before answering the private. "Beats me, Tim. I know Miss Greenleaf didn't help him. Jimbo said the man got free and attacked him, and nobody else was around. The only time she went near him, I was with her. She couldn't have passed him a weapon. Besides, she was with me when he escaped. He probably saw us together and decided to kidnap her for a hostage."

"It could be he got fond of her while holding her captive."

Pike scowled. "That's what has me so worried. If I've guessed right, he headed for Wilmington to throw us off the trail. If we're lucky, he's hiding around this place; so we had better scour it thoroughly. If there's one thing I learned from his capture, he does the unexpected and he's damned cocky. I just wish I knew who and what he is . . ."

"The sky's looking bad, sir. We'd best git started with the search. We'll be mighty cold if we git wet."

The soldiers went in their assigned directions. For half an hour, the Rebels diligently examined the house and grounds. Blane could hear the progress of the troops and Pike's angry bursts of words as each man reported a failure to discover them or any clues. He had heard the first talk between Pike and his men, so he knew Pike was laboring under false impressions or wishful dreams. He kept aware of the soldiers' progress as they searched the house, yard, barns, and sheds.

Knowing how badly Pike was aching and lusting for Shannon while he was making sweet, brazen, savage love to her within a few feet of that man drove Blane wild with excitement and power. He drove sensuously and feverishly into Shannon's body, being careful not to release her mouth or to remove his hands from her ears. He moved within her in such a way as to tease and to heighten her passions but not appease them. He didn't want her crying out from ecstasy, not yet. Besides, he wanted her totally distracted from the peril around them. He was glad to hold her captive in a dreamy world of rapture.

Blane heard one of the men again warning Pike of the rapidly approaching storm, but the obsessed officer brushed off the nettling caution. He heard Pike order men to search the nearby woods and fields in all four directions. He prayed the troop would not get stranded here, but they might if the storm broke before Pike's head cleared. Blane could envision Shannon's reaction if the soldiers camped on or near the porch.

The Texan berated himself for his selfish, arrogant behavior. He should have ceased this passionate madness and let Shannon dress the moment he heard the soldiers approaching. Now it was too late for her to obtain garments and slip into them. The loudness of Pike's baritone voice indicated he was standing near the front steps. Blane could not allow any noisy movement that might alert the persistent officer to their proximity. He raged at the idea of Shannon being found like this.

Shannon loved Blane so deeply and he was so talented at lovemaking that she was unaware of the danger surrounding her. Since Blane did not seem worried about their position and survival, she was confident they couldn't be located. Blane was driving her mindlessly wild with his movements and kisses. Her heart—or was it the pulse from his palms—pounded madly within her ears. Her body was a blend of blissful torture and fiery pleasure. All she wanted was more of him and his lovemaking. Afraid to move or make a sound, she lay in their shadowy Elysium, allowing him full rein over her body and passions.

Blane comprehended her thoughts and behavior. He knew he had full possession of her; that she was overpowered and intoxicated by sensation. His manhood was thriving on the sheer joy of pleasuring her, but it was beginning to beg for release. Blane knew Shannon was the first woman to whom he had truly made love, for this fusion of bodies and spirits was far more than having or enjoying sex. Blane dared not drop his guard for an instant, lest he drive savagely and urgently into her body to seek a joint victory over this rapturous battle.

Pike's next words caused Blane's heart to skip several beats. "Did you men search beneath the house?" the vexed Southerner inquired.

"I think Tim did, sir. I'll check with him."

Pike headed for the largest barn to make certain no corner had been left uninspected. As Tim joined Jeb and Gareth at the well, the tawny eyed Texan strained to hear their words, dreading them. He greedily assailed Shannon's mouth and rhythmically entered and withdrew from her body to hold her attention on their lovemaking.

Even though he was hard-pressed to master his desire, he resolved not to stop his blissful torment. Yet he knew if he did lose his control and if they were located, he would surely die a rapturously happy man!

"Tim, Lieutenant Pike asked if you searched under the house."

"I looked everywhere I could see or git. What does that man want from us? Hellfire, those two are long gone from this area. You saw that Yank's mettle. He ain't no fool or coward. Pike's just got a burning stick troubling him. I wouldn't mind diddling her myself."

"Me neither," Jeb concurred, rolling his eyes and licking his lips as that lustful fantasy filled his mind.

Gareth grinned lewdly before asking, "What about the porch?"

Tim pointed at it. "Look over there. Them bushes are planted tight against it. Ain't none of them got broken limbs and there ain't no loose boards or nails. The steps are solid backed. If anybody did git under there, they didn't do it within the last few hours. 'Sides, I peeked in from all sides. I didn't see or hear nothing. You want me to rip up a few of them boards just to make Firepants happy?"

Jeb shrugged and ventured sullenly, "Ain't no horses within a mile. What man with any brains would run off his horse so he couldn't escape fast if he was seen? And why would he stop to hide here? We done looked high and low, in and out. If we don't git to riding, we're gonna be dripping with cold rain. Don't Pike realize they ain't around?"

"All he knows is how much he wants to git that flaming-haired lady on his bunk." The men exchanged lewd remarks and sooty jokes before Gareth suggested, "Why don't we forget to search there? We should be gittin' ready to break camp. Let's go tell 'im we didn't find nothing. It's time for the noon meal and we're hours

AFFIX
STAMP
HERE

SPLENDOR ROMANCES

ZEBRA HOME SUBSCRIPTION SERVICE, INC.

120 BRIGHTON ROAD

P.O. BOX 5214

CLIFTON, NEW JERSEY 07015-5214

FREE BOOK CERTIFICATE

Yes! Please send me 4 Splendor Romances (formerly Zebra Lovegram Historical Romances), ABSOLUTELY FREE! After my introductory shipment, I will be able to preview 4 new Splendor Romances each month FREE for 10 days. Then if I decide to keep them, I will pay the money-saving preferred publisher's price of just $4.00 each... a total of $16.00. That's 20% off the regular publisher's price and there's never any additional charge for shipping and handling. I may return any shipment within 10 days and owe nothing, and I may cancel my subscription at any time. The 4 FREE books will be mine to keep in any case.

Name _____

Address _____

_____ Apt. _____

City _____ State _____ Zip _____

Telephone ( ) _____

Signature _____
(If under 18, parent or guardian must sign.)

SP1097

4 Free BOOKS are waiting for you!
Just mail in the certificate below!

Take advantage of this offer to enjoy Zebra's newest line of historical romance novels....Splendor Romances (formerly Lovegrams Historical Romances)- Take our introductory shipment of 4 romance novels -Absolutely Free! (a $19.96 value)

Now you'll be able to savor today's best romance novels without even leaving your home with our convenient and inexpensive home subscription service. Here's what you get for joining:

- 4 BRAND NEW bestselling Splendor Romances delivered to your doorstep every month
- 20% off every title (or almost $4.00 off) with your home subscription
- FREE home delivery
- A FREE monthly newsletter, *Zebra/Pinnacle Romance News* filled with author interviews, member benefits, book previews and more!
- No risks or obligations...you're free to cancel whenever you wish...no questions asked

To get started with your own home subscription, simply complete and return the card provided. You'll receive your FREE introductory shipment of 4 Splendor Romances and then you'll begin to receive monthly shipments of new Zebra Splendor titles. Each shipment will be yours to examine for 10 days and then if you decide to keep the books, you'll pay the preferred home subscriber's price of just $4.00 per title. That's $16 for all 4 books with FREE home delivery! And if you want us to stop sending books, just say the word...it's that simple.

from camp."

Ominous thunder roared loudly nearby, shaking the timbers of the house. Lightning flashed menacingly across the pewter gray sky. Horses stamped their hooves and whinnied in rising tension. Soldiers quickly reported no findings of any kind. Pike could tell that the men were becoming annoyed with his persistence. Unless one of the men had been careless, searching further at this location would be fruitless. They had left camp before dawn, before breakfast. It was noon, and a violent storm was brewing. The men were hungry, weary, and irritable.

The thunder and lightning increased in volume and frequency. The wind had become brisk and chilly. Pike had no choice but to order the men to return to camp until the storm passed. At the end of the side road, Pike sent his unit back to camp and headed for Wilmington alone. He instructed Jeb to inform General Moore of their search and of his return from town by tomorrow night, in time to pull out Sunday.

Blane's mind surged with happiness when the troop mounted up and rode away. He couldn't have requested better timing, for his control was nearly gone. Thunder rolled noisily across the heavens as Blane moved his hands from her ears. He shifted his position to suckle ravenously on her breasts as he worked his hips swiftly and rhythmically. He groaned in rising anticipation, knowing how close they were to the ultimate sharing. "They're gone, love. Come to me, Shannon, or I'll soon go mad," he urged breathlessly.

Their mouths fused as they labored together to bring each other fulfillment. They were as dry logs in a roaring fire, being consumed by hungry flames. Their bodies meshed perfectly as they raced up passion's spiral. At the summit, they worked feverishly, extracting every ounce

257

of pleasure before yielding to a climactic release that tumbled them over rapture's cliff and sent them falling, floating on airy wings of bliss until they touched the earth again in the peaceful valley of contentment.

Blane collapsed atop Shannon, unable to move or breathe normally. He couldn't believe how wonderful he felt or how thrilling their union had been. He shifted to rest partially over her moist body. His mouth couldn't halt itself from pressing kisses over her damp face and neck and chest. His lips and tongue brushed over one breast and then the other. His left hand stroked up and down her limp frame. It had been the most powerful and satisfying release he had ever known. It left him thoroughly sated even as it inspired a fierce craving for more of her. It was a curious sensation, a good one.

He rolled to his back and sighed contentedly. Placing his arm around Shannon's neck, he drew her along with him. Then he clasped her snugly against his damp torso, obtaining delight and serenity from their contact. He enjoyed the way her supple leg felt when casually thrown over his thigh to nestle intimately between his legs, and the way her arm calmly rested across his steadily rising and falling chest. He knew she felt totally at ease with him, and that conclusion was gratifying. He closed his eyes and was soon fast asleep, deeply asleep.

Thunder rumbled loudly outside their safe haven. Shannon sat up and looked down at Blane. He didn't move. Her eyes wandered up and down his magnificent body and her heart fluttered. How could she understand or explain such crazy emotions? He had just pleasured the very core of her being, yet she found herself desiring him again. Her hands itched to reach out and caress his body—all of it. She wanted to kiss him and to snuggle tightly into his embrace. He was so handsome and virile. He was totally engrossing. He was hers.

The storm struck with full fury, but Blane's slumber

258

wasn't disturbed. He slept as peacefully as a child in a parent's arms, safe and secure and surrounded by love. Shannon was glad she had never been afraid of severe storms. She listened to the thunder and pelting rain. The air began to cool steadily and rapidly and she shivered.

Shannon quietly slipped over to their pile of belongings. Oddly, she didn't feel guilty about using the stolen items. She took a handkerchief and soap from one haversack and moved over to the bucket of water. She bathed leisurely, then dried her fragrant body, delighted and amused by the soldier's choice of soaps. Taking a comb and brush from one of the sacks, she untangled her hair and plaited it, using an extra shoe lace to secure the end. Then the shapely redhead donned the stolen Rebel shirt and secured most of the buttons. As she put away the items, she stretched and yawned. She felt calm, refreshed, and relaxed. She carefully joined Blane on the blanket. After covering his naked flesh with the last blanket, she went to sleep.

Hours passed, and so did the violence of the thunderstorm. Yet a heavy rain continued to fall beyond the lovers' refuge, acting as nature's defense against the arrival of more intruders. The gray sky and impending October dusk steadily diminished the natural light. The temperature dropped and the air beneath the porch became cooler and damper with each passing hour.

Shannon was drawn to the warmth of Blane's sleeping form, and her movements and sighs awakened him. The groggy Texan lifted his head and rapidly assessed the setting and situation. His astonished gaze swept over the woman who was snuggled against him, her body freshly scrubbed and her hair braided neatly. He glanced at the blanket that partially covered them. Smiling raffishly, he grasped its edge and lifted it. She was clad provocatively in nothing but a faded gray shirt that had risen high over her hips, exposing creamy flesh. The furry covering around her private region almost appeared a tiny breechclout made from a red fox's luxurious pelt. His blood flamed as he noticed the heedless way her lower body was pressed familiarly against his, as if she lacked any restraint and shame where he was concerned. They were in nearly the same position as when he had fallen asleep.

Enthralled for a time, he allowed his mellow gaze to travel up her slumbering figure appreciatively and very slowly until it reached the exquisite face that rested without care or thought on his powerful shoulder. His yearning gaze wandered over each compelling feature. Despite her sharp wits, he wondered if she truly realized the full extent of her beauty and appeal. Her expression was soft and tranquil, yet he could feel the powerful pull of her magnetism. As his gaze lingered on her parted sensual lips, his respiration and pulse quickened. He could feel his heart beginning to thud heavily and his loins beginning to throb with swiftly rising desire. He licked his suddenly dry lips and questioned the beads of perspiration that had curiously formed above his upper lip and on his forehead. His body had tensed and he felt a strange turbulence inside. Was a mere glance at her all that was required to send his constantly smoldering passions beyond the boiling point?

His gaze defensively shifted toward the small openings to the outside world. He listened intently for any and all sounds. He could smell the effects of the waning storm that hadn't aroused him, and he was astounded by his total loss of awareness. He had slept so deeply that the world could have ended and he wouldn't have known it! Never had his wits and instincts been so dulled and clouded, especially in the midst of enemy territory. What was the matter with him lately?

Shannon Greenleaf . . . She was wreaking havoc with his wits, instincts, emotions, and self-control. All he wanted to do was to keep her safe, to retain his hold on her, and to spend time with her. He knew this attitude was wrong and selfish. He was losing sight of his duty and responsibilities, finding excuse after excuse to dally with her.

They could have outrun those Rebel soldiers. But anticipating that they would have to separate in Wilmington, he had intentionally avoided a hasty arrival. He had wanted and needed this time alone with Shannon to increase and strengthen his grip on her emotions. She had become an obsession, and he was afraid something or someone was going to steal her from him. He was afraid that somewhere around one of the next bends in their path they would confront either Corry or Hawke.

He mentally and disgustedly scoffed, *Afraid?* That wasn't like Major Blane Stevens at all. It was alleged he had a heart and nerves of stone. Maybe that had been true before meeting this enchanting redhead. He wasn't worried about Travers, for he would slay that lecherous snake before allowing him to touch Shannon even casually.

It was that unknown personage called Hawke who intimidated and alarmed him. He dreaded the day Hawke might unexpectedly appear before her and blind her to the passion she had shared with Blane. If only he knew the circumstances surrounding her romance with Hawke and the details of his disappearance and fate. He dared not question Shannon about his mysterious rival, for that would refresh her memory of Hawke.

The only thing he could do—or wisely should do—was wait for Shannon to reveal Hawke's identity and the facts about their past relationship. But he could also attempt to make certain that she was securely committed to him, bound so tightly that nothing Hawke could say or do would matter.

There were three methods, he concluded, used together or separately, to accomplish such a goal: love, marriage, or a baby . . .

Blane's rampant thoughts traveled to Texas and his sister. Even without Corry's love or the security of marriage to him, Eleanor Stevens was bound eternally to Corbett Greenleaf through their child. Because of what they had shared, Ellie refused to think about other men. The son she had borne as a result of that fiery romance had inherited his father's features. According to Ellie's last letter to him, she could never forget Corry, for she saw him each time she gazed at their son, which kept his reality alive and potent. No matter what Corry did to her, she would always love him; she would always have a part of him, a bond to him.

Blane's gaze roamed Shannon's features. Yes, a child was the perfect chain to imprison her. Even if Hawke did reappear, she would never desert the father of her child. Yes, a child would forge the strongest possible bond between them. Maybe that was the answer for everyone. When Corry was confronted by their child, surely he would crave his own son. How could he possibly deny his responsibilities to his brother-in-law's sister and their child? How could he dishonor himself before Shannon? This provocative scheme was perfect; it could solve all of his problems. Besides, there was only one way to create a child.

Blane grinned as he decided his sensuous course of action. He deftly unbuttoned her shirt and pushed the concealing material aside. His lips began to tease sultrily at her breasts. His talented hand slipped between her thighs and began to play enticingly in that sensitive area. Shannon moaned and squirmed, which delighted and encouraged him. A thrill shot through him when his name, not Hawke's, softly escaped her lips as she gradually awoke from her dreamy world.

Although it was only five o'clock, all light had vanished. Shannon opened her eyes to wintry blackness. Panic filled her. "Blane, it's so dark and scary." As she shivered from the chilly air, she asked, "Can we build a fire? I'm cold."

Blane shifted his nude body and brought his mouth close to hers. "I'm sorry, love, but we can't build a fire; the smoke would strangle us. Listen; it's still pouring out there. No one will be coming around again tonight. Relax and let me warm you," he entreated huskily, then nibbled provocatively at her lips.

His searing kisses and artful caresses captured reality and sent it spinning out of her reach. His mouth shifted back and forth between her lips and breasts, inciting both to quivering anticipation. His adroit hand persistently and cleverly encroached upon the fuzzy borders, smooth valleys, rigid peak, and moist cave of her private domain, which she willingly and eagerly surrendered to his pervasive exploration. She lay on the blanket as a dry sponge, greedily absorbing numerous blissful pleasures and torturously sweet enticements.

Blane was determined to become her only reality, to make himself unforgettable and irreplaceable and matchless. He wanted to awaken her somnolent passions to a higher level of awareness and hunger than she had known before. Then he would titillate those fierce yearnings and kindle those smoldering desires until her body was pleading for appeasement and ready to burst into roaring flames. When she had experienced the ultimate in tantalizing pleasure, he would assuage her voracious appetite with ecstatic sensations that would attack and conquer any lingering inhibitions she might have about her relationship with him. He wanted to provide a full range of erotic pleasures and intense feelings. His hands and lips wanted to explore and taste every area of her enticing figure.

Three times Blane stimulated her to writhing anticipation, and each time patiently and lovingly appeased her in a different manner. He touched her and thrilled her in ways she had never imagined, ways that might have been shocking or embarrassing at this first discovery if they had not been surrounded by darkness and if Shannon had not been consumed by blazing passion. As it was, she was too enthralled by the urgent cravings and rapturous sensations he was creating, whetting, and feeding to protest or prevent him from doing as he pleased. She was so mesmerized and ensnared by his loving assault that she could do nothing but permit it and enjoy it. After skillfully driving her up passion's peak and twice pushing her over its edge, he finally joined her on the third ascent to achieve a simultaneous climax that left both of them weak and breathless.

She felt utterly exhausted and contented. It had been a total experience with ecstasy beyond comparison or description. Even if a foe had arrived and had threatened her life, she would not have been able to find the will or strength to defend herself. From her head to her toes, her whole body felt aglow and at peace, as if every inch of her had shared in this enlightening and compelling discovery. It had been a strange and wonderful experience, powerful and all-consuming. She had eagerly and mindlessly submitted her flesh, her will, her heart to him. He had been in full control of her entire being, and she had not been frightened or restrained.

"Still cold and scared?" he inquired tenderly, sensing what she must be thinking and feeling after such an intense abandonment of will and body. Her trust in him had been complete.

"Neither," she replied, still breathing erratically. "I doubt anything could bother me right now, not even if a spider or two went traipsing across my chest or strung a web from my nose to my chin. What does one say following such an experience?"

Blane chuckled. "I'm glad to hear that I can distract and satisfy you as much as you do me. Lord, you play havoc with my duty and schedule. But don't you dare do anything rash to correct my new flaw."

"Frankly, Mister Stevens, you could use a flaw or two; then I would know you're human. Sometimes I can't believe you're real. Sometimes I wonder if I'll awaken to find you were only a beautiful dream. I hope not. You've become very, very special to me, Blane."

He was overjoyed by her words and her mood. "The same goes for me. You're very special, Shannon Greenleaf. But you needn't worry about me being a fantasy. I'm very real and human. Sometimes I'm too damn human. The problem is, I've been too indulgent and sweet lately, so you've forgotten what an ass I can be."

Shannon giggled and punched his arm. "No, I haven't forgotten, partner. You always find a naughty way of reminding me. But I think we're learning to accept each other's flaws, or at least to overlook them on occasion. A year ago—even a few months ago—I would never have envisioned myself in a . . . situation like this." She mirthfully accused, "You are a bad influence, Major Stevens. But I've never felt happier or more alive than I do with you. Despite my meager nineteen years, I've met plenty of men, but none such as you, Blane Stevens. You're an exceptional man, and a perfect partner. I'm awfully glad I met you and I'm here with you. You've taught me so much about myself, about emotions, about life. Thank you, Blane."

"For what, Shannon?" he asked in an emotion-laden voice.

"For being you," she stated simply.

"I wonder if you would feel and say that if you really knew me. We've been together for months, but we're still

265

strangers in many ways. Why, I don't even know your favorite food or color or place, or your nickname," he teased to lighten the heavy turn the conversation had taken.

Shannon sensed Blane's skittish nature surfacing again. She would keep her words light and easy for now. Whether this carefree male knew it or not, she was going to snare him forever! She was special to him; that was as clear as a sunny day in June. She smiled mischievously, knowing he couldn't see her in the dark. "Roasted duck. Red, green, and black. Let me see . . . Favorite place . . . That's a choice between New Orleans and your arms. Sometimes my brothers called me Vixen because my hair is the color of a female fox's coat and I can be sly and stealthy. What else do you want to know, stranger?"

"Who's waiting for you back home? Surely a woman with your looks and bloodline must have countless suitors chasing her. If I'm going to run into competition in Savannah, I might take a long time getting you there," he declared amidst chuckles to hide the gravity of his query.

"Alas, I fear I was much too impetuous and obstinate and arrogant and bratty to capture and hold any exceptional man's attention. And a Greenleaf can't marry just anyone. I fear I must be heading for spinsterhood, for I've never been betrothed or wed . . . or in love."

Blane was relieved that Shannon couldn't see his reaction to those last few words. He didn't know how to interpret them. Again, Hawke's image—alive or dead— loomed between them. Maybe he was mistaken; maybe Hawke hadn't been special to her. Yet the picture and things she had said in the past indicated otherwise. Although it would have been an incredible coincidence, perhaps Hawke had done the same thing to her that Corry had done to Ellie. Perhaps she wanted to forget the dark-

266

eyed individual whose picture stimulated strange stirrings and anger in Blane. Perhaps she didn't want to admit she had loved him and lost him. Or her denial might be a defensive measure if he no longer lived. But how would she feel and react if he entered her life again?

"What about you?" she hinted to break the oppressive silence, hoping he hadn't taken her remarks in the wrong way.

"I like blue skies, blue water, blue uniforms, and beautiful blue eyes. I also love green grass and anything red. I'm partial to rare steaks cooked over a campfire out on the range or in the high country, with lots of coffee or a canteen of Irish whiskey. I don't have a favorite place, unless it's Texas or most places away from civilization. I like to roam, and I suppose I always will. Pa always said I had trail dust in my boots. I guess they've never been emptied."

She wanted to keep him talking to learn more about him, so she asked several questions. "Who were your parents? Where is this new ranch you mentioned? How old are your brothers and sisters?"

"My mother was Lorna Marie Morgan, the prettiest and feistiest female in all of Ohio. Pa, the handsome and devilish Samuel Clayton Stevens of northern Virginia, met her when she moved to Texas with her brother Frank and his wife, Cora Beth. Ma and Pa married in '29, a month after they met. They settled west of Fort Worth, which turned out to be a bad idea; the Comanches raided that area at least once a year. With five sons and two daughters in eleven years, they did fine with the Rocking S until '51. Then those renegade Comanches struck like crazed dogs while Jory and I were off getting supplies. Eleanor was eleven at the time. Ma and Pa hid her in the cellar to keep her from enduring a fate worse than a quick death from a tomahawk or an arrow. Some females, no matter their ages, are raped and enslaved; or they're

267

raped and tortured before they're killed."

As Blane talked, Shannon could hear the love and pride lacing his mellow tone. "Ma could shoot as good as Pa and my brothers; in the wilderness, that's necessary. She insisted on helping defend our ranch during that savage attack. When Jory and I got home, we found Ma, Pa, Kirby, and Daniel slaughtered in the front yard. Kirby was only sixteen and Dan had just turned thirteen. That's a grim sight you never forget . . . or forgive, or even understand. Thank God, Lucy was married and gone. Lucy's a pretty gal. Those savages wouldn't have treated a lovely twenty-year-old with any mercy. She was lucky to avoid that kind of abuse and degrading slavery. I think I told you she's living with her husband, Lieutenant Edward Connor, in the Dakota Territory. She and Ed have two sons, or did the last time I heard. Let's see . . . fourteen and five if memory serves me tonight."

She could hear Blane shifting his position. She wished they had a fire so she would have light and warmth. Yet she didn't want to distract him from his painful revelations by requesting a small one just to locate something for supper. She was hungry, but they could eat later. She listened intently, comprehending his many reasons for loathing Comanches. For certain, she would have to keep Hawke's existence a secret. Blane might feel contempt for anyone with a half-Comanche brother.

"Clay had managed to roll under the front porch and conceal himself. We found him bleeding like a stuck pig with two arrows in his back. He was twenty-one at the time and had been married to Sue Anne for two years. Clay's thirty-four, three years older than I. He has four children: three girls . . . fourteen, eleven, and four, and one son, nine. 'Course those figures could have changed by now. Clay's like Pa; he likes a big family. During that raid, the Comanches took most of the cattle and horses, but they forgot to burn the house after they set a torch to the barns. The bastards stole everything that wasn't nailed to the floor or walls and couldn't be yanked loose."

He inhaled loudly before continuing with his tragic tale. "We didn't get Eleanor out of her hiding place until we buried nearly half of my family. Lord, that's one of the hardest things I've done to date. It isn't something a young girl should see. I guess Fate isn't totally cruel. If those bastards had burned the house, Ellie and Clay would have died too. Another good thing was that Sue Anne and their first child were visiting her people near Houston that terrible day.

"It took us awhile to get things going again. As soon as it seemed safe for the others, I took off with the idea of killing every Comanche within two hundred miles of the Stevens ranch. I figured the only kind of Indians who couldn't massacre more innocent ranchers and settlers were dead ones or those on the run from the white man. By then, we were getting help from the Army and Texas Rangers and other local groups. Things improved steadily, and I started branching out farther and farther from home. There was always the promise of more exciting and challenging adventures over the next hill, so I kept riding and seeking them. Jory met Martha and married her around '57. They've got twin sons who are five and one daughter about three. Including Ellie and her three-year-old son, I got me a big family again."

Blane hurriedly moved the conversation away from his younger sister. "If you like romantic tales, Blue Eyes, Clayton and Sue Anne's story sure is one. I doubt Clay could have survived if he had lost Sue Anne. He still claims she's the air he breathes every day. Ma took Clay with her in the summer of '49 to visit her brother Frank and his wife, Cora Beth. They hadn't seen each other in years. Clay had a pleasing surprise waiting for him there; Uncle Frank and Aunt Cora Beth had adopted this beautiful girl named Sue Anne, with hair the color of a chestnut mare and eyes as green as spring grass. Sue Anne had a smile on her face that will melt snow. Her folks had been killed and she had no other family. Clay and Sue Anne took to each other from the moment they met. When Ma returned to the ranch, Clay had a new bride with him. I've never seen two people any happier than Clay and Sue Anne. They're still acting like they've only been married a week or so."

Blane chuckled as he recalled that swift romance and the way his older brother had behaved. Of course, love had not been appealing to a strapling sixteen-year-old boy.

"Things were getting pretty bad on the ranch by the early part of '60. Clay and Jory lost cattle and horses to rustlers and disease. That summer was a scorcher, and most of the crops were singed in the fields. Most of the wild game had taken off for cooler parts. They were looking toward a bad winter when good luck arrived—if you can call somebody's bad luck your good fortune. Seems Fate has this way of being kind to everyone at least once."

He explained slowly, "There was a buckboard accident on Uncle Frank's ranch. Aunt Cora Beth was killed and Uncle Frank got a busted leg that never healed properly. He asked my brothers to sell the Stevens ranch and to move their families in with him. He asked them to take over the running and ownership of the Box *M* Ranch. Uncle Frank had a beautiful spread on the Brazos River, a massive ranch where he raised cattle and grew cotton and corn. It's near Richmond, not too far from Houston. When I got home for a visit at the end of September of '60, they were packing up to move. I hung around for a couple of months to lend a hand with the moving and to give them protection on the trail. Ellie was showing by then, six months pregnant by that low-down snake," he sneered bitterly.

Blane sat up and wrapped his arms around his raised knees. "It took me a lot of time and effort to drag the story out of her. For some crazy reason, I was the brother she chose as her favorite. She used to pester me like mad, dogging my every step and jabbering constantly. Clay and Jory told me they couldn't get anywhere with the man who duped her. I promised them and Ellie I would handle him; either he was going to do right by her and the baby, or he was going to die. A weasel like that doesn't deserve a good woman or to live, but Ellie still loves him and wants him. The move came at a perfect time. It seemed like a good thing for Ellie to make a fresh start where no one knew about her trouble. I took off in early December to join the Union. Before I reached Washington, I had seen enough to know the South was going mad with wild dreams. Before mid-February, they had captured over ten forts and arsenals from Texas to the Carolinas. Secession had started before I was in Louisiana. When I passed through Alabama, they were celebrating Davis's presidential appointment."

Silence filled the black area for a time as both Shannon and Blane sank into pensive thought.

The man who had been steadily and persistently tracking Shannon since she had run away from Boston in August sat before a cheery fire in his hotel room and sipped brandy. Simon Travers was leaning back in the plush chair with his legs stretched out toward the dancing flames that reminded him of Shannon's tumbling curls. He was grinning and thinking. He knew he was so close to Shannon that he could taste victory, and soon he would be tasting her sweet flesh and helpless surrender. He had leisurely bathed as he waited for his men to return with her. What did he care if that Rebel soldier was seeking her? He had known more than Pike;

271

he had known exactly where those two would go!

Along his journey from Washington to Wilmington, he had met with Confederate officers to pass along names of Union sympathizers, names that had allegedly been obtained by the beautiful and clever Rebel Flame. He had cunningly created two traps for the unsuspecting woman by spreading stories about both a Rebel Flame and a Union Flame. One identity would protect her until she was within his hands and the other would be used to coerce her into following his orders. Traveling with a group of hired men who owed fealty only to him and his fat purse, he had posed either as a Rebel agent working for Davis and the Confederate War Department or as a Union agent working for Lincoln, whichever the situation demanded.

At nearly every stop that Shannon and her handsome Texan had made, Simon Travers had stopped also, usually just behind them. Once there, he had destroyed any evidence, including people, that did not suit his purposes and he had created false clues to point in the directions he desired. He did not care which side won or was present when he caught up with Shannon. She would be at his mercy because he could be able to unmask her as either a Union or a Rebel spy.

Simon smiled coldly, congratulating himself on his cunning and daring. Shannon wouldn't have a chance of escaping his traps. He would blackmail her into marriage before this year ended, then he would have the Greenleaf holdings and Shannon. By the time he finished with his ruses, even Major Blane Stevens wouldn't trust her or help her for any price! She would have nowhere to run and no one to defend her. First he would punish her, then he would marry her.

Simon chuckled wickedly as he recalled his dealings with certain people during his pursuit of his delectable property. The soldier who had escorted Shannon out of

Washington had been easy to deceive and bribe. Having lost his selfish widow because of his time with Shannon, the soldier had betrayed her the moment he had learned of Simon's pursuit and reward. Naturally Simon had slain him for his loose tongue.

The Union camp near Alexandria had posed no problems or dangers for him, not with forged Union papers in his possession. And people along the trail had been eager to share information for a few coins or a hearty meal. Who could forget such a beauty with flaming hair and enormous blue eyes? But he had wasted time searching Alexandria, Fredericksburg, and Richmond before uncovering vital clues. Richmond had been so simple to enter and bleed for facts—once Simon learned where to look—that he wondered why the Union couldn't conquer it.

Another evil smile tugged at his lips as he remembered how much fun he had had duping Miss Van Lew, who believed herself a matchless Union spy. He wondered how long it would take her to discover that his fact-evoking gift wasn't from Lincoln in gratitude for her courage and cunning! She was the one to let Shannon's code name slip, just as she was the one to reveal names and places where "Lincoln's agent" could catch up with them for crucial news and a new assignment.

He had rushed to Danville to intercept Shannon and Blane, but they hadn't appeared. Deciding that Elizabeth had been mistaken or clever, he had headed back to Richmond less than two days before Shannon's solitary arrival in Danville! That second trip hadn't been a waste, for he had met and hooked up with Major Clifford's scout.

As for Major Clifford and that bumbling oaf, Thornton, he had dealt lethally with them for their treachery and deceit. If not for their stupidity and lust, he would now be home in Boston with Shannon! He had hoped his increasing the charges against Blane and Shannon would discourage them from using their secret identities and make them easier to track, for they always managed to elude him by a few days or a few hours. Either they hadn't discovered that someone was framing them or it didn't matter to that infuriating Union officer who was keeping her company.

At first he had plotted to get Blane and Shannon arrested as Union spies so he could waltz in and take command of her, but he had changed his mind. After hearing of the fiasco at Moore's camp, he realized she could be injured or slain by error if arrested. After all, he had supplied her with a large and dangerous role as the Flame. Thanks to Catherine Delany's revelation of Blane's lies to her, he had started disseminating hints that Shannon was a Rebel spy who was posing as the Flame to capture Union agents.

Simon was amazed by his enormous successes. Some of them had been most entertaining. He thought about the woman near Raleigh. That cheap whore had tried to sell him information for a thousand dollars in gold and the promise that Blane wouldn't be harmed. She had made it clear she didn't care what they did to Shannon. By the time he and his men had finished with her, she had been pleading to spill her guts. As Simon couldn't have her exposing or selling information about Shannon, he had his men toss her body into the well before they left her burned home. Since he wasn't totally unpatriotic, he had forced names and locations of Rebel safe houses from her and had turned them over to Federal authorities, compliments of the Union Flame . . .

Simon had dealt differently with the names and locations of Union safe houses. He had turned them over to Confederate officers, compliments of the Rebel Flame . . . He was digging her pit cleverly and steadily, and it would be one from which only he could withdraw her. She would be only too happy to return with him to Boston! He didn't even feel badly about torturing facts from that old couple near Fayetteville before he burned their house and barns. He made sure that Colonel Childs at the armory there gave Flame the credit for exposing the Thomases.

Being only a day and a half behind them then, Simon had assumed he and his men could travel faster than Blane could with Shannon and cautions slowing him down. Simon had wanted to catch up with them before they reached town. He had known their destination from the information provided by Joseph Thomas. Luckily he had obtained train rides for him and his men and their horses, claiming, of all things, a pursuit of the notorious Union Flame!

When the train halted for a long stop, Simon had presumed they were ahead of Shannon and Blane. He and some of his men had made camp and rested, and one man was sent to scout the area. The man learned that Blane and Shannon were captives in a Rebel camp only two miles from where he was, but before he could return to Simon's camp he was waylaid and robbed by human scavengers. By the time the man stumbled into camp and they could head out, Shannon and Blane had escaped.

Simon had underestimated Shannon's mettle and stamina. He had come so close to catching them. He had reached Moore's camp at dawn, in time to place maps and notes in her discarded belongings that "proved" she was working for the Confederacy. He had explained to Moore why she had freed the Union agent: to continue tracking the Union spy system in order to destroy it. He had instructed Moore not to send out a notice for her arrest or to reveal her identity, which he said would dash her cover and mission and endanger her life. Pike had already left seeking her, but Simon had boldly ordered Moore to recall the searchers and to dismiss them, and Moore had finally agreed.

It had been simple to discover where Pike was looking. Simon and his man had galloped past the road to the old mansion and had reached town shortly after two. Simon had spent most of the afternoon seeking the beautiful woman. When darkness fell, he had ordered his hired men to continue the search. If they didn't find her tonight, he felt certain they would in the morning. A woman like Shannon couldn't go unnoticed. He had been alerted to Pike's arrival and investigation but hadn't interfered. Instead, he had had Pike followed, in case someone revealed information to the handsome officer in a Rebel uniform. All he needed was time. Soon, Simon vowed eagerly, she would be in his hands.

Blane asked, "Ready to eat? We haven't had anything all day."

"Blane, what about this man you're seeking? Are you so positive he doesn't love your sister or want to marry her? What if there is a logical reason for his refusal? What if he is, or was, in love with another woman? What if he was already married? Or is by now? You said they moved while she was pregnant. What if he returned and couldn't locate her? There are so many possibilities. Are you still planning to slay him?" she queried anxiously. Killing a man in battle couldn't be helped, she told herself, but stalking and slaying a man . . . What if Blane was wrong about the incident? What if Ellie was lying? What if Ellie had shared her favors with several men? What if the one she had chosen to take the blame for her condition doubted the child was his? What if that stranger had made a careless mistake and had yielded to Ellie's wanton pursuit? What if Blane's sister had seduced this stranger to entrap him? Should the man's life be ruined because of her desires and wickedness?

276

Blane exhaled in a manner that exposed his annoyance, with the topic and the man involved, and with her bold questions. "I read the letters from him, Shannon. He was told everything. He knows where to find Ellie. In fact, he's the only one who was informed of her new location. My brothers have given him three chances to prove he's an honorable man. They've reasoned, argued, explained, pleaded, and threatened. No approach has worked. He even refuses to come and see his child, or to offer any support, which he can easily afford. The least he can do is give the child his rightful name. My brothers checked on petitions to legitimate a child born out of wedlock. It's a simple matter to obtain a bill to legalize his son. What honorable man would brand his child a bastard? He wouldn't even agree to a marriage just for one day. He was given the Stevens' word of honor that no demands would be placed on him after he gave the child his name. He was promised a bill of divorce, told he could claim refusal of sex because Ellie feared pregnancy and childbirth. That claim's been used successfully countless times. I think he's scared Ellie will try to hold on to him or try to make her son his rightful heir. He's made it clear he wants no part of the boy or Ellie. I owe the bastard a licking for the filthy names he's called her. And he claims he's never met her. He's a clever rogue; he's made certain there's nothing in his letters that could be used as evidence against him. He steadfastly proclaims himself an innocent being wrongly accused and Ellie a cunning whore. He's ripped my sister apart for the last time. Like you, Shannon, she believes there's some good reason for his rejection. Even if that were true, which it isn't, that doesn't excuse his cruelty. The boy will soon be old enough to start asking about his pa. What then?"

"You actually know this man?" she probed, more intrigued.

"I know who and what he is. I know where he lives,

how he lives, and what he looks like. And I could find him if it weren't for this bloody war. I've done a lot of checking on him. He isn't married or engaged; he doesn't even have a sweetheart. What he does have is a roving eye, a beguiling manner, an irresistible smile, a rich family, a bloodline as blue as a Federal uniform, and a talented blade that he can't keep in its sheath. He plays with women, charming them and seducing them. There's no acceptable reason why he can't marry my sister. And if he doesn't, then I damn well intend to slay the lying rake."

Chapter Eleven

"I doubt we'll have any more company tonight, especially in this foul weather. But just in case I'm wrong, you should cover up with that shirt. Never can tell when robbers and deserters might be nosing around. I'm going to light a candle just long enough to get us something to eat, then out it goes. You want me to pour you some of this fine whiskey to warm your bones, or are you planning to stick with water?"

"I was planning to freshen up before we eat," Shannon remarked.

He instantly replied, "Oh, no, you aren't. You've already had one bath too many. Do you realize that's all the water we have for drinking? It might have to last for days. I can promise you, thirst is an awful way to suffer or die. That's one of the Comanches' favorite tortures. The water is for drinking, nothing else," he stressed firmly.

"I'm supposed to eat with dirty hands and stay . . . unbathed for days?" she questioned in disbelief and dismay.

"What difference do clean hands make? You'll be eating out of a can with utensils." He didn't comment on the musky odor of lovemaking that clung to both of their bodies. He would let her bathe before they left for

Wilmington. His groin began to tighten and kindle as he inhaled the stimulating fragrance of sated passions. He commanded himself to get moving before supper was delayed again.

The candle that he took from one of the stolen packs could only remain lit for a brief time. He hurriedly searched for canned foods that could be consumed cold.

Then Blane went behind the suspended oilcloth and fumbled around in the shadows. She could hear the clanking of metal as he retrieved something from the corner. Blane pulled the barrier aside and informed her, "There's a . . . chamber pot back here when you need it." He returned, dropping the cloth into place and supplying privacy.

Shannon didn't like their predicament, but she had to accept it. She positively was not going to behave like a silly female or a spoiled child. She was darn lucky to be alive and to have things this good, and extremely fortunate to be able to share time and privacy with Blane. She pulled on the dark cotton shirt and tucked the lengthy tails between her legs, which were crossed at the ankles.

After opening the cans, he mischievously placed hers in the triangle formed by her barely concealed buttocks and bare legs. "That should help you locate them in the dark," he teased, grinning with amusement. He placed his cans on an area of the blanket near her feet. "Don't kick those over, or you'll have to divvy your share with me. No telling how long we might be trapped in here. We can't afford to waste anything." He rejoined her and blew out the light, but not before he had sent her a dazzling smile and his eyes had made a rapid sweep of her face and figure.

"Don't expect me to argue those facts," she cheerfully replied. "You're the expert. In fact, I'm demoting myself to your assistant. I have come to realize I am not qualified

280

to be your partner—not yet. In a few months, after lots of special training and ample experience, you can grant me a promotion. Until then, my superior commander, I will follow your every wish and order." She gingerly groped for a can and started to eat a most unappetizing meal.

"Be careful when making such tempting offers, Flame. Only a fool wouldn't take advantage of a devoted servant. What if your superior commander is a selfish, demanding, beguiling rake? What if my orders have nothing to do with the war, but only with satisfying my insatiable desire for you?" He chuckled before lifting his first can.

His rich voice and roguish laughter caused tingles of excitement to race over her body. "Since you aren't a fool, that means I can depend on you to carry out that delightful threat," she boldly responded. "Besides, a vital agent should be kept happy and calm so he can function at his best and safest. How can he have a clear head to perform his duty if he's besieged by hungers and distractions? As your loyal and dedicated assistant, surely it's my duty to the Union and to peace to provide you with whatever you require. After all, supplies and weapons can go only so far in keeping a man alive and healthy, in body and in mind. Isn't that right, sir?" Shannon took her second can, trying to keep her thoughts on this playful conversation rather than on the food.

He jested huskily, "Say one more enticing word, Blue Eyes, and I'll be disrupting your supper with one of those demanding and selfish orders. You've got me simmering over here now. You can bet I'm going to hold you to your word and offer, every chance I get."

"Don't agree too quickly, Major Stevens. Before I take on my new role of obedient assistant, you have to make me a promise."

Between chuckles, he taunted, "I knew there would be a catch, my fiery temptress. What is your demand, sly

281

demoness? My soul?"

"There isn't a single part of you I don't crave to own, but my request is a simple one. When you locate this man who . . . whom Ellie loves—whether it's during the war or afterward—promise me you won't gun him down like an animal. Please give him time to explain, time to change his mind about marrying her or at least legitimating his child. If it's possible, will you let me try to convince him to do right by Ellie and his son? Perhaps I can shame him into accepting his responsibilities to them, or clarify any confusion. Please."

Blane stared forcefully into the darkness, unable to pierce it. He wished he could see her eyes; eyes always talked louder than words, he knew, except where a skilled deceiver was concerned. "That's asking for more than one promise, Flame. Why should you become involved with him?"

"Because I don't want you killed during a confrontation with him, or imprisoned for his murder. You said his family was wealthy and powerful. That isn't the kind of man you can run around making accusations against or gunning down without proof of his crimes or evil intentions. It's Ellie's word against his. If he's been warned about your search for him, he'll be prepared to fight you. Or he might have hired villains awaiting you somewhere. If he's as wicked as you believe, you mustn't underestimate him. Please, Blane, let me help you with this problem. Don't get yourself slain or risk murdering an innocent man. Don't you realize this could be a terrible mistake? You could be stalking the wrong man. Blane Stevens, I don't want you dead or in prison."

"You've got some excellent points, Flame. You're more cunning and intelligent than I realized, if that's possible. Let me clear up one thing for you; Ellie isn't the only witness against him. It would be very simple to prove the man I'm tracking is the same one who came to

Texas and compromised my sister. You see, Flame, lots of people met him and observed their budding romance. Any of those people could swear in all honesty that Ellie wasn't seeing any other man that spring. Besides, he had papers and possessions to prove he was who he claimed to be. There is no way I could be seeking the wrong man.''

"There's still the danger of his entrapping you and killing you. You have to be careful. If he's the kind of man you say he is, then he's probably experienced similar situations before and knows how to deal with women or families who won't be discouraged.''

"You're right. I figured that when I caught up with him he would deny the truth and fight me, but I never thought about him turning the tables on me. He wouldn't battle me with words or guns if he could have me imprisoned or shot for attempting to kill him. It would be my word against his, in his territory. I'm certain he's a crafty bastard. I wouldn't put anything past him to entrap me. Why, he might even convince his sister to accuse me of kidnapping and raping her. Her family would have me hung before I could prove it was a trick. That would be one way of scaring off Ellie and my brothers.''

"My heavens, Blane, is his sister as wicked as he is? Do you honestly think she would conspire with him to carry out such an evil scheme? Who is this man? Perhaps I've heard of him or met him?''

"Tell you and risk having you try to solve this problem for me? No way, Flame; this is a dangerous and private affair. But thanks to you, I will be more alert. I promise I'll even talk to the bastard before I punish him.'' Blane sat up straight and stiff. "Of course! Punishment instead of death . . .''

"What do you have in mind?'' she inquired, her curiosity piqued.

"What torment could be worse than death for a

lecherous man, for any man? What action would prevent him from ever beguiling and seducing and deserting another naïve girl, short of slaying the son-of-a-bitch? Yes, there's only one way to sever his arrogance and lust and keep him from creating more nameless children or taking advantage of innocent victims. The perfect punishment for his black deed . . ."

She knew Blane was referring to castration. "Wouldn't a man die of such an injury? How could you get away with doing it?" she probed anxiously, recalling how she had dealt with Major Clifford in a similar manner. If that sadistic beast hadn't been found or gotten loose before that horrid night was over, his penetrating weapon, which had probably tortured many helpless women, would now be injured beyond evil use!

"Some ranch and farm animals have to be castrated for certain reasons. There's a simple and safe way to carry out the procedure. I would sneak up on him and then keep him blindfolded. He wouldn't know which of his victims was to blame. Besides, I know a wealthy and powerful Southern family. Surely this ravishing Greenleaf would protect me," he ventured, reaching out and finding a curl to yank gently.

"This Greenleaf, your devoted assistant, would swear you were with her night and day during his . . . unfortunate accident."

"You would tarnish your name and reputation to save my life?"

"I would do anything for you, Blane Stevens," she vowed softly.

Blane's reaction was to fling the cans out of their way so he could pull her into his arms and smother her lips with urgent kisses. Within moments he was making feverish love to her, as if it had been many weeks since he had taken her and was starving for her. After their passions were sated, they fell asleep snuggled together and slumbered peacefully until noon of the following day, Saturday, October 26.

By dawn of that same Saturday morning, Pike realized he had been cleverly duped by the fleeing Yankee agent. He had checked with Timothy and Annabelle Marlowe in case the rogue had taken Shannon there and left her, but to no avail. Now Pike suspected that the Yankee agent had surmised how the Rebels would reason out the facts and that they would follow the wrong trail. And since Shannon had mentioned that her captor had been heading for Fayetteville and Raleigh, it would have been logical for the Rebels to think he was now running in the opposite direction. But that was the beauty of the Yankee's clever plan. Who would suspect an enemy of heading exactly where he had told you he was heading! It would be just like that cunning Yankee to hide somewhere close to camp, spying on them, until they left the area. Then he could go along his merry way. Pike fumed. There was no need to scour Wilmington, but he believed that the old mansion did bear another look.

When Simon Travers awoke late Saturday morning, he was greatly angered by the news that greeted him. Shannon could not be located, and Pike had left for camp! "That Reb did not seek her at all this morning?"

"No, Mister Travers. Fact is, he did little searching here."

"Why would Pike come here claiming to look for them and not do so? Could be a decoy ruse. Could be those two know I'm on their tails," Simon murmured thoughtfully. From what he had heard in camp, Pike had been smitten with Shannon and had been determined to locate her to prove her innocence. "It all seems a little strange, seeing as Blane and Shannon surrendered to Pike. And Pike was with Shannon when those two escaped. I wonder . . . I think we should return to General Moore's camp and speak with Lieutenant Zachary Pike. I want to see just how much he knows, or claims not to know."

Saturday night, General Moore sent for Pike to come and answer Special Agent Simon Travers's questions. Pike had heard the strange tale that this unsettling man told his commanding officer. He hadn't noticed any maps and papers left behind in Shannon's belongings! If Shannon was the legendary Flame and she had helped Major Blane Stevens escape, then why was this man searching for her? Wouldn't that spoil the secret cover Travers was demanding they protect at all costs? If Shannon was that brave and cunning, she didn't require help from anyone! Besides, if she were a Rebel spy, she could be in danger from that handsome Union agent with her. Pike did not care for the look in Simon's eyes or the tone of his voice or the shaking of his hands when he talked of Shannon. Pike did not believe for a minute that Simon was a Confederate agent, or that he was seeking Shannon for good reasons, and Pike remained alert as this man chatted socially.

Pike lit a cheroot that he had purchased in Wilmington. He had become weary of polite banter about families, properties, and businesses. He knew this man was eyeing him intently, and he wanted to learn why. He leaned his chair back on its two rear legs, and asked, "You think Miss Greenleaf is safe traveling with this Major Stevens?" he inquired as he scrutinized Simon. He noted that the man did not seem afraid, even surrounded by so many Confederate soldiers, but something was awry . . .

Simon smiled too genially. "I've been trying to tail them for her protection, but Stevens moved too swiftly after their last stop. Don't worry about Shannon. She could beat most men with guns, knives, sabers, or arrows. She can also outride and outfight most of them."

"If she's in no danger, why are you tagging along to help her?"

Simon grinned again, turning sideways in his chair to prevent Pike from staring into his face. He chose his words carefully. "Because of Stevens. He's a different breed of Union agent. He's smart and he's fearless. You witnessed his skill and cleverness during his capture. I was told he surrendered to you. I said Shannon could best most men, and Stevens isn't average. Too bad he sided with the Union. When you searched Wilmington, you didn't find any clues to their whereabouts?"

Pike caught the challenging inflection in Simon's voice as the man spoke. He decided to test his veracity and knowledge. "I didn't ride into town after I left my men. I rode around searching areas that might appeal to a man who wanted to disappear for a few days. The storm slowed me down. I had to hole up in this shack for hours. I was tired and hungry and soaked. I figured the rain had washed away any tracks, so I returned to camp early this morning. It's my guess they're heading for Raleigh and Fayetteville. Stevens got an eyeful here, so I'm certain he'll want to return to the Yanks as quickly as he can. I could be wrong; Wilmington would be the perfect place to hide. If we weren't pulling out for duty in the morning, I would head there and search for her, with General Moore's permission. Like you, sir, I don't trust this Major Stevens. And I would like to see her."

"You think I should ride into Wilmington and look for her there?"

"If I were you, that's exactly what I would do," Pike responded.

Simon forced himself not to glare at the deceitful officer as he silently raged. The fool should realize he and his men knew about his futile search there—or was it his clever ruse to mislead any pursuers? Clearly, Shannon and Blane had not headed for Wilmington. This Pike was a liar! Was he also their accomplice, another Union agent? "You said you're from Charlotte, Lieutenant Pike, but you talk Western, like Stevens. He's from Texas. You know anyone over Charlotte way who would hide them?"

"Haven't been home since this war began, so I wouldn't know about suspected Union sympathizers. The authorities in Wilmington might be able to answer that question when you get there."

Sunday morning, when General Moore and his Confederate regiments moved northward, Lieutenant Zachary Pike was listed as a deserter. But miles from the camp, Pike was being beaten and questioned by Simon Travers. Pike knew this man was going to kill him, no matter what he said or did. He perceived great evil in Simon, and an alarming urgency to locate Shannon Greenleaf. Pike decided that Simon and Blane Stevens were Union agents who were trying to unmask and slay the beautiful Flame, the woman who had kissed him beneath the tree that night before vanishing in the control of her foe. Pike determined he would never betray her to this evil monster.

As Pike and Simon argued, Pike tried to make it obvious that he was attempting to avoid the subject of Charlotte. By doing so, he succeeded in convincing Simon that it was probably where Shannon and Blane were heading. Then Pike tried to discover Simon's motives by pleading with Simon to let him help find Shannon and rescue her from Blane. When he claimed he would do anything Simon ordered just so he could have Shannon as his reward, Simon laughed coldly and wickedly, and gave Pike an explanation that proved to the Rebel soldier he had been right about the mysterious Simon Travers.

Simon sneered and informed him, "Shannon is mine, you lowbred Reb. But she'll wish you had found her first when I get through with her." Simon jabbed a knife into Pike's stomach and twisted it cruelly. "Just so you know, Reb, she is the Flame, and all I said about her skills is true. That's how she got away from me." Simon plunged the knife into the left side of Pike's chest and twisted painfully. "I suspected you were helping them, but I didn't know why." He plunged the knife into Pike's right side and brutally sliced downward. "You should know that after you die, I plan to put her sign on you and give her the credit for your murder. You see, Reb, I'm collecting evidence on her to force her to marry me. I also plan to carve a little blade on your cheek. With luck, I'll convince everybody that Stevens is the infamous Blade. That should get him killed." Though Simon was unaware that he had accurately guessed Blane's secret identity, the dying officer sensed something of the truth in the murderer's words.

Suddenly Pike saw certain facts clearly. Shannon and Blane were a team, and Simon was after them for reasons that had nothing to do with the war. Shannon had risked her life for Blane; she obviously loved him. Blane had risked his life for her and therefore loved her as well. Pike grinned, then he murmured weakly, "Blane will never let you get her. When you get to Charlotte, he'll be waiting. He'll kill you, you bastard. You're a f-fool if you think she'll take you after having Blane Ste . . . vens." Pike's head dropped forward as death claimed him.

"You're the fool, Pike, if you think anyone will stop me from finding and taking her. Thank you for pointing us in the right direction. You men know what to do. Make sure there's no doubt who committed this foul deed. And

289

make sure the body is placed where it will be found before our evidence rots away or some vulture feasts on it. I'll be ready to leave for Charlotte when you return to our camp."

When Shannon and Blane awoke Sunday morning, they were facing each other. All it took was an entreating gaze from each to ignite desire's flames. As they lay nestled together after sating their passions, Blane cautioned, "I want you to be very careful in Wilmington. It's one of the most crucial supply and defense areas for the Confederacy. If the Union could capture Fort Fisher, Wilmington, and the entire Cape Fear section, they would be destroying one of the South's largest and most successful blockade-running businesses. North Carolina not only provides countless soldiers but also a vast amount of the supplies and arms used by the Rebels. Some of the most noted runners operate out of Wilmington or the Cape Fear area. Remember these names: the *Pet*, the *Siren*, the *R. E. Lee*, and the steamer *Lillian*. Then, you've got the *Kate* and the *Mary Celeste* working out of Charleston. The raiders carry out cotton, wool, tobacco, camphine, and lumber; then they return with munitions, supplies, whiskey, medicines, and money to pay soldiers. Jeremy told me the Union captured their most famous and largest runner, the *Advance*, on the tenth of last month."

When Shannon suddenly shivered with a chill, Blane pulled the blanket over her arms and shoulders and cuddled her closer against his warm body. "Jeremy also told me that General Hoke has been moved across the James River to defend Richmond against Grant's invasion. Outside of Lee, Hoke is the Confederacy's best officer. If those two were on our side, the war would have ended in less than a month. Jeremy's been collecting newspapers from the surrounding areas. He's keeping them hidden until he can pass them to me. I'm anxious to read what they have to say about the situation in this area and in other places. They have five major papers around here: The *Raleigh Register*, the *Raleigh Standard*, the *Fayetteville Observer*, the *Wilmington Herald*, and the *Wilmington Journal*. Agents get as much information from careless papers as they do from their investigations."

"Is that why you were sent to this area?" she queried, snuggling even closer to Blane, for the air seemed to be getting colder by the hour.

"If I can check these supply ports and privateering firms, I can estimate their strengths and weaknesses. I might be able to uncover their schedules and signals. It sure would help matters if I could find a way to help sever those connections. Those raiders sail back and forth through Admiral Lee's blockade like it wasn't even there. Grant's trying to come up with a plan to use naval and land troops to attack strategic points like Fort Fisher and Cape Fear simultaneously. If we can capture all major ports, the Confederacy supply lines will be crippled. Lord, I'd be satisfied if I could only discover how to make Fort Fisher pregnable to the Union's impending attack. Jeremy is sending a report to Grant and Lincoln right now about those troop movements we encountered. With luck, Grant or one of his generals will be waiting with open arms for Moore's battalions."

Shannon shuddered violently.

"Still cold, love?" he asked.

"No, it just sounds so terrible to be sending all those men into a trap. Do you ever get accustomed to such an awesome responsibility?"

"This is war, love, and one side will become the victor. We have to make certain it's the Union. I know this must be difficult for you, but think of it this way; somewhere out there, a Rebel temptress is doing the same things to help the Confederacy become the winner. You're only balancing the scales of justice, or shifting them in favor of the Union. Speaking of your duties, ma'am," he continued, "when you reach Wilmington, try to become acquainted with Governor Vance's family and Mrs. Armand J. DeRossett. But don't take foolish chances."

Shannon remained silent while he explained.

"Vance is the one who gives the officers their instructions, so you might pick up a clue or two about troop movements and assault plans from them. Just don't cast suspicion on yourself by asking questions or snooping around. Understand, woman?" After he felt her nod her head, he went on.

"Mrs. DeRossett has a female society that ministers to wounded soldiers passing through Wilmington to hospitals. She and her ladies go to the train depot and tend the injured. They change bandages, offer comfort, and perform tasks such as laundry or small baths or letter writing. They provide garments, medicines, treats, and much-needed smiles and affection. With wounded men coming from every direction, you could gather vital information from them. Even if you don't obtain anything useful, your conscience should be appeased by the help you're providing, and it will supply you with a protective cover while I'm gone."

"Where will I be staying? How would I reach you if I discovered something vital that needed to be passed along without delay?"

"You'll stay with Sarah Jane Sinclair and her sister, Molly Ryan. They own a hotel called the Resting Place. There's only one catch; they believe I'm a Rebel agent, their most important contact to Davis. They pass Union secrets to me. That way, we always know what they know or think they know. To them, you'll be Rebel agent Cockade. You know what that is?" he asked, referring to the red ribbon that had been worn by Southerners favoring secession.

After she responded affirmatively, he explained, "We'll say you're having a much-needed rest before continuing with your duties. After all, winter is wrapping its cold arms around us and you are a delicate lady. They'll be thrilled to have you as a guest at their hotel. But as I said earlier, be alert and careful at all times. Wilmington is filled with soldiers and Southern patriots. But it has many dangers because of the blockade-running companies. Some of those men won't stop with less than robbery or murder to establish their wealth and power. The crews from some of those ships are made up of cutthroats and criminals, the slime of the world. Stay off the streets after dusk. I don't care if you come across the one clue that could end this war tomorrow, stay clear of the wharves and privateering firms. If some sailor doesn't decide to carry you along as entertainment on his next run to Nassau, one of the merchants might see you as a money-making jewel for some foreign brothel or lecherous sultan."

"We certainly can't have someone running off with Major Stevens's prized possession. I shall be most careful, my greedy master. But, tell me, when you left me in Farmville with that horrid beast, Clifford, where did you go and what did you do?"

"I was supposed to be investigating troop movements, supply lines, arsenals, and enemy strongholds between Sheridan's and Grant's lines. They want to meet and shake hands as soon as possible. There seems to be a concentration of Rebel troops in that area. If the Union could conquer and hold a line from Louisville to Norfolk or Nashville to Williamsburg, Richmond would be cut off from the South. Then the Federal troops could start moving and pressing southward until they conquered the crucial areas of the Confederacy: Virginia, South and

North Carolina, Georgia, and Tennessee. If we defeated and controlled those states, the Confederacy would fall."

"Did you succeed?" she inquired nervously as the words "conquer Georgia" echoed in her mind.

"I'm afraid not. When Clifford's men tried to murder me in my sleep, I had to assume he knew or suspected who or what I was. I was forced to kill all three men to keep them from revealing that I had survived and escaped. Since my cover was gone and I figured you were probably in danger, I tracked you as quickly as possible. I was real nervous when I discovered you had left Farmville with those troops. It didn't take much skill to trail you to Danville. I saw you sneaking out of the hospital with your things, so I was waiting for you in the woods."

Blane felt Shannon stiffen and tremble. He guessed why, but he decided to set her mind at ease by misleading her. "I knew you would head south, so I made my way in that direction. I was afraid if I tried to get to you, I would startle you and you would expose us. I almost got to you too late. I should have been there before that Thornton stopped you. Another minute or two, and he would have been hauling you back to Clifford. Next time I'll move faster, Flame."

"I'm glad you moved slowly that time. James was calling me awful names and making vulgar threats. I even promised to marry him if he would let me escape, but he was certain I was lying because he knew how much I detested him. I'm sorry I ruined things for you. What about your mission for Grant and Sheridan?"

"Another agent was assigned to complete it. With Thornton and Clifford and Travers in the area, we couldn't hang around. Besides, my work here is just as important. I have to keep my par . . . assistant out of danger. Settle down," he encouraged when she trembled again. "I've been leaving clues and false trails to send

294

them in the other direction. If any of them are still after us, this is the last area they would search. Trust me, Flame; I won't let any harm come to you."

Time, Blane mused silently, was all he needed, time to earn more of her trust and affection; then she would confide everything to him and he would find the courage to do the same with her. First, he needed her to love and want him so strongly that nothing could part them. And he already sensed that she was beginning to feel at home in his arms and life.

For the next fifteen hours, Blane and Shannon spent their confinement talking, making love, and eating foods that were barely noticeable to appetites running in other directions. The rain had ended just after five the afternoon before, too late for troops to come seeking them. It was nearing midnight of their third night beneath the porch when Jeremy Steele arrived. It was still Sunday, October twenty-seventh.

"Major Stevens?" the voice filtered into Shannon's dreamy mind.

"I'm coming," Blane replied and moved in that direction.

"Moore broke camp early this morning and headed northwest. I waited until I was sure they were gone before I came for you and Flame. That Lieutenant Pike ain't rested a minute since you two escaped. I thought General Moore was gonna have to hog-tie 'im to make him leave this area. He's got it bad for Flame. I'll go after the horses and be back in an hour or so; then you can make Wilmington before daylight. I checked the area good and ain't nobody around. You want me to let you two out so you can loosen up a mite?"

"If you'll dig up the bushes and remove the covering, I can do the rest while you're gone." Blame figured Jeremy knew how close he was to Shannon, but neither man would embarrass her by acknowledging the fact aloud.

Shannon wrapped the blanket around her naked form, then waited for Jeremy to depart so she could light a candle to bathe and locate her garments. After the sound of Jeremy's departure ceased, Shannon jested, "Is it all right if I use the rest of the water for bathing?"

"It's dark outside. How about if you come with me to the well, soap up all over, then let me rinse you good with a few buckets of fresh water? Think it's too cold out there for a quick bath?"

"Are you jesting? It could be snowing and I wouldn't mind."

"Good. When you finish, you can return the favor."

They gathered a few supplies and crawled from beneath the porch. Both stretched and inhaled deep breaths of fresh air. Blane took her hand and guided her to the well, for a selfish moon was not sharing much of its light. While Shannon wet her flesh with the last of the water in one bucket and lathered up with the fragrant soap, Blane drew another one. He chuckled as he heard her teeth chattering.

"Is that noise from cold or fear?" he asked mirthfully.

"B-B-both. It's win-ter and we're s-s-sort of de-defenseless sta-standing here li-like this. You re-ready?" She shuddered violently.

"Why don't you dress first? You're shaking like crazy."

"The-then I would get w-wet again. Le-let's hurry, p-part-ner."

Blane took one blanket and gently dried Shannon. He rubbed his hands briskly over her body to chase away part of her chill, then wrapped another blanket around her shuddering form. "Go light a candle and get into some warm clothes. I can manage alone." When she tried to protest, he turned her and nudged her toward the porch. "Git, woman. You won't be any good to me sick. You can repay me another time, in a warmer location."

He grabbed a bucket and dumped it over his tawny frame. As rapidly as possible, he scrubbed and rinsed. After drying himself, he went to dress.

When Jeremy returned with their horses, Shannon and Blane were dressed and packed to leave. While the horses were being watered and saddled and Shannon waited patiently nearby, Blane, who was clothed in a gray wool shell jacket and blue trousers, and sandy-haired Jeremy Steele exchanged genial words and important information.

Snuggled into a butternut wool shell jacket that had been part of a Rebel uniform, a pullover white flannel shirt, and blue jersey trousers, Shannon felt refreshed and warmed. What she didn't care for, but found necessary in this cold weather, were the ill-fitting leather shoes called brogans. She felt as if she were wearing trimmed-down hat boxes! How she longed for her expensive slippers or her comfortable boots. She had brushed her thick hair, then twisted it and stuffed it into a slouch hat. She could not help but wonder how they would explain this Confederate garb when or if they met anyone on the road. She focused her attention on the men, wishing they would hurry.

Jeremy was saying, "General Hood did his best to halt Sherman before he reached Atlanta. He's still harassing the Federals in the area, trying to lure Sherman into chasing him. I was told George Thomas and John Schofield have been sent after Hood and Johnston. Looks like the Rebs are fleeing back into Tennessee. Seems Sherman plans to make sure there's nothing left around Atlanta, then he might split his units and send half toward Macon and half toward Athens to get rid of those arms factories. Then, they're supposed to rejoin to hit that powder works in Augusta. Ole Sherm's making sure the Rebs don't have any food, weapons, ammunition, or supplies. He plans to clean out Georgia, then do the same

297

with South Carolina. Tarnation, sir, he makes me ashamed to be a Unionist."

Blane turned the conversation away from Georgia and Sherman's march toward Shannon's home. "What's happening around here, Jeremy?"

"There's a lot of munitions and troop movements going on. Vance has ordered whole battalions to Georgia and toward Richmond. He's pulled Hoke out of Fort Fisher and has him heading to aid Lee in defense of Richmond. That Lee's a treacherous man; he's refusing to let Grant take the Confederate capitol or Petersburg. Looks like those Rebs have locked in for a long and bloody fight. The coastline from here to Georgia is still in Rebel control, and I mean tight and strong control."

"Any good news for our side?" Blane inquired sullenly.

"On the fourth, our *Washusett* defeated that Rebel runner, *Florida*. She won't be sinking no more Union ships like the *Jacob Bell*. I don't think I told you Rose Greenhow didn't make it back from England." His voice revealed excitement and a tinge of pity as he related the tragic, and perhaps foolishly heroic, story. "She was coming home the end of last month on the *Condor*, a fast steamer. Before they could reach Wilmington, Union gunboats saw 'em and attacked. The commander at Fort Fisher did all he could to keep the Union ships back until the *Condor* could slip into port. Rose and two other passengers were put in a small boat to row ashore. The gales were too strong, though. She was weighed down by her clothes, secret dispatches, and over two thousand dollars in gold. She wouldn't release anything, so she drowned. They had a funeral cortege march right down Wilmington's main streets on the first. She was given a military burial with a gun salute, flagged casket, and everything."

"Any news on Lincoln's reelection?" Blane queried anxiously.

"Farragut's conquest of Mobile and Sherman's storming of Atlanta look like the victories he needed to invigorate those war-weary Yanks. Ain't no secret McClellan's gonna give him a fast, hard run. Around these parts, Carolinians are getting a mite edgy. With that stunning defeat at Winchester and the Union's determination to take Fort Fisher, Wilmington and Charleston, you can't blame 'em. They've been supplying the Confederacy with men, supplies, and weapons, but there ain't been no real bad fighting in this state. Now that the Union is setting her sights on occupying her, folks are gettin' scared. You two be real careful; some folks are switching sides and others are pretending to change to entrap traitors. You'd best get riding if you're gonna make town afore dawn. The new password is 'turkey-stride.'"

Blane glanced at Shannon. Her creamy face and very dark blue eyes were illuminated by the glow from the camphine lamp that Jeremy had brought with him. As the wind picked up strength, its invisible fingers yanked off her hat. Coppery curls whipped around her head and the lamplight caused their fiery color and wavy texture to resemble bright flames dancing erotically in the breeze. At times like this, she looked like a half-wild and sultry creature who lacked all restraint but radiated an enticingly soft, romantic aura. His heart lurched madly and his body stirred uncontrollably to life.

His alluring gaze seemed to melt into a warm amber liquid that flowed over her and encased her in a protective and caressing golden shell. Shannon's molten blue gaze met his and seemingly dissolved into it, allowing their spirits to meet and fuse. All else became irrelevant.

Jeremy stopped talking, but neither Blane nor Shannon noticed. Intrigued, Jeremy glanced back and forth between the two mesmerized people. He had never seen Blane's face with such a strange and powerful glow, such an intensely tender and possessive expression. Jeremy hastily studied Shannon's matching response. It was Jeremy's opinion they were deeply attracted to each other. From the way those blue and tawny eyes caressed each other, there was no denying or ignoring the intimacy and intensity between the two. Instead of being pleased, Jeremy was alarmed and vexed, for his friend and fellow agent had lost all concept of his surroundings and duties! Presently, and probably for the last few days, his friend had been thinking of nothing except being with this flaming-haired temptress! Anger and envy chewed at the twenty-three-year-old man, who had lost his wife to another man during the first year of the war. This wasn't any time or place for Blane to be wooing this ravishing beauty. He hadn't been too injured to escape. Jeremy fumed. Didn't Blane realize how perilously distracting she was? Maybe it was his duty to his friend and the Union to get rid of this consuming Flame . . .

Jeremy gingerly ended the dismaying silence. "Sarah Jane and Molly are expecting you two at the hotel. I told 'em what you said about Cockade and her needing to get out of the fires she's been lighting and flaming in Virginia and Tennessee. I also told 'em she wouldn't be able to share any secrets with them, so they wouldn't get suspicious when Flame couldn't answer some of their questions. I told 'em she just needs to rest and stay out of danger for a few weeks. They're so excited about giving aid to the famous Rebel spy, Cockade, they can't stop giggling and planning. Sarah Jane said they're getting the best room at the Resting Place ready for her."

Shannon smiled at Jeremy, then Blane, just as Jeremy

put his defensive scheme into motion. "Watch yourself and bolt your door every night, sir, 'cause Molly's still got her heart set on snaring you. She has since her husband was killed two years past. Tarnation, I don't think she ever cared for John C. like she does for you, Major. She's a pretty woman with lots of money and a good social position. This war ain't going on much longer, so you'd better romance her a mite harder this trip. Every time I see her, she brags about that cameo you gave her. She's got it real bad for you, sir." Jeremy's chest rumbled with laughter.

Despite Blane's frown, Jeremy cleverly entreated, "Flame, you protect our friend over there or Molly'll be leading him into the church for wedding vows afore he can leave Wilmington. Once he gets his mind on a new bride, he'll forget all about us and the Union. You keep reminding him he can take advantage of that opportunity after the war. You make sure he keeps a clear head and cool blood around her."

With deceptive innocence, Jeremy teased mirthfully and slyly. He knew Blane would be nettled by his revealing words but not suspicious of them. After all, he hadn't been told about Blane's feelings for Shannon. Too, he was speaking on this side of the truth and they had always joked about Molly's hot pursuit. Jeremy wondered if Blane had ever appeased his manly needs inside that more-than-willing female who bordered on being the prettiest woman in these parts. When Jeremy spoke his last directive to Shannon, he did it in order that they would both realize how dangerous it could be if they carelessly exposed their passions to and inspired jealousy in Molly Sinclair Ryan.

While Jeremy waved farewell to the departing couple and remained to clear away the evidence of their stay at the old mansion, Blane and Shannon galloped down the

301

shadowy road until they came to the one that eventually entered Wilmington. Then Blane reined in his mount and called out for Shannon to do the same. Grasping her mount's bridle and tugging gently on it, he brought them closer. As they sat beside each other in near darkness, he said in a reluctant tone, "I think I should explain about me and Molly Ryan before we get into town."

Chapter Twelve

"That would be an exceptionally smart idea, Major Stevens," she replied in a peevish tone. Had he made love to her for three days while heading for a woman who was eagerly awaiting his arrival? Had he stopped to enjoy her before reaching Wilmington, knowing that she would terminate their affair upon learning about his relationship with Molly? "It isn't wise or safe to let me keep walking blindly and ignorantly into these kinds of private situations, as you did with Catherine Delany. Exactly how many beguiled women do you have waiting and pining for your next visit along our route?" she inquired sarcastically. She was angered by her tormenting suspicions about Blane's misconduct while carrying out his secret missions.

Before he could reply, she scoffed, "I thought you told me you despised men who used their charms and lies to take advantage of naïve and gullible women. I thought you didn't go around intentionally breaking hearts. If you sleep with some, or most, or all of your female sources, how do you know one of them doesn't have a devoted brother searching for the father of his sister's bastard child, just like you're doing for Ellie? With your stamina and appetite and extensive travels, you could have several bastards waiting and hoping for their pa to do the honorable thing. The kettle seems as black as the pot he's seeking."

Blane was hurt and angry. He was also surprised and disappointed. Because he was unaccustomed to exposing and defending his personal thoughts, actions, and feelings, Blane's voice had a razor edge when he responded to her insulting and accusatory remarks. "I see you've lowered your opinion of your partner very rapidly, without even giving him the benefit of telling his side. Since you've already judged me so black and guilty, maybe I shouldn't waste my time and energy exonerating myself. But I will, because this matter is important. Considering how close we've been, how could you compare me even slightly to that low-down snake I'm seeking! Lord, Shannon, if you think I'm that kind of man, you don't know me at all; and you sure as hell shouldn't be traveling and sleeping with me," he scolded her rashly.

He took a deep breath and continued. "Believe it or not, I've never slept with Cathy or Molly, or any of my female sources. Jeremy was only teasing me about her because she's always after me. If he had known about us, he wouldn't have done it. Maybe I am guilty of romancing vital information out of some women, but only when it's absolutely necessary. Surely you've learned enough lately to know that romancing a woman and making love to one aren't the same thing. I'll admit I've had my share of female flesh before and during this war, but only from those who knew what was happening and knew how to protect themselves from unwanted complications. Every town has houses with experienced women who provide such treats for hungry men. I don't go around charming and seducing naïve girls. The only innocent and trusting woman I've taken advantage of is Shannon Greenleaf, because I found her too damn

304

irresistible. I don't have any illegitimate children. But if I did—love the mother or not—I would marry her and give my child its rightful name."

When Shannon tried to speak, Blane harshly silenced her. "Just listen! I've always let Molly carry on with her flirtations and enticements because I needed a safe house and help in Wilmington. But I've never given her any promises. I haven't shown her more than gratitude for her assistance and friendly affection and enjoyment of her company. The same goes for Cathy. Damnit, Blue Eyes, this is war, not a game!" he verbally exploded, then berated himself for his loss of temper.

Again he silenced her attempt to speak, this time gently. "Please let me finish explaining this mess. Maybe I shouldn't let them have even scant hopes or dreams about me, but I can't bluntly or brutally spurn them. Maybe I am guilty of using them, but I'm doing it for the best of everyone, to get this country back together. Don't you see, Flame? To women like Molly and Cathy, I'm somebody unique and appealing, somebody totally different from their husbands and brothers. With few unattached men available, they turn to me. In case you haven't noticed, I'm not bad to look at and somewhat charming. Me and my work make them feel alive. We give them hope for peace and survival. We supply a little happiness and exictement. We make them feel important and useful, even patriotic. To them I'm a dashing rogue and a hero, a brave and clever spy, a man of mystery and prowess, a good catch for a future husband or current lover."

Blane leaned toward Shannon and captured her hand. "Unless Molly's found someone else to focus her attentions on, she'll still be after me. Don't you see, Flame; we're too close to victory to endanger our lives and covers. We must let Molly carry on with her shameless pursuit, and we'll have to keep her in the dark

305

about us. Otherwise we could be letting ourselves in for bad trouble. Until we leave Wilmington, we have to put aside what's between us."

"But, Blane, how—"

He pressed his fingertips over her mouth. "Don't argue about this matter, Flame. You promised to obey my orders, and this is an order. And don't you go getting riled over how I have to behave with her and you, and show your jealousy. I had enough trouble settling down Cathy. Lord, Flame, Molly would see you arrested and hanged before she'd let you take me away from her right under her own roof." His tone became husky and tender as he urged, "Please, Flame, don't interfere in Molly's games and dreams. Please believe me when I swear you're the only woman I want in my bed and my arms. I'm mad and I'm hurt that you would believe such vile things about me. To tell the truth, I had forgotten about her with you around to claim my attention. She isn't the reason we halted. I knew Pike would turn Wilmington upside down looking for us. I couldn't risk us being seen entering town."

Shannon imprisoned his fingers in her hand. "Will you listen to me for a moment or two, Major Stevens!" she demanded sharply. "I do believe you, and I apologize. It was foolish and unfair of me to attack you out of jealousy. When we get to Molly's, I'll try to obey your order, but it won't be easy. How will I look at you and be around you without the truth being written all over my face for Molly to see, especially when she's pawing you or fawning over you? You ordered me not to go to the wharves for any reasons; well, the same applies to you where her bed is concerned. I'll allow her romantic dreams, but nothing more, partner, understand?" she asked, using one of his favorite expressions.

Blane chuckled and lightly pinched her cheek. "Possessive little thing, aren't you? You needn't be jealous, Flame; I belong to you. Lord, you're right about one thing; it's gonna be torture keeping my eyes and hands off you for weeks."

Shannon tried to master her edginess. Her head and back were aching, which she assumed were effects from her previously cramped quarters and lack of exercise. She smiled. "You're a clever and resourceful man. I'm sure you can think of something if your hungers grow too large and painful. Let's get moving. I can already envision myself relaxing for hours in a big tub of warm water and lots of bubbles, then relishing a delicious hot meal and sleeping in a soft bed."

He kissed her palm. "Woman, you are a tormenting tease. What more could I want than to join you for all three?"

"To end the war and to find Ellie's errant lover," she unthinkably answered, then wished she had not said those things.

"My priorities are the war, you, then . . . Ellie's beguiler."

"Since nothing I say or do could possibly win or lose the war, I'll discard that priority. The same is true of Ellie's trouble; I could make the situation worse if I interfered. That leaves one. My priority would have to be to stay alive until I can make myself your first priority."

"Nothing could please me more, Shannon Greenleaf. Maybe that's why I can't bring myself to leave you anywhere for long; I'm afraid you'll find somebody to replace me, to change your priority."

Shannon caressed his jawline as she murmured, "In fear of swelling this handsome head, I speak reluctantly when I say you are irreplaceable, Major Blane Stevens. Unless you want or find someone to take my place, you're stuck with me. Until I find Corry, you're the only thing of value in my life. I've lost so much since this war began that I'm almost afraid to want you and need you. I'm so

307

afraid I'll look up one morning and you'll be leaving without telling me why you're going or where, just like that man did to Ellie."

She hurriedly went on to avoid any misunderstanding. "Not that I don't trust you, Blane, because I do. But all I have is your word that you want me too. Ellie loved and trusted . . . that man. Will you promise me one thing? If you want or need to leave me, don't go without telling me. I wouldn't try to hold you; I wouldn't cry or plead or give you any problems. If you have to go, do it openly and honestly. Please don't ever deceive me or betray me or desert me."

Blane thought he understood the meaning behind her words. "I promise, Shannon—open and honest, if I'm ever foolish enough to let you go. Will you do the same with me?"

Without hesitation, she vowed, "I promise."

Blane quickly went over the changes in his orders and new facts he had learned about their roles and assignments in Wilmington.

Having been alerted to their pre-dawn arrival by Jeremy, Sarah Jane was up and preparing to carry out her daily chores when Shannon and Blane rode up. Because they had encountered no person or obstacle along the way, they had covered the distance quickly and appeared without detection at the Resting Place just before six o'clock. Shannon was surprised to find that the hotel was large, beautiful, and well kept. The lovely, serene structure softly and quietly suggested money and elegance. Shannon was most impressed and pleased.

No sooner had the younger Sinclair sister told them that she rose early and handled the morning chores while Molly rose later and handled the evening tasks when Molly gracefully stepped into the receiving hall, all smiles and sparkling eyes for Blane. The ebony-haired beauty warmly greeted Blane before turning her curious attention to Shannon. Molly's smile froze. Her green eyes narrowed like a feline's stalking its tiny prey. It was obvious to the others present that Molly found Shannon's youth and beauty disturbing and objects of envy. Clearly she did not care to have such matchless competition around Blane, especially traveling with him. The twenty-eight-year-old widow visually appraised Shannon as if considering her purchase on the auction block.

Comprehending the woman's distress and suspicion, Shannon tried to dispel such hazardous feelings immediately. Her weary gaze swept over Blane with cool disinterest. "I'm so delighted to arrive finally. Major James has driven me as if I were a beast of burden heading for market. President Davis should recall him for lessons in courtesy and kindness. Perhaps it is this horrid war that causes fighting men to forget they should remain gentlemen at all times. I would never survive if the War Department paired me up with such an inconsiderate slave driver. I do hope this is the last time we shall be called upon to work together, sir."

Blane grasped his part in her cunning ruse and retorted nonchalantly, "It isn't my fault I was assigned to get you to a safe and comfortable resting place. As you can see, Cockade, you arrived in perfect condition, despite all of your grumbling and complaints. It astonishes me how you get anything done with that sorry attitude."

"Not only are you a beast—a crude and hateful beast—but you are also a fool. Never use my code name where it might be overheard. Very few people are as trustworthy and courageous as these two ladies. I shall not warn you again of such recklessness, sir. Anyone would think you an amateur at this dangerous and crucial business. I shall file a full report on your despicable

309

behavior when I return to Richmond."

Molly hurriedly inserted, "But Miss Greenleaf, you judge Major James too quickly and harshly. Perhaps you are overly tired from your journey and work. I can assure you, Steven is a fine gentleman and an exceptionally brave man. We are most honored to assist you both."

Shannon sighed heavily as she critically eyed Blane. "Perhaps you are right, Mrs. Ryan. I am thoroughly exhausted and out of sorts. I have a head wound that still pains me occasionally. Perhaps I am being hard on him. Surely he cannot be as terrible as I imagined if you speak and think so highly of him. Nor can he be a bad judge of character, since he has selected you two as good friends and helpers. We have traveled swiftly under frightful conditions, so there has been little time to get acquainted. I apologize to you, your sister, and Major Stevens for my silly and offensive behavior. I am most grateful for your patriotism. Your hotel is lovely. I know I shall enjoy my visit."

Grinning playfully, she teased, "Perhaps there will be enough time for a little entertainment. I hear many handsome soldiers are on duty in your fine city. How I long to hear the rustle of satin, the tinkling of wine glasses, the sound of lovely music, and the laughter and flattery of a handsome man. How exciting to think of dancing and dinners and smiles and fun. Wilmington seems so far from the noises of cannons, and gunshots, and exploding mines, and screams of pain and death. Perhaps I shall become spoiled here and never leave."

After introductions were made and genial banter was exchanged, the younger sister took command of the situation. Knowing they must be exhausted, the plump and jolly Sarah Jane immediately showed them to their rooms, returning to Shannon's with a hot meal and warm water for washing her hands and face. Shannon gazed around the spacious bedroom of the suite that Sarah Jane

Sinclair and Molly Sinclair Ryan had insisted she use without charge during her stay in Wilmington. She astutely presumed that Molly was tending to Blane's food and water, and she vowed she would not feel or show jealousy toward the buxom female who was half-owner of the establishment.

After devouring the tasty meal and freshening up, Shannon slipped into a flannel gown that Sarah Jane had given her. She smiled and sighed peacefully as she stretched out under the covers. Ignoring all sounds and thoughts, she slept tranquilly until mid-afternoon.

Upon awakening, she stretched over and over. How she wished Blane were lying beside her. How wonderful it would be to marry him and to awaken at his side each new day, she reflected silently. She could almost feel that last feverish kiss he had placed on her lips just before they had entered town. He had pulled her across his thighs to embrace and to kiss her a final time. He had reminded her to call him Steven James and had cautioned her to do nothing more than what they had previously discussed. He had released her horse with its identifiable markings and had disposed of the incriminating Confederate gear. They had arrived riding double.

Shannon got out of bed and walked to the windows. From the third-story suite, she had a marvelous view of the city and riverfront, and she saw that both were very busy. She noticed boats and ships of varying sizes. Perhaps she had a bit of the sailor in her as Corry did, she mused, for such sights always thrilled her, especially viewing the tall-masted sailing ships. A burst of anticipation and energy surged through her. She wondered if Sarah Jane or Molly knew any of their captains. It would be so exciting to tour one of those beautiful frigates. Surely she would be safe on the wharves if escorted by a powerful sea captain and friend of the Sinclairs.

311

She mentally reviewed the tale that Blane would relate about them. She prayed that Blane had been right in ordering her to use her real name. She also prayed that Jeremy Steele had been right when he had assured them that Moore's troops were gone. She mentally prayed for her two brothers, her home, divine guidance for Lincoln and all soldiers, and for her beloved. She prayed for the courage to confide in Blane, and for his understanding.

There was a knock on her door before Sarah Jane let herself in to deliver Shannon's meal and to see if she needed anything before she began her afternoon chores. The woman's entrance warned Shannon that she would have to bolt her door from the inside from now on. She smiled warmly at the woman who was eyeing her with fascination and respect.

"Good afternoon, Sarah Jane. This is most kind of you, but you shouldn't go to such trouble because of me. I can take my meals downstairs. You must be busy, and I don't wish to impose."

The hazel-eyed woman quickly retorted, "Impose? Heavens no, Miss Greenleaf. It's an honor to serve you. I know you must be exhausted, and I hated to awaken you. But we have strict dining hours; once lunch is served, no food will be available until six. I wanted you to eat before everything was chilled or discarded. You see, what isn't eaten or can't be saved is given to the poor or to soldiers. I told the cleaning woman not to disturb you until you were ready for your room to be straightened and to have your bath prepared."

"Could you join me for a cup of tea while I eat?" Shannon inquired, knowing the woman was bursting with questions. She knew it would be best to begin her stay in a genial and trusting atmosphere.

Sarah Jane beamed with pleasure and appreciation. She poured the tea and arranged the table while Shannon slipped into her garments. After joining Sarah Jane,

Shannon sighed heavily. "Please excuse my clothing. I fear I have nothing else to wear. What wasn't stolen along the way or discarded during moments of peril was left in Richmond. Do you think I could help with chores to earn money for a few items?"

"I couldn't possibly allow someone such as you to do menial chores. You are here to relax, Miss Greenleaf. My sister and I have numerous gowns and undergarments. We will be more than happy to share some with you. We owe you much for your services to the Confederacy. I'm sure I can obtain needed items from other ladies without revealing your identity. Don't you worry; I'll handle everything. By tomorrow, your closet will be bulging, but your colorful name will still be a secret."

"You are far too generous, Sarah Jane. Accepting charity comes hard at times, for so many Southerners and soldiers are sadly lacking in food and clothing, and even weapons. Please, call me Shannon."

"Major James told us what a terrible time you had getting here. I'm so happy you arrived safely. Your missions must be difficult when you don't know whom to trust."

Shannon stopped eating to respond. Knowing this woman might have heard of General Moore's search for her, she thought it would be wise to make a valid explanation of that episode. "They are, Sarah Jane," she concurred, then briefly related the occurrences in his camp before swearing her to secrecy. "That incident was most distressing. He deserved to know who we were, but it was too dangerous to confide in him. With clever and desperate spies everywhere, our missions and identities must be guarded at all times. We had no choice but to allow him to think he'd captured a Yankee spy with a vulnerable hostage. Now either he believes Major James took me captive again, or he suspects I was his Yankee accomplice. Here, you and your sister are the only two people who know I'm Cockade. You can imagine what the Federals would do to get their hands on me. It's so hard being on alert all the time, being suspicious of everyone, running and hiding. I need this rest and peace. I cannot begin to express my gratitude."

"After what happened to Rose Greenhow, I can't blame you for being afraid and wary. That handsome Lieutenant Pike went around giving your description and asking for news of you. Molly and I kept a sharp watch on him like Jeremy asked. You're lucky he didn't give your name or tell why he was seeking you, especially to General Holmes. Otherwise, you would be spending this rest time being questioned and trying to prove who you are. After a while, he seemed satisfied you hadn't come this way. What if you two hadn't escaped? What if General Moore had tried to execute you?" the woman asked worriedly.

"Those are the risks agents must take to help end this war. It isn't that we didn't trust Moore; it's just that damaging information is too frequently dropped by unthinking officers when they're drinking or bragging. Even if I had told Moore the truth, our release would have inspired hazardous curiosity. Or worse, he probably wouldn't have believed us; then we would have faced hours or days of badgering questions. We could have been sent to a fort or prison until our identities were proven. I was too exhausted to endure that. We can't let anyone discover we're in this area. I would be vulnerable to danger and the major's work would be thwarted. No one knows I'm Cockade, or that Cockade's a woman. You and Molly mustn't drop even a tiny clue about me. After the war, you can tell everyone how you helped me and Major James."

Sarah Jane smiled at her new friend. "You shouldn't feel guilty about deceiving General Moore. I'm sure he would understand."

"He should, considering he almost let me die in the line of duty. War causes men to think and behave stupidly. You can imagine me trying to tell him who I am. Many soldiers take one look at me and laugh skeptically. The only way I can convince them is to use certain code words. Evidentally, General Moore hadn't received the new list, because he didn't respond to my signals and I didn't know the old ones for his area. Besides, our capture and escape should make them more alert and careful. Men can be such cocky, stubborn creatures. Some of them detest taking suggestions or orders from a woman. General Moore seemed like one of those overly proud males. One thing for certain, our actions were good practice for a real capture and escape."

"You and Major James make a good pair. He seemed so concerned about you when you arrived. He's really kind and well bred. I'm sorry you found him so disagreeable. He's very handsome and manly."

Shannon realized this woman was perceptive and still harbored doubts about her. She decided that partial honesty would win Sarah Jane's loyalty and affection. "That false behavior was a wicked thing for me to do. I hope you don't think badly of me, but I wanted to avoid any problems or needless anguish. It was clear how Molly feels about Major James, so I tried to ease her worries. I'm sure she doesn't realize I travel with many handsome and virile men. I didn't want to give her cause for alarm about me and him. You see, the man I love and plan to marry as soon as this war ends is not Major Steven James. When she looked so concerned, I wanted to tell Molly outright that I'm not a barrier between her and the object of her desires. But I've learned from past experiences, verbal protests and denials only cast more suspicion. I know little about Major James. Are they very close? Did I do the right thing?"

Sarah Jane grinned, totally disarmed and deluded. Her

sister was a spoiled brat who thought she could captivate any man she wanted. Maybe with her looks, wealth, and ripe figure, she could ensnare almost any man, but not Major James. He was just too nice to spurn her! Molly could be so vain and bossy, and she used her age and past marital status as excuses. At times, Molly refused to do her share of chores, assigning them to their hired servants. Sometimes Sarah Jane wanted to strangle or spank her older sister. She wasn't fooled as to why Molly wanted the late shift of chores. It was the hour when numerous men came to dine and to chat with friends. She wondered how Molly was going to take to having this beauty around for competition, for Molly could be a spiteful thing. She liked Shannon, and would warn her.

"Molly would like for them to be close, but I doubt Major James feels that way. He's much too kind and well mannered to hurt anyone, even that flirty and persistent sister of mine. I think he's hoping she'll find other prey. But Molly has her heart set on trapping him. Unless you really come to like him, it would be best if you continued that false behavior around my sister. When riled, she can get nasty," she advised pointedly.

"You're a very bright and unselfish person, Sarah Jane. Is there a man in your life?" Shannon inquired genially as she sipped the tea.

Sarah Jane blushed and grinned, then sighed in frustration. "I'm waiting for the day when Jeremy Steele forgets his wife and learns to trust again." She went on to explain the tragic tale of Jeremy's betrayal.

"Perhaps we can find some reasons for Jeremy to visit frequently while we're staying here. He seems very nice and cheerful. Does he know you find him attractive, that you want him?"

"How does a woman let a man know such things without acting badly?" she questioned seriously.

"When he comes around, talk to him, smile at him. Prepare something special for him to eat, perhaps a treat to carry home. Ask about him; lonely people miss conversation and kindness. Don't be afraid to look him in the eye. Words and feelings can be exchanged with a special look. If he's been hurt, he needs to feel your affection and understanding. Besides feeling anger and bitterness and wariness over his wife's betrayal and desertion, he must have lost some of his self-esteem and confidence. Maybe he's afraid to trust or love another woman, afraid she'll do the same. Let him feel your love and warmth. Let him know you're hurting for him. Find ways to touch him accidentally, to remind him of forgotten feelings. Smell good and look pretty to snare his nose and eyes. Work on the physical side first, because you've got to catch his attention before you can catch his heart."

"You know so much about men," the woman declared in awe.

"I had three brothers who talked a great deal about women, feelings, and such. They wanted me to understand those emotions and situations. The average woman doesn't realize how scary it can be for a man to approach her, to risk being an amusement or diversion, to challenge rejection. Men can be just as shy or intimidated. They told me that it helps encourage and relax a man if you boldly show interest and affection. You have to encourage and relax Jeremy."

"I'll try my best, Shannon. Sometimes I wish I were more outgoing, like Molly. But if I were, I would never snare Jeremy." She laughed after speaking that naughty conclusion aloud.

"I'll speak with Major James and see if we can't get Jeremy to come here for some reason. I'll help you win him. It'll be fun."

317

Sarah's joy faded instantly. "But Major James left this morning. I heard him telling Molly he wouldn't be returning for two or three weeks. By then, it'll be freezing or you two will be leaving."

"He's gone? Without telling me?" she asked incredulously. That wasn't their plan! What about his recent promise to warn her of separations? She promptly mastered her emotions and poise. "That shouldn't surprise me, but I thought he was going to rest a few days. We aren't partners, and I did treat him rather hatefully last night. He doesn't owe me explanations, and he probably enjoys thinking he's put one over on me. Men—they always have something to prove to themselves or to others. Damn such pride and ego. Since he's left, that means I'm truly on a much-needed rest break. Wilmington seems so far from the battles and suffering and peril. I suppose I'll feel guilty every day for wallowing in this lap of luxury."

"You look as if you need rest, Shannon."

Shannon nodded as she replied, "I do. My head and back ache, and my stomach is crampy. Probably all of this riding and eating on the run. I would love to soak in a hot tub if you don't mind. And don't worry about Jeremy. We'll think of something. He'll be courting you before Thanksgiving," Shannon remarked confidently, then grinned.

"Only a month? I hope you can work that quickly. I've made no progress with him in two years. I'll send Mattilu Walker to help you. She's a free black woman who works for me. While you're here, she'll see to your food, bath, laundry, and cleaning. You'll like her. Just ask her for whatever you want or need."

After Sarah Jane Sinclair left the spacious room, Shannon went to lie down until Mattilu came to prepare her bath and to strengthen her fire. The days were growing colder and windier. In this hotel, Shannon felt safe and warm, but she fretted over the fact that her love was somewhere battling the enemy as well as this rapidly changing weather.

She massaged her temples. Her head hurt, but not unbearably. She felt tense and irritable. She was depressed. She stood and stripped off her pants, which seemed tighter today, and she was reminded of how and where she had gotten them. She wrapped a coverlet around her body and walked to the fireplace to stare into the almost serene blaze. She smiled as she recalled her chimney adventure with Blane. She couldn't imagine where they would have hidden if that fireplace had been in use. She sat in the rocker, again recalling another adventure: the night she had met Blane and he had tied her to a similar chair to interrogate her. So many things reminded her of Blane Stevens.

Shannon leaned her head against the chair and closed her eyes. She began to rock and to hum. So many images filled her mind: home, her brothers, her adventures, her perils, her dreams, her missing lover. How she longed for this war to end so she could start a new life, hopefully at Greenleaf with Corry and Blane, and Hawke . . .

When Mattilu arrived, she suggested that they prepare a tub near the fireplace instead of in the cool bathing closet. Shannon instantly agreed. The buckets of water were passed up from the kitchen by way of a pulley and shaft enclosed in a special cabinet and available for use on each floor. Shannon didn't mind using the large tin tub rather than the oblong one, for she had no patience for a lengthy soak today. She wanted to bathe, then return to bed.

As Mattilu assisted her, Shannon conversed with the woman to distract herself from her increasing misery. "I was told you're a free woman. How long have you worked for the Sinclair sisters?"

The forty-year-old, brown-skinned woman replied softly, "I's been wif Missy Sarah Jane since she wuz born. I used ta works fur her family. They's said I cud be free when them two girls growed up. Missy Sarah Jane kept her papa's word after he died. Missy Molly wanted Mattilu ta stays a slave. She gived Missy Sarah a bad time onnacouna of 'leasing me. I's been workin' fur her ever since. I's gonna enjoy hepping you, Missy Shannon."

Shannon turned her head and grinned at the attractive woman. "You can drop the ruse and false talk, Mattilu. I'm not a Molly or a tattler. I don't believe in slavery. So you don't have to pretend with me."

Mattilu laughed. "How did you guess?" she inquired.

"Some of your word choices and pronunciations. I know this must be a difficult time for you, but things will change after the war. You don't have to be afraid or devious around me. The way things are going, you won't have to conceal your sharp wits much longer. It must be taxing to playact all the time to keep people from getting nervous."

The woman stared at Shannon, who blushed and looked away. Mattilu warned, "I'm not the only one who should watch her words, Miss Shannon. Be real careful around Molly."

"What do you mean?" the redhead inquired anxiously.

"Much as I hate fooling Miss Sarah Jane, I hate slavery more, and I want it ended for all my people. Miss Molly has been asking lots of questions about you. She's upset because you're so beautiful and you've been traveling with the man who's got her planning and plotting his bewitchment, but she won't get him. Miss Sarah Jane is different. She's sweet and kind, but she's mighty patriotic." Mattilu's voice changed as she revealed, "Major

Stevens has been kind and generous to me. I've been helping him in little ways, if you understand my meaning. You can find rest and safety here. I promised the major to watch after you. Whatever you need, just call Mattilu—nobody else."

Shannon caught the name she had used and the clues in her statements. "You're smarter and braver than I realized, Mattilu. Like I said, playacting all the time is very hard and dangerous."

"I keep my eyes and ears open all the time. I try to help the major, but I don't take risks. We'll have to be careful, 'cause we don't want anyone hearing us talk. This town's full of Rebel soldiers and Southern loyalists, so you have to be real careful when you go out."

"I'm glad you're here, Mattilu. Now I won't feel so alone with Blane gone. Did he say anything to you before he left?"

"He asked me to look after you until he gets back. He told me how you two had to fool Molly. If I had to make a guess, it's love what put that gleam in his eyes and that cotton in his voice," she teased.

Shannon smiled, then laughed. "I hope so, Mattilu. I surely hope so." She continued with her bath, silent for a time.

"Miss Shannon, I forgot to tell you; nobody knows about me save the major and Mister Jeremy. I want it kept that way."

"I understand, Mattuli. I should explain a few matters to you." Shannon related how she had met Blane, some of their joint adventures, her search for her brother, and the Cockade ruse. She also explained the story they had told the Sinclair sisters. "Do you think Jeremy has any special feelings for Sarah Jane? I wouldn't want to encourage her if you think it's wrong or unwise. They *are* fighting for opposite sides."

321

"I've seen Mister Jeremy watching Miss Sarah Jane when she wasn't looking, and I've seen her do the same. I think something's budding betwixt them. 'Course Mister Jeremy might think it best to wait until the war's over to ask her hand in marriage."

"Perhaps that would be for the best. The war does have a way of coming between lovers even when they're working for the same side. I hope Blane isn't away too long. It's getting cold outside."

"One of the ladies sent a wool cape for you. Miss Sarah Jane has collected lots of clothes as well—pretty ones. Would you like to try them on after your bath?"

"Not yet, Mattilu. I haven't been feeling well today."

Shannon stood up and stepped out of the tub onto the mat placed there by the serving woman. Mattilu wrapped a drying sheet around her. "I think I'll lie down for a while. I'll look at the clothes later." As Shannon patted the water from her body, the edge of the bath sheet turned red, which instantly explained her symptoms.

Mattilu noticed her problem and smiled. "I'll get you some hot tea and monthly cloths, Miss Shannon. You just take it easy."

While Shannon awaited the other woman's return, she realized why she had been feeling so terrible yesterday and today. Suddenly she became aware of another fact—one which might have frightened her if she had thought of it sooner: this was her first monthly flow since August, making her long over a month late. She was delighted it had occurred here in the hotel and with Blane gone. She decided to follow the suggestions of Blane, Mattilu, and Sarah Jane to rest and relax for the next five days. She would sleep, rest, read, eat, and stay warm. Nature's timing couldn't have been more perfect. Considering how many times she had made love to Blane, she was fortunate not to be pregnant. She realized she would have to give that part of their relationship deep thought, or she

322

could find herself wearing ill-fitting shoes, similar to those Ellie Stevens was wearing. She loved Blane, and she suspected that he loved her. But what if something happened to him and she was left carrying his child? She smiled. If anything happened to Blane, that's exactly what she would want!

Chapter Thirteen

During those five days when Shannon chose to remain in her room, Mattilu brought her meals, saw to the cleaning of her room, assisted with her baths, took care of her laundry, exchanged genial banter, prevented Molly's visits, and delivered reading material. It was the newspapers that distressed Shannon. Not only was the news grim, but she realized that Blane had been withholding alarming facts from her.

Rebel agents had captured letters, Northern newspapers, and telegraph missives and had intercepted messages that the papers printed for all Southerners to read, knowing such quotes would inspire more courage and determination to battle such grisly foes and to win the war. After reading such pieces, words such as truce, peace, compromise, or surrender were soon forgotten by provoked and embittered Southerners, even those who had grown weary of the fighting and killing.

Shannon was staggered by the grisly facts and shocking orders. Grant was quoted commanding Halleck: "Send everything that can be got to eat out of Virginia, clear and clean as they go, so that the crows flying over it will have to carry their provisions with them." She read Grant's message to Sheridan: "Carry off stock of all description, and negroes, so as to prevent further planting. We want the Shenandoah Valley to remain a barren waste." Was this the price and reality of war? Was this how the North intended to accomplish a peaceful reunion?

Tears filled Shannon's eyes as she read Sheridan's response: "I have burned two thousand barns filled with wheat and corn, all the mills in the whole country, destroyed or driven off every animal, even the poultry, that could contribute to human sustenance. Nothing should be left in the Shenandoah but eyes to lament the war." Shannon wondered how the innocents—women, children, elderly people, the injured—could survive, especially during the freezing winter that was almost upon them.

But it was the horrors in Georgia that terrified and panicked her. That beautiful city of Atlanta had been destroyed—thousands of homes, farms, businesses, buildings . . . Nothing was left but "smoke and flame!" The Union soldiers were boasting of looting, burning, pillaging, and Heaven only knew what other foul deeds. It distressed her to read of Sherman's intentions to burn anything he couldn't use or carry with him. He had boasted, "Instead of the people there furnishing provisions for the Confederate Army, President Davis will have to supply them or they will starve." How could Lincoln allow such crimes? How could ordinary men commit them?

Sherman's aide-de-camp, Major Nichols, told how the Georgians—especially women—were vulnerable and defenseless. He said that "the rebel inhabitants are in an agony. The soldiers are as hearty and jolly as men can be." He spoke of the plundering as "one of the pleasantest excitements of our march." How could honorable officers allow such cruelties? Order them? How could average men—most with families left behind—turn into such monsters, or be so brutal and heartless? What of the innocents? What of the loyal Unionists, their lives, their families, their homes and properties? What of the desolation and death left behind such a wild rampage? Clearly the Union's strategy was to devastate the South into surrender—financially, socially, economically, industrially, and murderously.

Shannon's heart thudded heavily as she continued her reading. Sherman had written to Grant: "I can make Savannah, Charleston, or the mouth of the Chattahoochee. I prefer to march through Georgia, smashing things, to the sea. The utter destruction of its roads, houses, and people will cripple their military resources." *Savannah?* she fretted. What of the Confederate treasury at the Hay House in Macon? The munition works in Athens and Augusta? The rescue of Union prisoners at Andersonville? Where would that destroyer head next?

Shannon read about the torpedoing of the Confederate ram *Albermarle* on the Roanoke River by Lieutenant Cushing. That event had caused fear to race through the area. She read the reports on the upcoming election. Would Lincoln win again? Should he? She found herself delighting in General Lee's tenacious hold on Richmond and Petersburg. She read of daring battles between Union gunboats and Rebel blockade runners. Curiously, she felt a deep pride over those victories. Perhaps it was because she hadn't known of the Union's "win at any and all costs" strategy. Even during wartime, some deeds were evil.

When Mattilu revealed General Bragg's assignment to the Cape Fear defense, Shannon wondered if she should contact him. If so, how should she behave? What should she say? She was a Union agent! How could she betray another of her father's friends, knowing how her information might be used by men like Sheridan or Sherman? What if she saw or heard things that should be

326

reported to Blane? Could she? If not, what if he discovered she was concealing facts? She decided it would be better not to uncover information that might divide her loyalties.

If there was one thing that distressed Shannon as much as the atrocities committed by the Union officers and troops, it was the Union's refusal to exchange or to aid prisoners. Here she was, trying to help her brother escape, when the Confederacy was begging the Union to exchange captured men—if only the wounded or sick! The Confederacy had been trying to take "Christian" care of the Federal prisoners, but supplies and food were desperately low and medicines almost nonexistent. What a horrible choice: to feed and tend one's own people or the enemy's?

President Davis was deeply concerned over his inability to provide the captives with proper care, food, clothing, shelter, and medicines. In 1853, he had been the United States Secretary of War. He had loved this country and had fought for her during the Mexican War. He hated to see any of her people suffer needlessly. He had offered to turn over fifteen thousand sick or wounded prisoners without any exchange; the Union had refused to accept the men! The Confederacy had offered to buy medicines with gold, tobacco, or cotton; again the Union had refused, fearing the medicines would be used on Rebel instead of Yankee soldiers! Wasn't a dying or wounded man deserving of help, no matter his loyalty?

One paper told of how a group of Union prisoners was sent to Washington from Andersonville to plead for help and provisions; they were refused! They were told, "No, go back. You are rendering your country better service by staying at Andersonville than you would by being exchanged." Since all knew of the conditions of that horrible camp, how could Washington make such ridiculous statements and cruel demands? Those politicians and seat-warming soldiers wouldn't have spoken so foolishly if they had been Confederate captives for a month or so! What if Corry had been one of those pleading prisoners? Surely he would have escaped before returning to such injustice!

Five thousand more who could not be fed or tended properly had been released and sent to the Federals in Florida; they too had been ordered to return to the prison camp. Despair, dejection, and death had resulted for many of them. What barbaric, inhumane strategy was being practiced? The more Shannon read or heard, the more depressed and confused she became, and the more ashamed for her meager part in this matter. In view of such facts, how could she and Blane—both Southerners —side with the Union and aid such misery?

That first week of November was cold and damp. Shannon had kept to herself much of the time, claiming lingering fatigue and "female troubles." Molly Sinclair Ryan had visited her once, to share local gossip and to stress her claim on "Major Steven James." Shannon had played her indifferent, but respectful, part convincingly. Molly had left her suite all smiles, laughter, and confidence. Since Molly actually did very little work, Sarah Jane stayed too busy to visit more than a few brief times, during which they talked mostly about Jeremy Steele.

The majority of Shannon's time was spent alone or in the company of Mattilu. The two women became good friends, frequently exchanging tales of their past lives. As Mattilu was acquainted with Blane and could accidentally drop a clue before Shannon herself could confide in Blane about Hawke, she was careful not to mention him.

As everyone expected, Lincoln was elected President again. It was proclaimed that the military victories by Sherman, Sheridan, and Farragut had won him that political triumph. Shannon decided that Lincoln was either receiving terrible advice or being kept ignorant of the deplorable actions of his army, for surely he would not have permitted them. How she wished she could return to Washington and open his eyes.

Newspapers continued to declare that neither side would yield. Lee was holding Grant at bay, refusing to allow the Union's conquest of the Confederate capitol and the strategic city of Petersburg. But Grant was determined to win that area, though losses on both sides were awesome. Both armies were exhausted and embittered but seemingly resolved to battle to the death of every man present.

Another week passed, and Sherman was reported on the move again, heading southeast and cutting a wide path of devastation across Shannon's home state. His men had rested and feasted in Atlanta until the twelfth; they were said to be in excellent health and high spirits now. Rapaciously foraging along their trail to the sea, they would remain healthy and strong while weakening or destroying those left behind in their path. He was doing more than trying to break the Confederacy's spirit and sever supply lines; he was trying to cripple or destroy the South, to savagely punish all Georgians regardless of age or sex or guilt.

The Seventy-seventh Regiment and companies of artillerymen were ordered from North Carolina to the defense of Savannah. Hood had tried valliantly to lure Sherman out of Atlanta and Georgia, using himself and his men as decoys. True, Sherman wanted to defeat Hood, but his voracious appetite for Georgia's destruction had been whetted. When Hood headed into Tennessee to attack Nashville, Sherman sent Thomas in pursuit to defend and hold that conquered area.

On November fifteenth, Shannon took her first

evening meal downstairs, much to the surprise and pleasure of several officers dining there, and much to the vexation of an envious Molly, whose emerald satin gown the copper-haired beauty was wearing. To further irritate her sister, Sarah Jane introduced Shannon to the officers and to other couples present, then seated her at a table with five important guests.

Shannon smiled and spoke genially with men who were serving under Whiting and Lamb at Fort Fisher, as well as the messenger between Governor Vance and Fort Fisher, Mrs. Armand DeRossett of the Ladies' Relief Society, and Captain Elisha Carter of the blockade runner, *Rebel Gate*.

Mrs. DeRossett entreated Shannon to join her Ladies' Relief Society and help them with their mercy mission until she left for home. Shannon accepted the woman's plea for help, but not for the reason Blane had suggested. She would not spy on those wounded men; she would nurse them and comfort them. Mrs. DeRossett was to send word when trains arrived. On Tuesdays, the society met to roll bandages and to collect helpful gifts from the local residents.

The strength and importance of Fort Fisher and Wilmington were discussed proudly, as if the Confederacy's victory would be won or lost on their survival or defeat. Governor Vance's messenger seemed delighted to share news from other locations, news that should only have been for the ears of the governor and military officers. Shannon suspected the man's lips had been loosened by too much wine and the jovial company surrounding him.

Shannon boldly and coyly teased, "Sir, if I were a Union spy, I would have many valuable facts to report to my superior. Perhaps you should be more careful with your talk, for I fear that Federal agents lurk everywhere. We certainly don't wish to entice the Union Army or

Navy to attack our lovely and peaceful city or crucial fort."

Lamb's aide looked chastened and glanced around to see if anyone had been observing them too closely. He smiled at Molly and Mattilu nearby, then returned his attention to the exquisite redhead with large blue eyes.

When the messenger and Mrs. DeRossett departed, one of Whiting's lieutenant's encouraged, "Eli, tell us some stories about you and your raider friends. I'm sure Miss Greenleaf would find them fascinating."

With only three men left at the large table, Shannon had been about to rise and leave, but she was halted by the stimulating suggestion. She coaxed with a bright smile, "Oh, please do, Captain Carter. It sounds so exciting. Have you been to Savannah lately? Is she all right?"

Molly was pleased with the way Shannon was looking and smiling at the handsome and rugged sea captain. She decided it was to her advantage to encourage a friendship, and perhaps a romance, between them. With two of the serving women absent tonight, both she and her younger sister had been compelled to help with the evening meal. She smiled flirtatiously as she hinted, "Captain Carter, why don't you take your friends into the private parlor? It's more comfortable and quieter in there. Here's the key; you know where it is. I'll bring a bottle of sherry and four glasses, compliments of the hotel. I cannot tell you how delighted I am to see you make Shannon laugh and smile. She's been spending far too much time alone since her arrival."

As Elisha nodded agreement and gratitude, his green eyes gleamed with admiration for his dinner companion. The tall and muscular seaman rose agilely, then assisted Shannon with her chair. Taking her by the elbow, he escorted her into the private sitting room. Shannon sat on the sofa beside him, while the two officers claimed chairs nearby. Mattilu was the one who delivered the sherry and glasses. After pouring and serving the golden liquid, she left the room. To make sure they were not disturbed by other hotel or dinner guests, Lamb's aide bolted the door and returned to his chair.

Elisha lifted his glass and stated in a spirited tone, "Let's toast the health and happiness of our beautiful visitor and victory for the Confederacy." He lightly touched his glass to Shannon's, then took a long swallow. His fertile green eyes never left her liquid blue ones.

She replied, "You gentlemen are most kind and entertaining. I toast your health and happiness, and a swift and merciful victory." She took a sip from her glass, then smiled at the charming man beside her. He looked and acted as if he would be at home anywhere. His skill and courage were obvious, as were his breeding and intelligence. She could envision him standing on the deck of a tall-masted ship, shouting orders, using enormous cunning and bravery, his sable hair blowing wildly about his sun-darkened face, his forest green eyes sparkling with vitality and excitement, his white teeth gleaming in a triumphant smile. The tall twenty-seven-year-old had told her while they had dined that he had been born and bred to ships and the sea, coming from a wealthy and influencial family of shipbuilders and sea captains. No doubt his love for the sea and adventure explained his bachelor state, for he seemed a man to attract the female eye and to win most any heart.

Perturbed by Blane's behavior and absence, Shannon forced aside thoughts and yearnings for him. She and her mysterious Texan had no claims on each other, she rationalized. He had left without telling her and hadn't contacted her in over two weeks. For all she knew, he might not be returning, intentionally or unintentionally. For all she knew, she could be on her own. Since they were partners and lovers, he shouldn't be treating her

332

this way! Maybe what he needed was a spark of jealousy, such as those he had given her on several occasions. Besides, this captain was a real man, a brave and daring adventurer who was both appealing and charming. Who better to have as a friend if there were trouble or if she needed a pleasant diversion during her stay in Wilmington?

"Molly was right; I have been too sad and sluggish of late. I fear it's the cold weather and this ceaseless war. I'm becoming more homesick and worried over my family every day. Is there no end in sight, Captain Carter?" she inquired softly, addressing her question and focusing her attention on that compelling man.

Elisha smiled at her before responding, "I wish I could say all will be fine very soon. But I'm afraid it looks bad on land and sea. We've lost countless ships and supply lines, but Savannah was holding her own the last time I sailed into her port. She's a beautiful city, as special as her people. After the war, I would love to visit your plantation; your description made it sound like a paradise. Perhaps I could entice your family's shipping business to deal with my father's firm."

He and Shannon laughed. "I'm sure my brother would be delighted to meet and talk with you about such an arrangement, Captain Carter. A speedy and dependable shipping firm is vital to us. I shall be honored to have you as our guest and to introduce you to Corry."

Elisha eyed her curiously. "How do you plan to get home, Miss Greenleaf? Don't you think it wiser and safer to remain here?"

"I plan to rest for another few weeks, then head for Charleston by train. From there, I hope to obtain passage on the train home. If you're referring to Sherman's march toward Savannah, who better to protect my home and lands than the owner? Hopefully those men will tire of their destruction before reaching my city and the plantation. I will slay the savage beast if he or any of his ferocious animals sets one foot on Greenleaf land. I'm hoping the Rebel Army will defeat them or turn them aside. Somebody has to stop his wanton destruction."

Elisha forcibly relaxed and nodded as he observed the angry glitter in her eyes. "I'm afraid it requires an evil devil to defeat another powerful and wicked devil, and heaven be thanked the Confederacy doesn't have beasts such as Sherman and Sheridan."

"Someone or something must halt him. What of God's help and guidance, and Rebel prowess?"

"From what I've seen and heard, Miss Greenleaf, either God is not interfering in this conflict or He's sided with the Union. We have plenty of men—brave and clever soldiers—but soldiers cannot fight without supplies. Railroads, boats, and bridges have been destroyed, so we can't get things moved inland. Union spies get hold of missives and telegrams, so we can't send word where to come for supplies. All we can do is send out as many supplies as can be carried or transported when regiments pass through or near ports like this one."

"What about using flatboats on large rivers in the middle of the night? Or using pack mules overland with advance scouts? Surely there's some route the Yankees can't block? We can't leave men and land defenseless. Why do you risk your life running the blockade and challenging the shoals if the supplies are going to sit on wharves?"

"Because we plan to find new ways of getting the supplies to our men. I'll pass your suggestions along. I do have a plan to deliver a load to Richmond by docking at a Union port and coming from the North, disguising my men as Federal soldiers who are heading to resupply Grant."

Shannon beamed. "That's very clever and daring, Captain Carter. Surely it would work. Who would suspect such a ruse? If you could get other captains to do the same, supplies could be filtered into every area under attack. Your plan could save the Confederacy. You should guard this plan carefully, sir; Union spies could be anywhere."

"I know, Miss Greenleaf. I've come across several who were trying to uncover how we run the blockade. I even had one slip aboard my ship and try to burn her. It'll take more than a Union spy or traitorous Southerner to destroy the *Rebel Gate*, or capture me."

"What do you do with such men?" she inquired, trying to hide her anxiety. Blane had listed such a mission for this area. She feared to imagine a battle between Elisha Carter and Blane Stevens, for they appeared nearly matched in strength and skill and size.

"Men, I hang from the yardarm; women, I send to prison," he responded, leaning back against the sofa and watching her intently.

"Women?" she echoed in astonishment. "There are women who attempt such tasks? How could a woman hope to go unnoticed on a ship?"

He chuckled at her reaction. "By posing as a whore or a friend, or a patriot trying to get to Europe to raise money for the Confederacy. I even had one Yankee sympathizer claim to be a runaway from a savage uncle while her father and brothers were off fighting the war."

"I'm sure they all claimed innocence, so how do you know who's telling the truth and who's lying?" she asked, intrigued and dismayed.

"This is a depressing subject for such a delicate lady. Let's just say I have my way of unmasking spies. I heard you agree to help Mrs. DeRossett with the wounded passing through by train. That can be a difficult and

335

unpleasant task, dealing with wounded men who will surely become enamored of your loveliness."

"I am stronger than you realize, Captain Carter. I'm sure I can handle the situation. Being reared as the only girl in a family of four older males, I've had plenty of nursing practice and dealings with the opposite sex. Don't worry. I'll be fine."

One of the soldiers informed Shannon, "I'm not sure you can get home by train, Miss Greenleaf. The lines between Wilmington and Florence, those from Florence to Charleston, and those connecting Charlestown to Savannah are still intact; but we don't know for how long. Most trains only allow soldiers, munitions, and supplies."

Shannon smiled coquettishly. "I'm cunning, so I'll find a way."

Elisha related several of his most daring and exciting adventures before the two officers were compelled to leave, reluctantly. After their departure, Shannon was even more aware of how Elisha dominated the room and captured her attention. He poured them another sherry.

Shannon felt uneasy being alone with this disarming rogue. Blane and her wits seemed so far away. As he offered her the glass, she smiled and told him, "No thank you, sir. It's late. I must return to my room. Thank you for a lovely and relaxing evening."

He gently grasped her hand and drew it to his lips for a kiss. He smiled as she quivered and blushed, then lowered her lashes demurely. Desire and fascination filled him. "I have never met a more enchanting lady. Must you leave so soon? Stay for a talk and another sherry."

Shannon was tempted to comply, but this stimulating man made her nervous and wary. "I cannot, sir. We've just met tonight, and we're alone. I wouldn't want to cause gossip during my visit."

Elisha squeezed her hand appreciatively. "I can assure you that you're perfectly safe with me. Since most fathers and brothers are away, the code of conduct for ladies has altered. They must select their own behavior and companions. No one would slight you or darken your name for being with me. You see, I'm considered rather a hero around these parts; most blockade runners and raiders are. When we're in port, many women pursue me or send their daughters after me. In their eyes, I can do no wrong."

Shannon laughed at his rakish expression. "That could be true for local women, but I'm a stranger. Perhaps I would be viewed as a rival for those daughters and treated as an unwanted intruder."

"Your last statement might be accurate, but don't let it color your decision. When a man faces danger and death nearly every day, he finds little peace and happiness such as you've given me tonight. You inspire a man to defeat the foe just to earn your affection and respect. Dare I hope you are willing to see me again?" His green eyes were entrancing and entreating. "Please, Shannon, spend time with me during these next few days, perhaps my last on earth."

Shannon realized that if Blane hadn't stolen her heart, she would be encouraging this man's pursuit. He was dangerously attractive and immensely sensual. His smile could make a woman's heart flutter; his gaze could turn her body to liquid. What if she had need of a quick escape or protection? What if Blane were killed or captured? "Please don't say such a terrible thing," she scolded him, impulsively pressing her fingers to his lips as she mentally discarded her last thought. When he kissed them, she quickly moved them, then flushed as she lowered her hand. "Perhaps we can have lunch or dinner tomorrow," she boldly ventured.

Elisha's dazzling smile could have brightened the

darkest corner of any room. "Perhaps we could have both. In between, I could show you around the city or give you a tour of my ship. I saw how your eyes lit up each time a ship was mentioned."

"Sailing ships are so beautiful, like graceful birds that are swift and adventurous. My brother Corry has always wanted to be a sailor, but Papa refused to let him." She grinned as she suggested mischievously, "Perhaps you could attract the Greenleaf business by promising he could sail with you on occasion. That would win him over."

Elisha laughed, and the sound of it seemed honest and vital to Shannon. "Perhaps his sister would agree to come along with him?" he hinted as he locked the door behind their exit, reminding himself to return the key to Molly.

"Perhaps she would. What time shall I meet you for lunch?"

"Here, at the foot of the stairs at noon. I'll escort you to your suite," he stated politely and eagerly, unwilling to rush their separation.

She shook her head as she replied, "That isn't necessary, Captain Carter. The hotel is perfectly safe, and it wouldn't look appropriate. Tomorrow, if you would be so kind, I would enjoy a tour of the city before dinner. Perhaps I can see your *Rebel Gate* in a few days, before she leaves port. It has been an honor and pleasure to meet you."

Elisha caught her implication; she would wait until she knew him better before daring to venture aboard his ship. "I understand, and I must reluctantly agree, if you'll call me Eli."

"Good night, Eli. And thanks for brightening my evening." As Shannon mounted the steps, she did not realize that three pairs of eyes were watching her and making decisions that would affect her destiny.

Molly was consumed with a mixture of envy and relief. She had given up her pursuit of that magnetic rogue long ago, but he continued to stir her heart and blood each time she saw him. If Elisha was as smitten with Shannon as he looked and sounded, the redhead would offer no threat to Molly's desire to have Steven, for Eli always got what he wanted, one way or another. But the main reason she wouldn't worry over Shannon's rivalry was the Georgian's behavior toward that roguish privateer. If Steven made a play for Shannon on his return, she would make certain he learned of the romantic interlude between the Rebel agent and the blockade runner during his absence. Perhaps she should fan Eli's spark of interest by revealing who and what Shannon was, then swear him to secrecy. The daring and ravishing Cockade might provide a tempting challenge for the rakish captain. Molly smiled triumphantly and headed for her room, delighted by tonight's victory.

Elisha also watched Shannon until she vanished from sight. He passed his tongue over his lips as if licking away the sugary remains of a tasty treat and astutely decided there was far more to this woman than met the eye. Since she was the only woman who had ever stimulated his thoughts and feelings beyond concerns for duty or casual sex, he vowed to discover more about her before he sailed again.

Mattilu observed Shannon, Elisha, and Molly as well.

That next day at noon, Shannon descended the stairs to find Captain Elisha Carter waiting for her. As their eyes met, each smiled. They shared a lengthy and cheerful lunch before entering a rented carriage to tour the city. Elisha pointed out the many sights and amused her with tales about each one. He was careful to keep the conversation away from the war. He told her he would give her a tour of the wharves and shops another day, if she was interested.

Shannon smiled and told him she would like to visit them, as she felt safe with him at her side. The outing was exhilarating and refreshing. Shannon was able to push all problems and fears to the back of her mind. Annoyed with Blane, Shannon was determined to have a good time with this handsome and arresting man. She delighted in Elisha's attention and admiration. She relished his company, wit, conversation, and charm. She enjoyed feeling alive, feeling desirable, feeling safe and happy, feeling clean and warm and well fed. She even enjoyed the chilling mid-November temperature.

At dinner, Elisha couldn't refuse to allow two high-ranking officers to join them at their table, but he resented the impolite intrusion. The men competed with each other to obtain and hold Shannon's attention. Elisha sat back and watched Shannon charm them while making it known that he was her companion for the evening. To draw him into the talk, she continually addressed statements or questions to him. When one of the officers made a query, Shannon would reply, then asked Elisha's opinion. Sometimes it was nothing more than a "Did you hear that, Eli?" or "Isn't that funny?" or "Don't you think that's strange?" just to keep the other men from monopolizing the conversation and her attention. Elisha was enchanted by her behavior.

When the officers made no attempt to depart and the hour grew late, Shannon announced she was retiring for the night. "Thank you so much for a lovely lunch and special afternoon, Eli."

He grinned when he realized she hadn't mentioned this evening's dinner engagement. "I'll walk you to the stairs. If you gentlemen will excuse us," he remarked courteously, rising to help Shannon with her chair.

One of the officers said, "We'll wait here, Captain

340

Carter. There is a matter or two we'd like to discuss with you."

"I shall return shortly." Elisha guided Shannon around the tables and out of the room. He noticed Sarah Jane watching them oddly. Then, his keen gaze caught Molly and the black serving woman doing the same. He mentally shrugged, assuming it was his colorful reputation with the ladies that had them worried. This was one time it wasn't necessary. Shannon Greenleaf was a special and provocative woman.

"I'm sorry about that, Shannon," he apologized at the steps.

"Don't worry about it, Eli," she softly commented.

"Can we have lunch, tour the docks and shops, then have dinner tomorrow night?" he inquired, smoothly filling her schedule.

"I promised to help with the train passing through tomorrow at midday. Could we do those things Friday?" she compromised.

"Can we at least have dinner?" he coaxed persistently.

Shannon smiled. "That would be lovely, Eli. Seven o'clock?"

He nodded, then watched her ascend the stairs. He turned to find Molly standing behind him. She asked if she could speak with him. He nodded, then followed her into the private parlor. He dreaded to discover what she wanted, yet quickly changed his mind.

The next day was cold and windy. Shannon bundled up snugly in the wool cape that had been given to her by one of the local ladies. The brisk walk to the depot put color into her cheeks and caused her to breathe rapidly. Upon her arrival, Mrs. DeRossett cordially greeted her and thanked her for her assistance before introducing her to the other ladies present. She escorted Shannon around, showing her where to find things on the long tables and cautioning her on proper conduct around these emotion-starved men. She smiled as the woman hurried away to take charge of other matters and giggling females.

The train would be in Wilmington for several hours while the Ladies' Relief Society ministered to the wounded men. Those able to walk left the train to mingle among the ladies and to feast on hot food and special treats. Smiles, laughter, gossip, and news were exchanged. Men in need were given new garments and little items to enjoy while confined in the hospital. Letters were written for those with injured hands. Clean bandages replaced dirty ones. In some instances, emergency medical attention was required to save a life or to ease agony. Those too weak or injured to leave the train were nursed aboard it. Medicines were adminis-tered. Food, treats, and gifts were brought to their makeshift bunks. More letters home were written, and often a last will and testament. The women worked and shared unselfishly.

The sights and sounds at the depot were similar to those in the hospital at Danville, Shannon soon realized, and they refreshed horrible memories of that terrifying episode in her life. Shannon wondered if Major Clifford had sent anyone after her or news about her. Then she began wondering about General Moore and Simon Travers. If only her looks didn't provide such a revealing description! Maybe it was a mistake to be using her real name, for it would make her easier to trace. What if one of those villains arrived during Blane's absence? What if she were taken prisoner? She would have to be very careful to do nothing to incriminate herself. If she tried to get to General Bragg or General Holmes, her actions might endanger Blane upon his return, whenever that might be. He had been gone for twenty-one days—three weeks without a word! Maybe she would require Elisha's

342

assistance and protection after all, for she couldn't remain here as a guest indefinitely. She needed and wanted to get home—Sherman or no Sherman, war or no war!

To distract herself from her own cares in the presence of such misery, she chatted with the wounded while she tended their needs. "Is there any news from Georgia? From Savannah?" she inquired.

The man whose chest she was wrapping replied in a raspy voice, "He's a mean one, that Sherman. Pickin' Georgia clean as a buzzard o'er a carcuss. He's takin' his ease through 'er. I hear tell Wheeler's cavalry is dancin' afore him and harassin' him every step of the way. They's sendin' supplies up the river from Savannah to Augusta. Once they gits there and the Rebs pick 'em up, they's gonna head across to cut 'em off about midways. They's moving the treasury from Macon to somewheres in Alabama. Them *bummers* is doin' more lootin' and killin' than Shermy's men. What's done happened to men?" he fretted aloud.

"What are 'bummers'?" Shannon questioned in confusion.

"That's them marauders which rides on Shermy's flank. Nothing but deserters and renegades if you askst me. Shore wish Jackson and Stuart wuz still alive. They'd stop them devils in three steps."

"What about Beauregard? I've heard nothing of him recently."

"You ain't the only one. He's practically dropped outta sight. Some says he's battling sickness. Some says he rubbed Davis wrong. Can't win no war when leaders are being kilt and soldiers are desertin'. These is sorry times, miss, sorry times. What we need is help from the likes of that Blade and Flame that the Yanks have. 'Course we got us a Flame now, but nobody knows who or where she is."

343

Shannon trembled and paled. "Who did you say?" she asked.

"You ain't heard of 'em? Whyst they goes everwhere stealin' our secrets and slippin' through our lines. Can't nobody catch 'em. They say she looks like an angel with hair like flames. Like you, miss. But they's got hearts of ice and nerves like stone. Theys best be leavin' this area. Theys got three murder charges aginst 'em."

"What?" Shannon blurted out incredulously. "Three murders?"

"Yes'm. Theys kilt a Major Clifford and one of his men, a Reb named Thornton. Then theys kilt Lieutenant Pike, one of General Moore's officers whilst he was chasin' after 'em. Yes'm, cold ones them two," he remarked, lying down as she finished her task.

"James Thornton and Lieutenant Zachary Pike?" she probed.

"Yes'm, that's them, all right. Theys kilt 'em deader'n a rock."

"That's impossible. Who said they did such evil things?"

"Theys left their marks, like always."

"I don't understand," she pressed anxiously. "What marks?"

His response shocked and dismayed her. "Theys draws a knife and a flame as their signs. On bodies, theys carves 'em with a blade. Ain't no purty sight. We shore would like to catch 'em."

"Where are they now?" she asked fearfully.

"Word is theys been kickin' up a ruckus all around this state lately. The Rebs'll git 'em. I heared we got us a Flame now. Don't know much about 'er, but she's makin' havoc of them Yankee spies. Shore would be somethin' to see them two Flames at each other."

Shannon moved on to her next patient, afraid to ask more questions and praying this man was mistaken.

344

Confused and alarmed, she knew she had to get those deaths off her mind. She hadn't committed those deeds. Where had she gotten such a reputation? Two of them! She was so wrapped up in her thoughts that she was unaware of the green eyes that watched her every move. When she completed her chores, she was exhausted mentally and physically. She was surprised to find Captain Carter waiting to escort her back to the hotel. When she questioned his presence, he told her he was worried because it was nearly dark. Shannon smiled and thanked him for his concern and kindness. She tried to cancel dinner, claiming fatigue, but Elisha urged her to eat a good meal before retiring.

That next day, Elisha coaxed her into taking a ride around the city, but he couldn't persuade her to visit his ship. Following a rushed dinner and a stroll, Shannon returned to her room, leaving a frustrated Elisha watching her mount the stairs wearily. He decided he should talk with Molly again, for he was sure something was troubling Shannon deeply.

Molly suggested, "Perhaps she's afraid you're falsely trying to charm her rather than seriously romance her. You two haven't known each other long, so she doesn't know if she can trust you. Considering her work, Eli, you can hardly blame her for being wary of people. She has to be careful and alert for Union spies trying to unmask her. If I had done the things she has, I would find it hard to relax around people."

"Maybe I should talk to her," he suggested.

"No, you mustn't! She would panic if she learned you knew the truth. She would be furious with me, and so would Sarah Jane. You gave me your word," she angrily reminded him.

"Are you positive she's a Rebel agent?" he pressed skeptically.

"I swear it. Just court her; don't question her."

345

"Are you positive there isn't something between her and James?"

"Yes. Steven is mine. I would know if she had eyes for him. Besides, if she did, would she be seeing you?"

Elisha wasn't convinced that Molly was telling him everything. He decided there was only one way to uncover the truth. The next day he took Shannon to the shops owned and operated by some of the blockade runners. He tried to purchase several gifts for her, but she politely refused them. He tried to discuss the war many times, but Shannon would not allow it. For an agent, she certainly wasn't interested in obtaining information, at least from him . . .

After dinner, Elisha walked her to the stairs as usual. "I'll be sailing with the morning tide, but I'll return in a week or two. I'm using that plan I told you about the other night. We're taking a load of supplies up the York River under the Union flag and dressing in Federal uniforms. We have to get them to Richmond for dispersal. Lee needs them to hold off Grant." He awaited her response as an agent.

"Eli, do you realize how dangerous that is?" she asked worriedly.

"Somebody has to do it. We'll get past the Union lines by claiming they're supplies for Grant. They're practically breathing on each other, so we'll get through. Don't worry about me, Shannon. I sail through Union lines on every voyage."

"Everyone's luck runs out sometime. Don't go, Eli, please."

"You're my luck, lovely lady. I might as well be honest, Shannon; I fully intend to return and make you my wife."

Shannon stared at him in disbelief. "You what? Surely I did not hear you correctly," she probed apprehensively.

"I'm not an impulsive or reckless man, Shannon. But I

do know what I want when I see it, and these last four days with you have shown me what my life and heart were missing. I'm afraid circumstances prevent me from having the patience or the time to court you properly. I've never met a woman more perfectly suited to me and my lifestyle. If I'm lucky, I'll obtain your promise of marriage before I sail. Of course, nothing would suit me better than to marry you tomorrow and to have you waiting here for my return. If you'll agree, I'll arrange everything, then wait to sail with the evening tide."

Shannon was stunned, but intrigued. "Eli, we only met a few days past. You know little about me and my family. This is a very serious matter. I hope you don't feel that I've led you on or behaved falsely. I couldn't possibly accept. How can you propose to a stranger?"

"I've known plenty of women, Shannon, but none as special as you. If I leave without telling you such things, I could lose you before having a chance to win you. If you can't agree tonight, at least give me time to prove I would make a good husband for you. I've faced death enough times to know who and what I am. Do you have someone waiting for you in Savannah? Are you betrothed?"

"No, but I cannot give you false hopes. We are strangers in too many ways. You should not speak of such matters so soon and during such times. We are at war. At this very moment, my brother's life and our home are in peril. I cannot think of such things as courting and marriage. You ask too much, but I am deeply flattered."

"We are at war, Shannon; that's why I am forced to speak so bluntly and quickly. A man would be a fool to sail off without telling you how much he wants you. At least promise to grant me the time to prove my honesty and feelings, time to prove my suitability as your husband. If there were time for wooing you slowly and properly, I would do so. Forgive my rush, but please understand it. Destiny has thrown us together, and I won't give you up without a battle. When this war ends, you may be left without family and a home, Shannon. You might need me, as I need you." Elisha's eyes searched her face for clues to her emotions. He had perceived her attraction to him and her fear of it. He wanted her as his wife, and he would have her.

"I'm sorry, Eli, but I cannot make such promises. It wouldn't be fair or right. I am very fond of you, but I haven't fallen in love with you. Please don't delude yourself about me and my feelings."

Behaving as the masterful gallant he was, Elisha confidently vowed, "I'm going to win your heart and your hand, Shannon Greenleaf, and you won't be sorry for losing either. I won't press you or panic you further tonight. Just know if you need anything—anything at all—you can have it from me. Prepare yourself for my siege when I return." With those staggering promises, he smiled and left whistling.

Jeremy Steele watched the man swagger out of the hotel, then focused his keen gaze on the beautiful redhead who was staring at the man's back. He glanced at Mattilu and frowned. "We need to talk, Matti," he informed her after Shannon's departure.

From the clues Simon had obtained through cunning, deceit, strength, or purchase, he saw what Major Stevens had in mind. Blane was scouting Charlotte, Columbia, and Charleston before joining up with Sherman in Savannah. He wondered how Shannon would feel about Blane's part in the destruction of her state, town, and home, just as he wondered how Blane would be affected by the news of the destruction left behind him and Shannon.

Major Blane Stevens was a force to be reckoned with,

to be turned against Shannon. By the time he and his men reached Savannah—hopefully before Blane and Shannon—neither Shannon nor Blane would trust or like each other! The moment Blane left her side at Greenleaf—if he escorted her that far—Shannon would be helpless within his grip. Even Silas Manning wouldn't believe he hadn't been duped by this ravishing and tempting Rebel spy! Shannon would yield, or else . . .

"Mister Travers?" one of his hired men called to him. When Simon turned to listen, the men reported, "Major Stevens has left town, sir, but he's heading for Wilmington, not Savannah."

Simon digested those facts. Suddenly he flushed red with fury. "Damn that Pike! She's been in Wilmington all this time! I wonder if he wanted us chasing Stevens to get him out of the way or because he was trying to protect Shannon. Doesn't matter neither way. We'll head for Wilmington at first light. Without any problems, we should be there within a week. If Blane's gone after Shannon to take her to Savannah, they won't get past us. Five hundred dollars extra to the first man who sights them," he announced, hoping to increase their alert.

Simon fumed over his errors. He had gone from town to town, thinking he was right behind them. After locating Blane in Charleston, he had ordered one of his men to shadow the Union agent until he led them to Shannon. No wonder no one had seen the ravishing redhead along the way! She was safely hidden in Wilmington. No matter, for he had left evidence for or against her along his way.

"Jeremy, what are you doing in Wilmington?" Shannon inquired when she answered the summons at her door shortly after leaving Elisha's company. She smiled genially, but she was curious about this late and unexpected visit. "Do you have news about Blane?" she asked, suddenly excited and tense.

"No, I haven't seen him since you two left the mansion." Jeremy didn't say he hadn't heard from him, for he had several times. "I was hoping you had uncovered some facts I could send out in my next missive."

Shannon didn't have to consider the consequences of her reply before making it. "No, Jeremy, I'm afraid not. I haven't been asking any questions because I didn't want to draw any suspicious attention to me. I have met a few people, but they haven't revealed anything vital."

"Did you help with the hospital train?" he inquired.

"Yes, but the men didn't say anything we don't already know. I was never alone, so I kept silent except for friendly conversation."

"Have you met any of the Confederate officers?" he probed.

"A few. Like I said, I've been afraid to snoop. I'm sorry, but there isn't anything to pass along," she alleged, wondering why he was pressing her and staring at her oddly.

"Sarah Jane told me you met Captain Carter; said you two had become good friends," he hinted in a strange tone.

"Is that a problem? I do want and need friends, even if they're Rebels. I'm sure you know all about Eli . . . Captain Carter. Surely you don't expect me to try to extract information from him? The moment I started asking such questions, he would suspect me of spying. I'm alone here, Jeremy. I'm vulnerable to discovery. I must be careful." Shannon started to tell him what the wounded soldier had related to her, but she didn't like Jeremy's attitude and behavior. She decided to wait for Blane's return, then let him handle that hazardous matter. "Do you know where Blane is or when he'll

350

return for me?"

Jeremy shrugged, then remarked as if he didn't know, "Can't say. I guess if you don't have anything to tell me, I'd best be going."

Shannon wasn't fooled by Jeremy's reaction. Why didn't Jeremy or Blane want her to know of his location and assignment? It was almost as if they didn't trust her! "I would like to mention one thing, Jeremy. I know this is none of my business, but do you realize how deeply Sarah Jane cares for you?"

Jeremy stared at her. "Cares for me? How so?"

Shannon sighed heavily. Were all men blind except Eli? "She's afraid you haven't gotten over the loss of your wife, so she's afraid to let you know how she feels. She's in love with you, Jeremy."

"You mean she ain't just being kind?" he inquired in surprise.

"She's trying to reach out to you, but she's afraid of how you'll take her overtures. Women have to be careful when they expose their feelings. Some men mistake their reasons and actions."

"When she learns how me and Blane've been fooling her and Molly, she won't feel that way much longer," he stated sullenly.

"Then don't tell her until the war's over. But you should let her know you're interested in her as a woman, before some man snaps her up and away from you. A man can keep a woman dangling and guessing only so long before she looks elsewhere."

Jeremy gazed at her, then grinned. "I suppose you're right. I'll make sure she knows I'll be available after the war. I wouldn't want some officer or sea captain stealing her away. When Blane returns, give him this note. Make sure no one reads it but him—no one, Flame. According to our plans, he should be returning within a few days."

Jeremy bid her good night and left. Shannon stared at

351

the sealed note in her hands, then impulsively opened it. She fumed, for it was in code and totally indecipherable.

Sky is red. Flames are burning. Lovebirds flown away. Sparrow spiked. Many are flying to no returns. An eye behind. One More was wrong. One side is wrong. Our blood runs. A well of surprises.

Chapter Fourteen

The weather was stormy on Tuesday, so Mrs. DeRossett canceled the society meeting at her home and the collection of goods. Thursday, another train of wounded men halted in Wilmington. This time, injuries were fresher and more severe. The Ladies' Relief Society volunteers labored unselfishly until each man had been tended, and most did not complete their tasks until after the dinner hour. Shannon watched the train depart from the station with relief and sadness. She couldn't help but wonder if Corry were facing similar conditions elsewhere. Blane had been gone for twenty-six days. Elisha had been gone for three. She had never felt so lonely, so miserable, so weary, or so vulnerable.

One of the ladies insisted on having her carriage drop Shannon off at the hotel. Shannon was too fatigued and depressed for company or food. Carefully avoiding guests and her two hostesses, she went to her room immediately. She was delighted to find a tub of hot water awaiting her before the fire. She quickly stripped and sank into the soothing tub. She closed her eyes and tried to relax her aching body. She didn't know how much more suffering she could stand.

"Yes, Blue Eyes, you can steal my tub if you need it

353

that badly," a mellow voice teased from behind her.

Shannon opened her eyes and whirled around to find Blane hunkering down by the tub. "What are you doing here?" she asked in undisguised astonishment. "How did you get in?"

"Those questions sound awfully familiar. Let me see . . . Now where did I hear them before? Alexandria?" he jested merrily.

"Is that all you have to say after being gone for weeks? Why did you leave without telling me? Where have you been? Why didn't you send word?" She impatiently stormed him with questions.

Blane chuckled. "I see you've been missing me and worrying about me. Good, because I've been doing the same about you. It was a sudden move, and I didn't realize I would be away so long. But it did solve our little problem of how to fool Molly."

Shannon stared at him. He hadn't answered one of her vital queries. She decided not to probe him. From the looks of his face and neck, he had been shaving in the bathing closet during her arrival. His grin warmed her. "I've been so lonely. When can we leave here?"

As he dried the water and traces of lather from his face and throat, he responded, "In a couple of weeks. I have one more short trip to make; I'll be leaving at dawn. It looks as if the Union's going to try to take Fort Fisher next month. If all goes as planned, they'll move on to capture Wilmington and Charleston. If that plan works, Shannon, it'll all be over. Then we can concentrate on our private lives."

A surge of joy raced through her at this last statement. She eyed his bare torso and her gaze locked with his as they admired each other. "Does Molly know you're here?" she inquired anxiously.

"No, and she won't. Matti's bringing my food up here. Do you mind if I share your room tonight, since you confiscated my bath?"

"Your bath?" she echoed in confusion. Suddenly she blushed as reality struck her. "She knows you're staying here with me?"

"I could hardly conceal the fact, Blue Eyes. Don't worry about your reputation. Matti understands our situation," he jested unwisely.

Shannon's cheeks grew red with anger and embarrassment. "I'm sure you don't care about flaunting our relationship, but I do. I don't want anyone, including Mattilu, thinking badly of me."

Blane's expression became serious, as did his tone. "What's wrong, love? You don't appear happy to see me. I came a long way just to be with you tonight. Perhaps I should have sent a letter instead."

Tears stung her eyes. "I'm sorry, Blane. I'm so tired and scared. I want this war to end. I want to go home. I don't like this spy business. Please don't be angry, but I can't do it anymore."

"What's happened while I've been gone?" he inquired softly.

Shannon tried to explain her mixed emotions. "I'm sorry, but I can't be responsible for death and destruction. You do what you feel you must, but leave me out of it. I've seen too much suffering to help you."

Blane caressed her cheek and smiled. "Don't worry, Flame; I'll be happy to retire you from service. That way, I'll know you're safe. I always knew you had a tender heart beneath that tough facade. You relax here until my return, then I'll take you to Savannah."

"You promise?" she entreated, ecstatic with that news.

"I promise. Now hand me that cloth and soap and I'll give you a refreshing scrub." Blane bathed an exhausted Shannon then dried her. After placing her on the bed, he insisted she drink his brandy. Pressing her to her stomach, he gently and firmly massaged her entire body. As he stared at her sleeping form, his heart filled with love and pride. He stripped and bathed before Mattilu returned with his meal. He asked her to remove the tub and water in the morning, explaining Shannon's fatigue. He also asked for her to slip him a large breakfast at dawn, before he sneaked out again.

Shannon was awakened by stimulating sensations over her body. She smiled and wriggled as hands and lips teased over her flesh. Opening her eyes, she could barely see Blane in the soft lamplight. "I guess I fell asleep," she remarked drowsily. She yawned and stretched.

"For a few hours," he replied cheerfully. "It's morning—well, almost morning. I didn't think I should leave again without telling you."

Shannon grinned. "You're getting smarter every day. Do you mind if I say be careful for the hundreth time?"

"I would mind if you didn't," he responded. "We have about one hour before Matti brings our breakfast and I have to leave. What should we do with it?" he inquired huskily. "Anything you want to talk about?" he asked, propping his dark blond head on arms folded behind it. He stared at the ceiling and waited in suspense.

Shannon rolled over and fell across his chest, her fiery locks falling around their faces. "Now I see why you rudely awakened me so early. Let's see, exciting topics . . . The only one I can think of is Blane."

"Good, because the only one I can think of is Shannon. You notice I prepared for such a stirring conversation?" he hinted, wrapping his arms around her and running his fingers over naked skin that quivered beneath his touch. When they playfully tickled her ribs, she wriggled again, her bare flesh stroking his and inflaming him from head to toe. He moaned as his body loudly declared its needs.

He flipped her to her back, then tossed the cover aside

356

to gaze down at her. "Do you have any idea how beautiful and tempting you are? We're perfect together, Shannon. Lord, I've missed you, woman."

Blane nuzzled her neck, causing her to giggle and squirm. He spread kisses over her face and mouth and neck. He was thrilled by her responses this morning. He had been worried about the sea captain whom Mattilu had mentioned to him, especially after learning that Shannon had refused to expose the man's supply voyage. But from experience, Blane understood how hard it was to betray someone you knew. Mattilu had explained how deeply distressed Shannon had been over the news of Sherman's and Sheridan's wanton destruction. He realized that Shannon must have guessed he had been keeping those facts from her. Clearly her loyalties were becoming divided and confused. But to turn to another man, a Rebel, a dashing blockade runner? Hoping it had been nothing but a ruse to mislead Molly, he held silent on that unsettling topic. Maybe Shannon had been lonely and afraid, as she had told him. Maybe, like any woman, she had enjoyed the masculine attention. Maybe she had been angry with him.

Blane prayed she wouldn't discover how Mattilu and Jeremy had betrayed Elisha Carter to the Union. He wished he had been here to stop them, because it was unlikely that the captain could have succeeded in such a wild scheme. A trip up the York River to sneak past Union lines with countless supplies? The idea was too absurd for a smart man to consider! By now, the *Rebel Gate* could be sunk or captured and her captain could be in prison or dead. That wasn't his way of getting rid of a rival, even if the man had proposed to and was hotly pursuing his woman. He understood how Elisha must have felt, but only one man could have her. He knew if Shannon discovered Elisha's fate, she would blame herself. No doubt Elisha was blaming her right this moment, if he was still alive. God forgive them all for the terrible things they were compelled to do to win this tragic war.

He gazed down into Shannon's lovely face and mesmeric eyes. No, he couldn't blame Elisha Carter for falling in love with this woman. And he couldn't blame Shannon for refusing to bring about the man's capture or death. He had seen the anguish in her eyes and had heard it in her voice when she told him it was over for her. She possessed such a gentle soul and tender emotions. He could never force her to go against her conscience or beliefs. At least she wasn't asking him to cease his work and forget his duty. He would be just as understanding. Blane assailed her again with kisses, caresses, and tickles.

Shannon tried to stifle her laughter, fearing they would be overheard, but Blane was stealing her senses and control. It felt wonderful to be in his arms again. What did it matter if he had secrets he must keep from her? Everyone had his private thoughts and moments that could not be shared—even with a true love. She loved him enough to accept him as he was. They needed each other; they depended on each other. Their values were similar, if not alike. Each was tolerant of the flaws in the other. Their passions matched. They were creating a deep and strong relationship, a blended history, beautiful memories. They were comfortable together. They trusted each other, even with their lives and happiness. He was accepting what she could not do, and she was accepting what he had to do. They were changing, growing, sharing, meeting on all emotional levels.

Despite Blane's fiery kisses and warm caresses, Shannon noted that the air in the room was chilly and the fire was nearly out. "Are you trying to freeze me?" she asked mirthfully, yanking on the discarded covers.

"Surely you can't be cold at a time like this?" he wailed comically. "I'm burning up, woman. Want to share my heat?"

"Emotional fires do not warm the physical body, especially not during winter. Do you realize today is Thanksgiving? And Christmas isn't far away? Give me some cover, you beast. I'm freezing."

"We should be giving thanks for our good fortune," he ventured, refusing to move off her while he covered them. As she winced and frowned, he taunted, "Next you'll be accusing me of mashing you. Complain, complain, complain. I knew it was going to be like this when I was forced to bring you along. Be grateful woman; it's Thanksgiving."

"If you were to tell the truth, Major Stevens, you would admit that this is the last thing you expected when you agreed to become my partner," she responded, drawing his head down to fuse their lips. After kissing him feverishly, she murmured, "Now, will you please take advantage of me and this enticing situation before Mattilu brings our breakfast?"

"Who needs food when I have this luscious body to feast upon?" he replied, slipping below the covers to find her breasts with his mouth.

Shannon closed her eyes and savored the blissful feelings he was creating within her. She let his lips and hands wander freely and greedily over her body. When she could no longer stand the bittersweet pain of being separated from him, she urged him to enter her and possess her. The sensation of his flesh being engulfed by hers was staggering to her senses. She felt as if every nerve in her body was alive and throbbing. She craved him fiercely and completely. She refused to think of his imminent departure.

Blane felt ecstatic within her. Her body molded to his as if they had become magically joined. He had thought of this moment every night since he had last seen her. Raging jealousy had flooded him when he had heard of another man's pursuit. If he hadn't known before how much she meant to him, he certainly knew it now. He feared to admit he would have betrayed Elisha Carter to the enemy before allowing him to have this woman. Again, thoughts of Corry and Hawke tried to push themselves into his mind, but he resisted.

Knowing there was time to make love only once, they did so with tenderness and leisure, until passion's fires were burning too brightly and fiercely to be controlled. Blane timed his release to match hers and their gazes fused to visually share this special moment. As the last wave of rapture flowed over them, he sealed his lips to hers and kissed her with such gentleness that her heart surged with emotion.

She didn't want him to leave, but she could not beg him to stay. What would she do if anything happened to him? He had become her life, her present, her future, her existence.

There was a soft knock at the hall door. Blane looked down at Shannon and grimaced. He rose, slipped into his pants, then answered it. Soon, he returned to ask her to join him in the other room to eat. He didn't have to make his request twice. Shannon got out of bed and wrapped the blanket around her shivering body. Blane apologized about the fire, but each knew there wasn't time to warm the room.

Blane had placed the tray on a table. Shannon grinned as she joined him. "I'm starved," she confessed at the realization.

"Good, because that's what you and Matti will use to explain the feast if anyone noticed it. You did miss dinner last night."

"Your perception and cunning never cease to astound me, Major Stevens. I suppose you have dear Matti keeping a close eye on me for you," she playfully teased, sipping the hot coffee to warm her.

"Naturally. Surely you don't expect a smart man to leave his woman at the mercy of panting suitors." From the corner of his eye, Blane saw her flinch slightly. He waited for her to deny or admit to her new friendship with Captain Elisha Carter, but she did neither. He prepared her plate and passed it to her. He did not miss the way her hands were shaking and prayed it was from the chilly air. He had also realized how few times, if any, she had mentioned her brother lately. He immediately scolded himself for his doubt and concern. He knew the fear of losing her was making him insecure. That was ridiculous. Hadn't she proven her feelings countless times?

Shannon wondered if Mattilu had mentioned Elisha to Blane. What did it matter? She did not owe Blane a report on her behavior during his mysterious absence. She had done nothing wrong. She was allowed to have friends and to distract herself from her worries. If Blane doubted her love and attachment to him, he would have to deal with those feelings privately. Besides, he might think she was only trying to make him jealous or force him to remain with her. She would ignore the subject of Eli and concentrate on them and her food.

Shannon's mind roamed as she silently and eagerly devoured her meal. She had purposely not mentioned Corry, because she had feared it would plunge her into despair and she would behave like a child in front of Blane. He was so strong and brave, and surely he expected her to think and behave in a similar manner. It was so hard. No one had told her it would be easy or swift, but no one had warned her it would be this difficult! Her childhood world had been lost forever.

Her brother was on her mind constantly, especially when she helped with the injured men and read accounts of furious battles in the newspapers, and during holidays. Holidays had been such special times at home. Other than Blane, what did she have to be thankful for today? Even if Corry were alive, there was no guessing his condition or suffering. She had come to fear she might never see him again.

Shannon had stopped eating and was staring at the floor with narrowed eyes, clenching and unclenching her teeth as powerful emotions washed over her. She was eating a farewell breakfast, one that could easily mark a permanent farewell. Blane had vanished for nearly a month, then had returned unexpectedly and secretly. Now he was heading off on another mysterious assignment without explaining. If he didn't return, she wouldn't even know in which direction to seek him. Like a cunning thief, he had sneaked into her room, stolen a night of passion, and was sneaking out again. Did he have to do so much spying and scouting? He wasn't Lincoln's only agent.

Shannon was becoming angry with the men who were continuing this futile war, angry with her father for dying, angry with him for placing her in Simon's care. She was angry with Hawke for not returning when he was needed desperately. She was angry with herself for being so rash, so helpless, so torn between the two sides fighting this war, and perhaps so selfish in wanting to seize this happiness and protect it. She was angry with her brothers for their sorry fates. She was angry at Blane for playing such a large role in certain victories. She was angry with God for allowing this bloody conflict to continue this far and this long. Yet, she was fiercely trying to master her depression, to understand both sides of each issue. All she wanted was for their lives—what was left of them—to return to some semblance of normalcy.

"Shannon, is something wrong, love?" he queried gravely.

She lifted misty eyes to fuse with his troubled ones. "Do you have to leave, Blane? Can't you stay or take me

362

with you?"

Her questions surprised him. "It's important, love. And I want you to stay here where you're safe. I'll return shortly. I promise."

"Where are you going? What's so vital?" she probed.

"I'd rather not discuss it this morning. I'll tell you when I return."

"If you return," she scoffed. "Why are you suddenly so secretive with me? Have I done something to diminish your trust? I know I said I didn't want to help, but I do want to know what's happening. I worry so about you. I wouldn't even know where to look for you."

"You'll have to trust me, Shannon. You'll understand later."

"Are you afraid I'll carelessly drop clues in the wrong ears?"

"No, but this matter is very delicate."

"And very dangerous," she added fretfully.

"Not for me, love," he said, trying to appease her fears.

"You aren't invincible or immortal, Blane. Can't you let someone else take this mission? Can't we forget the war for awhile?"

"I wish everyone would forget the war, but they won't, love—not until one side wins. I have to do all I can to make certain the victor is the Union. We can't have a split country, Shannon. I was an Indian scout, so I have skills most of these agents don't. I can accomplish more and faster than several of them. Don't make this harder for me."

"Hard for you?" she debated. "I'm involved too, Blane. I can't stand this waiting and worrying. I have to get home. Please take me."

"Is there more to this change of heart and mood than you're telling me?" he asked, pushing aside his empty plate to listen.

Shannon sighed heavily. Maybe he was right. Wasn't he always? Maybe she was feeling guilty for withholding facts from him, about the information she had obtained here and about herself. If he was worried about her, he could be perilously distracted. "I'm sorry. I suppose I sound selfish and cowardly. It's so damned lonely without you. I worry about you all the time. I couldn't bear to lose you, Blane."

Blane stood and pulled her into his arms. He held her tightly and possessively. He almost revealed his love for her, but he feared it might encourage her to beg him to stay. He captured her head between his hands and lifted it. Their gazes locked and he smiled. "There's no way you'll ever lose me, Shannon. Give me five days, and we'll be heading for Greenleaf."

Shannon smiled and hugged him. Greenleaf! That was where she would tell him everything about her life and her feelings. There, they would be safe and happy . . .

Blane murmured, "I have to leave; it's getting light outside. Be careful, love. It should be over soon. The South can't hold out much longer. I'll get you home; then I'll find Corry."

Blane's pervasive kiss concealed Shannon's reaction to the way Blane had voiced her brother's name and the way he had looked. But as her senses became ensnared, she allowed her concern to slip from her mind.

Blane dressed hurriedly, then drew her into his embrace again. "Anything else before I leave?" he inquired. "Matti said you had a note from Jeremy for me."

"Note from Jeremy?" she repeated, then brightened. "I forgot about it! You do steal my wits at times like this, Major Stevens."

Shannon went to the dresser and knelt. She reached under it and fingered around until she located the paper that was wedged there. She smiled as she handed it to him. She jested, "He put it in code so I couldn't read it. What does it say?" she asked seriously.

Blane read the note for a second time. Was Jeremy crazy, confused, or mistaken? This message couldn't be accurate! Shannon couldn't have betrayed him and those other people. Catherine and the Thomases were dead? Moore had let them escape? Everyone along their path had been exposed? A traitor on his back? In his arms and bed?

Shannon noted his reaction and dreaded to question it. Was he heading into peril? Had he been unmasked? Were they both in danger? "Blane, what is it? You must stop keeping secrets and answer me!"

Blane looked up from the paper, which was shaking in his grip. He had to think quickly; he had to lie. "Moore sent out messages about us. We're lucky, 'cause they're searching the roads between Charlotte and Richmond. The Union's suffered a few defeats, but we've claimed heavy victories. Sherman's been ordered to take Columbia and burn it. A lot of the Rebels are changing sides or deserting."

Shannon had the oddest feeling that Blane wasn't telling her the truth, and it hurt her deeply. She was astonished by his next words.

"My plans have changed. I'm going to see Jeremy, then I'm coming back for you. Be ready to leave in no more than three days."

Shannon was tormented by his chilly voice and frozen gaze. What about that "important" and "delicate" mission? Why visit Jeremy? Why flee in a few days? "Can I ask you something?" she inquired, recalling a curious discovery. When Blane nodded, she asked, "Have you seen James Thornton and Major Clifford?"

Blane looked bewildered by her question. "No, why?"

"You haven't slain them? Or ordered them slain?" she asked.

"What? Get to the point, Shannon," he commanded brusquely.

Shannon related what the soldier had told her on the train. She couldn't understand why Jeremy hadn't mentioned Pike, as he seemed to know so much about General Moore. "Who would murder them and put the blame on me and this Blade? I don't even know him." The moment Shannon made that statement, the truth dawned on her.

She gaped at Blane. "It's you, isn't it?" she stated incredulously.

"What's me?" Blane asked coldly. He prayed as he had never prayed before in his life. He prayed Jeremy was wrong. He prayed those two men hadn't been slain as a ruse to unmask him to her.

Shannon walked to the fireplace where only a few low-burning coals remained. She stared at it, trying to understand this situation. She turned and looked at Blane. Of course, it all made sense—the mysteries, his scouting skills, his Indian training, his matchless prowess. Her eyes slipped to the ever-present hunting knife that was strapped to his gun belt. If he was as talented with a knife as Hawke was, his code name was appropriate. "You're the Blade. That's why you can't walk away from this business, not even for me, for us. Of course they couldn't replace you. I should have realized you're the best, and only the best could be the legendary Blade. Why did you kill them? And, Blane, why put our marks on them? I mean, I've heard you always sign your own deeds, by why include me? Why endanger my life and freedom? Do you realize what they would do with me?"

Either someone was setting them up for his own purposes, or she was the cleverest agent and coldest woman he had ever known. Heaven help them both if the latter were true. Was she too good, too perfect to be real?

366

No, he wouldn't believe these charges until they were proven. Shannon couldn't do such things. If she had started out to entrap him, she had dropped that scheme when she had fallen in love with him. Was that it? Her superiors were out to get her for quitting? Had she decided she didn't want to work for their side, for either side?

"I didn't kill any of them, Shannon, but not because I didn't want to. Evidently someone wanted them dead, so they gave us the credit. Maybe this will all make sense when I talk to Jeremy. Stay in your room while I'm gone. I'll ask Matti to bring your meals to you. Refuse to see anyone. Claim you're ill. Understand me, woman?"

He hadn't admitted to being the Blade, and he hadn't denied it. But surely he had insinuated it. Shannon tried not to view him in a different light, but it was inevitable and uncontrollable. The Blade had a reputation for getting his work done any way possible or necessary, and at any cost. She had given him a perfect cover. Who would suspect the solitary fighter of traveling with a woman . . .

"Shannon, do you understand me?" he pressed firmly.

"Yes, Blane, I think I do," she replied sadly. If he suspected that someone knew their identities and was entrapping them, why would he leave her alone and in danger? Did she know this man at all?

"Will you be all right until I return?"

"Yes, Blane."

"Is there anything else you've forgotten to tell me?"

"No, Blane."

"Will you wait for me and keep that door locked?"

"Yes, Blane."

He suddenly exploded with vexation. "Yes, Blane! No, Blane! Perdition, woman, this is serious! Stop acting like a wounded rabbit! You've known all along there were things I couldn't tell you. You're out of it, so stay out of

367

it! I don't want you getting hurt."

"And I don't want you getting hurt," she replied honestly.

"Follow my orders, and we'll both come out of this alive and healthy. Just give me three days," he stressed, holding up three fingers.

"I will. Blane," she began hesitantly, "you can trust me. I would never tell anyone about you. To make sure I can't drop even a tiny clue, I won't leave this room until you give the order. I swear it."

Blane seized her and yanked her into his arms, embracing her and kissing her fiercely. Afterward, he held her against him for a time. "Listen to me, Shannon," he whispered in her ear. "Don't forget how much I want you and I need you. Whatever happens, I'll protect you. Don't panic and run out on me. I'll clear up this mess."

Shannon's arms tightened around his waist and she snuggled closer to him. "Please come back to me, Blane." She lifted her mouth to his and kissed him hungrily. The cover slipped from her body.

Passions soared to a torturous peak. Blane gently grasped her arms and separated them. "I have to leave, Shannon; it's nearly daylight. Be waiting here for me, woman, or you'll be sorry," he teased in a ragged voice. Lord, it was agonizing to leave her like this.

Blane kissed her briefly, then gathered his things. He left while she was still trembling with desire for him. She walked to the fireplace and leaned her forehead against the mantel. "Please keep him safe. I need him," she prayed softly.

Observing the naked figure at the fireplace, Mattilu asked herself if she should return later. Hearing the young woman's words, she smiled and stayed. "Miss Shannon, are you all right?"

Shannon whirled and looked at the brown-skinned

368

woman whose expression held such sympathy and understanding. "I don't think any of us will be all right again until this war is over." She retrieved the blanket and wrapped it around her. "Blane must think I'm a terrible coward. Sometimes I behave so selfishly and foolishly. Oh, Matti," she wailed in anguish. "Sometimes I don't know what's right or wrong anymore. I feel so helpless. Whatever I do for one side, it hurts the other. Yet, how can I remain netural? It sounded so simple when I offered to help the Union. But that was before I witnessed the ravages of war and met the people involved. How can I steal facts and betray people I know? How can I be responsible for tragedy and death? I'm so confused. I feel as if I'm being torn apart. My heavens, I'm a Southerner, but I'm helping to destroy my land and people."

Mattilu came to where she was standing and laced her arm around Shannon's shoulders. "You're just tired, and worried about Major Stevens. Why don't you get back into that warm bed and sleep a while longer? And don't you go opening this door to anyone but me. Come along," Mattilu instructed, guiding Shannon to the bed and tucking her in like a child. "You stay right there until I bring your lunch."

Before leaving, Mattilu added kindling and coal to the dying fire. When they caught, she added several large pieces of wood. She gathered the dishes and left the room, locking the door behind her. Shannon laid her cheek on the pillow and cried herself to sleep.

When Mattilu returned just after one, she had to arouse Shannon to eat the hot meal. While doing so, Mattilu prepared a relaxing and refreshing bath before the cheery blaze. Shannon soaked for half an hour before drying off and slipping into a flannel gown. She would follow Blane's orders and do nothing but rest. What else could she do? She had no money for shopping, and reading the papers depressed her.

Around four, Sarah Jane came to visit and found Shannon in bed. She apologized for disturbing the napping female. Shannon smiled faintly. "Perhaps I'm just overly tired. We did work hard yesterday. It seems to get worse with each passing day. Don't concern yourself over me. I plan to be lazy for a few days. Major . . . James and I should be leaving soon, so I had better get all of the quiet and rest I can."

As the other woman was leaving, Shannon called after her, "Sarah Jane, wait a moment. Don't say who told you, but Jeremy was speaking of you the other day. He seemed to think you were only being kind and tolerant of him. He said he plans to let you know he'll be available after the war. I believe his words were, 'I wouldn't want some officer or sea captain stealing her away.' I hope you don't object to my encouraging him to expose his feelings for you. I'm sure he's only wary and insecure because of his wife's actions. He couldn't believe a fine and pretty lady like Sarah Jane Sinclair could be interested in him. Like so many men, he's afraid to make any commitments or promises until this horrid war is over. You've nothing to fear, my friend; he is yours for the taking. Just move slowly for now."

Sarah Jane hugged her affectionately. "Thank you, Shannon. If you hadn't come along, Jeremy and I might have sidestepped each other until it was too late. Do you know when he'll be visiting again?"

"I think in a week or two. Perhaps I can get a message to him through Major Ste . . . ven James. Excuse me for stammering this morning, but my throat is a little scratchy. Probably talked too much yesterday," she blurted, cleverly concealing her partial slips. "Why don't you invite him to have Christmas dinner with you? Why not ask him to spend the night Christmas Eve, then stay all day? I'm sure he's lonely out there and would love to spend those special days with you."

"Heavens, what would he think if I asked him to stay the night?"

"He would be thrilled, of course. Give him a task or two, such as getting you a Christmas tree and helping you decorate it. How can a hotel survive holidays without wood to cook the meals? Give your woodsman a short holiday, then ask Jeremy if he could please help you out of a bind by filling in for a few days. Tell him you'll repay the generous deed by feeding him and giving him a free room. Or you could imply that men get rowdy during holidays and you need a strong man around to keep them in line, to protect you and your female workers. Even if he guesses it's a ruse, he'll go along with it."

"I'm scared to death, but I'm going to do it. I'm sure Molly will have a fit, but I don't care. I do enough work around here to earn the right to have a free guest. You are the smartest woman I know, and I'm glad to have you as my friend. I shall hate to see you leave."

Shannon strolled around her room, feeling better after playing Cupid. It would be good for Sarah Jane and Jeremy to get married. Perhaps after spending time with her during the holidays, he might decide not to wait until after the war to announce his romantic intentions. He could move here and carry out his spy business without arousing her suspicions, just as he had been doing since the war began. Considering her intimate relationship with Blane, she realized that if Blane could fool her about his secret identity, surely Jeremy could keep Sarah Jane in the dark.

Having slumbered so much of the day, Shannon couldn't get to sleep until nearly dawn. She paced the floor, wishing she had a stiff brandy to settle her down. There was absolutely nothing to do, and she couldn't seek anything during the middle of the night. Finally exhausting herself, she slept most of the day, only to have the same trouble that night.

Determined to straighten out this nettling problem, Shannon forced herself to stay out of bed after Mattilu delivered her breakfast, even though it gave her four hours of nothingness. If she didn't rectify this contradictory behavior by the time Blane returned, she would be too fatigued to keep up with him. By four, Shannon could hardly keep her eyes open. She took a bath, which relaxed her rather than stimulated her. At six she ate hot soup, warm bread, and steaming tea, all of which further increased her drowsiness. By eight, Shannon was lying across the bed on her stomach, dreaming of days past.

Just before midnight, strong hands grabbed her shoulders and flung her to her back. A man straddled her body at the waist, pinning her to the bed and her arms to her sides. One weather-roughened hand clamped over her mouth and nose, preventing a scream for help or a plea for an explanation. His other hand spread over her throat and began to squeeze, leisurely and vengefully.

Shannon stared at her attacker, knowing this was not a bad dream. The lamplight was low, but she could see every line of emotion on his face. His eyes were so cold, so full of anger, so full of accusations, so full of hatred, so full of bitterness. He was gritting his teeth so hard that she oddly wondered what kept them from shattering under such pressure. He was so strong and his grip was unbreakable. She could not swallow. She could feel the blood pounding inside her head, causing her face to grow warm and red. No air could reach her lungs and they began to ache.

Tiny bright lights danced before her line of vision, which was darkening ominously. She tried to struggle, but it was futile. He kept watching her eyes, waiting to see her die beneath his hands. Her face tingled and her flesh felt strange. He was going to kill her. She didn't know why, and he wouldn't allow her to ask. Tears slipped from the corners of her eyes and rolled into her hair. She drilled her gaze into his, mutely pleading for an answer to this madness.

The man suddenly released his pressure on her throat, as if content to smother her with his bare hand. She tried to free her nose and mouth, if only for one gasp of air. She had never imagined she would die this way, because of this man. Shannon closed her eyes to let the blackness claim her warring senses.

Chapter Fifteen

Just before she lapsed into unconsciousness, the man removed his hand from her mouth and nose. Shannon inhaled sharply and deeply in a desperate attempt to refill her lungs with life-sustaining air. She began to breathe heavily and urgently to arouse herself. Her heart was pounding and her pulse was racing. Her vision gradually cleared. By the time she was breathing at an almost normal rate, her lips and throat were dry. She looked into the tormented expression of the man still hovering over her—the man who still held her imprisoned between his legs.

In a voice filled with anguish, he asked, "Why, Shannon? Why did you betray me? I thought I could trust you. I thought you were something special. She told me you were a Confederate agent. It's a lie. You're working for the Union. They were waiting for us when we reached the mouth of the York River. They blew my ship to hell and back. Nearly all of my crew was killed or captured." He grabbed her by the shoulders and shook her violently as he sneered contemptuously, "My God, I was taken in by a bewitching vixen. I wanted to marry you. That's like taking a viper into my arms and bed. Even if you didn't love me, didn't you at least care about

374

me? Did my life, my crew, my ship, those men awaiting my supplies mean nothing to you? I should kill you, woman, but I can't," he hoarsely admitted.

He flung his leg off her and sprang to his feet. Seizing her right arm, he forcefully yanked her from the bed and tersely ordered, "Get dressed. I'm turning you over to General Holmes. We'll see if he's as generous with your miserable neck as I was. I can't slay you, but I can't allow you to destroy more lives with your bloody spying."

Shannon was rubbing her sore throat and staring at him. "I don't know what you're talking about, Eli. I didn't tell anyone about your plans. I swear it on my life and honor."

"You don't have any honor, you bloody traitor. And soon you won't have a life—not one to speak of. If they don't hang you, they'll let you rot in prison. I trusted you and I loved you, Shannon. Why? Damnit, you owe me an explanation! For once, be honest with me."

"I don't know who betrayed you to the Yankees, Eli, but it wasn't me. Don't you remember how I begged you not to go?"

"Yes, I remember. It was because you knew you would be sending me into a trap. There were only three people who knew about my plans: me, General Holmes, and General Bragg. Until we pulled anchor, not even my crew knew where we were sailing or why. I didn't want any of them getting drunk and dropping clues. It had to be you. Molly told me you were an agent for our side, but that isn't true. You're here to help destroy Wilmington and Fort Fisher, aren't you, Flame?"

Shannon paled. "Perhaps General Holmes told someone. Why don't you ask General Bragg about me? He's known me since I was a child. He was a good friend of my father's. In fact, why don't you talk with Molly again? She can tell you I haven't been out of this room except once, and that was to help nurse a trainload of wounded

Rebels—Rebels, Eli, not Yankees. I don't know what Molly told you or why, but somebody's lying. Not I, Eli. I did not betray you," she stressed, tears rolling down her flushed cheeks. "You asked me to marry you before you left. If I had known you wouldn't be returning, why wouldn't I have agreed to marry you and become your wealthy widow? Why wouldn't I have agreed to marry you later just to fool you? Listen to me, Eli; I have not used you. Please believe me."

His frosty, hurt expression didn't change as she continued. "Don't you remember how I tried to silence Vance's messenger when he was revealing privileged information downstairs? If I had been after information, would I have tried to hush him? And you—when have I probed you for information? Never! Have you forgotten you mentioned this plan and trip in the parlor that first night we met. Either of those lieutenants could have told someone. How do you know it was a trap? Maybe they were awaiting any ship."

"Are you saying you didn't tell Molly and her sister you're a Rebel spy? You aren't staying here as their guest, relaxing until your next assignment? That is, if you aren't doing one here. Would you like to know what the Yankee captain shouted as he sent the last volley into my ship?" he sneered in simmering fury. "He said he owed the capture of my ship and crew to the beautiful temptress called Flame. I was lucky I got away; most of my men didn't. I heard what that soldier said to you on the train, and I saw how you reacted. Can you swear you aren't the notorious Flame," he scoffed bitterly.

Shannon's heart thudded painfully. She recalled that Jeremy had visited her after Elisha's departure that day. The attack on his ship had to have been a result of Jeremy's eavesdropping. Who else could have known about his voyage and blamed her? He must have sent word to Blane, telling him of their friendship, and of Eli's daring plans, and of her suspicious silence. They had almost gotten this man killed. Were they also responsible for incriminating her? Who else could know so much about her activities?

Shannon sank to the bed and sighed heavily. Her gaze lowered to the floor and more tears slipped down her cheeks. She didn't know what to think about the Blade, her cherished lover. Partial truth seemed the only way out, and perhaps Elisha deserved that much from her. She had to find some way to extricate herself and to protect Blane. "It's a long and complicated story, Eli. I've heard of the Flame's black deeds, but I'm not responsible for them. I admit I was given that code name in August, but I haven't used it or earned it. I did know those three men who were murdered, but I didn't kill them or help do it. And I don't know why that Yankee captain blamed me for your attack. If you'll listen, I'll try to explain. When I finish, I'll dress and you can take me to General Holmes. I won't try to stop you, and I won't try to escape. Maybe I should discover who's trying to involve me in these crimes, and why."

Shannon stood up to pace while she talked. "When it all started in Washington a few months ago, it sounded so patriotic, so logical, so simple and exciting. Lord, I was ignorant, and impulsive, and egotistic. I thought I was doing what was right for me and my family, for my country. I was reared to respect and obey authority. My father and brother had sided with the Union, so naturally I assumed my loyalties and duties lay with them. After my father and older brother were slain and my younger brother was taken prisoner, I was terrified of losing everyone and everything I loved. When I went to see President Lincoln, I naïvely thought I needed his permission and approval before I set out to locate and rescue Corry. I didn't know anything about war or what was happening in the South, but I did know I would need

377

help with weapons and supplies and safe places to hide and rest. I had read the glorious accounts of agents like Rose Greenhow and Belle Boyd. I pictured myself as a fearless heroine who was going to save her brother and home. I even foolishly believed I could become a clever agent who could help end this miserable war."

Shannon sighed heavily, then drank water to soothe her dry throat. "After what happened to my family, I didn't think I owed the Confederacy anything. To me, the South and the Confederacy weren't the same thing. The South was good, my home. The Confederacy was bad, a pack of renegades. My father had convinced me that the United States had to be reunited; I still believe that's true."

Shannon halted by the windows and stared outside at the full moon. She decided to color the truth slightly by telling Eli she had actually met the President. "When I met Lincoln, I was most impressed by him. He agreed to my working for the Union in exchange for their help with Corry. I was flattered by his confidence and faith in me. I felt I would be doing something important. Maybe I was deluding myself all along. I do know he helped me out of a terrible situation. There was a man chasing me, trying to force me to marry him. Lincoln helped me get away from him. It all happened in a big rush. When I left the White House, I only wanted to free my brother from a Confederate prison and get home to Savannah to escape that evil Simon Travers. I don't know how things got so confused."

She looked over at him, her lips and chin quivering. "You're hurt, Eli. Can I bandage your wounds while we talk? If I do anything wrong, you can shoot me." She asked him to remove his tattered shirt and let her examine his injuries.

Elisha did not agree to her ministrations because he was in pain, though he was; he agreed because he wanted

378

to observe her while she worked, while she was touching him. He sat in a chair as Shannon bathed and dressed his wounds from her medical supplies. He had several small burns, but they were easily tended. His arms revealed many cuts and abrasions, but what stitches were needed would come later. She did the best she could, relieved that he had survived this treachery.

"You aren't talking, woman," he stated evocatively.

Shannon was finished with her bandaging. She moved to the sofa and sat down, facing him. "My deal with Lincoln was simple. In return for getting me to my brother, I was to pass them any information I could gather about the Rebels. But I've never performed my task. I have not sent any missives to Yankees or reported to any agent. All along the way, I've worked doing things to aid the Confederacy, like helping with those trains of wounded. I never learned anything that the papers hadn't already printed. I really don't think Lincoln intended for me to be anything more than a cover for his male agents. Most of the time, I've been running and hiding, living in constant fear of discovery and often under awful conditions. I don't know why, because I never did anything wrong, despite what they claim I've done."

Shannon told Elisha about her talk with President Davis and how she knew him. She told him about her nursing in Danville and about Major Clifford's attack. She explained who James Thornton was. "They were evil men, but I didn't kill either of them. I swear it, Eli. I don't know who did or why. Nor did I kill Zachary Pike. He was very kind to me, a good man."

Shannon snuffled as she remorsefully recalled the lieutenant. "There was always something happening to keep me bound to the Union. Sometimes it was nothing more than the challenge of proving myself, of showing my gratitude to Lincoln and my partner. The closer I got to home and the more times he saved my life, the more I felt I owed him my loyalty. Maybe I'm just gullible and trusting, but he kept me alive. When I had time to read papers and gather news, the truth of this war struck home. I told my partner I couldn't help the Union because of the terrible things Sherman, Sheridan, and Grant were doing."

Shannon told him, "They said I could quit, if I promised not to reveal any of the things I had learned about their agents. I don't know who's making up these tales or committing these crimes, Eli, but it isn't me. Do you honestly believe I could do such horrible deeds?"

Elisha was watching her closely. "Who brought you here?"

Shannon was forced to lie to protect Blane. "After I refused to keep my part of the bargain with Lincoln, the agent with whom I was traveling dropped me and headed toward Charlotte. If I fail to keep my word, he'll look me up and get rid of me. While I was hiding and trying to decide what to do, I met a Confederate agent who let me travel with him because I told him I was working for President Davis. About all I've done is serve as his cover, sometimes playing his sister or nurse or wife. He left me here to rest and stay safe until he finished a mission for General Lee. When he heads for Savannah, he promised I could go along. Sarah Jane and Molly allow Rebel agents to stay here, so I claimed to be one. Ask anyone if I've done anything suspicious. I want this war to end, Eli, but not by helping the Union destroy the South. I swear to you I haven't gathered any information here in Wilmington and passed it along. I swear to you I told no one about your trip. I won't spy for the Union, but I cannot betray the people I met who are working for the Union. They helped me and defended me many times."

"Where is your brother? Did you find him?" he inquired.

"No. The men at Danville told me he's either at Andersonville or he escaped on his way there. Surely you've heard about that awful place. Can you blame me for wanting to help him escape? But when I saw what my help involved, I couldn't go through with it. As to who's playing the Flame, I don't know. Maybe it's some kind of trick to elicit my aid, or a punishment for refusing it. Maybe somebody's using the elusive Flame to cover up his own crimes. Why don't you do some checking around? I'm willing to bet this false Flame has committed crimes while I've been here. That should prove it isn't me."

"How do you explain my betrayal?" he questioned.

She candidly admitted, "I can't. Someone could have been spying on me and overheard what you said. The others might have been responsible. Damnit, it wasn't me."

"Does Steven James know all of this?" he asked.

"If you tell that Confederate agent about me, he'll . . . There's no telling what he'll do if he learns about what I've told you. Please, Eli, you mustn't tell anyone what I've said tonight. If you don't believe me, you can imagine what he'll think. Heavens, he'll probably think I'm spying on him! Why did I get myself into this mess? What do I have to say or do to convince you I'm innocent?" she entreated.

"Marry me," he responded, to her surprise and his own. "I couldn't turn in my own wife, could I? And that way, I would be sure you were retired from Union duty."

Shannon looked at him in dismay. "I can't marry you, Eli. I am very fond of you, but I don't love you. It would be wrong to marry you without love and under duress. Turn me in, if you must. Perhaps I can prove my innocence to the authorities before they do anything drastic. But why should strangers believe such an incredible story when you won't? Of course it sounds too improbable to be true. At least they'll know I'm blameless when this false Flame commits another crime while I'm in prison, or after I'm executed."

"Do you realize what prisons are like for women?" he asked her.

"I've heard stories. This is one of the dangers of being an agent. When someone discovers your identity, he uses it to blackmail you. I should be thrilled and flattered. Major Clifford demanded sex for survival; and James Thornton wanted to ransom me to Simon. At least you and Pike were honorable enough to demand marriage."

"Would marriage to me be as bad as prison?" he persisted.

"Under these circumstances, perhaps it would. I can't let you do this to either of us, Eli. We don't deserve being punished for someone else's crimes. Without love and trust, we wouldn't have a real marriage. I cannot wed you as a bribe to avoid arrest."

Elisha's gaze critically surveyed the woman before it. He had watched and listened intently as she related her remarkable story. He mentally envisioned those days he had spent with her and around her. "Either you're a damn good actress and a brazen bluffer, or you're telling the truth. Which is it, Shannon Greenleaf?" He inhaled deeply, then slowly exhaled as he made his decision.

Shannon's somber gaze unwaveringly met his percing one. "During the last few months, I've been all of those, Eli. I'm sorry about your ship and friends. I've suffered losses too, so I know how you must be feeling. Believing I betrayed you must make it harder. I am glad you survived, Eli." She noticed his hesitation. "I realize this is a difficult decision for you. I have no evidence to prove my innocence. You don't know me, so you have no reason to trust me. All I can say is I'm not that treacherous Flame. Maybe someone created a heroic image to stir men's spirits. Maybe someone's using Flame

382

to distract enemies from the real agent. Maybe someone's after me. I don't have any logical, or perhaps believable, answers. If you would rather not assume the responsibility for my guilt or innocence, I'll understand. Do what you feel is right. I won't blame you or hate you."

Elisha ran his fingers through his mussed sable hair and absently chewed on the inside of his left jaw. "I hope I'm making the right choice, Shannon, because I'm not going to turn you in. I'm afraid the authorities might not be as trusting as I am. Prison is a horrible place, and I wouldn't want you harmed."

Shannon closed her eyes and exhaled loudly in relief and gratitude. Tears began to roll down her cheeks. "You are indeed a very special man, Elisha Carter, but I knew that when I met you," she stated sincerely. "I promise you won't be sorry for believing me."

"Then show your appreciation by letting me stay here tonight." When he saw her face pale and her eyes fill with anguish, he clarified, "Not to repay me for saving your hide by sleeping with me. I lived on my ship, so I have no place to go. It's late and I'm exhausted. I won't touch you, Shannon; you have my word of honor. I just need to sleep. I'll look for a room in the morning."

Shannon's indecision was visible. "What if someone sees you coming out of my room? I already have that notorious Flame reputation to deal with. This could make matters worse for me." She sighed heavily. "But you're right. I do owe you for protecting me, and I could be partly to blame for your misfortune. Eli, can I ask you one question without your taking offense?" she queried anxiously.

"Ask," he replied, wondering at her curious look.

"This trip and attack—they did take place, didn't they? This wasn't a trick to unmask me or to ensnare me, was it? I know it must sound awful that I ask such things, but I've become so wary."

Elisha knew she was being honest with her questions. "Look at me, woman. Are these injuries false? I thought you were a Rebel agent, Shannon, even if you did act strange for one."

"What do you mean?" she probed in bewilderment.

"You never asked questions and snooped. You didn't reveal yourself when I told you about the voyage. Little things like those."

"That was intentional. I didn't want to do anything to incriminate myself, and I didn't want to uncover facts that could divide my loyalties. If the Union contacted me or tried to force my aid, I could then swear I had nothing to report. I'm tired of running and hiding and being terrified. You can have the bed and I'll take the sofa."

"No, I'll take the sofa, if we can't share the bed like two adults," he jested, grinning at her.

Shannon smiled. "That's the problem, Eli; we are adults. I am not in love with you, but you are dangerously attractive. I'll take the sofa because I'm shorter and smaller. I'll fetch the extra covers."

Shannon went to the closet and withdrew another blanket. She retrieved one of the pillows. "Good night, Captain Carter," she said, then walked into the other room. She placed the pillow on the sofa and lay down, covering her trembling body with the blanket.

"Good night, Shannon," he murmured tenderly from the doorway. "I should warn you that I'm not giving up my pursuit of you. We'll talk in the morning. Sleep well, angel."

"Eli?" she called out softly. "Thank you."

He smiled and warmed. No, he wouldn't give up on her yet.

Shannon lay awake for another hour, trying to make sense of this dilemma. What was happening? Who was doing this to her? What if Blane returned tonight? How would she explain Eli to him, or him to Eli? With luck,

Blane wouldn't appear until tomorrow as promised, and Elisha would be out of her room and bed. At last, she slept.

Early the next morning, Molly found Mattilu preparing to take a tray to Shannon's room. The woman was becoming suspicious of the redhead who was enjoying free room and board. She decided it was time to find out why that Rebel agent was spending so much time in her room alone. Perhaps if Shannon was still asleep, she might discover notes or messages left around. If not, she was eager to have a chat with the ravishing spy. She wanted to know if Shannon had heard from Steven and if she knew when he would be returning. For certain, something odd was going on where that vixen was concerned.

Molly informed the serving woman, "You see to your chores, Matti. I'll deliver our guest's breakfast. She certaily likes to take advantage of our good nature, lying about and being waited upon."

Mattilu calmly and genially protested, "You don't needs ta trouble yoreself, ma'am. Matti kin takes care of it and be right back."

Molly stared at the woman and scoffed, "Stop your slavelike talk with me, Matti. I told you, it's for the customers. Do as you're told, or else I'll fire you. Then you'd be in a predicament. No one else would hire a smart-mouthed Negro woman who doesn't know her place. You've been spending too much time waiting on that bitch hand and foot. It's time she started taking care of herself and earning her keep."

Mattilu dared not interfere when Molly was in one of her crazy moods. She nodded but didn't apologize for her words or behavior. She hated this woman, and looked forward to leaving this place.

Molly took the tray and walked to Shannon's room. Using her passkey, she let herself into the suite, for Shannon had forgotten to use the inside bolt after Mattilu's departure the night before. Shannon had awakened and was in the bathing closet freshening up and dressing, with the door closed. Molly left the tray on the hall floor and slipped into the room, failing to notice the pillow and blanket on the sofa. She tiptoed to the bedroom door and peeked inside.

The woman's eyes widened in shock as they swept over the man sleeping peacefully in Shannon's bed. She noticed his garments, which had been tossed over a chair. Her appreciative gaze roved his naked torso and handsome face. It looked as if he had been in a fight while he was away. Upon returning, he had rushed into this bitch's arms and bed for comfort! This settled it; Shannon wouldn't be sleeping with Elisha if there was anything between her and Steven. Molly eyed the virile man once more, then hurriedly and silently left the suite. She didn't want Shannon learning of her startling discovery when she left the bathing closet. But she would make certain Steven did, just in case he had his eye on this cheap little tart.

Molly locked the door and stood near it, grinning. So, Shannon Greenleaf wasn't such a perfect lady after all. In less than ten days, she had begun carrying on wickedly with a man whom she had just met. Molly envisioned Elisha's naked body beneath that blanket. No doubt he was handsome all over and was a skilled lover. Her body flamed with desire, for it had been a long time since she had sneaked a passionate night with a man. If it weren't for her fear of getting pregnant out of wedlock, she would take at least two or three men into her bed a week! How she missed a man's arms and lips and body. If Steven didn't come to her soon, she would be forced to look elsewhere for masculine attention. Perhaps to Elisha after Shannon left, if this was nothing more than a wanton affair between them.

Molly waited a few more minutes, then tapped lightly on Shannon's door. When the redhead answered it, Molly could tell she was dismayed to find her standing there. "Matti's busy, Shannon, so I brought up your tray. I hate to rush, but we're expecting several new guests this morning. Just let me know if you need anything else."

Shannon was stunned by Molly's friendly behavior. She couldn't believe the woman didn't want to come inside and harass her. She took the tray, thanked Molly, and watched the woman leave. Something had to have happened, for Molly was happy as a lark and it was still early! She placed the tray on the table, deciding to let Elisha eat this meal. She would find some way to eat something later.

Shannon went to the door and looked at the man slumbering in her bed. He was indeed attractive. She was fortunate that he had believed her and hadn't taken advantage of his information. "Eli?" she called softly to awaken him. When he opened his eyes and met her gaze, he smiled and stretched. Shannon's eyes slipped over the brawny shoulders and arms, bulging with muscles earned from honest and daring work. "Molly brought a breakfast tray. Why don't you come and eat it? I can get something later. We need to sneak you out of here before the hotel gets busy. How do you feel this morning? You must locate a doctor to tend some of those injuries. You need a few stitches and proper medicine. You can't risk infection," she chatted nervously.

Elisha hadn't moved or spoken. He was content to observe her. When she flushed, he grinned. "Do you realize how beautiful you are in the morning? Your husband won't be able to get out of bed and start his

387

chores until noon. No doubt he'll keep you chained to him when he does. Shannon, Shannon," he murmured huskily. "What I would give to have you as mine."

Shannon looked worried. "Eli, please don't—"

Elisha laughingly interrupted her. "Don't worry, angel. I won't press you this early in the day. But I won't give up the chase."

"You are impossible," she teased him.

"Oh, no, my lady, impossible I'm not—not where you're concerned," he refuted playfully. "But if I don't get dressed and get out of here, I might change my mind about storming your fortress wall."

"Hurry, before your breakfast gets cold." Shannon went into the other room and prepared his meal on the small table. She poured the coffee into the cup on the tray and in one left behind from her last meal, which she had rinsed in the bathing closet.

Elisha came up behind her and slipped his arms around her waist. He kissed her on the neck and hugged her longingly. "I surely would like to begin every morning like this, angel. I'm not a bad catch. At least give me consideration."

"That's all I'll give you, Captain Carter, if you don't sit down and eat," she replied mirthfully.

He merrily cautioned, "Watch out for hasty bargains, ma'am. The last one in Washington got you into lots of trouble and danger."

Shannon admitted instantly, "No one knows that better than I do."

Shannon nibbled on a biscuit with jam and sipped coffee while Elisha leisurely devoured her meal. After freshening up, he told her he would call on her for dinner. Shannon peeked into the hall to make certain no one was about when Elisha departed. After seizing her and kissing her thoroughly, he gingerly crept down the back stairs to head for his leased dwelling a mile from the hotel, a dwelling he hadn't bothered to mention to Shannon.

Shannon fretted all morning, wondering how to solve her predicament. When Mattilu came to bring her lunch, Shannon told her apprehensively, "Matti, Eli was betrayed to the Yankees and he thought I was to blame." She hurriedly outlined last night's confrontation with the captain. Assuming no one had seen Elisha come and go, she kept their innocent sleeping arrangements a secret. "I have to see him for dinner, or risk offending him and renewing his suspicions about me. What am I going to do, Matti? Blane is expected to return for me today. If he arrives tonight while I'm with Eli, you'll have to explain matters to him. We can't afford a complication at this late date."

"Miss Shannon, you shouldn't have told Captain Carter all those things. What if he changes his mind? What if he starts spying on you?"

"I didn't have any choice, Matti. He caught me off guard and tried to kill me. I was so terrified I couldn't think clearly. I had no way of knowing how much he knew about me. I couldn't risk being caught in a lie. Don't you see, it could have been a ruse to entrap me! We'll have to be very careful until Blane and I leave town. Damn that Molly Ryan," she suddenly declared. "Part of this is her fault. She told him I was a Rebel agent. She may have told others, the witch."

"We had better watch her closely, Miss Shannon. She's been acting a mite queer of late. You be real careful around Captain Carter, 'cause he's got his mind and heart set on having you."

"I know, Matti, and that has me as worried as his

thinking I had betrayed him. Who's posing as the Flame and getting me into trouble? Why are they doing this to me?"

"Miss Shannon," Mattilu began speaking hesitantly, "why didn't you tell Mister Jeremy about Captain Carter's trip?" Although Shannon had been confiding in her, Mattilu wondered if she would answer.

Shannon looked at her as she replied frankly, "Because of what actually happened. I didn't want to be responsible for the lives of those men, especially Eli's. I like him very much, Matti. If it weren't for Blane . . ." Shannon went silent and blushed. "Does it sound awful to be attracted to two men simultaneously? It's strange, Matti. They're so different, yet so much alike. I honestly didn't think Eli could succeed, so what did it matter if I withheld that information? Blane knows I'm not an agent anymore. I explained my feelings and guilt to him. He agreed it was best for me to stop spying."

"'Cause he's afraid for you. Did you tell him about you and the Captain?" When Shannon shook her head, Matti warned mischievously, "He's gonna be mighty upset and jealous if he comes around tonight."

Shannon grinned. "Maybe that will be good for him, Matti. He's always making me jealous with other women, so why not let him stew and worry for a spell? I'm teasing," she laughingly confessed. "If Blane doesn't know by now how I feel about him, he's blind and stupid. As we both know, he isn't either one. I only wish Eli weren't so taken with me. I really haven't encouraged him, Matti. In fact, I said everything possible to discourage his pursuit. Considering what he knows about me, I have no idea how he might react if I spurned him, even nicely. Oh, Matti, whatever shall I do?"

"You can't blame him, Miss Shannon. You're the most beautiful woman I've ever seen. No wonder Major

Stevens is trying to hurry back."

At seven-thirty, Shannon was dining with Elisha in the cozy private parlor. "How did you manage this service and privilege?"

"Molly and I are conspiring," he openly and devilishly announced. "I want you, and she wants your partner, Steven James." He surmised enviously, "He is that Confederate agent you mentioned last night? I hate to imagine you two traveling alone, especially playing husband and wife. Think I could steal his position?"

"You know I can't answer your first question. For all I know, Captain Elisha Carter, you could be a Union spy probing me or a Rebel agent testing me. As for taking my partner's place, it isn't necessary. I told you last night, I'm out of the spy business. It's too dangerous and demanding. All I want is to get home, since I can't seem to help my brother. If he escapes, that's where he would head. Besides, I don't trust that malicious Sherman. You know what he did to Atlanta."

"Don't you realize how perilous a trip to Savannah could be—not to mention staying there alone with those marauders terrorizing and plundering the countryside? I can't let you endanger yourself like that."

"That's my home, Eli. I know plenty of people there. I'll be safe. We have an overseer handling things until we return."

"What if he's taken off since you've been gone? Tarnation, angel, he could have robbed your place blind by now. Worse, you might have Yankees in residence when you arrive. I've seen what pirates do when they attack a ship with women aboard, and Sherman's men are worse than any pirates born. You'll be lucky if they only arrest you."

"I'll have to take that chance, Eli. I can't continue to accept charity, and I can't keep running and hiding. I want to go home. I need to go home," she stressed. "Now eat and stop staring at me."

Elisha chuckled. "You should be used to being stared at. What man could keep his eyes off you? You've already confessed to being attracted to me, so I have to take advantage of any weakness you have."

"You are a devil, Elisha Carter," she accused with a smile. "You should not behave so wickedly on Sunday."

"Guilty as charged, ma'am. Who is more in need of an influential angel than a devil such as I?" His green eyes sparkled with mischief.

"Elisha Carter, you are im—" Shannon didn't finish her jest, for Eli interrupted.

"That's right, angel. But I'm not impossible where you're concerned."

Shannon tried to change the subject. "What about your ship? How can you run the blockade without one? What will you do now?"

"Tuesday, I'm sailing—"

Shannon instantly injected, "Don't say another word! I don't want you accusing me of betraying you if something happens on this trip. Don't tell me anything," she firmly commanded.

"I'm not going on some dark mission, so relax. I'm sailing to Charleston on Tuesday with Captain Sellers of the *Majestic Maiden*. I have another ship there—my brother's. Denton's laid up with a broken arm and leg, so he won't mind my taking over the *Angel Wings*. I should return in a week. Can you stand being without me that long?"

"I can probably use the rest from all of your harassment, sir," she saucily informed him. "Eli, you will be careful," she urged.

"More so than ever. Perhaps my absence and your worry will endear me to your heart. I'll keep hoping

392

and praying."

They completed their meal while Elisha related sea adventures he had experienced before the war. Shannon relished the tales of other places and people. Catching her intense interest and pleasure, Elisha offered, "Come with me on my next voyage, and I'll show you sights you never dreamed existed. If you marry me, you can sail with me on every trip." He looked entreatingly at her, then grinned raffishly.

Shannon laughed. "That's a tempting offer, kind sir— you and the whole world. I shall give it my deepest consideration."

"I see I have a greedy, spoiled woman on my hands. Marry me, angel, and you can have whatever your heart desires. I'm a very wealthy man, so this isn't an empty promise. I can get you away from all this death and destruction and peril. Anything, Shannon."

"If I married you, Eli, it would be for love, not money. If I married you, you would be the only thing I desired. Wealth and station and travel mean nothing without love and passion. Those are not emotions a person can force on himself or on others. Nor can he halt them even when they are directed at the wrong person."

When the hour grew late and the wine bottle empty, Shannon told him, "I have to rest, Eli. For some reason, I didn't get much sleep last night. The dinner was lovely, and the company splendid."

"I'm sorry about what I did last night, Shannon. I lost my head. After I swam ashore, all I could think about all the way here was punishing you." He noticed the high neckline on her dress. "Are you all right? Is there any damage?"

She touched her neck and shuddered at the grim memory. "A few bruises. That's expected; I have fair skin. I'm glad you couldn't kill me, Eli. I can imagine what torment you would have suffered when you discovered I wasn't guilty, which you will. I know you're trying hard to trust me and believe me, but I know that isn't easy. Until my innocence is proven, you'll always have little doubts and qualms. Whatever happens, I'm glad I met you. After seeing and meeting so many vile men since this war began, it's good to find one like you. Be safe and be happy, Elisha Carter; you deserve both."

"You sound as if you're saying good-bye."

"No, just things that need to be and should be said between friends."

"Will you have dinner with me tomorrow night before I leave?"

"I would be delighted," she accepted cheerfully. Blane would just have to understand that this last dinner was necessary. "Could we make it at six? Then we could take a carriage ride or stroll after dinner."

Elisha beamed happily. "Six it is, my radiant angel. If you have to leave me, I'll walk you to your room."

"I don't think that's a wise idea, Eli. People will notice how much we're seeing each other, so they'll be watching us with curiosity. I'll meet you in our usual spot at six." Shannon stood and walked to the door, then waited for Elisha to accompany her.

"Would it be insulting or alarming if I kissed you good night here in private?" he inquired, pulling her into his arms as he spoke.

"Eli, I don't want to mislead you by—"

Elisha's mouth closed over hers, sealing their lips in a tender and heady kiss. He embraced her urgently but did not allow his eager hands to roam beyond her back. To his surprise and pleasure, the kiss continued.

Shannon allowed Elisha this coveted moment. She didn't want to spurn him or push him away. She would wait for the kiss and embrace to end, then politely and

394

quickly exit. After all, both were most stimulating and enjoyable. Like Blane, Elisha was talented in this area. Both men were so unlike those who had courted her previously, with their clumsy ways and repulsive gropings. Elisha could never know he might have won her heart and hand if Blane had not entered her life first.

When Elisha and Shannon parted, their gazes met. She moved her fingers over his lips, marveling at their ability to entice her to such madness. "I'd better leave," she stated a little breathlessly.

Elisha dared not press her, but he thrilled to her response. Watching her mount the stairs, he smiled and plotted her surrender.

"I see all went well with your little private dinner," Molly commented dryly behind him. "But why did she go upstairs alone?"

Turning to frown at his obliging assistant, Elisha said, "Because she's a lady, and ladies marry men before sleeping with them."

Molly smiled skeptically. "Don't be foolish, Eli. I've never seen any woman more infatuated and bewitched by a man than she is by you. She would probably do anything you wished if you followed her upstairs and worked those abundant charms on her. I won't tell."

"I already know how you can't keep your word and confidences," he stated in a barely veiled insult. "When the time's right, she'll be mine," he stated smugly.

"She already is, my blind and foolish rogue. She's just being coy, or you're being too cautious and insecure. When you aren't looking, her eyes are all over you. I suppose you're going to tell me that flush on her cheeks just now was because of the heat."

"Mind your own affairs, Molly. Foolish words and ideas are dangerous. You wanted Steven, so take him. You don't have to worry about Shannon stealing him.

She's going to marry me within the month."

"She's agreed?" Molly queried, angered and relieved.

"Yes," he stated confidently, tasting the remains of her kiss. "But don't go spreading the news until I tell you it's all right," he warned.

Molly nodded in vexation, then left him standing there. No doubt he was planning to sneak up the back stairs after convincing everyone he was gone! She couldn't wait to relate this news to Steven.

Chapter Sixteen

Monday dawned cold and crisp. That afternoon, a letter was delivered to Shannon. Mattilu brought it to her room the moment the roughly dressed man departed. Anticipation and excitement filled the redhead, for she knew it had to be from Blane. Shannon ripped open the seal and hurriedly read the stunning message. Her eyes widened and her lips parted as terror washed over her. She paled and trembled. She read the missive slowly and carefully, withdrawing and analyzing hidden messages.

"What's wrong, Miss Shannon? Is Major Stevens injured or captured?" the woman inquired fearfully.

"No, Matti, I suppose he's fine. The letter is from him. He wants me to come to Charleston immediately and secretly. He says the Rebel forces are tracking us. They've checked Raleigh, Fayetteville, and Charlotte. They'll be here in a few days. I have to get away. There's train fare inside. I can't let Simon locate me with Blane gone."

The older woman did not reason long before protesting, "I don't understand, Miss Shannon. Major Stevens was to come back here for you. He wouldn't tell you to meet him somewhere so far off. You can't travel alone. Are you sure that letter's from him?"

"It must be, Matti. It's signed with both of his initials. Who else would know his real name and code name? Besides, the clues are too clear for it to be from anyone else. I need to check the train schedule before Eli comes to dinner. If he discovers I'm leaving, he may try to stop me. I'll have to deceive him until he sails tomorrow."

Mattilu peeked over Shannon's shoulder to read the letter while the younger woman was staring off into space. She read:

Shannon,

Your Uncle Charles is longing for you to visit as we planned. Please come immediately. He secretly looks for you each day as his health goes worse. I have enclosed train fare. Leave today if possible, as death is near. I was telling him about our last trip through many towns. Now, our valiant soldiers are traveling that same route. Perhaps they'll enjoy Raleigh, Fayetteville, and Charlotte as much as we did. They should be arriving in Wilmington by Wednesday or Thursday.

A friend told me our lawyer, Simon Travers, will be arriving with the troops. I know he's eager to see you and discuss that problem back home. Uncle Charles said he wouldn't burn any of your letters because he has friends who might want to read them. I am well and eager to see you.

Major Steven Bs James

Even if Shannon's attention had not been distracted by pensive deliberation, she wouldn't have guessed that the ex-slave could read and write. "Miss Shannon," the woman called to her and interrupted her ruminations. "You had better take care of the train ticket. It's getting late. I'll have your bath and clothes ready when you return. Be careful."

Mattilu did not stop Shannon when she read her the letter and explained the clues. "I'm supposed to burn it so no one can find it and read it." She walked to the fireplace and tossed the letter into the flames. She watched the paper until nothing was left of it. Then she placed the money in her dress pocket and hurriedly departed.

Shannon was gone for over two hours. When she finally returned, Mattilu was nearly frantic. She observed Shannon's dejection. "Where have you been, chile? The depot is a short walk. I've been scared silly."

Shannon tossed her woolen cape over the sofa and sat down wearily. "It's awful, Matti. I don't know what I'm going to do. There won't be any trains until Thursday; and then I'd need a pass from General Holmes to ride it, if it's an emergency. I checked on buying a horse. There are none for sale or rent. I checked on stages and carriages. There aren't any, Matti. Unless I walk or find a horse to steal, I can't leave town. I dare not travel with soldiers as a nurse; the word must be out on me by now. You know I won't be difficult to locate. What shall I do, Matti? There is no other path to escape." Shannon didn't think to mention that she had spoken with Sarah Jane and had asked her friend if she knew of a deliveryman whom she could hire to transport her, for the woman had offered no help or advice.

The moment she made that statement, her gaze locked with Matti's and she saw the answer clearly. "Captain Carter is sailing to Charleston at dawn. Dare I ask him to take me along? You know what he'll think. Heavens beware, for I have no choice. Oh, Matti, I wish you could come along to protect me from his romantic pursuit. I so wanted you to come to work for me."

"You convince Captain Carter to take you to Charleston, and I'll be right there with you. I'm ready to leave this place. I'm smart and I'm an excellent worker. I won't have any trouble finding me a job. I promised Major Stevens I wouldn't let no harm come to you."

"You'll go with me?" she asked incredulously. "I would take you to Savannah with me, but I don't know what I'm going to find there. If we can get you a job in Charleston until I get matters settled at Greenleaf, I can send for you to come and work for me."

"Nothing would suit me better, Miss Shannon. I'll get you and me packed, 'cause I know you can persuade the Captain to take us aboard. Just don't you go promising him something you don't plan to give. Thanks makes a man terribly dangerous and unpredictable."

"First, we need to create a plan to convince Eli to help us. I'll need writing paper, pen, and ink. We'll prepare a letter that will convince him I'm in danger. We'll use the envelope from Blane's letter. See if you can find paper he won't recognize."

Her brown eyes brightened with mischief. She remarked, "We have a guest who will aid us, and he won't even know it! I saw a writing set with plenty of unusual paper. I'll go fetch you two pieces right now. You get all pretty for tonight."

When Matti returned with the pen and ink and stolen paper, Shannon had completed her bath and was wrapped in a blanket. How she wished she had her own clothes. Her silk robe would feel marvelous. She told the woman she would write the letter before dressing.

"What if Captain Carter recognizes your handwriting?"

"I can write with both hands, Matti. I used to do it to entertain myself. My scripts are different. He'll never guess the truth."

"I hope not, Miss Shannon. We don't need another problem."

"Listen very closely to the plan, Matti." When the

woman sat down beside her, Shannon related the details of her scheme.

Elisha leaned against the railing at the foot of the stairs. His alert gaze kept shifting upward as he eagerly anticipated Shannon's arrival. It was twenty minutes after six o'clock, and Shannon had not appeared. He decided to wait until six-thirty, then go check on her.

Molly unwittingly aided Shannon's ruse when she noticed Elisha's presence and approached him. She was furious with Shannon and Mattilu. "If you're waiting for that haughty bitch who's been eating and boarding free, she's packing to leave; and she's taking my best serving woman."

"What are you talking about?" Elisha inquired in puzzlement.

"You mean she hasn't told you? She's leaving tomorrow, and she's stealing Mattilu from me. They're both ungrateful bitches."

Elisha glared at the offensive female, then mounted the steps rapidly. He knocked on Shannon's door several times before Mattilu finally opened it. He could tell the black woman was distraught. "What's wrong, Mattilu? Molly tells me you and Shannon are leaving town."

The woman called on her deceitful accent and sly wits to elicit Elisha's aid. "Yessir, Captain Carter. I wuz suppose to come tell you she can't come downstairs to eat with you tonight, but I wuz afeared to leave her alone. She's mighty upset and sceered. Poor Miss Shannon, if'n that chile ain't got enough troubles with her papa and brothers, now some terrible man is after her. He's acomin' with legal papers which says he can force Miss Shannon to go with him. The soldiers are gonna help him steal that chile. Poor Miss Shannon can't find no way to escape 'em. Ain't no trains or horses or stages or nothing.

I got to hep her git her away from him," she vowed cleverly.

"When is he arriving?" Elisha questioned.

"That letter told her Wednesday or Thursday, sir. Miss Shannon wanted to run off afore he got here, but she can't find no way. I give 'er some brandy to hep settle her down. Lawsy, Captain Carter, I don't know whats to do. I wuz goin' with her to her papa's house to work. I done tole Mrs. Molly I wuz quit aworkin' for her."

"You fetch us something to eat and drink, Mattilu. I'll talk with Shannon and see what this is all about. Don't worry. I won't let anyone harm her. Where is she? Who was this letter from?"

"She's alyin' on the bed, sir. She's been acryin' and aworrin' ever since she came back from the train depot. I been tryin' to comfort her. This Mister Travers must be a wicked man. It ain't right he kin hunt her down like an animal and force her to live with 'im."

"You run along, and take your time. I'll take care of her." Elisha watched Mattilu's departure. He opened the door and entered the bedroom. He found Shannon lying stomach down and facing the wall. She was weeping softly into her pillow. The letter that Mattilu had mentioned was crumpled beside her glorious red mane.

He sat down beside her and began to stroke her hair. His other hand reached for the letter. He read it without asking permission:

Shannon,

You saved my life two times, so I owe you. Something crazy is going on and I can't make it figure. There's "fire" everywhere and doing things even war don't allow. How can this be, as you sit there? I been doing some checking and I don't like what I'm hearing and seeing. If I didn't know you, I would say you was guilty of these matters.

The man you spoke of to Mister L. is riding with troops. He's gonna find you there by 28 or 29. You ain't got no chance against him and his papers, if the troops don't arrest you for these crazy charges. My advice is to git like a fox from a chicken pen. If you come to Uncle Charles, I can help you get home. I can look for you on December 5 to 12. Don't stay and fight cause you can't win this one. I know you thought you were out of this mess. I'm sorry, but ain't no word on Corry. I think he got free.

I'm sending a little money. Get a train of you can or use it for supplies. Wish I could help more. Can't get to you. I can promise to try and clear your "name." I hate to say it, but the evidence looks real and bad. Git while you can. Stay safe and happy, Shannon. I pray I see you soon.

Your partner

As Elisha continued to stroke her hair silently, Shannon put the remainder of her desperate and clever plan into motion. "I've really made a mess of my life, Matti. I was so impetuous and foolish. I was going to prove I had guts and patriotism like my family. I had visions of doing wonderful and noble things for the Union, but all I did was help nurse Rebel soldiers and be a part of other agents' disguises. Now, I don't know what's happening or how to stop it. Where did it go wrong? Where did I fail myself and others? I'm no help to either side, Matti, because they're both wrong."

Her hand pounded the bed as she faked a rush of anger and frustration. "It makes me so mad. I haven't done anything wrong, but they won't believe me. Who's doing these terrible things to me? Who's using me to hide his own crimes? I would have been safer staying with that

403

Union agent, but I couldn't without helping him. I can't betray the South, Matti—not when I see and hear what the Union's doing."

She wiped real tears from her face, for she was suddenly terrified this plan would go awry. "If I stay and try to battle this so-called evidence, Simon will catch me. I can't return home with that beast, Matti. He's already stolen my family's holdings, and now he's trying to steal me. He practically owns me, Matti; and the law is taking his side. If only I could get to Charleston and Savannah, I know Corry would find me and help me. If he can't, I've got friends who would hide me and help me. I'm sorry, Matti. I know this isn't what you expected from me when I hired you."

Shannon sat up and turned as she said, "Even if we have to walk—" Shannon stared at the man beside her. Her body could not have assisted her ruse better, for she flushed and shuddered unconsciously. "Eli, what are you doing in here? I thought you were Matti. Where is she? I sent her to tell you I wasn't feeling well and couldn't join you for dinner." She looked at him as if praying he hadn't overheard her words. Her gaze fell to the letter within his grasp. She made a grab for it.

Elisha moved it out of her reach. "Why didn't you come to me for help, Shannon? Why run off without telling me anything?"

Shannon's eyes narrowed and flamed as she pretended to unleash her warring emotions. "So you could blackmail me into following your wishes? I'm tired of men taking advantage of me because of things I haven't done! Why must you all prey on defenseless women? I knew you wouldn't believe me. You tried to kill me because you thought I had betrayed you. I knew how this sudden departure would appear to you. I was hoping to get away before you revealed a dark side. Even so, I was going to leave a letter for you with Sarah Jane."

She breathed heavily. "It doesn't matter, because I can't find a way out of this town. I'm about to be unmasked, Eli. That should make you happy. Perhaps you are the one who told them where to find me. You might get to witness my death after all, because I will confess to being this legendary Flame before I let that foul devil take possession of me. Just go away and leave me alone. I have to think and plan. I trusted you, but you were only playing with me."

Elisha seized her arms and yanked her close to him. "What in tarnation are you talking about, woman? Stop talking crazy and in riddles. Why didn't you come to me? You knew I would help you."

"Yes, right into your bed," she accused, looking hurt. "Have you forgotten your little tale of living on your ship and having no place to sleep? I was going to come to you for help. I was going to beg you to take me to Charleston. What did I care about the blockade dangers with Simon stalking me and the Confederacy thirsting for my blood? I asked where a shipless captain would go to rent a room. I don't have to tell you what I discovered, do I, my honest and devoted suitor? That night you tried to kill me, you asked why. That's what I'm doing now, Eli. Why? What do you really want from me? Were you betrayed and attacked? Did you stay here Saturday night because you didn't trust me? Was it all a pretense to lure me into a false sense of security, to entice me to remain here until these troops arrived to arrest me? My heavens, my old partner trusts me and helps me more than anyone, and I did nothing to deserve it. It's all so confusing and frightening. I don't know who or what to believe anymore."

Elisha ruefully confessed, "I did deceive you, Shannon, but not for those reasons. I stayed here that night because I was afraid you would panic and run away from me. Tarnation, woman, look what I had done to you! I had to make certain you weren't injured. I wanted to stay here all night without touching you to prove to you I could be trusted. I won't leave you here in danger. You get packed and I'll take you to Charleston, if you'll promise to forgive me."

Shannon stared at him skeptically. "You'll take me there?"

"It's dangerous, but I can get you through their lines."

"What about Matti? I promised to take her with me. She's become my friend, and I need her. Besides, I couldn't travel alone with you and a crew of men. What would people think and say?"

"We'll take her with us. After we eat, you two get packed while I go see Captain Sellers. He owes me more than one favor."

"I can't go downstairs looking and feeling like this!" she protested, wiping the tearstains from her cheeks.

Elisha smiled. "Matti's bringing our dinner up here. You relax and let me handle everything. We sail at dawn."

As he spoke these last words, Mattilu knocked on the hall door to announce their meals. "You get freshened up while I let Matti in," he told her.

After placing the heavy tray on the table, Mattilu came to see about Shannon. The redhead excitedly revealed, "We're saved, Matti. Eli is going to take us to Charleston. From there, we can get home."

Mattilu turned and gazed suspiciously at the man leaning against the door frame. "Don't worry," Shannon informed her. "He explained everything. We can trust him," she stated, smiling at Elisha.

Elisha suggested, "Matti, why don't you go eat and pack, then return and help Shannon with her belongings. After we eat, I have to speak with Sellers and get things prepared for you two."

Mattilu grinned broadly. "I shore am glad I wuzn't wrong about you, sir. I'll take care of everything and Miss Shannon. See, chile, ain't nothing to worry about no more. They's still good men around."

Shannon smiled at Elisha again as she agreed. Suddenly the smile faded and Shannon turned away from him. After Mattilu left, the man questioned her change of mood. She looked up into his entreating gaze and asked, "How will I pay for our fares? What will you expect for this rescue, Eli?"

He caressed her cheek, for he grasped her meaning. "Only your safety and happiness, angel," he responded so honestly and tenderly that it pained her to delude him.

"If I could give you more, Eli, I would." She felt so guilty about using this man, who loved her, to reach the man she loved. She sadly admitted to herself that she had no other choice. "Forgive me."

"There's no need, angel. I won't give up hope for us, but I won't use your trouble to make you mine. I know it would spoil things."

"Oh, Eli, if things were different—if I were different—I would marry you tonight. You're one of the best friends I've had."

He chuckled and embraced her. "If you were different, Shannon Greenleaf, I wouldn't want you so much. Perhaps in time you might discover you can't forget me, or things could change. If that day comes, promise to look for me, because I know I won't be able to replace you any time soon, if ever."

Shannon gazed into his compelling eyes. "I promise, Eli."

After they had eaten and Elisha had departed, Shannon cried. Elisha was very special. She had to be careful not to deceive him more than necessary; she had to be careful not to encourage his love and desire. She entered the bedroom to complete her packing.

It was still dark Tuesday morning when Elisha and his helper came for the two women and their belongings. Shannon snuggled into her woolen cape to ward off the freezing weather that was teasing at December's door. The sky was black behind countless tiny lights. For some curious reason, the word "freedom" kept racing through her mind. Instead of being afraid and wary, Shannon felt calm and confident. She was happy and full of anticipation, and she knew it was because of Elisha Carter.

The ship sailed shortly after they were aboard and comfortably ensconced in Captain Sellers's quarters. Elisha had told them to remain there unless he announced otherwise. If there was trouble, they were to be passed off as prisoners, which reminded Shannon of the incident in Moore's camp. He had said the trip would require about three or four days, according to winds and Union obstacles. They could have made better time if it hadn't been necessary to sail inside the blockade lines so close to land contours and shore perils. She was astonished and delighted when Elisha revealed that he had left hints around town to imply she was sailing for Nassau and England with him. That information would halt or slow everyone's search for her! Her affection and respect for him increased, as did her remorse for duping him.

The first day at sea passed without a problem. Aside from a heavy breeze, the weather was pleasant, though cold. Shannon couldn't speak ill of the winds, for they blew in the ship's favor. Surprisingly, she and Matti fared well on the rough seas. The captain and Elisha joined her for the evening meal, which passed with good food and amusing sea tales. That night, Shannon slept peacefully.

The next morning, Elisha allowed her to come topside to enjoy the view and adventure. She stood at the railing and allowed his arm to rest lightly around her shoulders. She inhaled the cold air and smiled.

"You make an excellent sailor, Miss Greenleaf. Too bad your first voyage comes during such bad weather and conditions."

Shannon laughed. "Only the circumstances are bad, Eli," she corrected him. "Now I see why you and Corry are bewitched by this magic. How do I thank you for such a gallant rescue?"

"Your smile and joy are thanks enough, angel. Does the offer still stand to introduce me to Corry and to help me acquire his business?"

"More so than ever, Captain Carter. The sea gives one such feelings of excitement and freedom. I shall have to tag along." Shannon instantly scolded herself, for she was innocently misleading him again.

Elisha watched the wind whip through her hair and tousle it riotously. The morning sun beamed down on it, bringing it to fiery life. The sky and clouds were reflected in her large blue eyes, as dark and mysterious as the waters around the ship. She was exquisite. She was stimulating. She was complex. How he wished he possessed the courage to whisk her away to sunny and exotic Nassau! Perhaps after the war . . .

"I've never seen you so happy and carefree, Shannon. I wish I could have known you before this war, and I hope to know you after it."

"I have you to thank for this present mood, kind sir. Home, Eli—I'm finally going home," she stated wistfully. "It's been a long and hard journey." Tears stung her eyes and she lowered her head.

Elisha briefly tightened his hold on her. "It isn't over

409

yet, angel. But at least most of your troubles are behind us."

Wednesday afternoon, Simon Travers and his men arrived in Wilmington. It did not take long for them to uncover the false clues left by Elisha. He raged at Shannon's stroke of luck. Again, he had missed capturing her by one day! How many men was she going to enchant into helping her? She couldn't flee him forever. Simon pondered Blane Stevens's reaction to her little adventure with another man. Unless the man had wings, he mused, they had arrived before the dashing Union agent. Why shouldn't he leave a fatal surprise for Blane, compliments of Shannon? The handsome rake deserved death for stealing his property! That would ensure Blane's never joining her again. Besides, the Union was winning the war; it didn't require Blane's help. Before he and his men departed in the morning, he would send a message to General Holmes about that Yankee spy, and sign it from the Flame.

Simon fumed at this new delay, but he also questioned his information about Shannon's destination. He knew that Shannon wanted to get to Corry and Greenleaf. Suddenly the truth became clear. Of course! That's where the sly witch was heading! he realized triumphantly. It was time to stop pursuing her all over the South. The smart thing to do was head for Savannah and wait for her arrival. He could become part of the welcoming committee for General Sherman. The way that soldier was progressing, Savannah would greet Christmas as a Union conquest. When unsuspecting Shannon arrived—and he was certain she soon would, he would be waiting for her, waiting with the evidence to force the Rebel Flame into his possession.

* * *

Strange things were happening, things that caused Blane to increase his caution and vigilance. While Simon and his men were sleeping in a hotel not far away, Blane sneaked into the Resting Place to retrieve Shannon. He was alarmed to find her suite empty and clean. He wondered if that hateful Molly had assigned his love to a smaller and cheaper room. There was only one way to discover the facts.

Molly opened the door to her suite and sleepily gazed at the anxious man standing there, demanding to speak with her. She smiled and invited him inside, closing the door behind him. In the dim lamplight, she did not realize how harsh her features appeared.

When the woman tried to dally with him, he asked sternly, "Where is Shannon, Molly? I don't have all night."

Molly's blood and temper began to simmer. "She's gone. And she didn't leave any message for you," she added frostily at his concern.

"Gone?" he echoed in disbelief. "Where? How?"

The nettled woman responded angrily, "She got a letter, then packed and left. She sailed with Captain Elisha Carter yesterday. I believe he said for Nassau, then England. She certainly must be popular, with so many men and soldiers asking for her. If you're planning to chase her, I wouldn't recommend it. She's been sleeping with Elisha during your absence, and she's going to marry him."

Blane drew back his hand and almost slapped Molly before he could stop himself. "You vile liar. The only man she sleeps with is me," he snarled unwittingly. "Don't you ever besmirch her name again."

"You sorry bastard!" Molly sneered. "It serves you right to be fooled by her. I found Elisha in her bed one morning when I went to deliver her breakfast. He was naked and sleeping like a baby. I didn't have to ask why, and neither should you. I don't suppose you heard about

411

the attack on his ship? He lost it and most of his crew. He was hurt, but he survived. He came running back to Miss Shannon for comfort. You can say or think as you will, but I saw it with these two eyes. Matti had been waiting on her hand and foot and letting her other chores suffer, so I took up the tray to set her straight. She was in the bathing closet cleaning up and Elisha was sleeping. Neither of them saw me. If you find her, ask her. I dare you."

Molly was filled with rage and spite. She acidly scoffed, "She's only using both of you. And there's no telling how many other men she's snared with those looks and that body. She uses her charms and devious innocence to wrap you men around her finger. She did the same with Elisha, then sailed off with him yesterday. Ask around. You'll learn I speak the truth. What else would he be doing in her bed early in the morning without clothes? He only lives a short way from this hotel."

Blane scowled at the hostile woman. He knew her well enough to realize she was telling the truth, from her point of view. Yet he felt there was something strange about Elisha's return and his stay in Shannon's room. "What about this letter you said she received?" he probed inquisitively.

"Matti took it up to her. Some man delivered it just before lunch Monday. It couldn't have been a new assignment, or she wouldn't have taken off with Elisha. Unless he's her partner now."

"You're positive she didn't leave any message for me?"

"I'm positive she didn't. If you don't believe what I'm saying, go ask my sister. She was even more shocked by your Shannon's departure with another man. When Elisha was here, she spent nearly every minute with him. I can't blame her. He's handsome and virile and very rich. He asked her to marry him several times. She finally agreed. Or maybe she was just trying to avoid her duties. Two soldiers did come looking for her this morning. They seemed none too pleased about her taking off like that. Damn the bitch! She even stole Matti from us. Is that any way to repay us for helping her? No doubt the famous spy needed a personal serving woman. If you see her, you let her know she ain't welcome here again."

Blane's expression altered as he digested those additional facts. After telling Molly he wouldn't be returning again, he went to awaken Sarah Jane to test her sister's honesty and to glean more information. He was dismayed to receive almost the same story Molly had given him. Sarah Jane made it worse by telling him how sorry she was that Shannon had turned to another man for affection and help.

"Don't you think it was just friendship or loneliness?"

Sarah Jane lowered her lashes to conceal her disappointment with Shannon and the girl's behavior. "All I know is what I saw, Major James. They looked mighty close. I do know Elisha fell in love with her and asked her to marry him. He said she was considering his proposal. He told me he hoped they could return from England as man and wife. I know Shannon was afraid of something, but enough to marry Eli? . . . I thought there was something between you two."

"There was, Sarah Jane. I don't understand her actions." He felt traitorous asking if she knew about Molly's wanton charges.

"Molly told me what she saw. I didn't believe her until—" Sarah Jane's face went red and she halted her statement.

"Until what, Sarah Jane?" he pressed apprehensively.

"I'm sorry, Major James, but I did see Captain Carter sneaking down the back stairs very early that morning.

413

He must have just returned from his narrow escape with that Union ship. He had several bandages on his head and arms and hands. I wish she had left you a message, sir, but she didn't. I was hoping that letter was from you. I only saw her for a short time after she received it. Whatever it said, it made her afraid. She went to the train depot to buy a ticket to Charleston, but there were no trains due for days. I know she tried to buy or rent a horse or pay someone to drive her to Charleston. She even asked me to help her locate someone. When I couldn't, I assumed she would be staying here. Perhaps Captain Carter offered to help her get away," she speculated, feeling sympathy for the man standing before her, who was obviously distressed and pained over Shannon's loss.

Sarah Jane added, "They were to have dinner downstairs. He asked me to hold and prepare a special table. When Shannon didn't come down to join him, he went to her room. Matti served them there. She and Shannon have become close friends. I can't blame her for leaving to go to work for her. Molly did treat Matti badly."

"Do you know how long Carter stayed with her that night?"

"Probably only long enough to eat. I saw him leaving a little over an hour later. He came after them early the next morning."

Blane analyzed these new facts. "Are you sure they were sailing for Nassau and England?" he persisted.

"All I know is what I was told, sir. I did hear talk that it was true. They left on the *Majestic Maiden* with Captain Sellers."

Blane thanked her and left. He was standing beside his horse in the stable, getting ready to mount, when four soldiers entered the wooden structure and surrounded him. Blane eyed the guns leveled at him and wisely did

414

not reach for his Colt or his knife. His instincts and skills came to full alert as he sized up each man and the situation.

The stocky captain moved closer to Blane as his gaze swept over the tall, muscular agent. "You can drop your weapons, Major Stevens. You ain't going nowhere but to hell come sunup. Your spying days are over, Yank. Do it real easy, with your left hand."

Blane scanned the expressions and stances of the men before him, astutely obtaining facts about the courage and skills of each. He observed how each foe held his weapon and reacted to the situation. He didn't smile at the captain's mistake in ordering him to use his left hand. He casually and fearlessly used one finger to lift his gun from its holster, then dropped it to the ground in a calculated, though unnoticeable, manner. He did the same with his hunting knife. Like a cunning mountain lion, he remained poised and prepared to attack the moment their guards were dropped. He patted Dan's nose as the well-trained and intelligent animal smelled danger and shifted his hooves in mounting tension and alertness.

The Confederate officer ordered, "Up with those hands, Yank. We don't want to deny you a proper neck stretching at dawn. Rebel bullets are too quick and easy for scum like you."

Often under such conditions, Blane would unnerve and distract his opponent or opponents with taunting smiles and remarks. Tonight, he operated differently. He was in a hurry, and he had other things on his mind. He shrugged and lifted his hands slightly above his shoulders. "You got the wrong man, Captain. How about you explaining this mix-up to me?" he coaxed genially.

The sandy-haired man lowered his rifle. The private relaxed his grip on his weapon. The captain holstered his revolver as he laughed triumphantly. Only one soldier, a redhead, kept alert with his weapon poised for use.

The cocky officer teased, "You hear that, boys? Major Stevens thinks we caught us the wrong polecat. I would say Flame's description of him and his horse call him a bold-faced liar. We can't be mistaken, Yank. You showed up when and where she claimed you would. See that, boys? There's a knife scar on his left jawbone right where she said it would be. How many men do you think there are carrying a western Colt and a Cavalry knife and wearing a bandanna like a Texan? Brown and yellow hair and greeny brown eyes. You're him, all right."

"Who is this Flame? And what am I accused of doing, Captain?" Blane observed the men as three of the soldiers laughed and exchanged knowing looks. Only the redhead remained stiff and silent.

The private hinted mirthfully, "Why don't you tell him, sir? Maybe these Yanks are too dumb to know about our beautiful heroine."

"Only a fool doesn't know about Flame," the sandy-haired man scoffed, placing his rifle butt on the ground beside his right boot and holding the barrel steady with his fingers.

"Are you one of those fools, Major Stevens?" the private asked, then giggled like a young girl who was spying on her sister's first date.

"I must be, Private, 'cause I've never met her," Blane replied.

"Then how do you know Flame is a female, Major Blane Stevens from Texas?" the redhead scoffed, his rifle barrel still aimed at the Texan's middle. The man's blue eyes were as cold as frozen ocean water.

Blane shook his head in silent chiding. "Men don't usually refer to a male agent as a beautiful heroine," he retorted insultingly, paying closer attention to that

416

particular man. "Who is this woman, and why has she got it in for me? You do have legal charges against me?"

Amused chuckles escaped the captain's throat. "Oh, we got us plenty of charges, Yank. You traveled with Flame, so you should know her. Before she left town, she gave General Holmes a long list of your deeds, long enough to get you hanged at first light. Flame said she couldn't hang around"—he halted to laugh at his choice of words—"to watch you pay for your crimes. Said she found someone else to work on. If I was a Yank, I sure wouldn't mind her working on me," he murmured, grinning lewdly and smacking his thick lips. "She also gave him a list of your Union sympathizers. He's gonna take care of them as soon as he deals with you. Tell us, Major, is she as beautiful and clever as they say?"

Blane smiled wolfishly and seemingly admitted defeat as he answered, "More so, Captain. She could charm the rattlers off a sidewinder and never get bit. Hair as red as a fiery sunset and eyes as blue as a tranquil ocean. She has skin as soft and white as a winter ermine, and a body to drive a man wild with hunger. Beautiful isn't the right word to describe Flame. She's—"

While the Confederate soldiers remained enthralled by his confession, Blane struck swiftly and lethally. He flung himself to the ground and seized both carefully discarded weapons. Quicker than the eye or mind could follow his fluid movements, he lifted his pistol with his left hand and fired at the redhead, wisely and accurately dispatching the only real threat first. He agilely flipped to his back and shot the sandy-haired man before the shock-slowed soldier could recover his rifle and defend himself. Almost simultaneously, Blane's right hand skillfully threw the knife into the captain's chest as the stunned officer was trying to yank his revolver from its holster.

Blane nimbly shifted his body to the opposite side to fire into the heart of the white-faced private, who was lunging rashly for him. It wasn't necessary. Dan kicked out with his hind legs and sent the private staggering a few feet to slam his head into a wooden post, killing him.

Blane rapidly scanned the four men for life and found none. He grimaced as he reloaded his pistol and replaced his weapons. He hurriedly mounted Dan, knowing the gunshots would call attention to the stable. He glanced down at the captain and finished his last statement. "She's Destiny's Temptress, Captain." That described the traitorous Siren perfectly. She not only taunted and tempted her own fate, but that of others. "But she's tempted me and mine for the last time," he vowed coldly. He bent low over his horse, then kneed Dan into a fast gallop through the open stable doors, just in case other soldiers were waiting in ambush outside.

When no one fired at them or pursued them, Blane patted Dan's neck and murmured, "Thanks, old boy. You saved me again. Seems like you're the only one I can depend on. We've seen worse dangers than that one. Lord, I've killed more men at one battle than in there. Stupid bastards! They deserved to be defeated—except for that redhead. Damn shame he got this duty tonight with those fools."

He laughed satanically and narrowed his eyes. "Shannon forgot to warn them they'd be dealing with the Blade, a man who can put a whole band of Comanche warriors to shame. That little vixen hasn't got me fooled. I know exactly where she's heading. Carter better hope he's had enough of that witch by the time I reach her, because there won't be anything left to catch a man's eye. She's in for something worse than death, boy. I can slice her up until no man will ever want to look at her again, and I won't even have to kill her. Yessiree, Dan, I'll take something from Flame that means more to her than her miserable life. I'll scar that beautiful face and body so badly she'll repel anyone who looks at her. Every day of her sorry life she'll suffer for what she's done to me and others. And every time she looks into a mirror, she'll remember and regret betraying me."

Chapter Seventeen

Late in the afternoon of November 30, the *Majestic Maiden* sailed past Forts Sumter and Moultrie to dock at Charleston Harbor. Shannon was astonished by the number of ships stranded in the port and by the amount of cotton and goods that seemed to be rotting on the wharves, for only the most daring captains would challenge the Union blockade. Countless men milled around as if waiting for something to happen. What, she could not guess.

Shannon and Mattilu thanked Captain Sellers for his kindness and generosity. Fortunately, there had been no trouble and they had slipped between Union ships as if invisible. The captain seemed reluctant for the women to depart, as he proclaimed them his good luck charms.

Elisha escorted them and their belongings to a large hotel where Shannon was shown to a lovely suite with a private bath. Mattilu was given a regular room adjoining Shannon's spacious quarters. Shannon had protested the expensive lodgings until Elisha pretended to agree to consider the payment of her bills a loan. He told them to get settled while he went to visit with his brother, Denton. He warned them not to venture from the hotel grounds because the city was filled with soldiers and sailors who would be seeking mischief within the hour.

When the two women were alone and sipping tea, they laughed and talked about their adventures and good fortune. "I can't believe we made it, and so easily, Matti. No one would think to search for us here. All we have to do is wait for Blane's arrival."

"I'm proud of you, Miss Shannon. You are the smartest and slyest woman I know," Mattilu complimented cheerfully.

Shannon stated ruefully, "I really hate taking advantage of Eli. He's been so kind and helpful. I'll find a way to get the money back to him. I feel so wicked for using him like this."

"Don't you worry none. Men been using women for hundreds of years. Captain Carter wants to help you and protect you. It ain't your fault if you don't love him like he does you."

"But how will I explain Major Stevens to him?" she worried aloud.

"I would be thinking more on how to explain the captain to the major," the woman teased, her brown eyes sparkling.

"I'm sure Blane won't mind my taking the only path available to me. Besides, I had you as my chaperon."

Now that they were safe, Shannon's thoughts turned to the future. She knew she would want to spend time alone with Blane when he returned and on the way to Savannah, and she realized she would have to help Mattilu find a job quickly. "We don't know how much time we have before Blane arrives and we leave, so we'd best look for a new job for you tomorrow. I'll send for you the minute I have things settled at home."

At the dinner hour, Elisha returned briefly. He had had trays prepared and delivered for Shannon and Mattilu, as if they could not see to this simple task themselves. He informed Shannon that he had lengthy business dealings to discuss with his brother and needed to spend the evening with him. He gave Shannon the man's address, in case there was trouble. He handed Shannon a book from Denton to occupy her time and mind. Then he bid them farewell until morning.

By eight, Shannon was curled on the sofa before a cheery fire, completely engrossed in the book in her hands. Shannon read until her eyes refused to work a moment longer. She wondered if there was any significance to Elisha's choice of *Wuthering Heights* by a British novelist, as it was the tale of a woman trapped between two men. The story was so romantic and poignant, yet tragic. How sad to love so fiercely and potently and be unable to have your heart's desire . . .

The next morning, Elisha solved Mattilu's problem of finding work when he arrived to offer Mattilu a job as Denton's hired servant. After describing Denton's needs and injuries, Elisha offered her an excellent salary and promised good working conditions. He told her the position would be available on Tuesday. "He's invited us to have Sunday dinner with him. Mattilu can look around and make her decision tomorrow. Denton's looking forward to meeting you, angel. Just remember, he's a charming rake."

"Like his brother," she merrily retorted. "Older or younger?"

"Less than a year younger. Would you like to tour the city?" he inquired eagerly. "She's one of the most beautiful anywhere."

"I hate to leave Matti alone in a strange place. Why don't we just eat, then take a stroll outside?" she suggested reluctantly.

"Why don't we take Matti along with us? If she's going

422

to be living and working here, she could use a tour."

Shannon beamed with pleasure. "You are a wonder, Eli. Whatever would I do without you?" she declared impulsively.

"That's what I'm trying to teach you," he replied with a smile.

For hours they walked and looked, stopping here and there for rest or refreshments. The city reminded her so much of Savannah and New Orleans. The elegance, beauty, and flavor of the Old South was represented all around her. She could see and feel its captivating enchantment everywhere. She saw it in the architecture of the homes and buildings, in the live oaks with their dripping moss, in the swaying palms with their prickly bark, in the people with their grace and charm, and in the air itself. She immediately decided to add it to her list of favorites.

The air grew colder as dusk approached. Elisha had wanted to take her to a special eating establishment, but he couldn't with Matti along. It had cost him a pretty penny to get the brown-skinned woman—his "fiancée's serving woman"—the adjoining room in the hotel.

Upon their return, Matti ate in her room while Elisha and Shannon dined in the large and luxurious room downstairs. She was amazed by the air of wealth and relaxation that pervaded the room. People were eating, laughing, and conversing as if peace and joy ruled the land. Shannon was glad she was wearing the sapphire gown that Elizabeth Van Lew had given her, which had been repaired and cleaned by Mattilu during her stay in Wilmington.

Elisha couldn't seem to take his eyes from Shannon tonight. She was radiant and ravishing. Her hair had been brushed until it shone with vibrant life, then arranged in curls and ringlets that added extra elegance and appeal to her looks. Her eyes seemed a darker blue and sparkled with vitality. Elisha found himself wanting to whisk her away, to caress that silky flesh, to finger that flaming hair, to gaze into those expressive eyes, and to make love to her.

They sipped claret and listened to the music provided by a harpist and pianist. They talked about their families and homes. They discussed their travels and interests. They chatted about books and plays. They revealed their favorite places and activities.

Shannon was astonished to realize that she hadn't known or asked where he lived. It was Norfolk, a seaport conquered by the Union in 1862. He revealed how his father had managed to retain possession of their shipping firm by pretending to side with the Union and to perform duties for it. Fortunately, all of their ships had been at sea during the conquest and had avoided capture. He and his brother had become blockade runners to aid the South. Shannon could tell he felt deep respect and love for his family, their home, and their business. He joked lightly about his father's cunning pretense, saying they would fare well even if the Union won. He related his desire for her to meet his parents and brother. After that, they carefully avoided further talk of the war, and any decision of their relationship.

Sunday was a lovely, but chilly day. Elisha brought a carriage to transport Shannon and Mattilu to his brother's dwelling. It was a large apartment positioned over a carriage house and a small stable, and it had a private courtyard. Elisha explained that he worked out of Wilmington while Denton worked out of Charleston. The servant who greeted them was an elderly man who would soon be leaving to live with his son in Georgetown. His departure couldn't have been timed more perfectly for Shannon's and Mattilu's needs.

Within minutes, Shannon was aware of the vast similarities between the two brothers in looks and personality. She found the meal and the conversation delightful and realized that she hadn't had such fun in a long time. She teased Denton about the book he had sent over to her and learned it had been a gift to him from a female admirer.

"Do you think she was trying to tell me something?" he jested.

"I shall let you know when I finish reading it, if Eli permits me reading time. He's kept me busy since our arrival."

"I can see why. If I didn't have this busted arm and leg, I would be challenging him for your attention and company." Everyone laughed before Denton went on to relate the details of his accident.

While they chatted and dined, the male servant gave Mattilu a tour of the apartment and outlined her duties. Charmed by the man and the setting, the woman instantly accepted the position. She would move in on Tuesday and assume her new role.

Denton inquired, "How long will you be staying here, Shannon?"

She glanced at Elisha and smiled before replying, "Someone is meeting me here in a few days to escort me home to Greenleaf. When Eli comes to visit my brother and solicit his business, perhaps you can accompany him. I'm sure Corry would be thrilled to hear about your adventures and to work with you. As I told Eli, he has a sailor's soul."

"Excellent. Then our families should get along perfectly."

Elisha devilishly added, "That's what I've been trying to show her and tell her. Just remember, little brother, I saw her first."

The remainder of their visit passed swiftly and

cheerfully. As they were leaving, Denton offered, "If you're in need of a carriage or horse, Shannon, please feel free to use mine. I keep a sharp eye on them, as the Confederacy tries to confiscate all horses for duty."

"You are as kind and generous as your brother. Thank you, Denton. It has been wonderful meeting you and sharing today."

"You're welcome any time, Shannon, with or without that dashing brother of mine. While he's gone, let me know if you have need of anything at all," he offered sincerely.

"Gone?" Shannon repeated, looking inquisitively at Elisha.

Elisha smiled sheepishly. "I was going to tell you later. I didn't want you to worry. I have to sail at midnight tomorrow." He would not reveal that his voyage would take him to Savannah to deliver supplies and men to battle Sherman's imminent attack on her city. He knew this trip would be perilous, for that port was currently being watched and guarded more closely than the others. He had no doubt about his skills or success, but he didn't want to alarm her. He also wanted to observe the conditions in that town, before she began her journey there. If things were as bad as was rumored, he would hold her captive here before allowing her to go home. "I won't be away more than three or four days. You won't be leaving that soon. If any needs or problems come up, Denton will take care of them."

Wanting to retain his trust in case of trouble, Shannon asked no questions about his destination our purpose. "You will be careful?" she entreated with sincere concern and affection.

"I will be more than careful, angel," he promised warmly, not caring who was watching them. "If you recall, I have a wife to pursue."

To lighten the conversation, Denton wailed comically,

426

"I guess that's his way of telling me to keep my hands and eyes off you, Shannon. Don't worry, big brother, I'll take this treasure into the family any way we can get her. I know Mother and Father will be just as pleased with your choice." The two men exchanged smiles and laughter.

"She hasn't agreed to anything yet, Dent. Maybe you can work on her while I'm gone. Convince her I'm perfect for her. At least persuade her to let me chase her and woo her."

"If you two are this conniving and persistent in business, you must be very successful," she remarked with a laugh.

At Shannon's door, Elisha caressed her cheek and smiled into her upturned face. She beseeched him, "Please be careful on this trip."

"You have my promise, love. Before I sail tomorrow night, I have a special evening planned for us. From six until midnight, I'll make you forget everything but me," he boasted with a sly grin. After kissing her feverishly, he returned to his brother's home.

Before following the handsome seaman, Blane Stevens glared at Shannon through the narrow crack in his door. He watched her sigh heavily, then enter her suite. Riding nearly day and night, he had reached town the morning after they had docked. It had been simple to locate her, and to follow them. She could wait for her punishment until after her lover sailed. Right now, he needed to uncover and report the captain's plans . . .

Elisha and his brother spent most of the following day discussing their business and Elisha's impending voyage. That night, Shannon and Elisha ate an early dinner before he took her to the Dock Theater to see John E.

427

McDonogh's production of *The Seven Sisters*. At eleven, Elisha kissed her farewell at the door, unaware of the perils that would soon confront each of them.

It was nearing dawn when Shannon was awakened by strong hands gagging her mouth. She began to claw and slap at the dark form above her. The man seized her right hand and pinned it beneath his knee. Her assailant secured a rope around her left wrist, then tied the other end to the bedpost. Shannon squirmed and yanked on her right hand to free it. She needed to defend herself or pull off the gag to yell for help. He followed the same action with her other wrist, binding her outstretched arms to the bedposts. She twisted and kicked at the shadowy figure that hovered over her as he worked to render her defenseless. He grabbed one flailing leg and tied a rope around her ankle, then secured it to a footpost. He repeated his movements with the other ankle. Once she was bound and spread-eagled to the posts, he sat back on his haunches and exhaled loudly from his exertions.

He slid off the bed and lit the oil lamp. He watched shock and confusion register in her eyes as the light revealed his identity. She looked at his expression, then glanced at her bonds. She was smart, for he could tell she knew this was not a joke or trick. She watched him intently, waiting for him to expose his reasons. He sat in a chair and observed her, content to let her worry and wonder for awhile.

Shannon was utterly bewildered and alarmed by his inexplicable behavior. Had he gone mad? No. There was something about his aura, something about his expression, something about his posture that frightened her. He was serious with this conduct. A coldness and scorn seemed to emanate from him. Danger permeated her senses. She tried to reason out his actions. He had been rough with her. She could already feel sore spots that had been made by his strong hands and brutal treatment.

Shannon wiggled and grunted, but he didn't respond. He just kept staring at her with those icy hazel eyes. Blane had certainly acted strange before leaving her room that last morning in Wilmington, she reflected. Something in the note from Jeremy Steele had inspired a curious reaction. She had suspected him of lying during his brief explanation, and she had discovered his secret identity. Why had he lured her here to attack her? Had she unknowingly committed some terrible offense? Why didn't he talk to her? Why wouldn't he allow her to speak? What was he waiting for, grinning like a sadistic demon anticipating some evil ritual?

Twenty minutes passed. Again, Shannon yanked on her bonds and thrashed on the bed. She drilled her gaze into his, attempting to spur him into action. Nothing. Anger filled her. How dare he treat her this way! What about their relationship? Was this some test? Some punishment? Some lesson? For what? Why?

Shannon began to twist her hands to loosen the ropes. She worked until her wrists were raw and blood was running down her arms. Still Blane did nothing but stare at her. As tears of pain and anguish began to run into her tangled hair, she closed her eyes and prayed for enlightenment. Her fears and anger mounted. She began to struggle wildly, accepting the pain of her actions. Through the gag, she tried to make as much noise as possible. She finally obtained a reaction.

Blane walked to the bed and stood near her waist. While staring oddly at her, he withdrew his knife. Instead of severing her bonds as she expected, he cut the nightgown from her body. He held up the ruined garment as if it were a war prize, grinned victoriously, then nonchalantly dropped it to the floor. As he replaced his knife in its sheath, his sardonic gaze roamed her supple, helpless body from head to foot. As if he could not resist the impulse to touch her and to provoke her, he slowly passed his warm fingertips over her chilled skin.

To Shannon, his hands felt like punishing weapons whose fiery and lethal surface enticed searing chill bumps over her quivering flesh. His hand was exceptionally gentle as it caressed her face, as if gingerly exploring fragile features. Blane's fingers drifted down her throat, traveled her collarbone from end to end, and moved deftly up each outstretched arm and back again. He used those tightly controlled weapons to circle each breast. As he playfully teased the peaks with smoothly trimmed nails, he chuckled before bending forward to encircle and tease them with his burning tongue. Again he laughed softly and satanically as the peaks responded to him.

Blane returned his attention to his taunting journey over her body, relishing his power to arouse her. Using the back of his fingers, he guided them over her stomach, across each rib, around her navel, and downward to venture over the fuzzy red covering between her thighs. He glanced at Shannon's face when her body stiffened. It was a bright red, and she was crying with her eyes closed. Her reaction halted him.

Blane didn't continue his exploration. He sat beside her and scolded, "You shouldn't have forced me to punish you, Blue Eyes. As much as you need killing, I can't be the one to do it. Lord help you, Shannon, because somebody will do it before this war's over. I wish you had been for real." That night in Washington, he hadn't been able to frighten a confession from her. Tonight would be different. He knew exactly how to terrify information from her. First, he would have to convince her that he was cold-blooded and cruel, that he was serious about his impending actions.

Shannon's eyes opened. She stared at him. What was

430

he saying? He wanted to kill her? Like Elisha, he sounded as if she had hurt him!

"There's only one way to keep you from using your beauty and charms on other unsuspecting men. This will hurt, but it won't kill you," he hinted, holding up the sharp knife. "I learned many skills and tortures from the Indians. When I finish tonight, all you'll want to do is hide from everyone for the rest of your life. Even though your hair will grow back, the scars I put on your face and body won't ever go away. Not even the best doctors will be able to help you. It's the only way I can stop you from hurting and killing more innocent people."

Shannon's eyes widened in a mixture of terror and shock. He couldn't! He wouldn't! Could he? She shook her head and tried to speak. She jerked on her hands and ankles, causing more rope burns and bleeding. It was useless. Tears were blinding her eyes. She blinked over and over to clear them, to see him and to read his intentions.

His hand wandered into her hair and he relished its silkiness and vitality for the last time. "How can you be so cold and cruel? I know you disliked Cathy, but did you have to order her torture and death? And the Thomases? Lord, Shannon, they were old and weak. We spent our first night together in their home. I can understand why you had Thornton and Clifford slain, but the others? Why not have them arrested? And Pike. I can't imagine why you had Pike eliminated, unless he had guessed your evil and it didn't matter to him that you were on his side. You really had me fooled, Blue Eyes. I have to admit, you are matchless in getting your job done. Everywhere we went, you betrayed my friends and helpers. You've single-handedly done more in three months than half the Rebel spies have accomplished in three years. You've managed to destroy the Union spy line and you've unmasked the Blade. That alone should win you a medal

431

and a fat reward. All along you were using me and aiding the Rebels," he accused bitterly. He placed a hand on either side of her body and leaned forward to glare into her wide and tormented gaze.

He sneered coldly, "You think I don't know about those messages you left for Moore in your belongings! You think I don't know they let us escape from his camp! You think I didn't notice you found a way to speak privately with an officer everywhere we stopped! Just like I noticed how you kept trying to get away from me—until you realized who I was. Then you were willing to do anything to defeat me."

"You didn't really expect that trap you set for me in Wilmington to work, did you? I had to kill four men to get away. They were real impressed by the Flame and her work. They were real grateful for that letter you left behind that told all about me and my helpers. I'm afraid I had to deny them my capture and execution. I know agents do some terrible things in the line of duty, but to seduce me and then have me killed beats them all. I wonder if you're blindly patriotic to the Confederacy and you don't care what you have to do, or if I mean absolutely nothing to you. Damn you for being so cold-blooded and heartless, you traitorous and tempting witch!"

Shannon couldn't believe what she was hearing, nor what this man whom she loved had planned for her. Yes, the Blade would do anything necessary to perform his duties, even savagely brutalize her for crimes he should know she could never commit. Her tears blurred his face and body. She couldn't look at him with such hatred and contempt in his eyes. She turned her cheek to the pillow. How could he judge her guilty of such evil? How could he not allow her to defend herself? How could he bring himself to mutilate the same body he had made love to so many times? How could he ignore and destroy what they had shared and what they could share? Someone was digging a grave for her, and she could not imagine who or why. It had to be someone close, to know such details. Was it Blane? Was it time for the Blade to cover his tracks, all of them, in any way necessary?

Blane observed Shannon for a time. There was something in her eyes and behavior that baffled him. He watched the tears flow and her body tremble curiously. Of course she was frightened. But it wasn't the kind of fear and panic that would be natural under these conditions. He had outwitted or battled many opponents, Indian and white, male and female. She was not reacting like a guilty foe caught in a trap. She had looked genuinely shocked and distressed by his charges. She had looked puzzled and challenged. She had looked emotionally—not physically—defeated and injured. He couldn't be wrong . . .

Why not, his mind quickly debated. If he was right now, he had been mistaken for months! How could she have done such things? She looked so delicate, so gentle, so innocent, so fragile, so hurt.

He tried an approach to the truth, before he made a grave error. "At least I should be grateful you waited until my assignment before giving it your all. You were a virgin that night, weren't you?"

Shannon grimaced and stiffened, but she didn't look at him or open her eyes. She made no attempt to communicate with him verbally. He wondered what she would do if he removed the gag. He cleverly scoffed, "I wonder what Carter had to say about getting used goods. Molly and Sarah Jane told me about him sleeping in your room while I was gone. Did I get you so worked up that you needed two men to sate you? Or did you decide your *helpless* surrender would disarm and enchant him like it did me?" He watched Shannon's head jerk around and her eyes fly open. She sent him a pained and falsely accused look again. Damn her and those bewitching eyes! he raged inwardly.

"After I discovered what you really are, I could see why Carter didn't blame you for that attack on his ship. Too bad he survived to be used again. I hope you two had a pleasant voyage; it'll be the last time he sates his passion with you, unless it's in the dark. He won't be able to even glance at you, Blue Eyes, no matter how beautiful his memories of you. How much does the Confederacy pay for rendering such sacrificial service? Whoring and spying should earn double pay."

His last remarks elicited a different emotion: fury. She squinted her eyes as she glowered at him. So much turbulence filled them. He witnessed a change in her expression and mood. The anguish, shock, and confusion were giving way to hostility, and rage, and rebellion, and contempt . . . and hatred. "The truth bother you, Blue Eyes?"

Those emotions increased in intensity. She clenched her teeth and glared at him as she twisted her balled fists and pulled determinedly on her bonds. Bright red blood saturated the ropes and rolled down her arms. Still she denied the pain and continued to struggle for freedom. Tears filled her eyes, but she seemingly refused to allow them to leave their confining banks.

Blane glanced at her wrists and ankles. He knew how much she was hurting herself, all without a whimper or grimace. Accusation was exposed in her gaze, that and a mirror of betrayal. Could he slice and mar this beautiful creature? What if Jeremy had been wrong? Without giving it another thought, he severed the bond on her right arm as he murmured, "Let someone else get rid of you for the Union."

Shannon removed her gag. She reached for the knife, too distracted by her turmoil to be surprised by his release of it. She sliced through the bloody rope on her other wrist, then sat up to free her legs. She removed the ropes from her limbs and flung them to the floor. She glared at him. "Get out of my sight, you bastard, before I do forget how much you meant to me and I slit your miserable throat."

Shannon tossed the knife at his feet. "I can't wait for them to catch the real Flame. I hope you choke when you discover your vicious words are wicked lies. Is this why you sent me that false letter? To lure me here so you could play your malicious and sadistic games?" Shannon rolled off the bed and retrieved the money from a drawer. She turned to find Blane's gun in his hands, as if he had expected her to withdraw a weapon. She laughed derisively. Then she threw the money at him and declared with a sneer, "Take your filthy money. I couldn't get a train like you suggested. If you're such a damn good agent, Blade, why didn't you know about train schedules and restrictions? Leave Wilmington and come to Charleston as quickly and secretly as possible, Shannon. Simon and the soldiers are about to swoop down on you," she repeated sarcastically. "I don't know what this little game was all about, and I don't care. Just get out of my life and stay out. You don't have to do things like this to frighten me into silence. I would never betray you, not even after what you did tonight. But come near me again, and I won't be able to keep that promise. You said you would end it . . ."

As tears filled her eyes again, she bit her lip to control them. "A less terrifying rejection would have worked just as well. All you had to do was say, 'It's over, Shannon,' and leave. Even for the notorious Blade, it wasn't necessary to drive me away so skillfully and cruelly."

She inquired sadly, "Why didn't you leave me in Wilmington? Why lure me here? Afraid to display such

brutality and cruelty before Molly and your friends? I
wish your letter had arrived a day later. Then Eli would
have been gone and he couldn't have brought me here to
endure such despicable treachery. As for your insult,
Major Stevens, you can take it and go to Hell. I've never
slept with any man except you, and I'll probably regret
that for the rest of my life. All I did was bandage Eli when
he appeared in the middle of the night, injured and
determined to kill me for betraying him. He thought I was
the only one who knew about his trip. Somehow you
found out and exposed him. I had to tell him almost
everything about me to save my life. But I never exposed
you, not even to convince him not to strangle me."

She snatched up a blanket and covered herself. Being
naked before him like this made her feel so vulnerable,
and misused. "I can't help it if he's in love with me. I've
told him over and over I don't love him and I won't marry
him. But I do like him. He's been kind and gentle and
generous. I only wanted you, and you're not even real.
How gullible and stupid can a woman be? I trusted you. I
would have given my life for you. I even convinced Matti
to sail with me so I wouldn't be alone with Eli. When I got
your letter, all I could think about was getting to you and
being with you."

Shannon angrily brushed away the tears that raced
down her cheeks. "You didn't have to do this, Blane. I
would have let you go without any trouble. I wouldn't
have tried to hold on to someone who didn't . . . want me
or need me. If someone set you up in Wilmington, then
you'd better be careful, because it wasn't me. Do you
honestly believe I did those horrible things? Or is this
your clever way of spurning me? I never knew you at all,
did I? I was just a cover, a pleasing disguise. Why did you
have to bring me along? Why did you have to say all those
lies while we were trapped under that porch? Was any of

436

it real, Blane? Any of the words? Any of the lovemaking? Any of the feelings?"

Blane was looking at her oddly, worriedly. "What's this about a letter from me telling you to come here?" he asked reluctantly.

Shannon ignored him. She went to the basin, poured fresh water into it, and submerged her bleeding wrists. She winced as the raw flesh protested her action. After gently cleaning the wounds, she patted them dry, and tore strips from a sheet to bandage them. When Blane tried to assist her, she pulled away from him and warned, "Don't you ever touch me again, you vile beast. I don't need your help, and I don't need you." She wanted to scream, I hate you. She didn't because it was a lie and she was afraid he might guess the truth.

He seized her shoulders and whirled her around to face him. "I asked you about that letter. Now answer me, woman," he demanded.

"I suppose you're going to say you didn't send me a letter?"

"No, Shannon, I didn't. You promised to wait for me at the hotel. I returned a day late to find you gone. And with that lovestruck seaman! Then I was told you had been sleeping with him and was planning to marry him. I try to get out of town, and there are soldiers all over me and thanking Flame for exposing me. What am I supposed to think? You could have left me a message with Sarah Jane."

"Are you insane? Why should I leave you a message when you sent for me? And don't keep denying you sent it! Who else would know to sign it 'Major Steven Bs James'? Who else knows about Simon? Who else knew we were to head for Charleston next? Who else could list our previous travel route? Only you, Blane Stevens— you liar and user!"

"Where is this letter I supposedly sent you?"

"I burned it as you asked. If I hadn't, I would cram it down your throat." Shannon scornfully recited the letter almost verbatim, then finished with, "I see just how eager you were to see me! You are the lowest creature I know."

"Is that why you turned me in to General Holmes?" he accused, then charged her with being responsible for the episode in the stable, which he angrily revealed.

"That's a bloody lie! I wasn't expecting you back in Wilmington. You wrote me to come here. I was terrified when I couldn't find a way to meet you. And this is what I get?" She held up her injured arms.

"Lord, woman, you're telling the truth, aren't you! What in perdition is going on?" he stated irritably.

"I don't know, and I don't care anymore. Even if this is some crazy misunderstanding, it's over between us. You wanted to kill me. You were going to disfigure me. You shamed me, and hurt me. You accused me of many murders, or of being responsible for them. I am innocent, you bastard. I never did any of those things—to them or to you."

"Carter did those same things, and you forgave him."

"Eli doesn't know me. Eli hasn't spent countless days and nights with me. Eli has never made love to me. Eli has never heard my hopes and dreams. Eli has never touched my heart and soul. Eli has never deceived me or used me. Eli was no more to me than a friend, a good friend who almost got killed because of me and you."

"Shannon, listen to me; we've got to figure out this mess. If there is another Flame or someone who knows this much about us, we're both in danger. We have to decide what to do."

"If there is another Flame?" she sneered coldly. "There is only one Flame, Major Stevens, and it isn't me and never was me. When Eli returns, I'll persuade him to take me to Savannah. From now on, you're out of my life, and I'm out of yours. Forever, Blane."

Blane looked at her and shook his head. "No, Shannon, it won't be forever. I won't let you go—not now or ever. I have some investigating to do; then I'll return." He whirled and left the suite.

Chapter Eighteen

Blane stalked aggressively to Mattilu's room and persistently knocked on the door. There was no answer. He deliberated his next move. He decided to seek the woman, as he wanted this distressing matter clarified hastily. He confronted her as he was rounding a corner to the stairs. He saw her face brighten and warm.

"Major . . . James," she shrieked excitedly, alertly preventing a careless slip. "Miss Shannon will sure be glad to see you. She's been worried half sick about you. Don't tell her I told you how scared she was. I was just ordering her morning meal. I'm to go after it at nine. Miss Shannon wanted to sleep late this—" Mattilu halted her rush of words as she noticed how troubled he appeared. Comprehending his departing direction and distraught mood, she became confused.

"I need to discuss something with you, Matti. Now," he stressed.

"Let's go to my room," she suggested, leading the way. Inside, she inquired worriedly, "Have you seen Miss Shannon? What's wrong, sir?" she probed gravely as she watched the broody man pace anxiously.

He ceased his rambling and looked directly into the woman's bemused expression. "I don't know where to start or what to ask first, Matti. I'm confused, and I'm hurt, and I'm furious. Maybe it will help to clear my head if you explain what you and Shannon are doing here and how you got to Charleston. She was told not to leave Wilmington without me. Why did you two run off like thieves in the night?"

Mattilu's brown eyes filled with puzzlement and her forehead wrinkled. "I don't follow your meaning, sir. Your letter told her to get here as fast as she could. The only way was with Captain Carter," she replied, wondering if their manner of travel was provoking him. "Don't blame her, sir. Your letter said she was in big danger, and Captain Carter was the only path to escape. Did you fuss with her?"

"What letter, Matti?" he questioned sullenly. Had Shannon duped Mattilu, or slyly elicited her aid, or told her the truth?

"Why, the one you sent to her at the hotel," she responded.

"I didn't send any notes, letters, or messages to Shannon. Before I left town, I ordered her to wait for my return. I told her it wouldn't be more than a few days. There wasn't any letter from me."

Mattilu frowned in irritation and appeared skeptical of his words and motive. "I saw the letter, Major. I took it from the man you sent and delivered it to her. I was with her when she read it and figured out your clues in it. I helped her pack and get away."

"Listen to me carefully, Matti. I did not send any letter to her. If one came, it was from someone else. If Shannon told you it was from me and that I said to leave, it was a lie," he charged, hoping she would debate him and supply him with the information he needed to this enigma.

441

Mattilu stared at the handsome devil before her. "Major Stevens, why do you want to trick and hurt that chile? If this has somethin' to do with your work, it still ain't right to be so bad to her." Mattilu scolded him with revelations of Shannon's fears and worries, of her desperate attempt to escape Wilmington to meet him, of the messages in the mysterious letter.

"Maybe she's a Rebel spy and somebody warned her to get away before my return. I've been learning some mighty suspicious things about her. Maybe she just wanted to trick Captain Carter into taking her along with him. Maybe she doesn't want him to know she's chasing him as fast and hard as he's chasing her." He tensely awaited her reaction to his shocking accusations.

Mattilu displayed not only anger but disappointment. "How can you say such hateful things about her? She ain't no Rebel spy. She ain't no side's spy. I been watching her closer'n a flea on a dog. She ain't done nothing wrong." The vexed woman related what she knew about Shannon's relationship with Elisha. She explained how she and Shannon had used a trick letter to win the captain's assistance. She exposed everything that had happened during and following their sea voyage, proving that nothing intimate could have taken place between Shannon and Elisha. "Miss Shannon don't want nobody but you, Major. She ain't told you no lies or been bad. I can't believe you can say or think such things. If you repeats them to Miss Shannon, you'll have done lost her afore you finishes talking," she warned.

"Somebody is playing evil games, Matti. You and I can't afford to be tricked. The war is serious. Our jobs are dangerous. All you know is what Shannon told you was in that letter, which she burned."

"I knows what was in it 'cause I read it!" When he gaped at her, she declared, "That's right, Major; I can

442

read and write. I saw the letter and read it afore she told me what was in it. She didn't lie or trick either one of us. It was signed with both of your names. And it spoke of private things only you and Miss Shannon knows about."

Blane was distraught. "Let's go over everything once more, Matti, real slow and careful, and in detail. Something crazy is happening, because that letter wasn't from me. You and me had better figure out who's tricking all of us, and why."

Shannon slipped into the courtyard of Captain Denton Carter's home. After saddling one of his horses, she tied her belongings to it, as much as she could carry. To the saddlehorn, she secured the bundle of food that she had obtained from the hotel kitchen. Sighting a canteen, she placed its strap over the horn and allowed it to hang suspended on the other side. She disliked stealing Denton's military items, but she needed the bedroll and blanket she had found in the stable. She also felt a twinge of guilt over having to steal the match safe, utensils, candles, and other needed items from the hotel. She had listed them and left a note instructing the hotel to place them on her bill, to be settled by Captain Elisha or Denton Carter, said bill and kindness to be repaid later.

Shannon secured two envelopes to Denton's message board beside the steps to his lovely carriage house. The letter to Denton was an apology for the theft of his horse and gear and a promise to reimburse him. She asked him to take care of Mattilu until she could send for her, and to explain to her friend that she had found it crucial to leave town hastily and secretly. She told him to advise Mattilu not to worry about her, that she would explain matters later to everyone. The letter to Elisha was a carefully worded one of gratitude for his aid, friendship, and

443

protection. Again, she promised to repay Elisha for the expenses he had incurred on her behalf.

Knowing Denton's male servant would be leaving soon to fetch Mattilu from the hotel, Shannon hurriedly carried out her daring plan. Dressed in boots, shirt, and pants, Shannon mounted the horse and tucked her wool cape around her legs. She walked the animal from the stable beneath the apartment and held her breath as she prayed no one would hear or see her and attempt to stop her flight homeward. She had her gun, her knife, her passes, her skills, and her resolve.

At the entrance gate, she leaned over and fastened the latch. She walked the horse for two blocks, ignoring the stares and whispers of curious people along her way. Then she kneed the gentle beast into a slow gait until she reached the edge of town. There, she nudged him into a steady gallop toward Savannah, leaving the cobblestoned streets and her treacherous love behind.

Three hours later, Blane and Mattilu were actively searching for clues to Shannon's disappearance. At first, neither realized she had gone. The clever redhead had left garments and personal items lying on the bed and side table and peaking from a partially opened drawer to make it appear she was merely out for a stroll or on an errand. The two had sat in her room for over an hour, awaiting her return. The alarming discovery of missing possessions came to light when the apprehensive Mattilu began to gather, fold, and put away the misleading items.

"Major Stevens!" she shrieked from the bedroom. "She's gone!"

Blane rushed into the room and questioned Mattilu's words and findings. After checking the drawers and closet, the woman announced in dread, "She's took some of her things and left. She's out there alone, and hurting. Look what you've done to her, sir."

The two spoke with the desk clerk and fretted over his revelations. She had left hours ago, promising Captain Carter would pay her bills. The stuffy male had no idea where she had gone or why.

Blane and Mattilu searched the grounds and nearby area. They questioned people. Some had seen the beautiful redhead, but no one could give her location or destination. They went to Denton's, and there they learned she had taken the horse and supplies and had left two letters. Blane finally persuaded Denton to allow him to read both, convincing him she might be in peril. It was clear to everyone where she was heading. It didn't sit well with Blane when Denton suggested she might be going to join his brother.

Blane couldn't expose his knowledge of Elisha's past actions. He knew Denton was perturbed by his refusal to relate his reasons for pursuing Shannon or to reveal why he believed she had fled. However, Blane didn't mind telling the man he was going after her. Mattilu begged to go along, but Blane convinced her that it was unwise and would slow his progress. He promised to contact both of them with news of Shannon's location and condition.

The nerve-wracked Texan packed his saddlebags, checked out of the hotel, and once more raced off in pursuit of the impulsive female. He encountered heavy troop and weapon movements along the Carolina roads. He asked questions several times, stating he was looking for his commanding officer's daughter who had left home after a quarrel with her father. He jokingly told the men he had been ordered to bring her home any way necessary, even by tying her to his saddle. When one of the lieutenants declared that this personal matter was a waste of time and energy for a soldier, Blane

445

audaciously told him that the foolish girl was running off to meet one of Sherman's men to marry him. Blane said they couldn't allow such an outrage, or such a dangerous possibility. After all, the enemy could make use of the information inside that vain and silly female's head. Not only did that explanation get Blane out of a threatening situation, but it got him a pass and information about Shannon, as well.

Blane traveled all day, gradually and cunningly tracking her. He knew Shannon had also been slowed by the soldiers and sentries, and he knew she couldn't travel as rapidly as he. Without sleep last night—he winced as he thought of the reason—she should be halting soon from exhaustion and from difficult terrain.

For nearly thirty minutes, Shannon had struggled and argued with the two soldiers in mud-splattered gray uniforms, who were unloading her belongings, placing them beside the road in a curiously neat pile, and brazenly confiscating the animal stolen from Denton. One soldier apologized as he informed her that all available animals were to be claimed by the Confederate Army, to be used by the cavalry and advance scouts or used for transporting supplies or for pulling ambulances. All pleas, chiding, insults, and arguments fell on deaf ears.

Shannon shouted at them, pointing out her dire circumstances and the danger. "You cannot steal my horse and leave me stranded in the midst of a marshy wilderness! Look around us; there's no one and nothing here! Just wild animals and possibly horrid deserters! Night is coming and it's getting colder. I'm a woman. I'm alone. I have a pass from the President himself. This is outrageous! This is criminal!"

The persistent soldier showed her the official order for his action. "Sorry, ma'am, but it cain't be helped. We got to have every horse we can find. Won't nobody hurt no fine lady like you. You just keep walking down this road and you'll come to help. Or camp here until help comes along. We're leaving you your supplies. Our men need these horses. We got a war agoing on."

"You'll have a worse one on your hands if you take my horse, sir!" she shrieked at him, then reasoned in a softened tone, "Surely you have enough sense to realize that order does not apply to unescorted ladies who will be left behind in danger and darkness and cold!"

The second soldier spoke up as he visually scanned her beautiful features. "It says all horses, miss. We can't show favorites, now can we?"

Shannon pretended not to notice how he was looking at her. She swept off her felt hat and allowed her flaming curls to settle wildly and tantalizingly around her torso. As she flipped the edges of the wool cape over her shoulders to display a tempting figure, she falsely paced and fretted aloud to disarm and captivate them. "I cannot believe this is happening. I'm as much a soldier as you two. I've probably endangered my life as many times and made more sacrifices to aid the South. How dare you treat me in this unforgivable manner. I've been a nurse for years, and I'm heading to Savannah to help soldiers wounded by that vile Sherman. Without my horse, I cannot possibly get there by foot any time soon, if at all! Do you realize how many soldiers die from a lack of medical attention? I was requested to go there! You have no right to impede my journey, or to prevent it!"

"Some regiment will be along in a day or so. You can join one of them," the first soldier informed her stubbornly as he finished his task.

Having been told countless times of the power and

447

magic of her large blues eyes, she stood near the men and focused that weapon on them. "Sirs, you do a vile and wicked thing—to the Confederacy and to me. I have endangered my life and safety by attempting to get to Savannah to aid the wounded. Without my horse, how will I be able to travel or to flee peril? Marauders and deserters abound in these grim times. Savannah is over a hundred miles. I came from Wilmington. How will I get to either town?" she asked, stressing her sorry situation.

"A female don't travel alone unless she's brave and strong, miss. If you're gonna ride all over the land, you'd better learn to defend yourself or git back home where you belong. Besides, we ain't harming you," he said with a frown. "You females steal a soldier's attention from his duty and safety. You don't belong in our camps. Go home, girl."

Shannon was provoked by his scornful chiding. She sarcastically emphasized her first few words as she scoffed tersely, "If I had been home where I belonged, sir, countless men would have died from their injuries. The South has few doctors and surgeons. If you are wounded, I hope you do not find yourself dying for want of a woman who was ordered to return home and to forget her duty to the Confederacy. Perhaps you will have no one to change your bandages, to feed you when your hands are missing or do not work, to write home to let loved ones know you are alive, to give you water when your head burns with fever and you can't move or speak, or to do many other things that are too depressing and private to mention in mixed company! Perhaps you will discover we nurses are not distracting or irritating under those grisly circumstances! Take me to your commanding officer! I'm positive he will agree my mission is just as vital as your thieving one!" Suspecting they might consider her wrist injuries those of an escaped captive, she was careful to keep them concealed with her long sleeves.

The man bristled. "There ain't time, ma'am, and we got orders. They don't say nothing about exceptions. We got to locate twenty horses and take 'em to General Moore. Everybody has to make sacrifices during a war. You look strong and brave. You'll be fine. Let's go, Elmer. We can't stand here jawing all night."

Shannon had been about to announce herself as the legendary Flame, for they would never consider stealing that heroine's mount or treating her in such a terrible manner. But the mention of Moore's name prevented her from using that ruse or going to confront him. She dared not come into contact with him or continue a verbal battle that might be mentioned to him! Clearly these men were going to take the roan and leave her on foot, no matter what she said or did. She inwardly fumed and raged at their actions and her helplessness. Evidently conditions were more terrible than she had imagined, for otherwise they would not have demanded her horse. She had no choice but to acquiesce to their strength and determination.

"Just wait until President Davis and General Bragg hear about this," she threatened one last time. "Take the damn horse and get out of my sight, you villains! Surely the world has gone mad when Rebel soldiers begin preying on vulnerable women and conducting themselves so dishonorably. Pray you never fall under my care, sirs, for I shall return your kindness of today!" She had ridden since early morning and was tired—too tired and too tormented to be afraid.

The second soldier pointed to their left and suggested, "There's a railroad about a mile or two in that direction. Find the tracks and follow 'em. You might hitch a ride; if not, you'll come to people and a depot sometime tomorrow. You won't get lost if you follow the lines."

Shannon watched the two men ride off with her horse and four others, all having been taken by force from unsuspecting and defenseless people. What was the South heading to? What was happening to her people? She, a woman, had been left in the wilderness, in the dark, alone, and the temperature was dropping swiftly toward freezing! She glanced in both directions. She had not passed any homes or settlements that could be reached before night, and she dared not follow the soldiers to General Moore. She concluded it would be best not to remain on the barren road, where menacing human hazards existed. Without a mount on which to escape, she felt she would be safer inland. At least the railroad would provide direction as it snaked its way to Savannah by a longer route. Perhaps she could obtain a ride when they saw a woman alone, she mused hopefully.

Shannon searched her belongings and supplies for those items she would need the most, as she could not carry everything. She used the waning daylight to pick out the least difficult path. She inhaled deeply, summoned her courage, and left the road. She walked until it was almost dark. She hated to stop, for movement provided body heat, and the area was too wet for a campfire. But she realized it would be rash to travel when she couldn't see the ground. She had no choice but to halt for rest and sleep, and wait for the morning light.

She dropped her possessions on the damp earth and leaned against a tree. Slowly her aching body sank to the cold ground. She cuddled inside the long cape and closed her eyes to rest a moment before eating an unappealing meal. All day she had attempted to block out her anguish. Uncontrollably, it flooded her mind and body. Had her beloved been using and duping her from the first? Had she been a gullible, trusting, enchanted fool? What was

450

the truth about her odd letter, Blane's fight in Wilmington, Elisha's near catastrophe, and all the other insidious engimas that surrounded or implicated her?

Shannon tried to reason out these entangled mysteries. Who was to blame for her misery and peril, and why? Would Jeremy Steele act viciously without orders from Blane or another agent? If so, why destroy her and why delude his friend? Was Elisha deceiving and tricking her? She had recklessly divulged too much to him, and he could have uncovered other facts. What if Elisha had lured her to Charleston and had betrayed Blane to General Holmes? Revenge and lust were powerful motives. What if only the Blade was responsible for her predicaments?

A heavy thud sounded near her head, causing her to open her eyes and turn her head to investigate the startling sound. A knife was impaling a large and intimidating spider to the tree. Colorful fluids and viscera oozed from the gaping wound. The fuzzy creature's many legs waved about in panic and pain, as if it were performing a death dance. Its chelicerae wriggled frantically and defensively, and futilely. She gaped at the petrifying sight, which was only ten inches from her head.

"It's mighty dangerous to be wandering around here in the dark and alone, Blue Eyes. This area abounds in spiders and snakes and alligators and such. Need a ride to Savannah?" he calmly offered.

Shannon whirled and stared at the man approaching her on foot. His skill with a hunting blade was apparent, for he had struck his target accurately and from a distance. With Dan's reins clasped loosely in his left hand, Blane Stevens casually strolled toward the astonished redhead. "How did you find me? And why did you bother, unless to further harass me? I see you persuaded them not to confiscate Dan."

He grinned nonchalantly and replied, "I saw them first. But even if I hadn't, Dan wouldn't have allowed anyone to take him captive."

"Like master, like horse," she scoffed bitterly. She refused to show or speak gratitude for his preventing the enormous spider from crawling over her and probably biting her. "One of us isn't going to remain here."

He shook his sun-kissed head as he debated, "You're wrong, Shannon. Both of us stay here until we resolve some troubling matters. I talked with Matti while you were sneaking off, and I'm concerned over these riddles. I know it was stupid of me to stake you out like a Comanche captive, but I needed time to think before acting more rashly. Don't you know I could never kill you or injure you? I couldn't even stand to watch you hurting yourself. During a war, men think, say, and do crazy things. Blame my work or my past; I was raised hard and fast and wary and harsh." He halted and dropped Dan's reins, assuming a stance and expression that exposed his determination.

"I don't care what you say, or do, or believe, Major Stevens. I don't want to hear any more lies or be involved in your evil games. Our association and relationship are finished. I'm going home, where I belong. If there are any mind-disturbing riddles, you can solve them any way you damn well please. After your treachery and betrayal, I don't owe you any respect, or loyalty, or explanations. You accused me of horrid crimes and deeds, and you called me vile names. You deluded and humiliated me. You hurt me physically and emotionally. I have no forgiveness or understanding or trust left for you. How could you be capable of such brutality and deception? Why me, Blane?"

Without including the dark reasons from his turbulent

452

past, he explained why he had been afraid to trust her and how his suspicions had been aroused. "These crazy doubts about you intimidate me. Look at the evidence pointing to you, Blue Eyes. What was I supposed to think and feel? How could I ignore it?"

Shannon had pushed herself to her feet. She glared into his entreating expression. "By the same token, Major Stevens, consider all of the incriminating and traitorous evidence pointing to you. Consider, too, how we each dealt with our comparable suspicions and emotions. *Suspicions*, Major Stevens. Not hard facts," she stressed.

"Don't you realize I'm confessing my mistakes? I'm apologizing. I'm trying to explain and clear up this confusion. I'm not perfect. I'm human, fallible, mortal. I'm afraid for you, Shannon. I will be until I discover who's after you and how they know so much about us."

"Afraid of me and afraid for me . . . If those statements were true, you would be in a terrible mess. Let it go, Blane. It won't work anymore. I can't believe anything you say or do. You shouldn't have given yourself away with that signature. You're far too clever and alert to make such a careless error. Perhaps you assumed I was too stupid to notice it or recall it. If you're afraid of trusting me to hold silent about you and the Union, dispose of me here and now. If not, get out of my life and sight and let me go my own way."

"I can't, Shannon; not tonight or ever. Even when I thought you were guilty, I couldn't take your life. I couldn't even sit there and watch you hurt yourself while I was torturing myself for being unable to deal with your alleged treacheries. Help me get to the crux of this affair. At least try to view this situation from my side. I'm a man, Shannon—an ordinary human being. Don't I have the right to correct my errors, to change and improve my weaknesses and flaws? Are you so cold or perfect that you can't understand and forgive me?"

She challenged sadly, "See it from your side, Blane? There shouldn't be any conflicting sides between us. I thought we were a perfect team, not perfect people. I thought we had something special and honest developing between us. I was mistaken about you and us. This isn't a simple error that can be easily or quickly corrected. The fact that you thought I was guilty of such horrid crimes and acted on those flimsy doubts proves there is nothing unique or valuable between us. Or at most it must be something so weak and meaningless it isn't worth saving."

"You can't believe that, woman, not after what we've shared and endured together. Give me time to prove you're wrong to turn away from me. Stay with me, Shannon. I need you, Blue Eyes. For myself only," he clarified hoarsely, taking a few steps toward her.

Shannon retreated the same number of steps. "You're wrong again, Blane, if you think I don't feel that way. Obviously our emotions and thoughts vary greatly. Time would be useless, Blane; it wouldn't change anything. Don't you see? I didn't turn away from you; you cruelly and savagely rejected me, and I won't return to endure more agony. As for needing me, you don't and never will, other than for a pleasing diversion or a defensive cover for your missions. The Blade provides all you want or need. I'm tired. Please go away."

"Can I ask you one question, Shannon?" He continued even before hearing her response. "During all of these months, especially these past weeks and days, did you never once doubt me? Never once try to deceive me? Never once try to escape me? Never once question your own feelings and mine? Never once give me reason to mistrust you?"

Shannon looked him in the eye as she responded, "Yes, Blane, I did all of those things, with just cause. But I never betrayed you, or humiliated you, or accused you of vile deeds, or tried to kill you."

"Don't you realize there are vast differences in our backgrounds. Shannon. Most of my life I've been a loner and a fighter of some kind. I had to become self-contained, depending on my instincts and my wits and my skills. We grew up so differently. I learned to fight and kill and be wary at an early age. Since eighteen, I've had to survive on cunning and mettle. Sometimes I survived only because of mistrust." He smiled. "Then I met you. I'm trying to learn to share, to change my thoughts and feelings, to put someone else first. I'm trying to open up to emotions I didn't know I had inside me. I have to learn to trust women, particularly you. Years ago I was taught to be cautious around beautiful and daring females. A stunning Comanche creature put this scar on my face after I rescued her miserable hide," he revealed, rubbing his finger over the area. "Then you come along. Lord, Shannon, emotional lessons are hard and painful. Help me understand myself and our situation. I don't want to lose you."

Tears stung her eyes. She was so afraid to trust him, and more afraid not to. She had to remember he was a man, a secret warrior, a man who existed on his immense prowess and keen wits. She had to consider the evidence against her and decide if it justified his behavior. She had to realize he had been battling this war for years, and he had scars added on top of past scars to harden him and to make him leery. "I can't answer you tonight. I'm too confused and fatigued. Give me time to deliberate my feelings and our problems."

*　　　*　　　*

For a week they traveled through the countryside of South Carolina, staying clear of towns and Rebel camps. Blane's caution had increased, for things were getting worse all over the South. He would be glad to get her home, for she would be safe in Union-conquered territory. He wisely did not press Shannon, though he made sure she was aware of his presence. They rode double or walked in watchful moods, speaking only when necessary. They slept side by side, on separate bedrolls. They ate from his and her provisions. They both spent hours searching their hearts and observing each other intently.

The weather was getting colder each day. In less than two weeks, it would be Christmas. In a few months, the war would have gone on for four brutal and costly years. Each night, Shannon would snuggle into her bedroll and shiver until exhaustion claimed her. But each day, she was becoming more and more aware of her vanishing doubt and anger toward Blane. She was becoming more and more hungry for his stimulating lips, his comforting embraces, the warmth of his body and smile, the closeness and ease they had shared, the fiery passion that had been denied them for weeks. She hated this estrangement, this close proximity without touching all the ways she yearned to touch.

Two more tormenting days passed. They camped in the midst of several large rocks, which would provide protection from the cold winds and any passing enemies. Dan grazed and watered as if this biting weather meant nothing to him. After Blane and Shannon had completed a meal that nearly finished off their supplies, she sat with her back to a towering rock. Her teeth chattered and her body shuddered.

Blane looked around, then smiled to himself. He told her he would return soon, then disappeared into the trees. Within the hour, he had come and gone many times, carrying leafy branches and stacking them nearby. The pile grew taller and thicker with each trip. Finally, he propped limbs against small trees and bushes in such a manner as to create a shelter against the brisk winds for Dan. Sensing his master's care and concern, the animal nuzzled Blane's hand and chest. Dan was content to graze on winter grass in the leafy semicircle; and his owner was content to leave him alone, knowing he could defend himself.

Shannon watched Blane continue his task in another area, which was sealed off by huge rocks on three sides, like a miniature box canyon. Taking heavy branches, he covered the overhead area between the boulders, overlapping the limbs until they formed a barrier against the brisk wind and cold air. He retrieved his sleeping bag and unrolled it beneath the leafy ceiling, then deposited the rest of their belongings at the open end. He skillfully crisscrossed more branches until only a small entrance remained uncovered. He turned and smiled, inviting her to share his snug abode. Shannon's gaze revealed her qualms about sleeping so close together and in such a secluded and romantic setting.

Blane teased, "It's mighty cold and windy out there, and getting worse. You want me to pass out your sleeping roll, or do you plan to form a truce and enjoy my hospitality tonight? Hard as it'll be, I promise I'll behave myself. You haven't forgotten how many times we've shared bedrolls and kept to ourselves? Come on, Blue Eyes. You know you can trust me. Don't be obstinate and spiteful."

After Blane vanished behind the sturdy wall of limbs, Shannon eyed the enticing shelter for several moments. She kept going over his words in the hotel in Charleston and in the marsh. Her mind kept murmuring, *If what he*

457

said was true . . .

She stood up and went to the makeshift hut. She hesitated, knowing what would happen if she dared to sleep so near him. But wasn't that what she wanted? Wasn't he what she wanted, forever? If she believed there was a possibility that these weeks of mysterious misunderstandings had resulted from an enemy's interference, she could be losing her love and all of her dreams by refusing to listen and take a chance, or to compromise.

She stepped away from the entrance. If only it wasn't so frightening to risk her heart and soul on this unpredictable man! If only he hadn't treated her so savagely in the hotel. His harsh words were hard enough to forget, but his brutal actions were nearly impossible to rationalize or excuse. Was she insane to spurn him? Was she insane if she didn't? It was so complicated, and her decision could be so very costly.

Blane joined her in the icy breeze. He touched her shoulder and entreated, "Come inside, love. I won't harm you again. Remember how it was between us. Not just the lovemaking, Blue Eyes, but the fun and the laughter and the talking. It was so good and easy to touch during night or day." When she did not turn or respond, he asked, "I really made a mess of things for us, didn't I?"

Shannon turned and met his somber gaze. "Yes, Blane, you did," she concurred painfully as tears escaped her eyes. "I felt so safe and happy with you. You filled my mind and life and heart. I wanted you and needed you. Now, it's like . . . there's a cold, thick wall between us; and I'm not sure I want to remove it or can remove it. You can't imagine how much you hurt me that night, or how much you terrified me. When I look at you, doubts and fears attack me. It's almost as if you did slay me that night, or our relationship. I don't know you or

458

understand you, Blane. I don't think it can ever again be like it was. Perhaps that's the saddest part of all; you destroyed something very rare and beautiful."

"Don't close me out, Shannon. I love you. When this war is over, I want you to marry me. Please give us time to find what we had again. I was a bloody fool to let fears birth suspicions. Lord, woman, I was so afraid you wouldn't be for real, so afraid I couldn't win you and keep you. This is all new to me, Blue Eyes. Help me adjust to it."

Shannon stared at him. Had she heard him correctly? "Don't you realize I'm just as frightened of surrendering to you? Don't you see what a big risk I've been taking? I've given you all I have, all I am."

He captured her face and lowered his until their noses almost touched. "Then give me more, Shannon, or return what you've taken back. Give me your love and trust and loyalty. Marry me in Savannah. Marry me and wait there for my return. The Confederacy is folding like a morning glory at high noon. I'll complete my duty, clear our names, and come home to you. We're destined to be together."

Her eyes widened and searched his gaze for a glimmer of jest or deceit. "Are you serious, Blane?" she questioned in astonishment.

He smiled, then kissed her forehead and nose. "I've never been more serious in my life. Miss Shannon Greenleaf of Savannah, will you do me the honor and great pleasure of becoming Mrs. Blane Stevens on Christmas Day? Or no later than New Year's Day? Does that prove my feelings and intentions, partner?"

Shannon flung herself into his arms and hugged him tightly. After covering his face with kisses, she replied, "Yes, my love, it does and I will. Take me inside. I'm freezing."

Blane scooped her up in his arms, ducked, and entered their cozy haven. He rapidly sealed the entrance, enclosing them in a dim and fragrant paradise. They undressed swiftly and came together on the bedroll with an urgency born of fiery passion and newly confessed love.

Chapter Nineteen

Shannon and Blane traveled another four days, halting briefly along their journey to rest and to make love. Soon, the war would be over for them and their dreams could be fulfilled. In the midst of such misery, their love gave them hope. Most of the time they concealed themselves from the Confederate regiments heading for Savannah to defend the city against General Sherman or from those retreating to "tend their wounds and attack again," as they declared loudly to anyone they met along the way.

While seeking a place to cross the Savannah River into Georgia twenty miles above the town, they encountered a small band of wounded men who were being taken to the field hospital near Ridgeland. The men told of their skirmishes near Statesboro. They related horrifying tales of razed towns and plantations, of looting and killing beyond the point of warfare or punishment, of wanton destruction of life and property. They sadly declared there was no stopping Sherman; within two weeks, Georgia would be conquered and devastated almost past survival. They told of how Sherman and his men were planning to trample South Carolina—that "hellhole of

461

secession"—next, then move onward to stamp out rebellion in her sister state before joining forces with Grant to clean out any lingering nests of traitors.

Needing information on the war's path and progress and on any hazards before them, Blane and Shannon were compelled to stick to the roads and to bluff their way past any trouble. Travel was slow with so much activity occuring as the enemy swept through the area. Times were bad, and few questions were being asked, especially of those heading toward the line of fire. The strongholds and supply lines were being wiped out rapidly and thoroughly. Rebels were dying and deserting by the hundreds. The end was coming for the Confederacy, and most knew it or sensed it.

On Wednesday, December 19, Blane and Shannon learned of Hood's defeat in Nashville the Saturday before by Union officers Schofield and Thomas. News filled the air of incidents in North Carolina, making Shannon glad to be away from that frantic area. Governor Vance had sent the Armory Guards from Fayetteville and forty thousand men from Raleigh to the nearly defenseless Wilmington to cover for those men who were presently serving to defend Savannah, a vital supply port. Four battalions under Colonel Leventhorpe had been assigned to protect the Fort Fisher area. The Junior Reserves and Hampton's cavalry had been sent to repel Grant's men, who were attempting to tear out the rail lines at Belfield. Shannon was saddened to think of those young men, practically boys, fighting against twenty thousand well-armed and experienced Union troops. The weather in that area was reported to be intensely cold.

Blane knew about the planned assault by sea and land on Fort Fisher within the week. The powder ship *Louisiana* would be sailed against the earthworks and exploded. Once the fort and town were taken and

Charleston was conquered, it would all be over for both sides.

Blane and Shannon neared the outskirts of Savannah late Sunday, December 23, to discover that Sherman had entered the city on Friday. Blane insisted they make camp and not enter such a tense area at night. She waited in dread to view the despoilment of her city and home. She couldn't help but be grateful to the vicious Sherman when she learned of his decision to spare her beautiful city from being burned and plundered. However, she was dismayed to hear of his plans to remain there for a month while his men rested and prepared for their conquest of South Carolina and made certain they were in full command of the area. She astutely and bitterly realized how and where those men would regain their strength— by confiscating Southern homes and supplies!

As they mounted Dan for the last time early the next morning, Blane informed her, "We're going to present ourselves to General Sherman immediately to prevent any problems or troubles for us and Greenleaf. You need to make your loyalty and claim known to him."

Naturally Shannon wanted to head directly home. "We're so close, Blane. Please take me there first. You can return to town and see that monster. I don't care to ever meet him. At last, home, clean clothes, regular baths, hot food, and a warm bed," she hinted temptingly. "If we go into town, we can't make it home tonight. Who do you want to spend this evening with, me or Sherman?"

He chuckled and pulled her hair playfully. "We're too close to take foolish risks, Blue Eyes. We need to check out the conditions in town and make our identities known to General Sherman. We'll need passes and letters of defense for our safety and your property."

She protested, "But you can obtain those tomorrow, while I'm sleeping and stuffing myself. I want to see if

463

there's any word from Corry and . . . see how things are at home. Please," she wheedled.

Shannon's mention of Corry and her avoidance of the subject of Hawke ripped into Blane's confidence and happiness, reviving his concern over those two unresolved matters. He hadn't thought about either man in a long time, and certainly not as threats to his future with Shannon. She did not realize that her reasons for rushing to Greenleaf were the very same reasons he wanted to stall their arrival as long as possible.

"Don't be childish, Shannon," he scolded her sternly, surprising her with his coolness and firmness. "Right now, victory and our lives are more important than your first glimpse of home. We could be mistaken for locals or Rebels or Confederate agents. We have to settle matters with Sherman first. Besides, I have to report to him, for he's the superior officer in control of this area. I'm supposed to fill him in on the movements of troops and weapons between here and Charleston. We'll spend the night in town, then head for your plantation tomorrow."

"You're going to provide the information for that beast to raze South Carolina like he did Georgia? How can you?" she reasoned.

"It's my duty, Shannon. I'm a Union officer, and I want this war done with quickly. I have a woman to marry and take home to Texas."

"Texas?" she echoed. "It's a wilderness with Indians and outlaws. I don't know anything about being a settler. You never said we would live there."

"Did I need to?" he jested, observing her shock and distress. "Wives usually move in with their husbands, and my home is there."

"You could live at Greenleaf with me and my family."

"I'm a rancher, Shannon, not a plantation farmer. Don't worry. You'll love Texas and the Stevens ranch.

464

We'll be married and together."

Shannon remained silent as Blane urged Dan forward toward the city.

To his surprise, Blane had no difficulty getting into town or in to see General Sherman, as if he were well known and his visit expected. Shannon was peeved when she was told to sit in an office across the hall while the two men talked privately. As she waited for Blane, the victorious men's stares and whispers grated on her nerves, for she erroneously assumed they were laughing at her dirty and disheveled appearance. She didn't like being seen like this, especially in her home town. She didn't like being shut out of the conversation in Sherman's appropriated office. She didn't like Blane's current mood and conduct, and she didn't like the idea of leaving Georgia for wild Texas.

Noon passed, and still she waited. She was tired and tense. She wanted a hot bath and a meal. She yearned for a soft bed and clean garments. These ill-mannered Yanks hadn't even offered her hot tea or coffee; nor had they provided water and a place to freshen up after her journey. She longed to see her home and her brothers. Her anger and vexation increased by the hour, for it had been three since their arrival!

When Shannon could tolerate this treatment and her fatigue no longer, she tried to approach General Sherman's office to tell Blane she was leaving. The officer on duty halted her. After she explained her need to speak with Major Stevens briefly, the man informed her that Blane had left an hour before and was expected to return any moment. He smiled and said he would tell her when the major arrived.

Shannon was furious. How dare he take her for granted! How dare he behave in this inconsiderate and rude manner! "I'll wait for twenty minutes, no longer. If

Major Stevens doesn't arrive by then, you may tell him he can locate me at home."

Instead of returning to the office where she had been told to wait, she strolled into the entry hall and gazed out the window. From rooms to her right and left, she could hear tales of bloody battles and awesome triumphs. As the Union soldiers laughed and joked about their superiority and conquests, Shannon's fury began to mount once more. When they started to boast of their matching intentions for the Carolinas, she was sorely pressed to remain silent. She kept warning herself of the dangers to her family and property if she behaved like a rebellious and insulting Rebel. Under these conditions, she had to force herself to keep still.

Suddenly familiar names and astonishing facts caught Shannon's attention. She strained to hear the conversation between the officers standing at the foot of the stairs, twenty feet behind her. She was glad they were making no attempt to whisper. Why should they? They were bragging of another Union victory, in their headquarters. Her heart drummed heavily as the staggering information filtered over to her.

"As soon as Major Stevens returns," one officer was saying, "General Sherman wants a meeting of all head officers on duty. Right now, he's sending reports to General Grant and Admiral Lee. With the facts he's supplying us with today, between Sherman and Grant we'll have those Carolinas bagged and ready to serve Lincoln at his picnic on the first day of spring; and Admiral Lee will find that taking Charleston and Columbia will be as simple as plucking dead or stunned birds caught in his sails."

"Did the major say why he wanted to question the captain and crew of the *Angel Wings?* He's lucky Captain Elisha Carter survived the trap they set with Blade's

466

information. How does he get so much done?"

"Captain Carter or the Blade or Major Stevens?"

The other officers laughed. "Carter's been a pain in our blockade for years. They nearly caught him last month. Got to hand it to him; he's got guts and wits. Too bad he decided to work for the Rebs."

"Yep," the man who had just arrived agreed. "'Cause I just heard he died from his wounds. Sure was a waste. Handsome devil and money to toss overboard. Blade's gonna be rankled with the Navy. He told them to capture Carter, not sink his ship and kill him."

"Probably couldn't be helped. Carter isn't one to surrender. Did they learn anything useful from him before he died?"

"Now that you mention it, you know what the guard told me? He said Captain Carter kept mumbling about being betrayed by a bewitching temptress and being a fool for trusting her twice. From the threats he was vowing, she'd best be thankful he can't return."

Before the man could say more, another said, "Must have been some stormy romance gone sour before he sailed. At least we got one less runner to battle."

"We got the best runner out of our hair," the man corrected him. "But guess who Carter thinks betrayed him to the Union? Flame," he announced with an appreciative whistle. "From the way Carter was carrying on, he had to have known her. If she had walked into that cell, Carter would have forced himself from his bunk to slay the beauty. If there's such a thing as a ghost, his will surely haunt the Flame."

One of the men debated, "But it was the Blade who arranged Carter's defeat. The way I heard it, he sent word from Charleston even before Carter left port. I wonder if Major Stevens has met this Blade or Flame."

The men chuckled again. "Word is the Blade put that

Rebel Flame to rest, after he enjoyed her for months."

"Serves her right for trying to steal glory from our Union Flame. She had to be a fool to pit herself against the Blade."

"Who knows, maybe she enjoyed him as much as he enjoyed her. I wouldn't mind sharing a bunk or bedroll with either woman."

"'Cause you're crazy, Bo. That Rebel temptress would slit your throat and brand you like she done her other victims. Blade must have put her out of business. Ain't been no word or sight of her since her treachery in Wilmington. I bet Stevens didn't take kindly to her betrayal."

"I wonder if he killed her," a youthful officer suggested.

"Wouldn't surprise me none. Major Stevens and the Blade have one thing in common: they get their missions done any way they have to. Let's grab a cup of coffee before we start our meeting. Sounds like it's going to be a long one. Sherman says we take Columbia next."

"I hope we finish before dark. I plan to round me up a pretty little Rebel treat to feed this aching in me gut."

Lusty chuckles echoed in the room. "I must admit, these Southern belles are fine specimens of womanhood. If we play our cards right, we could find our stay here most entertaining. When females are scared and hungry and alone, they become real pliant."

Shannon was relieved to be dressed like a man, to be wearing a floppy felt hat over her fiery hair, and to be standing with her back to the men. Anguish filled her heart and mind. Elisha was dead, and he had died cursing and blaming her. And Blane—what was he doing and what had he done? The trip here had been an assignment . . .

Shame and fury flooded her as she thought of how she

468

had been discussed so crudely and openly. How difficult would it be for another agent, from either side, or for any clever person, to investigate and to prove she had been with Blane on countless occasions? It would be fairly simple; and it could be exceedingly perilous for her.

What would these lecherous officers think when Major Blane Stevens married a flaming-haired woman, one who had been traveling with him? She assumed she could prove her identity as the Union Flame, but could she disprove an accusation that she was the Rebel Flame? She tried in vain to push new doubts and fears from her mind.

If only she didn't feel so miserable. She was exhausted. She felt bloated, even though her stomach was so empty. She couldn't seem to get rid of the tension and nausea that had been assailing her for the past few days. But she felt certain that once she reached home, bathed, rested, and ate properly, her body would return to normal. There could also be another explanation for these physical problems, she realized, for her monthly flow was late again. And even if she was feeling somewhat light-headed at the moment, she would not ask for nourishment from these smug foes!

Shannon went to inquire about Blane's lengthy absence. She asked the officer for a pass as protection during her ride home. Her request was refused, and the man told her to wait in the other room until given permission to leave. Her glare challenged his authority and words.

"Major Stevens ordered me to guard you, Miss Greenleaf. I was not to let you venture out alone. There are Rebels and marauders lurking in and near town. You must wait for him."

When the officer left to respond to another summons, Shannon departed by the front door. To halt her exit, the

469

blue-clad man would have to arrest her! Dan was nowhere in sight. She frowned, then noticed a wagon moving southward. A triumphant smile brightened her dirty face and she ignored everyone to hurry after it.

"Mister Barnes," she called out as she approached the wagon's tail. "Mister Barnes, wait up, please. It's Shannon Greenleaf."

The wagon halted and the man turned to look at her. Shannon went to stand near the front wheel and gazed up at him. Tears of joy, relief, frustration, and turmoil made streaks down her grimy face. She tried to regain control of her breathing. "I finally made it to Savannah, sir. Can you give me a ride home? Has Corry or Hawke returned?"

The startled man gaped at the lovely and bedraggled creature. "Is that really you, Miss Shannon?" he asked in amazement.

She smiled, then laughed. "It's me, sir. I was trapped in Boston when the war started. Papa and Temple . . . are gone. I don't know where Corry and Hawke are. I've been trying to get home since August. It's awful everywhere, sir. The Union is devastating us. Can you please take me home?" she begged shamelessly.

"You sure you want to go out there alone?" he asked, knowing what she would view, unaware she was ignorant of those facts.

"I have to go home, Mister Barnes," she replied wearily.

He slid over and invited, "Climb up, Miss Shannon. But if you want, you can come home with me. We don't have much after those Yanks claimed most of our animals and supplies, but you're welcome to share what little we got left. Them devils ain't wasting no time stealing from us poor. I should warn you; because your family sided with them malicious Yanks, most folks here

470

won't be kind or forgiving or charitable. Even if them Yanks don't appreciate your loyalty."

Shannon did not question his meaning. She did not want to discuss her family's choices, right or wrong. She had her home and Blane. What more did she need in her future? Only her two brothers and peace.

The wagon traveled for an hour, reaching Greenleaf property by four o'clock. Shannon's blue gaze grew large and troubled as she viewed the increasing signs of vandalism. Fences had been torn down. Pasture sheds had been burned. Their lovely entrance had been marred by painted words, by the obliteration of their name and magnolia carvings, and by the crushing blows of tools on many tabby sections. "Which despicable villains did this criminal deed, Mister Barnes? How could anyone be so malicious and cruel as to wantonly damage or destroy such beauty? The wall and arch will have to be repaired and painted."

By then, they had reached the entry arch. Noah Barnes reined in his mule. "I can't take you any closer, Miss Shannon. You sure you want to go up there and look around? It ain't a pretty sight."

The unsuspecting Shannon glanced from the elderly man toward the house. She went pale and shuddered in rising panic. She could not be viewing her drive and home! This was some horrid nightmare, some wicked delusion! The moss-draped majestic live oaks that had formed nature's tunnel from the tabby arch to the yard had been mutilated. Yes, that was the right word for what her eyes observed. Some trees had been chopped down, others had been scarred with axe blows, and others had been set aflame—trees that had been large and beautiful and almost ageless. Worse, she could see what was left of her home, a blackened ruin amidst utter and wanton destruction. There was no sign of animal or human life.

471

The stench of smoke and soot remained in the still air, telling her that this evil despoilment had been recent. She feared she was going to faint in shock. "Why, Mister Barnes? Do our neighbors hate us this much? Did they do this before or after that sadistic Sherman conquered our city?"

The man looked at her oddly. "Your neighbors didn't do this, child. It was those Yankees, Miss Shannon." When he saw her disbelief, he related the stunning tale, "Me and Reverend Peters and Thad Jamison saw them doing it. The Yanks had us hauling supplies into town for their soldiers. We saw the fire and came to see about it. Jamison thought it was a good mistake, seeing as how the Greenleafs were Unionists. But me and Peters tried to stop them. We told them your family was siding and fighting with the Union. They said . . ." The older man shifted anxiously and fell silent.

Shannon probed, "They said what, Mister Barnes?"

"It ain't worth repeating, child. It was nothing more than crazy words to excuse their evil. I'm taking you home with me."

"Tell me what the soldiers said," she demanded. "And how can you be sure they were Union soldiers?"

"I know everybody around these parts, Miss Shannon. They were wearing Federal uniforms and they had papers with orders and seals on them. Besides, I've seen two of them in town with other Yanks."

"But why would they raze Greenleaf? It can't be true."

"They said you and Corry are . . . Rebel spies, Miss Shannon."

She was visibly stunned by his words. "That's insane! How could they destroy our home and lands based on wild suspicions? Corry's a Union soldier! As for me, the charge is too absurd to argue. Someone is going to pay for this crime," she vowed bitterly.

472

"That ain't all, Miss Shannon," he hinted worriedly. "They come by here every morning to see if you and your brother have returned. They told us you two will be arrested and . . . punished."

This time, Shannon swayed on the wagon seat. Noah seized her arm and steadied her. "This is all a terrible mistake," she whispered.

"You should be careful, child. Those Yanks said they had a long list of crimes and witnesses against you. I'm afraid you might not be able to prove your innocence before . . . before trouble strikes."

Shannon realized she might need this man's aid, so she did not proclaim her innocence by revealing her ties to the Union spy system. "Don't worry about me, Mister Barnes. Major Blane Stevens won't let the Union soldiers harm me. He'll learn who did this to us."

"Major Blane Stevens, the Union officer?" he probed fearfully.

"That's right," she replied, watching his alarm increase.

"That's who gave the order for all this," he told her, motioning at their surroundings. As she shook her head in a denial of his words, he informed her, "It's the God's truth, child. I saw his name and heard them say it. They claim he's arriving soon from Wilmington to make sure they carried out his instructions. I don't think you should be around when he arrives, Miss Shannon. He sounds hard and dangerous."

The distraught woman needed privacy to think and to vent her feelings. "I'll walk from here, Mister Barnes. Thank you for helping me and for trying to save Greenleaf. I'll be fine," she assured him.

After protesting and arguing her intention to remain here, the worried man departed. Shannon steeled herself for a closer view of this malevolence. As she trudged up

473

the private road, she tried to ignore the weather and landscape. She kept her moist eyes locked on what had been her home. Very little of the once elegant structure remained. She saw partial walls, stone foundation, chimneys, charred columns, shattered glass, ornamental stair railings, and blackened beams that had refused to be totally consumed by fire. Pictures, clothing, keepsakes, furnishings, and such were lost forever. Her gaze took in the markings painted on each towering column after the fire: Union flags and symbols, vulgar words, and a sketch of a knife . . .

Shannon slowly turned and looked in each direction. Everything had been destroyed or ruined, with the exception of the gazebo. She almost laughed hysterically as she stared at it, for it did not even need painting. She walked dejectedly toward the family graveyard.

Even that area had not gone untouched. The fence had been torn down. Headstones had been tumbled, or splashed with paint, or crushed, or demolished by all three actions. Shannon went to her mother's grave and knelt. Tears dropped from her face to her filthy garments. Was there anything left of her past world and dreams?

"Shannon, what in blazes are you doing here alone? I've been frantic since you ran off. I told you to wait for me in Sherman's headquarters. I rode like the wind to make sure you're all right."

Blane was infuriated and alarmed by the destruction around them. Remembering his past losses in Texas, he knew what his love must be feeling. He was angry with her for endangering herself and disobeying him. He wished he knew which spiteful neighbors or vengeful Rebels had wreaked such damage here and such suffering on his love. He knew she was shocked and depressed, for she hadn't heard his approach or calls. He had to get her away from such sights. He was hoping a dose of his anger would return her wits and stir her emotions.

He leaned over, grasped her arms, and pulled her to her feet. "It's late, Shannon. Let's get back to town."

She lifted turbulent eyes to his. Had he ordered this vengeance when he believed she had betrayed him? Was he making certain she had no place or person to turn to except him? Surely he didn't have lingering suspicions about her? "Why, Blane? I'm not a Rebel spy."

From where they stood, the Blade's symbol wasn't visible to Blane. "That's probably not the reason, Shannon, but I will check into it after we return to town. Somebody is punishing you for siding with us."

"You don't have any idea who did this or who ordered it?"

"Of course, not, Blue Eyes. Sherman told me he was leaving Savannah intact. I need to get you fed and bathed, woman. Remember what I told you about the Comanche attack on our first ranch? I lost my home and property and part of my family, so I do know how you must be suffering. I left a meeting to find you. Let me get you to the hotel, and you can rest and eat while I finish my reports. We haven't had privacy for days." He would tell her later, after she had settled down, that he had to leave at first light tomorrow. What a miserable way to start Christmas morning!

When he attempted to draw her into his embrace, she balked. "I'm home, and I intend to stay here. I have some thinking to do. You return to your meeting and friends. Leave me alone."

"You're coming with me, Shannon," he commanded forcefully.

"No, Blane, I'm not." She was testing him with her refusal. In sheer panic, she waited to discover the truth about him, their relationship, and her fate at his hands.

She was about to leave her love standing there when her misty eyes landed on her brother Hawke leaning against a tree, smiling at her and mutely beckoning her. Her eyes widened in disbelief as his name seemed to explode loudly through her mind. Was she dreaming? Were those his sparkling ebony eyes engulfing her? Was that his enchanting grin curving up the corner of his sensual mouth? His coppery bronze face displayed such awesome beauty and strength. How could he stand here so calmly just smiling at her after this lengthy separation? He looked so healthy and vital she felt stronger and braver just gazing at him. She was flooded with powerful emotions. All other thoughts and problems vanished from her mind. Joy and excitement surged through her body. She had to make sure he was real.

Blane caught her arm to halt her departure, unaware of the man behind him. Shannon tried to jerk away. When Blane tightened his grip, she shrieked, "Release me, damn you! It's Hawke." Stunning him, she managed to yank loose. She raced into the open arms of the man who could not have known how he had haunted Blane's dreams.

As his love shouted his mysterious rival's name, Blane whirled and watched her being lifted and hugged tightly in Hawke's strong arms. He observed them as they seemed to memorize every inch of the other's face. He watched them touch each other: faces, hair, shoulders, hands. He could hear their ecstatic laughter, but not their muffled words. He saw them cuddle, as if they had been two cats rubbing over and against each other. They caressed cheeks and embraced over and over. He spread kisses over her face and squeezed her until she giggled and squealed. He kept lifting her and hugging her fiercely. The joy and love between them was undeniable, just as their strong bond and rapturous reunion were

476

staggeringly potent and intimidating.

"Oh, Hawke, I'm so happy you're home," she murmured in his ear, crying and laughing simultaneously. She would visually engulf his face, then hug him tightly, only to repeat the action over and over.

Hawke bent forward to bury his nose in her hair. He held her possessively as he whispered, "You've grown big, little sister, and very beautiful. These eyes have hungered to feast on you and these ears have begged to hear your laughter. I'm home, Vixen. Tell me of our father and brothers." He pressed her wet cheek against his chest.

"Look what the enemy has done to our home. I'm so glad you didn't stay here to battle them. Oh, Hawke, they're so evil. There's so much to tell you. Every day I've prayed for your return. We have—"

Blane had mentally lived this moment several times in the past. He had dreaded it and feared it, for the reasons he was presently observing. He desperately called to his love, "Shannon! I'm leaving. Are you coming with me or not? Shannon! Let's go!"

Hearing the terse voice, Shannon parted slightly from the handsome man but did not remove her hands from around his body. She eyed Blane. Leave? She looked up into Hawke's stoic expression. How should she explain each to the other? She felt pulled between them. She needed to clarify things with Blane, but she wanted this special reunion with her brother. Right now, it was Hawke who pulled the strongest on her emotions. Right now, she was confused about Blane. Did Blane have nothing to say about his many treacheries of late? Was he going to keep silent about Elisha? About her home? About pretending to unselfishly escort her to Savannah when he was actually carrying out an assignment? What about his secrecy with Sherman?

477

"I need to stay here. We can talk tomorrow," she told him.

"We talk now, or never," he demanded, burning with jealousy.

Shannon whispered something to Hawke, then moved toward Blane. Hawke went to the gazebo and took a seat as she had suggested. Shannon looked up into Blane's frosty expression. "I'm sorry, Blane, but I can't leave with you tonight. Hawke and I have some matters to settle. Would you like to meet him?" she asked apprehensively.

Blane's hazel eyes grew colder and harder by the minute. "He's the last person I want to meet, Shannon, except for Corry. If you don't come with me now, I won't give you another chance."

Shannon was astounded by his words and behavior. "I can't leave now, Blane. Look around you. How could you make such a demand?"

"If you love me and want to marry me, prove it, Shannon. Get on Dan's back and ride away without looking back."

"I can't," she refused painfully. "Give me until tomorrow."

Blane glanced over at Hawke. The man's dark gaze was examining them intently. Blane wanted to slay him but had no just reason. He was determined to force Shannon to make a choice between them, here and now. He could never ride off and leave her to spend the night with Hawke, then take her back after she had tested her emotions and Hawke's. And if she had any doubts about her feelings for either of them, it was futile to drag her away. He watched as Shannon kept glancing at Hawke and smiling at him, as if she couldn't keep her eyes and mind off his rival. There was such a softness and radiance in her eyes when they touched on his bronze-skinned opponent. He fumed enviously.

"Shannon, I'll ask you one last time; come with me now. I have to leave at dawn. I want you to marry me tonight. If you refuse, I won't return to Savannah. I want Hawke and Corry out of your life."

She gaped at him. Did he want to take everything and everyone from her? Did she know this man at all? "I can't go with you or marry you tonight, Blane. And I'll never sacrifice Corry and Hawke for you or anyone. If you can't give me time and understanding, then go."

Her words were not interpreted by Blane as she had intended them, but neither one knew that. Blane swiftly covered the distance between the graveyard and Dan. He unbuckled the girth strap and removed the hidden pictures. He didn't have to retrace his steps, for she followed him to probe this inexplicable behavior. She didn't get the opportunity, for Blane reacted violently and recklessly in his state of anguish. He had thought he had finally won her love and fidelity. He now believed she was rejecting him for another man, and bitterly suspected she had duped him all along.

"You might want these back, Flame. I don't need them anymore. Make sure you guard your backside. You left a dangerous trail behind."

Shannon looked at the family pictures, then at Blane. "You've had them all along? You lied to me and stole them. Why?"

"I wanted to make sure I could recognize Corry when I met him, just in case we got separated," he sullenly replied. He had this irrational urge to make her suffer as he was suffering, to spoil her reunion and her life with his victorious rival. She had allowed him to fall in love with her and plan a future for them, then had crushed both dreams. The moment Hawke reappeared, she had discarded him for her former love.

479

Shannon began, "I don't understand. You sound as if—"

He sharply cut her off. "As if I despise the sorry bastard and want him dead? I do. When we met in Washington, the moment you exposed your name and home to Silas Manning, I recognized both; and soon I'll find and slay Corry. If your family hadn't taken off in '61 before my arrival, this matter would have been settled years ago. I agreed to let you tag along as my so-called partner because I hoped you would lead me to your brother. By the time I found those pictures, you were good company between the blankets and you were providing a superb cover. Besides, I wasn't sure which of those men was Corry."

Shannon was bewildered and pained. "From that first night in the White House, it was all lies and games? And why were you chasing Corry?"

"Because he's the man I've been seeking to kill, the one who ruined my sister's life in the spring of '60. He's had plenty of chances to accept his responsibilities. Even if I never locate him, I've amply repaid him, haven't I, Blue Eyes? I've been here three times searching for him since your family left. Too bad Greenleaf's ruined. Serves him right for refusing to share it with Ellie and little Corry."

Blane's keen wits were dulled by fury and anguish, but he noticed her reaction. "You look shocked, Blue Eyes. I'm surprised you haven't figured this out by now. I thought you said you and Corry were close. Did he keep such wickedness a secret from you, or have you known the truth since before we met? From the things you said each time this subject came up, I couldn't be sure about what you did or didn't know. Were you a clever trap for me? Did Corry send you to Washington? Or did you come up with this self-sacrificing scheme to save him

480

after we met? Are you sure you want Hawke so much that you'll risk Corry's life by spurning me? I suppose you could blackmail me with accusations of rape and abduction. But who would take the word of the Rebel Flame against mine?"

Shannon did not make any attempt to conceal her anguish and tears. "If I lived forever, I wouldn't have guessed you capable of such treachery and cruelty, or such stupidity. You're wrong about everything, Blane. Corry isn't responsible for Ellie's troubles, and I had never heard of you before that night in Washington. And even if he were guilty, you had no right to make me pay for his sins. How wrong and wicked you are. What kind of satanic beast are you, Blane Stevens? Your revenge has succeeded beyond your wildest dreams. If you're through tormenting me and gloating, why don't you get the hell out of here?"

The sight of her agony vexed him. "Do you expect me to believe it was a mere coincidence that *you* entered *my* room that night? I promised Ellie justice. When you see Corry, make sure he knows the Stevenses have exacted their revenge. And make sure he knows I still plan to slay him if he doesn't marry Ellie and legitimate his son."

"I would never tell my brother what you've done to me just to punish him. If Ellie is anything like you, the man who marries her is a fool. How blind and rash you are, Blane Stevens. If you had told me the truth, I could have proven you're wrong about Corry."

"You can stand there and scold me for lying and deceiving you? What about your lies and tricks? At least you owe me for saving your lovely neck several times, my tempting Rebel Flame. And what about Hawke?" he sneered, his smoldering gaze wanting to singe his rival.

"You know I'm not a spy for either side, so don't use that to excuse your wickedness. As for Hawke, I didn't tell you about him because of your feelings about bastards and Indians, and because that area of my life was painful and private. I didn't think he would ever come back to Greenleaf. Believe it or not, I was going to tell you about him tonight. I was going to tell you everything about me tonight," she added sadly. How would he react to news of their child? Would he deny that he was the father, or demand the baby for misguided revenge on her brother? She couldn't risk his answer.

"But Hawke returned today and changed your mind, didn't he? How can you choose him over me? He deserted you years ago, like Corry did Ellie. When I learned about him from you and Thornton and saw his picture, I was afraid this day might come." He told her what he had overheard in the past and his interpretations. "Were you using me to replace your lost love? Are you going to marry him?"

"Marry Hawke?" she echoed incredulously. "Are you insane?"

"What's the matter, Flame? He beneath you, like me? Papa's dead now, so he can't stand between you two. And that bastard Corry hasn't got the right to judge anybody! That night at the Thomases, were you really a virgin, Blue Eyes? Or was Thornton right? Were you sleeping with Hawke and me and no telling how many other gullible fools? Like brother, like sister. Once I get rid of Corry, you and Hawke can marry and have all of this to yourselves."

"Oh, Blane, you don't realize what you've done to me, to us. You don't know how wrong you are about everything. I loved you. I gave you my heart and soul. I was going to marry you."

"Until you discovered you could have Hawke again," he charged.

Her eyes examined his harsh expression and frosty

482

glare. "If Hawke was the only misunderstanding between us, I would shake some clarity into that stubborn head. But Hawke wasn't the reason you set out to use me and betray me. You didn't know about him for a long time. We had something very special, or we could have had something special. How tragic that you had to destroy it all because of lies and hatred."

She glanced at the destruction surrounding them. "You're responsible for all this, aren't you? When it looked as if you couldn't obtain your bloody revenge on Corry, you saw me as the perfect weapon for hurting him. I wonder how Ellie will feel when you explain how you carried out your promise to her. In her place, I would die of shame and anguish. I would be ill for having had any part in such evil. You've ruined everything, Blane. When you learn the truth of your errors, I hope it tortures you as much as it's tormenting me. Now that you have revenge, can't you be satisfied? Will it give you and Ellie joy and freedom? How could I have been so wrong about you? How could you hate me and spite me so cruelly? What of all those nights and days we shared? How could you be so blind and vengeful?"

Blane impulsively confessed, "It wasn't always Corry and Hawke. I didn't start out to hurt you, Shannon. I hated Corry and wanted to punish him. You just got in the way. Maybe it was your destiny to tempt me into using you as my weapon. Lord knows you're an irresistible witch. I'm not even sure Corry didn't sic you on me."

"You're mistaken, Blane. You couldn't have done such horrid things to me if you didn't hate me. You've destroyed my whole world, and you wanted to destroy me. If that isn't hatred and evil, I don't know what is. All I wanted was to love you and to build a life with you. When should I expect Sherman's guards to come and arrest me as the Rebel Flame? Will you be around for my mock trial and execution? Is that to be your finishing touch to this madness and evil?"

"You can relax, Shannon. I've cleared your name with Sherman."

"That was decent of you, considering you're the one who planted all the false evidence," she stated sarcastically. "Damn you, Blane!" she raged aloud, then murmured tormentedly. "Damn you. We could have been happy."

Blane watched as Hawke rose and flexed his muscular body. Though the man couldn't hear them, Blane knew he was observing them with those keen midnight eyes, ready to spring into skilled action. Blane had seen enough half-blooded men and women to guess that Hawke was one. He should have guessed from the picture. Clearly the man had been reared or partly reared in the West. Hawke's stance and expression told Blane plenty about him and his prowess. His jealousy mounted. "You have Hawke back. What could you want from me?"

"What I want, you cannot give me. Oh, Lord, you're so wrong; and it's too late to explain the truth to you. Just go away."

Her first statement pained him deeply. He realized there was one person who might put a damper on her reunion with Hawke. "I almost forgot about one of your lovers. I should tell you about Elisha Carter before—"

"Don't you dare tarnish Eli's name!" she shrieked angrily. "I know what you did to him both times. He was my friend, nothing more! Get away from me, you vindictive bastard!"

Hawke came toward them the minute she raised her voice. "Shannon, you all right?" he called out as he neared them.

Shannon rushed into his protective arms and replied,

"Yes, Hawke. Now that you're home, I'll be just fine. I've missed you so much. I was so afraid I would never see you again."

Hawke pulled the precious girl against him and looked over her head at the man who was glowering at them. He sensed a strained leash on the man's anger and temper. He sensed anguish and turmoil. "It's all right, Vixen. I won't leave you alone again."

Blane mounted Dan and looked at the embracing couple once more. "Don't forget to tell your beloved Hawke how you've been spying and whoring for the Union with me," he declared bitterly and rashly.

Hawke's body went rigid. His black eyes seemed flaming coals. His right hand pulled Shannon to that side. His left hand went for his knife. "I shall slay you for your insult, white dog," he threatened ominously.

Shannon rapidly grabbed his wrist and halted him. "No, Hawke, don't fight him!" she protested, fearing injuries or death for either man. She lifted her teary gaze to Blane's sullen stare. Her lips and chin quivered as she bravely confessed, to both men's astonishment, "Don't challenge him over my lost honor and shame. He's telling the truth. He's a Union agent, the best they have. I was his partner, or disguise, or whatever he needed. For the past few months, I've worked with him and traveled with him and . . . slept with him—but never as a whore. I thought I loved him and wanted to marry him. If I hadn't come home today, I would have, if his proposal had been honest." She looked into her half-brother's worried eyes and murmured, "I'm sorry, Hawke. Please don't hate me. I was a fool to trust him and sleep with him. I don't ever want to see him again."

Hawke pressed her wet cheek to his racing heart. He studied the resentful man on horseback. "I could never hate you, love. Don't blame yourself for making a mistake. Are you sure about this, Vixen?" he inquired, knowing something awesome had transpired between the two.

Shannon's body shuddered. "Make him go away, Hawke. I don't need anyone but you," she stated intentionally to fool Blane.

Blane inhaled raggedly, kneed Dan, and galloped away.

Chapter Twenty

Having already suffered through her horrifying
discovery of Greenleaf's ruin, Shannon was too distressed and exhausted after her confrontation with Blane
to relate the details of their entwined past to Hawke. Her
brother lifted her and carried her to the lean-to he had
constructed on Saturday near the stream on their land.
He had arrived late Friday night while their home was
still in flames, but it had been too late to prevent its
destruction or to see who was responsible. Parts of it had
burned rapidly; others still smoldered.

As they talked, he prepared food for her, then tucked
her into his bedroll. He reclined against her and held her
tenderly. Before falling asleep, Shannon told him of their
father's grief and remorse over his cruelty to Hawke. She
revealed the grim news of the family's losses, and they
grieved together for father and brother. She told him
about Simon Travers and her escape to find Corry. She
promised to explain her relationship with Blane in the
morning. Soon, Hawke lay awake, watching his sister
sleep restlessly.

Shannon awoke early. After eating and bathing, she
changed into garments from the bundle left behind by
Blane. As calmly as possible, she told Hawke the story of

Major Blane Stevens, leaving his charges against Corry and his bitter betrayal for last, knowing how unsettling they would be. "If the only problem had been his misconception about us, I would have bound and gagged him until he heard the truth. But it was all lies and tricks, Hawke. All he wanted was to get to Corry and kill him if he refused to marry this Elli. He's wrong, Hawke; Corry isn't guilty."

"You're right, Vixen. I'm the man he's searching for," Hawke admitted. "I wish I had known who he was yesterday and why you two were quarreling. We could have settled this matter peacefully. I'm sorry he hurt you and wants to end Corry's life because of me. I'm responsible for Ellie's pain and his false assumptions. I got her pregnant and never returned. I'm in love with Ellie Stevens. I would marry her today if I could find her. She vanished years ago. A son . . . we have a son."

"You and Ellie? How?" she demanded. "But they're seeking Corry, blaming him, trying to force him to marry her or die."

"Because they think I'm Corbett Greenleaf," he replied softly.

Shannon watched him intently. "I'm confused, Hawke. Did you know about the child and their search? Why do they think you're Corry?"

"It's a long, sad tale, Vixen. You know how Corry or I used to travel with Father to Texas or other places. That spring, Father had wanted Corry to go, but he had that broken leg that didn't heal for months. I took his place. We couldn't tell the men we were dealing with that I was Indian or part Indian, so we pretended I was Corry. That's when I met Ellie Stevens." His voice and gaze softened at the memory.

"She stole my breath and heart, Vixen. Trouble was, I didn't realize I was falling in love with her. We spent a lot of time together. At first I thought I was only having fun.

But we kept getting closer and tighter. After she told me about that Comanche attack on her family and ranch, you can understand why I had to remain Corry to her, for the same reason you didn't tell Blane about me. Before those two months passed, I knew I loved her and wanted to marry her. Father kept telling me she and her family would hate me for lying about my identity and for being part Comanche. He didn't want me to marry her and stay in Texas, and he didn't want me to bring her home. After Father called me a coward and rejected me, I returned to my people to prove myself. After I did, I looked for Ellie. I was going to reveal the truth about me and beg her forgiveness. It was too late. Don't you see, Vixen? They believe they're right about Corry. If I were Blane and you were Ellie, I would seek revenge as he has done. If Corry had gotten those letters you mentioned from the Stevenses, he would have told us. Father must have answered them and burned them. How she must hate me for leaving her to suffer alone."

"No, Hawke, she doesn't," Shannon refuted. She told him what Blane had said about his sister's feelings. She told Hawke how and where to locate Ellie and his son. "Go to them, Hawke—today. All of you have suffered too long. Find her and tell her the truth. She loves you and needs you. It won't matter about your Indian blood."

"Will my action repair the damage to your love for Blane?"

Shannon lowered her head and cried. "No, Hawke, it can't. If you want to bring your wife and son here to live, please know this is your home too. You are a Greenleaf. I won't blame Ellie for anything her brother's done to me. Find her and marry her, Hawke, before they convince her to accept another man in your rightful place."

"I cannot leave you alone," he protested. "What about Corry?"

She stroked his cheek affectionately. "Don't let her

489

suffer a day longer, Hawke. I'll be fine until you return. We'll need lots of help rebuilding our home and lives. I'll go into town and find work there. Maybe Corry will arrive before your return; if not, we'll decide what to do about him. This land is huge. He could be anywhere. Ask Ellie to write Blane in care of President Lincoln and tell him the truth about you two. That should keep him from stalking Corry." She removed the gold band she was still wearing and handed it to him. "Blane purchased this for her. Marry her, Hawke, and be happy."

"You must not hate or blame him. If I wed his sister, our families will be joined. It was an honest mistake on his part, Vixen."

"If that were true, Hawke, I would rush after him today. There's more you don't know about us. It's too late. Besides, even if it was a tragic error, Blane should not have sought revenge on me."

Hawke explained, "That is the Indian way, Vixen, and the law of western lands. All who carry an enemy's name and blood must also bear his guilt and punishment. He comes from such lands and beliefs."

"This is not the West, my precious brother, and he has betrayed me in other ways. I can never return to him. Do you know how good it is to see you alive and well?" she murmured, hugging him. "What have you been doing all these years?" she asked, allowing space and time to appease her emotional wounds before continuing their talk.

As he usually did when speaking of his Indian ties, Hawke unconsciously slipped into another dialect. "The Comanche grow weak and few, little sister. Treaties are broken by both sides. New forts are built each season to master and control the red savages as they did the black ones," he stated sarcastically. "A soldier named Van Dorn has made himself the chief destroyer of my mother's people. At Rush Springs and Crooked Creek, he slaughtered many good Comanches. Rangers now ride against us, and they are powerful white warriors. The American Army sends what are called 'Galvanized Yankees' to battle us while they fight Rebels. The soldiers become stronger and smarter under Sibley and Sully. But they also send white devils in the bodies of Chivington and Carleton. Many say when the Union defeats the Confederacy, they will send many more soldiers to settle the Indian wars. I cannot raise my son in such dangerous lands and times. Again, I will choose the white way. I will marry Ellie and bring my family to Greenleaf."

Shannon smiled and agreed with his decision. Now that he knew about Ellie and the child and where to locate them, she could see how anxious he was to claim them. There was nothing he could do here any time soon, except to go after Blane for the same reason Blane had been stalking Corry! She couldn't expose that dilemma and spoil Hawke's chance for happiness with Ellie. Besides, the best way to end Blane's hostility and to protect Corry was to solve the problems of the past. She had made mistakes, and she must correct them. She didn't want Hawke delaying his journey and worrying over her troubles while he could be attempting to repair his own life. She had learned a great deal during these past months. She was stronger and smarter. She could handle her life and safety for a few months.

"I tried to convince Blane he was wrong. Not that Corry is infallible, but I knew he would never turn his back on such responsibilities. I told Blane it was either a lie or a mistake, but I never imagined it could be you he was seeking. I remembered those months. From mid-April to July of that year, Corry was either in bed or on crutches. I'll never forget that time. He was an annoyance to everyone with his two broken legs. What did happen to Corry on his last trip west with Papa?"

"It was New Orleans, Vixen," he corrected her with a smile. "Corry should explain it. I will tell you it had to do with his falling in love with the wrong woman, and killing a man over her."

"Oh, Hawke, must love always be so difficult and painful? Why don't you prove me wrong by bringing home a happy bride and son?"

"Why don't you come with me?" he coaxed, hating to leave her.

"You can travel faster and more easily without me. Besides, I've been running and hiding for months, and I need to relax and recover. And someone needs to remain here to watch for Corry. I'll be fine."

Christmas evening, Shannon was sitting before a cozy fire in a Savannah hotel, sipping sherry and crying softly. Hawke had left for Texas at midday, after placing her in this lovely room. A hot bath and meal had done nothing to lift her low spirits. She had enough money from Hawke for room and board for three days. During that time, she needed to find work and make future plans. Blane had left town as he had vowed, or threatened; and the Federal officers refused to discuss him or reveal his destination. She decided against asking them to send word to him about Corry and Hawke. She was afraid she might discover that he wasn't coming back. It was time to decide how she felt, what she wanted, and how to get it.

Shannon didn't leave her room that next day to seek employment, because the weather was terrible and she was feeling awful. On Thursday, she finished a late breakfast in the eating room and went into the hotel parlor to see if any newspapers had been left behind by guests. Finding none, she was about to return to her room when the man coming down the stairs captured her attention. She was terrified but grateful for having

492

sighted him first. She fled into the empty hotel sitting area, whirling this way and that as she sought a hiding place. The heavy drapes offered a promise of concealment. She prayed the man would leave the hotel and allow her to escape his grasp. He did neither.

Simon Travers and his cohort sat down on a sofa within a few feet of her. She prayed she could restrain the nausea that was building within her throat. She listened as the repulsive man listed her sorry predicaments and how he intended to locate her and solve them. In horror, she discovered he was the one who had been tracking her, who had been planting false information about her, who had exposed and murdered all of those people along her journey with Blane. Simon—not Blade! He revealed the trap he had set for her and would spring if she defied him. It seemed he didn't know she was staying at the hotel, for he had his other men out searching for her.

As if she had been an emotion-filled cauldron, rage and thirst for vengeance began to simmer within her. Cunning and daring joined them. Resentment deposited itself inside the boiling kettle of turbulent feelings. When she considered the many times men had used or tried to use her and the grim situation she was now enduring, a shocking plan formed in her mind, a plan she had not considered since the day she had seen a lawyer before leaving Boston . . .

After Simon and his hired villain left the hotel, Shannon went to her room to prepare to combat his brazen plan. Simon owed her! Without the backing of her home and crops to support her, Simon would control her family's stolen holdings. She needed to recover at least some of their funds. She needed a name for her child before she started exposing her newly discovered condition. She needed money to escape that beast and a way to disarm him to carry out her flight to freedom. She needed to recover the false evidence he had created

493

against her. She needed revenge on him for many reasons. She would have it all, and humiliate Simon in the process!

At last, Fate was on her side. When she noticed Simon returning to the hotel, she put her plan into motion. She walked down the steps as if heading for the noon meal, her head and eyes seemingly lowered in sadness and worry. She slowly lifted them, then cleverly brightened her expression when her eyes touched on the man standing in her path.

"Simon," she greeted him joyfully. "What are you doing here? You couldn't have arrived at a better time. Things are so awful. Please forgive me for tricking you and running off like that. Take me home to Boston. It's so terrible here." She began to weep, and she took him off guard by moving into his arms for comfort and protection.

Between sobs, she told him, "They burned Greenleaf, Simon. They destroyed all of it. No one likes me because Papa sided with the Union. A Federal agent who was supposed to help me ran off two days ago. I can't find Corry, Simon. I don't even know if he's alive. I don't have any money and all of my clothes are gone. I've had to live on charity. What am I going to do?" she entreated, sounding totally helpless and subdued, totally ignorant of his crimes and evil.

Simon withdrew a handkerchief and dabbed at her abundant tears. He guided her over to a sofa, then scolded triumphantly, "You were a naughty girl, Shannon. I've been looking for you for months. You know you shouldn't have traveled alone with a strange man. You're a lady."

"He was mean to me, Simon. He was always making me go hungry and dirty. He wouldn't let me rest and he made me get hurt twice. He even threw away my clothes and things. He said I was dumb and spoiled. He said I couldn't do anything right. I tried, Simon, really I did. It was so scary trying to help him spy on the Rebels. I thought it was going to be fun and exciting. It wasn't. Most of the time he left me with his friends while he took off for days."

Shannon knew she could disarm and mislead Simon with childish and feminine chatter, just as she knew this man was ignorant of her wits and daring. "I showed him one time! No, two times! I beat up this major who tried to attack me. And I saved his life when he got captured. Do you know he made me hide in this dark hole under a house once? It was getting so cold and dangerous. He told me to stay here. But I don't have any money or clothes. I'm afraid of him, Simon. He acted so strange sometimes. He even accused me of spying on him and almost getting him killed. He said if I left Savannah he would send the Union Army after me. This war is making people wild and mean."

Simon cupped her chin and lifted her head, pleased by her subjugation. "What you need is a good husband to take care of you. The sooner, the better. I'll arrange things for us to marry tonight."

"You would marry me after the terrible things I said and did to you? Oh, Simon, you're much too forgiving and kind. But we can't marry until tomorrow. I don't have any clothes, and I want Reverend Peters to perform the ceremony. Please, may I have a pretty dress and a real wedding? I promise I'll be good from now on."

"You wouldn't be trying to fool me again?" he teased.

She shook his hand. "Don't be silly. You'll come shopping with me. I won't buy anything you don't approve. Then we'll go see Reverend Peters together and set the time. Do you think we could find any flowers for me and the church?" she speculated as if deep in thought. "And a ring, Simon! I'll need a ring. What if they don't have any in town? Gold and silver were confiscated many times during the war."

Simon chuckled. "I'll take care of the church, preacher, and ring, and the flowers, if I can locate any. You go shopping for a proper dress and some clothes. This is Harvey Franklin. He'll escort you where you need to go and back here. Buy whatever you need or want."

After he handed her a wad of money, she kissed him on the cheek and hurried out with her guard. She knew Simon was afraid to trust her but was too arrogant to believe she could dupe him twice. Besides, he didn't know that she knew all about him. Her plan was working!

Harvey stood guard at the front door of every shop she visited. Between stops, he held and carried her packages. At her last stop, she entered the front door and sneaked out the back to visit her old friend and a fierce Rebel, Floyd Weeks, at the stable next door.

After her return to the hotel, she concealed several purchases under her mattress, then burned the extra boxes. She spread out her new wardrobe to show to Simon when he came to retrieve her for dinner. As she anticipated, Simon appeared at four o'clock to tell her the wedding would take place as soon as she was dressed.

Shannon blushed and stammered demurely as she told him, "We have to . . . wait a few days, Simon. I . . . It's . . . We can't . . . Oh, heavens," she fretted nervously and modestly. "It's my female time. I'm sorry."

Simon chuckled. "We can still marry today, Shannon. I have the adjoining room. In a few days, we can share the marriage bed."

"Are you sure you don't mind, Simon? This is so embarrassing."

Simon didn't mind at all, for it proved that Blane hadn't left anything undesirable behind. "You get dressed. Peters is waiting for us."

Less than an hour later, Shannon became the wife of Simon Travers. They dined in the hotel and drank expensive champagne. She looked beautiful and fragile in her pale blue wedding gown. She kept eyeing the gold band on her finger and smiling at Simon. They made plans to return to Boston the following week. At nine, her feigned exhaustion won her a departure to her room. She knew a guard would be positioned outside her door. She didn't care, for it was Simon who was in for a big surprise!

She cursed Blane for deserting her to face this peril and problem alone. There was no time to search for him, even if she had known where to look. She was angry and resentful toward him. She changed and was ready to leave at eleven. Her tight bundle of extra clothes, canteen, and supplies were resting on the floor beside her bed. She waited eagerly for the signal from Floyd and Noah. It came just after midnight. The door into Simon's room opened and Noah peeked inside, grinning conspiratorially. She hurried to meet him.

"We took care of him," her friend whispered, pointing to the unconscious body on the bed in the adjoining room.

"Are you sure he'll be out long enough?" she inquired anxiously.

"He drank that glass of whiskey we set out for him with Doc's drug in it. Just to be sure, me and Floyd held his nose and forced half the bottom down him. He'll still be sleeping come noon tomorrow," he boasted cheerfully. "He never even looked under his bed."

"Thank goodness, or you two would be dead. You don't know how much I appreciate this help." She hugged each man and placed a kiss on each one's cheek.

"About time we helped out and had fun doing it," Floyd remarked.

"We should get busy and get you out of here," Noah advised. "With that guard posted, I sure am glad

497

Travers's door opens to a different hallway. If he obeys his order and don't move, he won't see you escape."

Together, they searched the room. Finding the false evidence against Shannon, they burned it in Simon's fireplace. The two men prepared Simon to appear as if sleeping peacefully, just in case anyone dared to check on a newlywed couple. Shannon took all of Simon's money and concealed part of it in each of her boots, for she felt this money was truly hers.

As they worked quietly and secretly, Noah informed her, "This man and that one in the hall are two of the soldiers who burned your home, Miss Shannon. Appears they ain't real soldiers, just evil men. I hope this dangerous plan of yours works. It sure is a clever one."

"You mean it wasn't Sherman's men?" she probed.

"Nope, it was him," Noah declared, nodding toward Simon. "Looks like he wanted you homeless and helpless. He's the one who laid the blame on the Union and that Blade fellow."

Shannon couldn't allow the time or emotion to analyze such news. If she had learned the truth about Blane sooner, it might have made a difference, but now she didn't know where to locate him, and there was always the possibility that he might not have believed all of her incredible revelations, if she had known where to find him. For now, she had done what was necessary for her survival and escape and that of her child. That reminded her of another detail. She took the marriage license, in case she had need of it. Shannon made a hasty check of her room as Noah and Floyd waited patiently. She felt faint when she heard Noah's next words.

"As soon as we get you away, we're going to rescue some other friends. Ever heard of Captain Elisha Carter, the blockade runner? Them Yanks are holding him and part of his crew captive. We been waiting for their wounds to heal enough. It has to be tonight, 'cause Floyd heard they were being sent to prison camp tomorrow."

"He's alive? But they said Eli died from his injuries."

Noah shook his head and smiled. "That was his first mate. They exchanged places to protect Captain Carter until he could escape. He's a valuable man. You know him?" he inquired at her reaction.

"We were the best of friends . . . until he was told I betrayed him to the Union. Please tell him I'm innocent. It was . . . the Blade. He was spying on both of us. Tell Eli to stay clear of Wilmington. The Union is attacking there by land and sea. He'll never get through."

"Why don't you come with us? You can leave with them, then you won't have to travel alone. Those men will defend you."

"It's too dangerous, Mister Barnes—for them and for me. I have to get word to the Confederate forces near Columbia."

Noah's keen gaze wandered over Shannon's face and hair as he absorbed her words. "You're the Flame, ain't you, Miss Shannon?"

She knew it would require too long to explain the truth. Why not let them believe they were assisting and protecting their famous heroine? She smiled heavily. "You can't tell anyone about me, Noah, Floyd," she whispered gravely, as if drawing them into her confidence by using their first names. "If anyone discovered the truth, my life and mission would be in jeopardy. You can't even tell Eli. He or his men could drop a dangerous hint in the wrong ear. There are spies everywhere. Tell them I said I'm heading for Andersonville to free Corry. I'll make sure our side has a big surprise waiting for Sherman when he crosses into Carolina. I would like you to give Eli something for me. Tell him to read page fifty."

Delighted she had kept it, she retrieved Denton's book and quickly wrote a message across the edge of that page, a message she prayed he would accept: "Eli, perhaps in time you will learn I did not betray you here or at York. I wish you a long and happy life, for you are very dear to me. Stay safe and well. S.G."

She gathered her belongings, leaving the blue dress shredded beneath the covers in Simon's bed. She could not resist taking ink and drawing flames on the villain's bare chest. When questioned about the strange deed, she vowed that Simon would show no one. As they sneaked out Simon's door, Noah hung the privacy tag on the doorknob.

Noah, Shannon, and Floyd slipped out the back door to the hotel and went to the stable. There, Shannon mounted the horse supplied by Floyd and stealthily left town. By two in the morning, Elisha and his men had been freed and were making their way toward Charleston. Their courageous helpers returned home without leaving a single trace of their participation or a clue to the escaped prisoners' destination.

January 31, 1865 was an extremely cold and windy day in Georgetown, a small city located on the Winyah Bay, fifty-six miles northeast of Charleston. It had been over a month since Shannon had vanished mysteriously and successfully from Georgia. She had decided against spending this painful interlude in Wilmington or Charleston, knowing both would be carefully searched by Simon.

After leaving Savannah, she had traveled to Hampton. There, she had met with Confederate officers. As the Flame, she had related every fact she had gathered about the Union's forces and plans. She had told them she was heading for Wilmington to flush out several Federal agents who were supplying information for an imminent assault on the entire Cape Fear River area. She had warned them to prepare for Sherman's attack on

Columbia and a Union siege on New Bern. She had asked them to send warnings to Fort Fisher, which was perilously low on soldiers. She had told them the thwarted Christmas Day assault on Fort Fisher had been a clever diversion to keep them off guard for the second one, which was being planned. The regiments under General Johnston had been delighted by her aid and awed by her courage.

Johnston had provided Shannon with a pass and an escort as far as Branchville, where his troops were ordered to the defense of the state capitol. He had told her how proud her father, his old friend, would be of her. Shannon had not revealed his death or his Union loyalty. From Branchville to Lake City, Shannon had been passed along from Rebel unit to Rebel unit. At Lake City, she had not continued her alleged journey to Wilmington; she had slyly headed south for Georgetown, to work in a Confederate hospital. She had decided to live there until the war ended and she could straighten out her life and emotions.

She had located a small and comfortable dwelling near the hospital and had begun her nursing again. For her, this was all she owed either side. For weeks, she had spent her days ministering to the needs of countless and seemingly faceless soldiers. She had spent her nights remembering her mistakes and crying over her losses, when she was not dreaming of Blane. There was no doubt she was pregnant and would be exhibiting that condition by the end of March or April, according to how her body dealt with that burgeoning situation.

On January 13, General Terry and Federal troops had attacked Fort Fisher; that vital stronghold had fallen to the enemy by the fifteenth. Rebel officer General Bragg had led Hoke's troops to battle Union forces at New Bern. Union Secretary of War Stanton had visited the conquered Savannah in December and the defeated fort

501

on January 16. Grant had made an appearance there on the twenty-eighth.

Without Shannon's awareness, crucial events were about to take place, far away and nearby. President Jefferson Davis had sent a message to President Abraham Lincoln that read, "I am ready to send a commission . . . to enter into a conference with a view to secure peace to the two countries." Lincoln had responded, "I have constantly been, am now, and shall continue ready to receive any agent . . . with a view of securing peace to the people of our common country." A meeting was set for February 3 in Hampton Roads, Virginia, aboard the steamship *River Queen*. Blane had been assigned to protect Lincoln's life during the conference with the Confederate Vice President Stephens.

On February 1, Sherman left Savannah to begin his rampage on Columbia. On the sixth, President Davis made a stunning revelation, telling his people, "The Commissioners . . . were informed that nothing less would be accepted than unconditional submission" of the Confederacy. A rally was held in Richmond where Davis verbally injected new fighting spirit and loyal resistance toward the arrogant Union. Two days prior to this, Major Blane Stevens had been wounded and taken to the hospital in Georgetown.

Shannon casually glanced inside the surgeon's private room when another wounded man was delivered. For a week, new arrivals had been heavy and frequent, but she refused to overwork herself. Her attention was seized by the fact that this gray-clad man was under guard. As she gathered fresh bandages from the supply closet nearby, she heard the men talking about the possible capture of a Union spy. Looking through a slit in the door, she made a startling discovery. As soon as she regained her poise, she skillfully handled the precarious situation.

Shannon knew the surgeon was busy at the field hospital a few miles from town. She calmly entered the operating and examining room. As she moved past the unconscious man on the table, she halted and rushed to his side. "Corry!" she shrieked in dismay. "What happened to him? He's hurt badly. The doctor is away. You must go for him quickly. Corry?" she called to him. "Can you hear me? It's Shannon."

One of the soldiers asked, "Do you know this man?"

As she pressed a thick cloth to Blane's head to staunch the flow of blood, she responded, "Of course, I do; he's my brother! Where did you find him? We'll have to notify President Davis immediately."

"Why?" the other guard inquired.

"Corry is one of his top agents. He's supposed to be dogging that beast Sherman. How did he get here? You must fetch the doctor."

"You mean he ain't no Union spy?" the first man queried.

"Corbett Greenleaf, a Union spy? Are you insane?" she scoffed.

"But your name is Travers," the second man reasoned.

Shannon held up her left hand and wiggled her ring finger in his face. "Because I'm married. If you wish to inspect my papers, you'll find I am Shannon Greenleaf Travers. This man is my brother, Corry. If you doubt my word, ask President Davis. He is a friend of our family. He's the one who asked Corry to become an agent."

"He had suspicious maps and papers on him, ma'am."

"What else would an agent be carrying, captain? If you know what's good for you, you'll forward them instantly to General Johnston or to President Davis. Look at him," she demanded, nodding to Blane. "He can't complete his mission. Someone will have to replace him. Tell General

Johnston the reports are from Greenleaf. He'll understand and handle everything. If Corry was shot, they must be critical."

The surgeon returned and hastily listened to the heated conversation taking place. Naturally he took Shannon's word and side, and dismissed the guards. He alarmed her when he said Blane's wounds needed stitching immediately, but he had two emergency operations waiting. He told Shannon she would have to tend her brother. He quickly issued instructions, then left her alone with Blane.

She did not have time to consider refusing. She anesthetized her love, cleaned the two gaping wounds, then stitched them deftly. After bandaging his right arm and head, she went on to tend the lesser injuries. When she finished, she asked two other nurses to help her get Blane into a bed in the adjoining ward, a bed at the end of the row, where he would have privacy.

She remained on duty until nine, but Blane revealed no signs of regaining consciousness. She was afraid to leave his side, fearing he would awaken and expose both of them. She finally made herself go home to sleep until five. She was at his side again by six. She checked her handiwork and waited. He looked so pale and vulnerable, so compelling.

At eight, a patient called her from her vigil. Shannon spooned medicine between his fever-parched lips and changed his blood-soaked fillet. As she worked, she glanced at the last bunk to find Blane stirring and moaning. Several nurses, a doctor, Confederate wounded, and two soldiers were near him. Shannon rushed to his side and dropped to her knees beside his bunk, careful to face the wall. She began to speak to him as if to encourage his awakening, but it was merely to prevent Blane from revealing himself during his weakness and confusion.

"Corry? Corry, can you hear me? It's Shannon. You're hurt badly. Try not to move. You're going to be fine. I'll take care of you."

Blane forced his eyes open and looked at the vision of loveliness who was bending over him, who was touching him with fiery caresses. He tried to clear his head, but it throbbed and whirled. He hurt all over and felt weak as a newborn pup. "Shannon? Where am I? What happened?" He looked at her and listened to her words.

"Corbett Greenleaf, I could strangle you! You scared me half out of my mind," she scolded him as a frightened and adoring sister would do. "You almost got yourself killed. Soldiers found you wounded and brought you here to the hospital in Georgetown. This is no way to treat your baby sister. Now that Papa and Temple are gone, you're all I have. Whatever were you doing in this area? I thought President Davis had assigned you to scout Sherman's trail. You're lucky to be alive. They nearly mistook you for a Union spy."

The doctor joined them. "I know your brother frightened you badly, Shannon, but he is wounded. Let me have a look at him." As the surgeon eyed her work, he smiled and remarked, "I couldn't have done better myself. You should be glad your sister is working here. She's the one who stitched you up while I was unavailable. She must be awfully talented with sewing. Come along, Shannon, and let Corry sleep and get well. Your brother will be just fine in a week or so."

"Shannon?" Blane called out to halt her departure. "Can I have some water, sis? My throat feels like it's full of cotton."

"Is it all right, doctor?" she inquired.

"Fine, Shannon. When you finish, I need your help."

Shannon fetched fresh water and carried it to Blane. "What are you doing so far from home? Where is Hawke?" he probed with seeming casualness.

As before, Shannon talked to the top of his head, to the middle of his throat, or to his feather pillow, but never to his eyes. "I left Savannah right after Christmas to avoid those horrid Union soldiers and their villainous leader Sherman. Is that enough water, Corry?"

"What about Hawke, sis? Where is he?" Blane persisted.

"Hawke left before I did, to marry the woman he's loved for years. Stop worrying over my suitors, big brother; I tried to tell you he and I were just good friends. He's a brother to me. He left to marry with my blessing. Get some sleep. I'm sure the soldiers will want to discuss those maps and notes with you later. I advised them to ask President Davis to replace you on this mission. With luck, his best agent won't be incapacitated very long."

"I should have listened to your last scolding. That leaves only two marriages to concern me: yours and Ellie's."

"You're late again, Corry. I've taken care of both weddings."

"Both?" he asked in bewilderment.

"I'm sure Ellie Greenleaf is ecstatically happy right this minute. As for handling my wedding, big brother, it isn't necessary. I married Simon Travers on December 28." The gold band glittered in his eyes.

Blane tried to sit up and demand an explanation. Fury sent blood rushing into his pale face. "You can't . . . be serious," he argued.

"I know you and Papa didn't approve of Simon. But it's my life, Corry, and I did what I needed to do. It's too late to scold me or lock me in my room. Settle down before you tear out my perfect stitches."

For five long and difficult days, Shannon played the devoted sister and talented nurse to Blane Stevens. As his wounds healed and his strength returned, he watched her

506

like an eagle. When Sherman's march on Columbia began to flood the wards with more wounded, the doctor suggested that Shannon take her "brother" home with her to provide another bunk for a soldier who was in worse condition. Blane would not allow her to extricate herself from the delightful trap.

The moment they entered her dwelling and closed the door, Blane seized her and kissed her feverishly. He ignored her struggles and protests. "Lord, I've missed you, Blue Eyes. I was a damn fool not to stay here and fight for you. I'm getting you out of this marriage to Travers; then you're marrying me. Why didn't Jeremy tell me about you and Travers when I sent him to check on you? Just wait until I get my hands on his miserable throat. All this time I thought you were living with Hawke! That's the only reason I didn't come back for you. Why the hell did you marry Travers?"

"Get your filthy hands off me, you traitor; then I'll tell you." She waited for Blane to sit in a chair before he collapsed. Omitting only the reason that lived beneath the hand resting over her abdomen, Shannon coldly and candidly related her many motives. She left out none of Simon's crimes and black deeds. "When the war ends, so will this mock marriage. I was being courted by a lawyer in Boston, so I know exactly how to walk away from him legally and financially secure. All I have to do is stay out of his reach until then."

Blane pulled her down into his lap. "If you fight me, I could be injured. Just sit still and talk awhile. I've got to know the truth, Shannon. Did you ever love Hawke and plan to marry him?"

"I never considered marriage to Hawke, for any reason. And I never loved him in the way you're thinking. Hawke is a brother to me, Blane. He has been ever since we met when I was eleven and he was fourteen.

I have no aversion to his Comanche blood, but that is one of the reasons I never mentioned him to you. Anyway, I had no idea you knew about him. The other is for personal family reasons. If you hadn't deluded me or concealed those pictures, we could have dealt with Hawke and Corry that day I was shot or that day at Greenleaf. You have what you wanted. You obtained revenge for your family's suffering, and Ellie has married my brother by now."

"That isn't all I wanted. I wanted—and needed—*you*. Think back, woman. Can't you understand how I was led astray by coincidences and false evidence? I was hurt and angry and jealous that day. I didn't mean all those cruel things I said. While we were traveling together, I was trying to figure out how to help Ellie and not lose you doing it. When I learned about this Hawke, I wanted him out of your life and mind. With the problems of Hawke and Corry solved, we can rebuild our relationship. We'll get you free of Travers, then we'll marry."

Shannon used all of her strength to force Blane to release her. She looked down at him and responded, "You are a damn fool, Major Blane Stevens. By the way, I helped Eli escape your trap before I left Savannah. Too bad I was already bound to Simon before I discovered he was still alive. If not, I would be a captain's wife today."

"I'm not responsible for what happened to your home, Shannon. I saw the Blade's mark on the columns as I was riding away. I was too mad to deny it. And I wasn't trying to lay blame on you."

"I know. Simon did those things. That isn't my battle with you."

"If you hate me and crave vengeance, why did you save my life?"

Shannon looked him in the eye as she shockingly answered, "I don't hate you and I don't want revenge. If there's one lesson I learned well from you, Major

508

Stevens, it's the high price and pain of seeking misguided justice. But the most important thing you taught me was how to love passionately, blindly, completely, and eternally."

"What are you saying, Shannon?" he asked in astonishment.

"That I love you, but it's over forever between us."

Chapter Twenty-One

"How can it be over if you love me?" Blane reasoned frantically.

"Because I don't trust you and I don't like you. And without those feelings, love and passion aren't enough to sustain a relationship."

"Do you have any objection to my trying to earn them? You won't be sorry, love. For the first time since we met, there won't be any people or secrets between us. We've been through all kinds of situations and emotional turmoil. Those experiences have got to make us stronger and closer. Give it time; make sure. Am I so despicable and unworthy? Let me prove you're the one who's wrong this time."

Shannon looked him over speculatively and mischievously. Once they parted this next time, they might never meet again. Why not enjoy him? Why not let him soothe her loneliness, and her fears, and her desires? He owed her relief from all of the shame and agony he had brought into her life! How fiercely she craved him. Besides, she couldn't get more pregnant than she was. She couldn't be used or hurt again, for she knew what to expect and what not to expect from him. "If you think you can accomplish such a feat, you can try," she challenged flippantly. "As I recall, you are 'good company between the blankets.'" She saw him wince at his own words.

When Blane attempted to rise and go to her, she halted him. "Not tonight, Corry. We're both too weary and addled. Give it a little time and care. You don't mind if I call you Corry so I can get accustomed to it and won't slip in public?" she teased. "I'll put you to bed, then I'll cook dinner. You are injured, love."

For two days, Blane was on his best behavior. They chatted about anything but the war and their past troubles. They ate together, and they slept in the same bed. Blane helped her with the meals and dishes. He hauled in firewood and removed the ashes. He was amused each time she scolded him for those exertions. He teased her about her artistic "parlor stitches" on his temple and arm. She jested in return that he should be glad she had not embroidered her name on him and marked him as one of her many conquests. He didn't want to tell her he was healing rapidly and easily, for he didn't want her to evict him.

As they lay in bed one night, Blane turned toward Shannon and stroked her hair. He watched the flames from the hearth dance on her silky tresses. He noticed how the firelight settled and glowed softly on her skin. His finger moved slowly and sensuously over her lips. He wished he could look into those expressive blue eyes, but they were closed. "I know I promised to be patient, but I want to hold you. Do you realize how hard it is for me to keep my hands off you?"

Shannon opened her eyes and looked at him. "Do you realize it isn't necessary? I said I didn't trust you or like you, but I never said I didn't desire you. I don't want you to keep your hands off me. For your record, Major Stevens, I was a virgin that night at the Thomases; and no man has touched me except you."

Blane gazed into her eyes. "I'm sorry for what I said that day with Hawke. I was angry and jealous, but I shouldn't have lashed out at you with such cruel lies. I wanted you to share my pain because I held you responsible for inflicting it. I was a damn fool. I love you, Shannon, and I'm sorry I've given you reasons to doubt it."

"So am I, Blane. It was so good between us. Is it lost forever?"

His lips came down on hers and they kissed tentatively. He kissed her eyes, her chin, her nose, and then her greedy mouth. For a long time, all he did was hold her, kiss her, caress her, and study her.

Shannon wanted him and needed him, so she encouraged him to quicken his pace with her entreating hands and lips. When his mouth closed over her nipple, a shock of sensation surged through her body. Her breasts were so sensitive to his actions. She tingled and warmed. It felt so wonderful to have his hands leisurely wandering over her satiny flesh. She closed her eyes and opened her senses to those blissful feelings.

Blane deftly heightened her passion until she was aquiver with urgency. He entered her body with skill and tenderness. He lovingly labored until she was susceptible to every movement and touch. He knew how much pleasure and rapturous torment he was giving to her. It thrilled him, pleased him, and stimulated him. When he carried her to the edge of sensual ecstasy, he drove powerfully and talentedly to send her tumbling madly and wildly over its exquisite precipice.

After he had sated her, she was breathless and weak. She grinned at him and nibbled at his lips. "That was a marvelous peace token, Major Stevens. Perhaps that's how I'll charge you every day for room and board—unless it proves too much for a wounded male."

"That's the best medicine and treatment I've had so

far, Nurse Greenleaf. If I get weak from overwork, you can carry out my stirring task. We do have a delightful partnership," he jested roguishly.

The following day, Shannon found herself eager to get home. She laughed merrily when she arrived to find her dinner prepared. "I knew you would be tired, sis, so I'm earning my keep."

"That isn't how I requested payment, Major Stevens."

Blane chuckled. "You misunderstand, Blue Eyes. I have dinner ready so we'll have more time and energy to work off my debt."

She returned his kiss and hug. "I always suspected you were very crafty and greedy; now I'm convinced," she retorted coyly.

They had made love twice before Blane told her reluctantly, "I have to leave for awhile, Shannon. Will you be all right?"

In a mellow tone, she replied, "I was fine before your sudden arrival, and I'll be fine after your departure. I had good training in self-reliance from my old partner. You've forgotten, I'm a temptress of destiny. I plan to force Fate to give me my due. Are you sure you're up to traveling, Blane? That head and arm haven't healed yet."

"I have a few matters to settle, then I'll return."

"I don't think you should return. I don't want Simon discovering our affair and using it against me during the divorce. I have it all planned, and I don't want you or anyone to spoil it. I have to be in control of the charges, not him. It's been marvelous having these stolen days with you, Blane. We've made peace. Why not leave it like that for now?" She waited tensely for his response.

"Does the money mean that much to you, Shannon?"

"It isn't *the* money, Blane; it's *my* money—Greenleaf money. Would you allow an enemy to rob you and your family? It has to do with justice and principals. Besides, you're forgetting a very vital point. Your sister is a

513

Greenleaf by now, so our estate is partly your nephew's. Would you want Simon to steal little Corry's inheritance?''

''He's dangerous, Shannon. I don't like the idea of your challenging him alone. Don't do anything rash until I'm around to help you.''

''This time, the law will side with me against him. I have plenty of valid charges for my petition, not the least of which are 'Cruelty' and 'Fraud' and 'Wasting property' and 'Attempt on petitioner's life'. If I'm lucky, I can find a way to prove 'Partner is fugitive from justice.' If necessary, I'll lie my head off. Any of those charges are grounds for divorce and obtaining a third to a half of his holdings. Don't intrude. Remember our relationship is physical, nothing more.''

''Maybe for you, Blue Eyes, but not for me. I love you, and I'm going to win you back.''

After making torrid love to her, Shannon watched Blane mount Dan and ride away. She couldn't help but wonder what he would have said and done if she had asked him not to leave, if she had begged him to stay. But she was determined to teach him to be honest and considerate. She had to let him see what it was like to have her, and to lose her. She had to know if she could trust him, depend on him, win him completely. She had to make certain she had no doubts that his past mistakes and cruelties had been unintentional or uncontrollable. She had to make sure that he had no doubts or suspicions about her.

On February seventeenth, Sherman's men conquered and razed Columbia. On Saturday the eighteenth, Charleston surrendered to the Union, an action that aided her survival. That same day, Shannon packed and left Georgetown with the Rebel troops who were heading by train to defend Wilmington, the last supply port. On Tuesday, Shannon was sitting on the sofa in Sarah Jane Sinclair's parlor and having tea.

Shannon told the woman what destruction she had found at home. She asked about Jeremy and their holidays together. Shannon listened as the woman reluctantly confessed her switch in fealty, due to Jeremy's influence and love. Shannon smiled empathetically as she explained her own divided loyalties. When Sarah Jane asked about the wedding band, Shannon exposed her clever scheme without shame or guilt.

"Can you obtain a divorce and settlement so easily?"

"I know the law, Sarah Jane. You mustn't worry about me."

"But that awful man is searching for you. He's been here twice. I wouldn't be surprised if he's offered a reward for you."

"He won't find me or harm me. Where is Molly?" she asked worriedly, knowing that the hateful witch would betray her at the first opportunity.

"She ran off to England with a sea captain. He was more like a pirate, if you ask me. That sister of mine is a fool."

Once more, Shannon found herself living in the lovely suite on the third floor. There wasn't time for her to look for work. On Wednesday, under the command of Union general Schofield, Wilmington peacefully surrendered to Generals Cox and Terry. As if by magic, Jeremy Steele arrived to protect his love. The hotel was crowded with Union officers, and Shannon volunteered to help her friend with the chores.

Meanwhile, in South Carolina, Sherman was viciously carving his way through the state as he headed toward Fayetteville. Reports were that he was chasing Johnston with a wild-eyed thirst for the Rebel's blood. And in

Virginia, Sheridan and Grant were attempting to snare Lee between them.

Jeremy took possession of Molly's suite of rooms on the first floor, a suite that adjoined Sarah Jane's. From the beginning, Jeremy informed the arriving conquerors of his identity and Union loyalty. As his fiancée, Sarah Jane, as well as her hotel, were spared any trouble. As for Shannon, she performed kitchen tasks to keep busy and out of sight.

For eleven days, the two women and Jeremy ran the hotel without problems. Shannon was continually aware of how closely and intently Blane's friend observed her. One day he made her so edgy with his stare and coldness that she demanded tersely, "Why do you dislike me, Jeremy? Why did you tell Blane all those lies about me?"

"Were they lies, Mrs. Travers? Do you really think you're good enough for Major Stevens?" he asked skeptically.

Shannon was stunned by his sharpness and words. "You sent that letter to me, didn't you? You wanted to drive me away from him. Why? What have I done to you? I know Sarah Jane told you why I married Simon. What right do you have to interfere in the lives of others?"

"Blane is my friend. When I saw how you were blinding him, I had to save him from you. You aren't fit to come near him."

"You planted the false evidence," she accused. "You wanted them to arrest me and execute me. How could you kill innocent people to hurt me?"

"I ain't done nothing to you but send that letter and tell Blane you was living with that Comanche. I knew that would end your spell, faster than telling him about you and Eli or you and that Travers."

"You malicious bastard! That isn't true. Eli is my friend and Simon is my bitter enemy! I love Blane Stevens, you fool!"

516

"Then why did you whore to Travers to get your way? No good woman would sleep with a snake for money and revenge. Why should the Flame be scared of false evidence, unless she's guilty? If you loved Blane and you was a real patriot and agent, you would have asked for Union help in Savannah. I know about tempting witches like you."

"How dare you," she shrieked contemptuously. "You're vile, Jeremy Steele. You don't deserve a woman like Sarah Jane or a friend like Blane. I've never been touched by any man but Blane. If you hadn't been creating these vicious charges against me and pouring them into his head, we would be married today. If you were such a damn good agent, you'd know I'm innocent."

"An innocent woman doesn't marry the man who supposedly tricked her and stole her money and burned her home."

"That's enough, Jeremy," Blane warned from the doorway. "She had no choice when I deserted her and left her at his mercy. I wish you hadn't interfered, because you're mistaken about her."

Shannon glanced beyond Jeremy to settle her burning gaze on the handsome man who was staring at her in such a curious manner. Did he believe what he had said? Or was it a ruse to disarm her?

"Don't be fooled by this tempting witch, Blane," he warned.

"Oh, she's fooled me all right, but not how you think." Blane purposefully strolled forward. He halted near Shannon and examined her with his keen gaze. "Why didn't you wait? I went to Georgetown looking for you, then I searched Charleston. I was just about to head for Savannah when a captive mentioned the ravishing redhead who had tended his wounds before heading to Wilmington. I found Corry."

Shannon paled and trembled as she witnessed his

517

accusatory expression and mood. She reached for the cabinet to steady herself. "You didn't . . ." She couldn't complete the terrifying question.

Blane forcefully drilled his gaze into hers. "You deceived me, woman. Isn't it time for the truth—every word of it?"

Jeremy stated, "I told you she was lying about that half-breed."

Blane watched the effect of his words on her. "Not lying, Jeremy, just keeping silent because she is stubborn and had been hurt. She never loved him or planned to marry him, because Hawke is her half brother," the angry Texan disclosed. "That's who you sent to marry Ellie, isn't it? Like you said, I was chasing the wrong man, or rather the wrong brother. Why didn't you tell me about Hawke in Savannah? How could you let me ride off thinking and feeling like that? Why didn't you explain in Georgetown? You knew I was still seeking the wrong man. Lord, Shannon, I could have slain Corry by mistake. All this time you knew you were letting my sister marry . . ."

Shannon went straight and stiff as she cut off the words she feared were coming forth, "Silence! He's my brother. Don't you dare call him names! He loves Ellie and she loves him. Stay out of it."

He insisted on finishing his statement. ". . . Marry the right man. I should have guessed the truth when I saw those pictures. Thank heavens Corry has chestnut hair and blue eyes. Ellie is a blue-eyed blonde. They couldn't possibly have a son with midnight hair and eyes who favors Hawke. Now I know why I found his looks disturbing. Why did you tell me Corry had gone to Texas to marry her?"

"I didn't. I said she was marrying a Greenleaf, the man she loved, the father of her child. That's Hawke Greenleaf." She smugly related how she and Hawke had figured out the truth and how he had left to marry Ellie. She didn't care if Jeremy was hearing Ellie's secrets. She told Blane about the romance between Hawke and Ellie and the reasons for Hawke's ruse, and why the truth about him had been withheld from Ellie and Blane. She told Blane that Ellie was sending him a letter of explanation via Lincoln, stating it was Ellie's right and duty to clear up this torturous misunderstanding.

"Your family sent their threatening letters to the wrong man; that's why Corry claimed innocence and refused to wed her. Or perhaps my father dealt dishonestly with Ellie's claims. He's dead, so we'll never know what he did or why. After we went to Boston, Papa disowned Hawke and sent him away for refusing to fight for the Union. Everyone involved has suffered enough. Please let Hawke and Ellie be happy together. He's bringing her to live with us, so you won't have to see him again. He can't help being part Comanche, just as he can't help what happened years ago with your sister."

"If Ellie and Hawke want each other, that's fine with me. Since he's your brother, he's got to be special. But you should have been honest in Georgetown. I thought Corry was with Ellie. When I confronted him, I was shocked and infuriated."

"You instantly assumed I had lied to you! That should teach you not to jump to hasty conclusions on crucial matters. Don't you see, Blane? How could I tell you about Hawke, knowing how you feel about Comanches? I wanted you to hear about their love and happiness from Ellie; then maybe you wouldn't mind their marriage. And I wanted you to deal with your doubts about me and him while you still viewed him as a rival. I wanted you to realize you're the only man I love and want, before I told you why Hawke was no threat to us. I wanted to see if you could love me and trust me on sheer faith. Did you hurt Corry? Where is he? How is he?" she pressed eagerly.

"Calm down, Blue Eyes. I only thought you were trying to protect him until we could settle matters. He's been with the Union Navy for the past seventeen months. His ship was docked at Charleston. We actually ran into each other. I recognized him instantly. Needless to say, we uncovered many truths during our quarrel. As soon as I made my charges, Corry started guessing the truth."

Blane chuckled. "Since keen intelligence runs in your family, Corry and I figured you and Hawke had also solved this mystery. But Corry knew something you didn't: he knew that Hawke loved Ellie and had returned to Texas to find her when Corry went off to war. It was clear to me he didn't know about the letters, just as Hawke didn't know where to seek Ellie. I was hoping you had supplied that information. I can understand why you kept silent, and I hope you can see why I did the same about chasing Corry. If I didn't know before Georgetown that you loved me and could be trusted, I sure learned my lesson there. Corry's safe and healthy. I didn't tell him about your troubles with Simon Travers. I thought you would prefer to explain them."

Shannon stated softly, "That was considerate and compassionate of you. You're sure he was all right? How long will he be in port?"

"He sailed before I left town. He said not to expect to see him before the war is settled. I also didn't tell him about your home. He can't do anything at sea but worry. I promised I would locate you so we could settle our differences and get married. He was most agreeable about me and my sister joining his family."

She shook her head sadly. "Just like that—forget and forgive the past? Heavens, Blane! How can I marry you when you're always ready to doubt me at the slightest provocation? What if Hawke hadn't been my brother or Corry had been guilty? Would you be here now? Why can't you have faith in me? When have I lied to you? When have I harmed you? I even told you that Hawke was a brother to me."

"Listen to me, woman. We've both been stupid and impulsive. You know perfectly well you implied the truth all the time, but you didn't speak it clearly and openly. How was I to know, Shannon. I admit I've been spiteful and mean at times. I'm sorry. I acted out of jealousy and torment. You and Ellie and this war have made me act crazy. The truth is out. It won't happen again. I swear it, Shannon."

"No more twisted code of honor and justice? No more making me suffer for the sins of others? No more suspicions and doubts and charges?"

"I'm not the only one guilty of those things, Shannon," he replied tenderly, rebukingly. "You have to accept some of the blame. We can't change our past actions, but we can have something special if you're willing to help me build it. We're a perfect pair, Blue Eyes."

"It's so hard to know what to do. I'm so afraid to trust you again," she confessed hoarsely. "I know about so many things you've done, like those two betrayals of Eli. How can I be sure you aren't still deluding me and using me? You said and did such awful things."

"I know I hurt you, Shannon. All I ask is another chance."

There was one way to test his love and faith. She looked into his eyes and inquired gravely, "If I told you I was pregnant, would you ask me who the father was? Would you have any doubt it was you?"

His heart thudded wildly and joyfully at her words. He grinned as he recalled mentally plotting to ensnare her with a child. Another thought shot into his head. Women had died in childbirth, including Shannon's mother. Could a daughter inherit such a condition? The smile faded as worry filled him. "Are you pregnant, Shannon?"

"You didn't answer me, Blane," she persisted.

His gaze shifted over her supple figure. "Surely you wouldn't have married Simon Travers while carrying my child? You couldn't possibly give our son that bastard's name."

"Not for any reason, Blane?" she probed. "Not even to protect your child after you deserted his mother? Not even to give him a name other than bastard? Not even when you couldn't be located to marry her? Not even for money to ensure his survival? Not even to destroy false evidence against his mother so he wouldn't be born in prison or die before he left his mother's body? Not even to reclaim his rightful maternal heritage? Not even because you hurt and shamed his mother so deeply that she couldn't tell you about him? Not even because she feared you wouldn't believe her, if she could find you?"

Blane tenderly caressed her damp cheek. "She would be justified in doing so, even if for only one of those reasons. I have no doubts, Blue Eyes. But you've made a terrible mistake. By marrying Simon, you've given him a claim on our child. Do you realize the law will be on his side? If he learns the truth, he'll use our child to hold you or to punish you."

Shannon's legs went weak and tremors swept through her. She had not taken her pregnancy into consideration when planning her divorce. Could Simon lay claim to her child? A pregnancy could have a dire effect on her charges. "I was planning to end the marriage before my condition became obvious. I was hoping to find you and marry you before the baby was born. I want your son to have your name. So much had happened during those few days: seeing Greenleaf destroyed, finding Hawke there, enduring that . . . situation with you in Charleston and at home, learning all about Ellie and Corry and Hawke, then Simon appearing with his blackmail

522

scheme. I was alone. I was so tired and hurt and confused. It all started while I was waiting for you in Sherman's office."

"What do you mean?" Blane asked, holding her tenderly.

She told him about the soldiers' enlightening conversations. "I was mad at you. I was hurt. I wasn't feeling well. That's when I realized I was pregnant. Maybe that's why I was so jittery. I had to get out of that vile beast's office. Mister Barnes took me home, and you know what I saw and endured there. What have I done?"

"Relax, love. I'll think of something. Until we can get you free of Simon, you'll have to stay hidden and keep the baby a secret." He glanced at Jeremy and asked, "Can I depend on you for help and loyalty? If you hadn't interfered, this might not be happening."

Without thinking, she unselfishly chided, "Don't blame him. He was only trying to help you. In view of all the false evidence Simon created, it's no wonder he didn't like me or trust me. We have enough trouble without you two splitting your friendship over me."

Blane speculated sullenly, "Lord, Jeremy, don't you realize the truth? Look at Shannon. Who are you really seeing and punishing?"

He looked at Shannon's hair and eyes and complexion and size. Shock registered on the man's face. "God, forgive me . . ."

"It's Shannon you've wronged, Jeremy. I should have guessed the trouble before now. She isn't anything like Cassandra."

Jeremy's remorse couldn't be denied. "I'm sorry, Shannon."

Blane stayed with Shannon for eight days. They talked and loved and made plans for their future. He was

523

afraid to leave her, even under Jeremy's protection. On March 5, Sarah Jane and Jeremy were married. Shannon was moved into Molly's old suite of rooms, which afforded secrecy of location and quicker aid from her two friends. As Blane checked news of the events occuring in the South each day, he began to realize it was selfish and wrong of him to be lazing around with his love.

Confederate General Johnston arrived in Raleigh and was greeted jovially by Governor Vance and his staff. General Schofield's Union troops were making a move on Goldsboro, having taken New Bern. On the sixth, General Bragg alerted Johnston to the Federal attack planned on Kinston. The following day, the Union Army was dealt a stunning defeat. Unfortunately Sherman was on the move . . .

Blane received orders from General Grant to resume his duties. He was relieved when Shannon did not argue or plead with him. During the last two hours they spent together, they did nothing but lie snuggled together, silently enduring their thoughts of this torturous separation. He made her promise she would remain inside Molly's suite until he came back for her.

During Blane's absence, Shannon read every printed word that Jeremy could provide for her. This war was such a tragedy, she thought sadly as she scanned the newspaper accounts one afternoon. It should never have begun! Most of the Southern states had not intended to secede. If only President Lincoln had not illegally instigated hostilities against certain states, others would not have been forced or compelled to go to the aid of their "Southern brethren." The North had actually invaded the South and had inspired this bloody conflict, she realized. Lincoln himself had admitted in July of '61 that "except perhaps South Carolina, a majority of the people were for the Union." All of this for male honor and pride?

General Johnston claimed a defense post at Smithfield, between Raleigh and Goldsboro, a hundred miles from Wilmington. From there, he could wait for Sherman or move to intercept him. When news arrived of Sherman's march toward Goldsboro, the Rebel forces went into action. Hoke's Division, Stewart's command, Bragg's force, Hampton's units, Hardee's troops, Kirkland's Brigade, the Junior Reserves, and other regiments prepared to surprise, confront, and defeat General Sherman at Bentonville on March 19. It was an awesome and costly battle for the Union. The Rebel strategy was cunning, but a lack of fighting men and supplies eventually forced their retreat. It was a glorious mark on Johnston's record, though he lost the town.

Sherman joined Schofield in Goldsboro, where incidents of looting and plundering and burning and slaying of men became common news. It seemed that Georgia, South Carolina, the lower half of North Carolina, and Tennessee were conquered territory. That left the upper section of North Carolina and most of Virginia to be defeated by the Union forces.

On March 23, Captain Elisha Carter sailed into the port near Wilmington, flying a Union flag. After meeting with Jeremy, the two men visited Shannon with dire news.

"Are you sure?" she probed frantically.

"He's on his way here with five men, Shannon," Eli told her. "If you don't come with me, you know what he'll do. He must have plenty of money and power, because he persuaded the soldiers to search Denton's home from top to bottom and his ship from stem to stern. It's the third time he's been to Charleston seeking you. I had one of my crewmen watch him. As soon as Simon headed this way, I came to make sure you weren't here. You can't remain in Wilmington. He'll find you."

"He has no legal right to claim me," she argued.

"If he didn't, the authorities wouldn't be helping him."

Jeremy advised, "Go with him, Shannon. I'll try to locate Blane and send him to help you. Travers is dangerous, and crazy."

"But I have you and Eli to defend me," she protested. "What can we do if the law insists you leave with him?"

"Blane will be furious if I run off with you, Eli."

"Look," Elisha reasoned, "Jeremy has told me you two are in love and planning to marry. I'm not trying to steal you from him—not that I wouldn't give anything to have you for myself. I only want to protect you. I owe you, Shannon, for helping me escape in Savannah and for misjudging you. Jeremy can tell Blane where you are. Besides, Matti would love to see you and take care of you."

In three days, Shannon was sitting in Denton's parlor. All three men had agreed this would be the last place Simon would look for her. The weather was improving and warming. Nature was busy making her changes. Shannon's tummy was beginning to round slightly and the waists of her clothes were getting snug. By her best calculations, she was a few days over four months pregnant. She prayed this harrowing ordeal with Simon would end soon and she could begin her life with Blane, before anyone doubted the child's paternity.

Mattilu Walker had been overjoyed to see Shannon. The first day, the two women had spent hours exchanging stories and making plans. Matti was thrilled by "the little bun" that Shannon was "warming." She insisted on waiting upon the laughing redhead who vowed she was in excellent health. For days, Matti worked on adjusting Shannon's garments and talked of her newly found sweetheart, smiling happily as she did so. Clearly Matti was not ready to leave Charleston

526

and Clem.

Shannon made certain no one caught even a glimpse of her at a window. If Denton went out at night, the apartment remained dark, for Matti had a small cottage on a dirt lane nearby. Shannon cautioned the adoring Denton not to buy anything unusual and warned Eli not to visit too often. Elisha and his brother took daring steps to prevent any hint of Shannon's presence. While Shannon concealed herself behind a sofa, Denton "entertained" a female companion until long after midnight. Another night, the two brothers hosted a lengthy card game while Shannon hid under Denton's bed. When and if those visitors were questioned and bribed, none would report a guest at Denton Carter's.

The end of March found President Lincoln visiting with General Grant at City Point and planning the final strategies. It was learned that General Sherman had met and talked with the two leaders on March 27. On the twenty-ninth, General Lee asked for supplies to be sent to Amelia Court House, as he could no longer battle Grant for the control of Petersburg and Richmond. Johnston was leading Sherman a vexing chase in North Carolina. On the thirty-first, the last Confederate victory in Virginia was enjoyed at Chamberlain's Run under Barringer.

April arrived with grim defeats for the Confederacy. The war raged fiercely in Virginia, the last Rebel stronghold. Grant and Sheridan tightened their noose around General Lee and that area. The battle at Five Forks cost Lee a third of his army. On April 2, Petersburg fell to Union forces. On April 3, Richmond—capitol of the Confederacy—was conquered and looted and burned. Grant pursued Lee across the state, while Sherman chased the elusive Johnston. With the capitol lost and all supply lines severed, the Confederacy was on the brink of total ruin. Rebel soldiers now functioned on

527

sheer grit and pride.

Amidst these struggles and agonies, Major Blane Stevens worked as an advance scout for General Grant. It had been over three weeks since he had left Shannon in Jeremy Steele's care. To avoid making a lethal slip, he had forced his wits and concentration to stay clear and sharp, for the end of the war was near and it would herald the beginning of his life with Shannon. When a medical officer removed his stitches, the man praised the fine surgeon whose work barely showed. In time, Blane would have nothing more than two slender white scars to remind him of that fateful incident.

After Blane reported Lee's reason to rush to Amelia, he asked Grant if he could send a message to his wife in Wilmington. He was concerned at being unable to contact his love and his friend. He wanted to make certain Shannon was healthy and safe. Grant gave him permission to send word to an officer there, who in turn was to deliver his message. As the telegram was passed from station to station toward his beloved, he was unwittingly supplying a clue to her location.

On Monday, April 3, it was Mattilu who carelessly exposed Shannon's current location to Simon's human watchdog. Excited about the baby, she had shopped for cloth and yarn and ribbon to begin making its tiny garments. Clearly a Negro servant would have no purpose or money for such items, and certainly a bachelor would not. Fortunately, Elisha's guard on Denton's home noticed the man who had followed Matti and then had hurried to send a telegram to Simon Travers in Savannah.

Mattilu wept at her foolish error, which also alerted the two seamen to Shannon's secret. On Tuesday, Elisha paid Mattilu and Clem to disable Simon's cohort while he slipped Shannon aboard another ship. He also told Matti to claim she was making the garments for Sarah Jane Steele, who would be warned to corroborate his story. Thirteen days after leaving Wilmington, Shannon was at sea again.

It had been decided by Elisha that the safest place for Shannon was in Norfolk with his parents. Surely Simon Travers would never think to go there! To avoid suspicion, Elisha sent her with Captain Neil Ruffin of the *Siren's Song.* Elisha would sail between Wilmington and Charleston, making sure he was in full view of witnesses.

Elisha's clever scheme was working perfectly. He had related the details to Jeremy and Sarah Jane, so they could tell Blane when he returned. Until it was safe, Shannon would live with the Carters. Her location could not be mentioned to anyone or written anywhere. No one was to be trusted with news that could endanger her life.

On the fifth, Lee arrived at Amelia Court House to learn that there were no critical supplies awaiting him and that Grant was eating his dust.

In Charleston on the sixth, nothing Simon's men did to Mattilu and Clem obtained a single clue to Shannon's whereabouts. There was no evidence to tie those two blacks to his injured spy, and he couldn't be convinced they were lying. He therefore assumed that neither Denton nor Elisha Carter was hiding Shannon. Evidently his henchmen had made a reasonable mistake.

That same day the telegram from Blane was intercepted by a greedy man who had been hired to do exactly what he did—inform Simon Travers of who might have information that could lead him to his missing wife. Simon was about to give up his search when the message arrived from Wilmington, via Savannah. Immediately Simon headed there. The villain he left behind to slay Matti and Clem was killed by Elisha's man before carrying out his orders. As prearranged, Elisha sent a coded telegram to warn Jeremy of Simon's impending approach and to make certain they had their stories straight.

Upon his arrival on Friday, Simon illegally purchased the two stolen telegrams for a nice sum in gold coins. He grinned evilly at the offensive thief, knowing his men would reclaim the coins within a few minutes and rid him of this witness. Simon's satanic smile broadened, for he saw that both telegrams were from men in love with Shannon and both were addressed to their mutual friend, Jeremy Steele . . .

Chapter Twenty-Two

On April 7, the persistent Union forces, who had been held in check briefly and skillfully, pressed forward into the confusion and skirmishes at Sayler's Creek. After retreating once more, the Rebels headed for Farmville, where Shannon had fallen into the evil grasp of Major Benjamin Clifford the September before. Lee knew the fate of the Confederacy would soon be decided, for he was down to ten thousand soldiers who were exhausted and dejected and lacked weapons and supplies.

On April 9 at Appomattox, General Lee admitted defeat and surrendered to General Grant. Apprehension and uncertainty hung heavily in the stillness, a stillness that resulted from the cessation of fighting and talking. To the surprise of the conquered men, Grant gave the astounding order that the Confederate soldiers be given food and a pardon and a dismissal. Another stab at peace was made when the honorable victor allowed the ex-Rebels to leave with their mounts and weapons, for he knew such items would be needed to supply game and to plant new crops.

Blane witnessed this meeting between two great men. Soon, all fighting would cease, and the Union would rebuild itself. Blane slyly requested that he be sent to

531

North Carolina to see if he might assist Sherman with clearing away the remaining Rebels in that state. Such an assignment would provide the opportunity for a quick departure from Virginia and the chance to see his love, if only for a few hours. He and Dan were permitted to ride the train to speed his arrival and much-needed assistance. Along the way, Blane made plans to expose the villainous Travers and to free Shannon.

At sea, a crippled *Siren's Song* was slowly making her way toward the port near Wilmington. A violent storm had broken one mast and had cracked another. Because Wilmington was the closest place available for repairs, Captain Neil Ruffin had ordered his disabled ship and loyal crew to head there. With calm breezes and lost sails, the voyage would take several days. And it was during those sluggish moments that the crafty Captain Ruffin conceived a possible solution to Shannon's dilemma. He realized that its success would require an illegal deception and perfect timing . . .

In Wilmington, Simon was biding his time until the Union soldiers left town to aid Sherman's assault on Johnston. Too many officers were staying at the Sinclairs' hotel, soldiers who might be persuaded to side with the ravishing Flame or Major Blane Stevens. Now that he had discovered a trail to his traitorous wife, he found the patience to wait and to plot. After all, Simon mused, anticipation and clever planning were almost as stimulating as success.

On Monday, April 10, the revelation of Lee's surrender and Johnston's continued resistance spurred most of the local troops into action. On the thirteenth, the Union regiments headed for Battle Ridge and

Sherman's command. It was the moment Simon Travers had dreamed of for days. At last, he would locate Shannon. Then he would make her and all of her helpers pay dearly for their treacheries!

Elisha and Denton Carter reached Wilmington in time to rescue Sarah Jane and Jeremy Steele from Simon's horrid plan for their deaths. Upon their arrival, the Carters had been alerted to something suspicious when they could not locate their friends in the hotel, and the hired servants seemed confused by the couple's unannounced absence. The woodcutter told of seeing five men entering the hotel around noon and seeing three of them departing fifteen minutes later. The two brothers sensed danger and trouble. Elisha and Denton sneaked into an unlocked window of the Steele's suit and killed Simon's cohorts as the two villains struggled to strip and violate Sarah Jane. They found that Jeremy had been beaten during his interrogation by Simon, for he had tried to remain silent.

The four prayed for a miracle, for Jeremy had betrayed Shannon's new hiding place to keep Simon's men from beating and raping his wife. The confession had been in vain, for Simon had announced his intention of having them tortured and slain despite Jeremy's cooperation. The two brothers listened in horror as the rescued couple described their terrifying experience and expressed fear over Shannon's peril.

Jeremy told how Simon's sadistic evil had exposed itself when he ordered two of his men to remain behind to rape Sarah Jane time and time again and to force Jeremy to watch every minute of her shame and abuse. Jeremy said the wicked man had laughed satanically as he had issued his final order before leaving. He had told his men, "When you run out of strength or get bored with her, slice their throats or whatever. Just don't leave them alive. I'll meet you back in Savannah within two weeks." With this, he had calmly departed to head for Norfolk. Jeremy couldn't thank the brothers enough for saving their lives and for preventing Sarah Jane's degrading violation.

The authorities in Washington and Norfolk were immediately informed of this crime and the one about to take place. The two brothers quickly and fearfully raced off in pursuit of Simon and his cutthroats, not wanting to chance the possibility of the villains getting through to their parents and Shannon.

Sherman entered Raleigh that same day. Confederate Generals Johnston and Hardee convened at Hillsboro to decide their imminent course of action in order to continue their resistance.

On the morning of April 14, Blane Stevens reached Wilmington to make his terrifying discoveries. Before he could gather supplies to head after his love and her satanic enemy, Captain Neil Ruffin arrived to halt his departure and to provide the scheme that would foil Simon permanently.

Ruffin escorted Blane to his ship and quarters and into the arms of Shannon. He explained his daring, ingenious solution to the startled Texan. Then he handed Blane a pen and showed him where to sign the paper and page, praising Fate for leaving two lines blank on that vital day. There was no danger of discovery, for it could be proven that all three people involved had been in Wilmington on a particular winter day. For the lovers' benefit, he hurriedly performed a wedding ceremony. When Shannon and Blane left the *Siren's Song* shortly thereafter, they were secure in the knowledge that the ship's log and the document in Blane's grasp stated that on November

22, 1864—the night on which Shannon had conceived their child—on this ship and by this captain, Major Blane Stevens and Shannon Greenleaf were married.

At the hotel, Blane and Shannon explained Ruffin's cunning ploy to Jeremy and Sarah Jane. "All of the documents declare that Shannon and I got married that day. All we have to do now is have her bigamous marriage to Simon nullified. Considering all of his crimes, it should be simple to prove he forced Shannon to marry him. We'll say he told her I was dead and that she was free to marry him. Naturally he was threatening to kill all of her friends and two brothers if she didn't obey him. We'll use the actual account of how she fled him, then found me alive in Georgetown. All of you were helping me hide and protect her until she and I could straighten out this mess. Now that the war's at an end, President Lincoln can help."

Shannon's eyes glowed as they settled on her love. "Simon and I were never really married. But Captain Ruffin did marry Blane and I today. Are you sure you two are all right? I'm sorry for getting you both into danger. You can see why I was too scared not to marry him in Savannah, and too smart to hang around afterward."

While Shannon and Blane were making passionate love in the Wilmington hotel on the night of April 14, they were unaware that President Abraham Lincoln was being assassinated by actor and Southern partisan John Wilkes Booth during a play at Ford's Theatre in Washington. Nor were they aware that it would no longer be necessary to extricate Shannon from Simon Travers's evil grasp. By midnight, the malevolent Travers was dead at the hands of Elisha and Denton Carter. It would now

535

be a simple matter to expose Simon's fraudulent claims on Greenleaf holdings, to have such holdings returned to their rightful owners, and to prove blackmail, which would nullify Shannon's marriage to him.

Gradually all Confederate uprisings were quelled. On April 26, General Joseph Johnston capitulated to General William Sherman at Durham Station. On May 4, General Richard Taylor, commander of the Mississippi and Alabama forces, surrendered to General Edward Canby. President Jefferson Davis was captured on May 10 at Irvinsville, Georgia. The charismatic man, whose fealty, enthusiasm, confidence, energy, and courage had given the Confederacy theirs, would be imprisoned at Fortress Monroe in Virginia until 1867. On May 26, the Confederate forces in Texas under General Kirby-Smith yielded peacefully to Union forces. In the South, it was time for recovery and reconstruction.

The first of June found the remaining Greenleaf heirs camped on the site of their devastated property, planning and rebuilding the lovely house. Corry had returned home and was seeing Temple's ex-fiancée, Clarissa Jamison. Hawke was there with his wife, Ellie Stevens Greenleaf, and their energetic and inquisitive four-year-old son.

As warm rain continued to fall and impede the rebirth of Greenleaf, Shannon and Blane Stevens lay on a thick bedroll in their large tent, which had been purposely situated at a distance that would allow privacy. She was lying on her back and gazing into her husband's sparkling hazel eyes. Blane was resting on his left side with his chin proped upon his left hand. His right hand was lovingly and gently stroking Shannon's protruding abdomen. It halted briefly when the baby shifted. A grin swept over his face at the slight movement. Awe, peace, and joy mingled to compose a heart-fluttering expression on his face.

Blane's mellow gaze lifted from his right hand to Shannon's face. She smiled at him and reached up to caress his cheek. "I think he's going to have as much vitality as his father. With luck, he'll be as handsome."

"What if he is a she, and she becomes a headstrong temptress like you? I'll have to remember never to try to control this tiny vixen's destiny. I had a hell of a time doing so with her mother. Lord, spare me from the trials of handling two ravishing and willful redheads at the same time," he murmured, passing his tongue over her lips as he deftly unbuttoned her cotton dress. His hand slipped inside the material to allow his fingers to playfully tease a receptive peak. His mouth sealed over hers in a kiss of contentment that swiftly changed to hunger.

After his pervasive kiss, Shannon replied merrily, "I can think of something better for you to handle, Major Stevens."

As Blane's lips replaced his hand at her breast, he speculated mischievously, "Better than this, my flaming enchantress?" His hand slid down her quivering body, up her silky thigh, and into a fuzzy paradise as he added roguishly, "Or better than this, Shannon Stevens?"

She closed her eyes and sighed contentedly as she enjoyed his blissful ministrations. "That's exactly what I had in mind, my cunning Blade." Never had she been happier than here with the man who had compelled her to tempt all dangers and demons to share his destiny.

Author's Note

For the history buffs who might question certain facts
and dates in this book, I would like to explain my
difficulty in locating matching sources. Although I used
at least seven history books and many other historical
research materials, I was amazed and distressed by the
many discrepancies I discovered—my first since becoming a historical romance writer. When I found a
conflicting fact or date, I checked another book. During
one such incident, I found that two books were in
agreement on a date, while two others agreed on a
different date. When a fifth book concurred with the
second set, I decided to use that date and search no
further. Among the discrepancies was the conflicting
date of Lee's surrender to Grant at Appomattox. Because
I had been taught that April 9—not April 6—was the day
of the actual surrender, I used that date in my novel. I
found Johnston's surrender to Sherman listed as April
18 and April 26 in two different places! I was vexed to
find the claim that Wilmington never fell to the Union
Army, when other sources listed its capitulation as
having taken place on February 22, 1865. I found that
Charleston yielded on February 17 and February 18, and
to Sherman's troops, who were razing Columbia on

February 17—110 miles away. The April 7, 1865 battle took place at "Saylers Creek" or "Saylors Creek" or "Sailors Creek"! Sources also seemed to vary in consistency by dates written and dates published; the older the work and the closer to the war, the more biased the writer's opinion and material. I do wish to say that I made every effort to check and recheck historical material used in this novel.

If you are missing any previous Janelle Taylor novels that cannot be found in your local bookstores, they can be ordered from Zebra Books at the address in the front of this novel. For a *Janelle Taylor Newsletter* and bookmark, please send a self-addressed, stamped envelope to Janelle Taylor Enterprises, P.O. Box 11646, Augusta, Georgia, 30907-8646. I do hope you enjoy this story and the exquisite Elaine Duillo cover.

LOOK FOR THESE REGENCY ROMANCES

WATCH FOR THESE REGENCY ROMANCES

BREACH OF HONOR   (0-8217-5111-5, $4.50)
by Phylis Warady

DeLACEY'S ANGEL   (0-8217-4978-1, $3.99)
by Monique Ellis

A DECEPTIVE BEQUEST   (0-8217-5380-0, $4.50)
by Olivia Sumner

A RAKE'S FOLLY   (0-8217-5007-0, $3.99)
by Claudette Williams

AN INDEPENDENT LADY   (0-8217-3347-8, $3.95)
by Lois Stewart

SPINE TINGLING ROMANCE
FROM STELLA CAMERON!

ROMANCE FROM HANNAH HOWELL

MY VALIANT KNIGHT   (0-8217-5186-7, $5.50)

ONLY FOR YOU   (0-8217-4993-5, $4.99)

UNCONQUERED   (0-8217-5417-3, $5.99)

WILD ROSES   (0-8217-5677-X, $5.99)

WATCH FOR THESE ZEBRA REGENCIES